THE
STARS
LIKE
GODS

ASTERION NOIR: BOOK 3

G. S. JENNSEN

HYPERNOVA
PUBLISHING
2019

THE STARS LIKE GODS

Copyright © 2019 by G. S. Jennsen

Cover design by Josef Bartoň, Obsidian Dawn and G. S. Jennsen.
Cover typography by G. S. Jennsen

Hypernova Publishing
P.O. Box 2214
Parker, Colorado 80134
www.hypernovapublishing.com

Publisher's Note: This is a work of fiction. Names, characters, places, and incidents are a product of the author's imagination. Locales and public names are sometimes used for atmospheric purposes. Any resemblance to actual people, living or dead, or to businesses, companies, events, institutions, or locales is completely coincidental.

The Hypernova Publishing name, colophon and logo are trademarks of Hypernova Publishing.

Ordering Information:
Hypernova Publishing books may be purchased for educational, business or sales promotional use. For details, contact the "Special Markets Department" at the address above.

The Stars Like Gods / G. S. Jennsen.—1st ed.

LCCN 2019905474
978-1-7323977-5-0

BOOKS BY G. S. JENNSEN

ASTERION NOIR

EXIN EX MACHINA

OF A DARKER VOID

THE STARS LIKE GODS

AURORA RHAPSODY

AURORA RISING

STARSHINE

VERTIGO

TRANSCENDENCE

AURORA RENEGADES

SIDESPACE

DISSONANCE

ABYSM

AURORA RESONANT

RELATIVITY

RUBICON

REQUIEM

SHORT STORIES

RESTLESS, VOL. I · *RESTLESS, VOL. II* · *APOGEE*

SOLATIUM · *VENATORIS* · *RE/GENESIS* · *MERIDIAN*

LEARN MORE AT GSJENNSEN.COM/BOOKS

For New Shepard and Blue Moon, for Starship, for Artemis.
May you all return us to the moon, then to Mars
and the stars beyond.

DRAMATIS PERSONAE

Nika Tescarav
NOIR Leader; Former External Relations Division Advisor
Dashiel Ridani
Industry Division Advisor; Owner, Ridani Enterprises

Perrin Benvenit
NOIR Personnel Director

Adlai Weiss
Justice Division Advisor

Grant Mesahle
Owner, Mesahle Flight

Blake Satair
Justice Division Advisor

Katherine Colson
Administration Div. Advisor

Joaquim Lacese
NOIR Operations Director

Maris Debray
Culture Division Advisor

Parc Eshett
NOIR slicing specialist

Lance Palmer
Commander, Armed Forces

Spencer Nimoet
Justice Division officer

Ryan Theroit
NOIR robotics specialist

Cameron Breckel
External Relations Div. Advisor

Selene Panetier
Justice Division Advisor

Julien Grayson
Justice Division Advisor

Harris Rosenthal
Justice Division Advisor

Gemina Kail
Administration Div. Advisor

Magnus Forchelle
Scientist

Francis Wallman
Justice Division Officer

Ava Zobel
NOIR weapons specialist

Maggie Zobel
NOIR member

Simon Granger
CEO, Briscanti Materials

Zhanre'khavet
Taiyok Elder

GUIDES
Delacrai (*Kiyora*)
Anavosa (*Mirai*)
Luciene (*Synra*)
Selyshok (*Ebisu*)
Iovimer (*Namino*)

GENNISI GALAXY
(MESSIER 94)

RASU STRONGHOLD

SOGAIN SYSTEM

III-E183-31B

MIRAI

NAMINO

ADJUNCT HACHI

KIYORA

EBISU

TOKI'TAKU
(TAIYOK HOMEWORLD)

SYNRA

HOKAN STATION

CHOSEK
(GHIZERU HOMEWORLD)

- ASTERION DOMINION AXIS WORLDS
- ASTERION DOMINION ADJUNCT WORLDS
- ✳ ALIEN WORLDS

ASTERION DOMINION
AXIS WORLDS

MIRAI   NAMINO   SYNRA   EBISU   KIYORA

View the Galaxy Map online at gsjennsen.com/map-tslg

THE STORY SO FAR

EXIN EX MACHINA

A woman wakes up in a rain-soaked alley with no memory of who she is or how she got there. Two strangers, Perrin and Joaquim, find her and offer to take her in. When asked, she tells them her name is Nika.

Fast forward to five years later. Nika leads an armed team, including Perrin and Joaquim, in an infiltration of a transportation headquarters on Mirai. They break into the data vault and corrupt the passenger records so they can travel without being tracked. A discussion back at their base, The Chalet, reveals the larger purpose of the group, which calls itself 'NOIR': fighting an increasingly repressive government and searching for people who have vanished in the last several years.

Dashiel Ridani, an elite Industry Advisor, discovers that shipments of his company's new product, a virtual limb augment, have been stolen while in transit to retailers. At a meeting between Advisors and the Guides—the leaders of the Dominion government— the Guides brush off the theft in favor of pressuring a Justice Advisor, Adlai Weiss, to apprehend the members of NOIR and bring an end to their disruptive activities. Afterwards, the Guides meet in secret, debating how they can shut NOIR down and hinting at some greater threat to the Dominion.

At The Chalet, one of NOIR's top hackers, Parc Eshett, shows off a new virtual limb augment he's installed.

Nika heads to another Dominion world, Namino, to purchase new equipment from a Taiyok merchant named Xyche. The Taiyoks are a winged alien species known for their cloaking capabilities. While on Namino, she spends an afternoon with her occasional lover, Grant.

Joaquim attends the criminal trial of a former friend. During the trial, he recalls the last time he'd seen his friend, when Joaquim's lover Cassidy was murdered during a police raid on their apartment. After the raid, Joaquim turned his back on that life to start a new one on Mirai.

Dashiel visits Chosek, the homeworld of the Chizeru, a diminutive, pre-industrial alien species. Chosek is rich in kyoseil, a rare mineral Asterions use to enhance their bio-synthetic bodies and many of their technologies, and the Chizeru mine the kyoseil for Asterion businesses.

Later, Dashiel replays a memory from five years earlier. In it, he and a woman make love; their pillow talk involves a series of outpost disappearances on Dominion exploratory worlds. She is worried the Guides are involved and plans to hack into government files in search of evidence. The next night, she disappears; Dashiel has searched for her ever since, to no avail.

On a distant exploratory world, Advisor Gemina Kail oversees the destruction of a lab outpost. The employees living there are gassed, loaded into stasis chambers and shipped to a secret space station.

Nika returns to The Chalet to learn that Parc has been arrested for burglary. She reaches out to a NOIR contact in Justice, Spencer Nimoet, who sneaks her inside the jail to see Parc. He acts very unlike himself—passive and unconcerned about his plight.

Nika, Perrin and Joaquim try to figure out what might have happened to Parc to explain his behavior. Nika and Perrin go see the merchant he purchased the new limb augment from, who tells them the manufacturer is Ridani Enterprises and gives them one of the augments so they can test it.

Another NOIR hacker, Cair, finds a hidden virutox in the augment software. It attaches itself to a user's OS then alters their programming, decreasing impulse control and emotion expression.

Nika, Joaquim and a NOIR robotics specialist, Ryan, infiltrate Ridani Enterprises in a bid to uncover more about the augment and possibly the virutox. Nika is hacking into the server in the CEO's office when Dashiel returns to work and discovers her there. During a tense standoff, her disguise fails, and he recognizes her as the woman from his memory, his lost love who vanished. He asks her to meet him the next day, then urges her to leave before security arrives.

At the meeting, amidst lots of angst on both sides, Dashiel tells Nika she used to be a diplomatic Advisor. He reveals she is a descendant of the fabled First Generation, who led the Asterions across galaxies in search of a new home when their rebellion against the Anaden Empire failed. After recounting the events leading up to her disappearance and his search for answers, he tells her about a psyche backup she kept.

Nika visits the bank where the backup was stored, but her account was emptied out the same day she woke up in an alley with her memory erased. She confronts Dashiel in his home, accusing him of being involved in her psyche-wipe. Devastated at the realization he will never get back the woman he loved and desperate to prove his sincerity, he asks her to experience ('simex') one of his memories from their time together. Secretly wanting to glimpse the woman she supposedly used to be, she agrees.

The memory is of a party at Maris Debray's loft nine years ago. Nika, Dashiel, Maris and Adlai are all clearly friends, and they banter for several minutes before Nika and Dashiel retire to the balcony together. They snuggle, kiss and drink champagne while they chat about an upcoming interstellar mission by the starship *Shorai*.

The memory leaves Nika disoriented and drowning in unfamiliar emotions. She tells Dashiel that woman is gone forever, then starts to leave. But the lingering memory overwhelms her, and she embraces him instead. In a torrent of passion and turbulent emotions, they make love.

In the dead of night, Parc is convicted and transported to the Zaidam Bastille prison. There, he and other convicts are herded into stasis chambers and knocked unconscious.

The next morning, Nika and Dashiel share moments both tender and troubled before going their separate ways. Dashiel tells Adlai about the virutox implanted in his stolen augments and implores him to investigate. He then goes to check on Parc as a favor to Nika, only to find Parc has already been sent to Zaidam.

Dashiel tells Nika the bad news, and they meet with Joaquim and Perrin. He and Joaquim instantly clash, arguing over the best course of action. Dashiel confides to Nika that his Advisor status will allow him entry to Zaidam, but to break Parc out will mean the end of Dashiel's career and turn him into a fugitive.

They are fighting about what to do when an explosion rocks The Chalet. They find the main floor on fire, with a crater at its center. Joaquim accuses Dashiel of causing the explosion, and Nika forces Dashiel to leave.

In the aftermath, it's determined that Cair became infected with the virutox when he studied the augment software; he caused a scene on the main floor before tampering with equipment until it exploded. Three people were killed in the explosion, including Cair. Using psyche backups they can theoretically be brought back, but NOIR lacks the resources to do it.

Adlai confirms the existence of the virutox in the limb augments. He informs the Guides, and is shocked when they order him to let the virutox propagate. They question how he discovered it, and when he repeats what Dashiel told him—that a contact alerted him to it—they order Dashiel and the contact to appear before them.

Advisor Iona Rowan participates in an illegal, underground competition where the participants temporarily switch consciousnesses to complete challenges. Unbeknownst to her, she switches with a man who had installed the limb augment and was infected with the virutox.

Nika reluctantly agrees to meet the Guides with Dashiel, but only if they use the opportunity to search the Guides' data vault for more information on her psyche-wipe. When they arrive at Mirai Tower, however, the Guides have moved the meeting time up, leaving them no time to conduct the search. Nika abandons Dashiel and sneaks into the data vault herself. She uncovers numerous files about her investigation into the outpost disappearances, including references to a 'Rasu Protocol.' She also finds proof that the Guides ordered her psyche-wipe, which was executed by Gemina Kail.

At this point, she's interrupted by security. Adlai and Dashiel reach the vault at almost the same time, and on seeing Nika breaking into the data vault, Adlai reluctantly tries to arrest her. Seeing no other option, Dashiel feigns ignorance and turns on Nika.

Nika escapes through a window, but she's shot by a drone as she does and is badly injured. Joaquim and Perrin mount a rescue effort; they are able to reach her before security forces and evacuate her to The Chalet.

She awakens hours later in a treatment tank, her wounds healed. Hurt by Dashiel's apparent betrayal and angry about all she's learned, she thanks Perrin and Joaquim for saving her then tells them she has to leave, to protect them and to find answers.

A Taiyok assassin ambushes Nika while she's on her way to Namino; she kills him and quickly leaves the scene. She asks Grant for a ship, but rebuffs him when he tries to kiss her. After an awkward exchange, they agree to remain friends, and he gives her a ship he's built.

Nika is about to leave in her new ship when Dashiel shows up at the hangar, bags in hand. She holds him at gunpoint while he explains that he hadn't betrayed her, but rather bought her time to get away and him time to withdraw funds from his accounts and transfer control of his company, all so he could come with her. Eventually he convinces her, and when they embrace she experiences a memory of the day she met him.

At the embassy on Chosek, Iona falls victim to the virutox and goes on a shooting spree, shooting multiple Chizeru, Asterion business executives and herself. Adlai is called in to investigate the massacre; he discovers she was infected with the virutox without the limb augment being installed, suggesting it is communicable.

Troubled, Adlai reaches out to Dashiel, but he's vanished. Adlai puts the pieces together and deduces Dashiel has joined Nika on the run. Faced with mounting evidence, he's forced to accept that the Guides are behind recent events and decides to take action.

Nika and Dashiel infiltrate Zaidam Bastille to break Parc out, only to be told Parc has been transferred to a vessel named the *Tabiji*, destination unknown. Nika hacks the Zaidam server, where she learns every convict has been transferred under the Rasu Protocol, and the prison is empty. Security forces arrive, and Nika is spaced while trying to reach their ship. Dashiel rescues her, and they escape the prison.

Later that night, Nika experiences another memory, this time of the final hours of the Asterions' rebellion against the Anaden Empire. She's a diplomat for the rebels named Nicolette Hinotori, who is bonded to an AI named KIR. Facing annihilation, the rebels flee the Milky Way on generation ships in search of a new home.

Gemina Kail pilots the *Tabiji* to an alien stronghold across the galaxy, where she delivers thousands of Asterions in stasis chambers to a mysterious alien species called the Rasu.

OF A DARKER VOID

Nika and Dashiel visit Ebisu, where Nika baits a Taiyok assassin who is tailing her into a trap then gives the alien a message to deliver to the Guides: that she will kill every assassin sent after her, but if instead they want to talk, she is willing to listen.

On Mirai, Adlai and Spencer confiscate limb augments from merchants in an attempt to prevent more people from being infected with the virutox. Later, Maris confronts Adlai and demands he tell her where Dashiel and Nika have gone and why, and he agrees.

The next morning, Adlai interrogates Iona to determine how she caught the virutox. She admits she interacted with a man named Tristan McLeros at a Disuta game. That night, Tristan breaks into the Mirai One transit hub, intending to fiddle with the transportation system as a prank. Instead, he accidentally overloads the power distribution system, causing the building to explode.

Adlai reviews surveillance footage and identifies Tristan as the perpetrator. He confronts the Guides with evidence that the virutox is responsible for the explosion and demands to know why they continue to allow it to spread. They refuse to tell him, and he in turn refuses to stop confiscating the limb augments, daring them to come after him.

The Guides confer on what to do about the deteriorating situation and the increasing number of rebelling Advisors; they elect to continue guarding the Rasu Protocol secrets. One of the Guides, Delacrai, privately believes this course will result in the destruction of the Dominion and decides to take action.

Later that night, Nika receives an anonymous message containing the location of the next outpost to be raided. She and Dashiel visit the Taiyok homeworld to purchase a stealth module for their ship, which they've named *Wayfarer*, so they can track whoever attacks the outpost. To prepare, Nika accesses an encrypted memory of the first Asterion meeting with the Taiyok leader 12,000 years ago. Afterwards, she confides in Dashiel about the memories she's been recovering and tells him she believes her former self deliberately encrypted the memories, then made him the decryption key.

Nika contacts Grant for help in installing the stealth module. While he talks Dashiel through updating the ship's systems to accept the module, Dashiel lets slip that Nika had been psyche-wiped 5 years earlier, which Grant did not know.

Adlai's people are able to create a vaccine against the virutox. He and Spencer debate how best to distribute the vaccine, given that the public no longer trusts Justice. Spencer confesses that he has contacts in NOIR and suggests asking them for help.

Spencer contacts Joaquim and asks him to meet with Adlai. Joaquim is deeply suspicious, and he and Perrin argue about whether they should do it. Joaquim reveals why he despises Justice: that Justice officers on Synra killed the love of his life and destroyed all her psyche backups.

The meeting takes place, and Adlai gives Joaquim a copy of the vaccine for NOIR to distribute. On the way back home, Joaquim is hit with a tranquilizer dart and kidnapped.

Perrin flees in a panic with the vaccine and returns to The Chalet. She and Ryan study the vaccine to ensure its genuine, then she meets with Adlai again. She tells him about Joaquim's kidnapping, and they reluctantly decide that they have to focus on getting the vaccine distributed before trying to rescue him, since Adlai is already in danger of being fired. Despite all the angst, they instantly hit it off and agree to work together.

Nika and Dashiel arrive at the outpost in time to see two ships show up; Gemina gases the outpost then orders dynes to transport the inhabitants in stasis chambers onto the larger ship. Nika sneaks onboard and tells Dashiel to track her. An interference field blocks her signal, though, so Dashiel plants a tracker on Gemina's personal ship, then barely escapes as the outpost is destroyed.

The ship Nika has stowed away on arrives at a space station, and she sneaks off to investigate. The *Tabiji* is docked there, and she breaks into its navigation records and copies its travel history. Then she steals Gemina's personal ship and meets Dashiel and the *Wayfarer* on a nearby moon.

They quickly tie the *Tabiji*'s journeys to the historical route of the *Shorai*, deducing that the *Shorai* must have discovered something at the terminus point of the *Tabiji*'s trips.

They follow the path the *Tabiji* has been taking and discover the stronghold of the Rasu. The aliens have built a Dyson lattice around a star to siphon off its energy. Thousands of city-sized platforms orbit the star, from where countless ships arrive and depart. They observe Rasu ships joining together to create larger vessels in a seamless fashion. This triggers a recollection by Nika, but when a Rasu ship opens a wormhole vortex that nearly drags the *Wayfarer* in, they decide they should leave.

Once they're safely outside of the Rasu stellar system, Nika recounts the story of something that happened to her 3 years earlier. She and Perrin went to a club, where a man offered them a simex depicting an alien invasion in which they are tasked with disabling the alien ship.

In the simex, they found themselves in a jungle as a ship—what Nika now recognizes as a Rasu ship—descended from the sky while burning the jungle with a laser beam. The ship landed and machine-looking aliens disembarked. Several natives attacked and were quickly captured. The aliens transformed into a variety of shapes and tools, the metal they were made of liquifying and resolidifying as needed. Perrin got injured, and they tried to exit the simex, but the exit command didn't work.

They sneaked on the ship and came upon the Rasu killing all the native prisoners. Perrin screamed, and the Rasu pursued them on a chase through the ship. They made it to the command center, where a huge plasma chamber powered the ship's main weapon. Before they could try to disable it, Rasu surrounded and killed them.

They woke up in the club and tried to get a refund for a defective simex, only to learn the man who gave it to them didn't work there. As they were leaving, Nika heard a voice in her head saying, '*Remember this. When the time comes, you must remember what you have seen.*'

Dashiel and Nika conclude that someone deliberately targeted her with information about the Rasu. They speculate that it might have been the Sogain, a mysterious, technologically superior species Asterions encountered 200K years ago. In that encounter, an Asterion vessel was forcefully ejected from the Sogain system by a cosmic force and warned by a disembodied voice never to approach again. Armed with their new knowledge of the Rasu threat, Dashiel and Nika decide to return to Mirai.

On the Guides' Platform, Blake Satair, a Justice Advisor, probes Joaquim's mind for information on NOIR. Joaquim's internal defenses block much of the 'interrogation,' but Blake is able to extract the name of Joaquim's former boss, the owner of The Chalet. He has the man brought in, extracts The Chalet's address and kills the man.

On the way to Mirai, Nika accidentally triggers another encrypted memory. In it, a man named Steven Olivaw tells her he intends to undergo a Retirement & Reinitialization, essentially committing suicide. She professes her love for him and begs him not to go through with it. He muses that perhaps she could find happiness with his next incarnation, but she tells him she won't accept a hack copy, and he leaves. When the memory is over, Nika lies to Dashiel about its contents. She realizes that Dashiel is a descendent of Steven and is troubled that for some unknown reason her former self clearly never told him this.

When they reach Mirai, Dashiel receives a message from his deputy at his company asking to meet. Nika suspects it's a trap, but he insists on going. They argue, and he leaves in anger. Nika tries to track him, but he's turned off his locator. She's wrestling with what to do next when she receives an anonymous message stating that NOIR headquarters has been compromised. She orders everyone to evacuate immediately then departs in the *Wayfarer* for The Chalet.

Dashiel arrives at the meeting and is ambushed by Blake. He's able to get a one-word message to Nika before Blake disables his comms.

When she receives it, she realizes it was in fact a trap and he's been taken prisoner. With no way to locate him, she has no choice but to continue to The Chalet. When she arrives, she blows a hole in the roof and evacuates people as Justice squads begin attacking on the ground floor. Several NOIR members are killed, but most are able to escape. Nika takes off in the *Wayfarer* then blows up the building, burying the attackers in the rubble.

After taking the injured to a clinic, Nika meets with the source of the anonymous messages, who turns out to be Guide Delacrai.

Delacrai tells her that Joaquim and Dashiel are being held on the Platform and, when pressed, reveals that in return for the Guides delivering them thousands of Asterions in stasis chambers every few months, the Rasu agreed not to invade and enslave Asterion worlds.

The Rasu are interested in the Asterions' unique physiology of bio-synthetic intelligence powered by kyoseil and quantum programming, though they have not disclosed why. The Rasu also claim to control hundreds of galaxies spanning this region of the universe. Nika demands the woman's help in getting onto the Platform and freeing Dashiel and Joaquim; Delacrai agrees.

Nika, Adlai and Spencer prepare for an assault on the Platform, while Perrin and Maris ready Maris' loft for the other half of their plan.

All the Advisors (except Adlai and Dashiel) arrive at the loft, ostensibly for a party, and Perrin locks the door and blocks all communications. Maris recounts everything they've learned about the Rasu, the outpost kidnappings, the virutox and Nika's psyche-wipe. Maris pressures Gemina until she fills in the gaps on the Rasu, their demands and the Guides' actions to comply since then.

Maris then reveals that the Guides are holding Dashiel prisoner, and that Nika and Adlai are currently rescuing him. On hearing this, Blake tries to disable the communication block to get word out, but Perrin and others subdue and restrain him.

Joaquim wakes up in an interrogation room. He frees himself from the restraints and searches the facility, worried Perrin was captured as well. Instead he finds Dashiel, whom he frees.

While hunting for a way off the Platform, they find the Guides' inner sanctum. There they discover that the Guides are using remote-controlled dolls instead of real Asterion bodies, with their psyches living inside massive servers. Such an existence is anathema to most Asterions, and in disgust Joaquim records a narrated video of the dolls and servers.

While Dashiel investigates further, Joaquim disappears into the power control room for a few minutes. When he returns, they exit the sanctum for the Platform's central chamber. The main entrance is locked, but they hear sounds on the other side and start banging on the doors.

Nika, Adlai and Spencer infiltrate Mirai Tower. Security fires on them, and they face resistance all the way to the Platform entry in the penthouse. Under fire from AEVs outside, Nika nearly electrocutes herself hotwiring the d-gate, and they flee through it onto the Platform. Once there, they hear a commotion in the central chamber. Unsure of what waits on the other side, they ready their weapons before opening the doors.

They find Dashiel and Joaquim on the other side. Nika embraces Dashiel and tells him she loves him, but before they can talk further, more security forces attack.

Once dispatched, they return to Mirai Tower. Joaquim insists they all go out on the balcony then sends a command. In orbit above Mirai, the Platform explodes. Adlai wants to arrest Joaquim, but Dashiel talks him down.

Nika and Maris reunite, though this is the first time Nika has met Maris since the psyche-wipe. Nika goes on camera in a live broadcast and, with Dashiel, Adlai, Maris and many other Advisors at her side, addresses the Asterion people. She tells them that the Asterion Dominion is in grave danger, and she needs their help to save it.

CONTENTS

THE
STARS
LIKE
GODS

LATENCY

240,000 YEARS AGO

MIRAI

Nika Kirumase settled onto a cushioned chaise beside the railing as the yacht's bow cut into the crest of a wave, sending a misty spray of cool water over her and the port side of the deck.

She wiped her face dry before responding. "Yes, we are pretty damn good at governing ourselves. But the fact remains that with the addition of a third colonized world, we risk descending into a quagmire of endless squabbling driven by conflicting priorities. Worse, we risk drifting apart from one another. To be strong—to protect ourselves—we need to remain united. As distasteful as it is to all of us, this means a pan-world governing body."

Charles Basquan returned from the bar, his hands full, and passed out frozen lime vodka cocktails to everyone onboard. "Not a whole government, though. Just a council of sorts, don't you think? A small body to decide issues affecting more than one of our planets. I wouldn't expect it to be a full-time job for those who serve on it."

Maris Debray nudged Nika's feet to the side and draped herself across the bottom half of the chaise, despite the two additional chaises waiting unoccupied elsewhere on the deck. "Charles, I admire your optimism—and your yacht, by the way, this is fabulous—but put two or more people in a room together and grant them the power to make decisions, and bureaucracy is as inevitable an outcome as sex." She sipped on her drink. "Still, it *is* needed."

Nika fought to reclaim a portion of the chaise for herself. "The sex, or the bureaucracy?"

"The *government*, my dear."

"Oh, right."

"And a military." Lance Palmer stood stiffly by the outer wall of the main cabin, holding his cocktail between two fingers like it was a contaminated lab specimen. "If I may interject, I assume this is where I give a speech on how the universe is an incomprehensibly dangerous place, and we need to be prepared to defend all our colonies against any number and variety of threats we might encounter. Which we aren't. Prepared, that is."

"How about we enter your statement for the record instead. You're not wrong, Lance, but it's a conversation for another day." Nika gave up the fight for ownership of the precious chaise real estate and swung her feet onto the deck. "Do any of us want to serve on this council?"

Charles scoffed. "I cannot think of a single worse notion than slaving myself to the whims of the populace."

"Give the populace a little credit. They've done rather well for themselves so far."

"You serve on it, then. Actually, now that I consider the idea, you're perfect for the job."

Nika studied her drink. He wasn't wrong…but like Charles, she suspected she'd chafe under the artificial constraints certain to accompany the position. She shook her head. "I have too much wanderlust to tie myself to a government desk job."

"But if it's only part-time—"

"No, Maris is correct about the bureaucracy. I am, however, willing to take point on organizing the creation of this council."

"Great. Being off the hook as I now am, I'm getting another drink." Charles disappeared into the main cabin.

Nika shot his back an annoyed look but raised her voice so he could still hear her from inside. "I think it goes without saying that, even if we're not official appointees, all of us should plan on supporting whomever *is* chosen. We'll owe it to them to step up and advise them on issues where we have particular expertise." No one objected, so she kept going. "What are we talking about here? A single representative from each of Synra, Mirai and Namino?"

Charles wandered back onto the deck, drink in hand, and collapsed onto one of the empty chaises. "I really don't think we need anything more complicated, at least to start."

Maris poked Nika's leg with a painted toe. "Ana would be a great choice."

Lance gave up scrutinizing his drink to frown. "Who?"

"Anavosa Kelaine. She's practically the mayor of Mirai One already. Smart, pragmatic but principled. Maris is right. She'd be a good choice."

"I adore it when you talk dirty to me."

She soft-punched Maris in the thigh. "You wish. What about for Synra?"

Blake Satair, who had been quietly brooding on the opposite side of the deck until now, perked up. "Luciene Toskav."

Nika groaned. "He's an ass."

"Yes, but an ass who gets things done. When so many people abandoned Synra for the—" Blake scowled at the lovely, powder-blue afternoon sky "—*allegedly* nicer climate of Mirai, Synra's societal infrastructure began to fall apart. Luciene stepped in, restored order and gave purpose to those who remained."

Nika had heard plenty of rumors implying the tactics Luciene had employed to do so bordered on the unsavory. But it was true he had probably saved Synra. Ends and means.

She regarded Blake skeptically. "I'm surprised you don't want the job."

"Oh, I do. But I'm a man of action. I prefer to be on the streets, making a difference on a daily basis outside of the, yes, inevitable bureaucracy."

Frankly, she was relieved. He was far too much of a zealot to be entrusted with the keys to the kingdom. During the SAI Rebellion, he'd exhibited a troubling absolutism which veered toward blind narcissism. He and Steven had clashed regularly and had come to blows twice in the dark final days of the doomed rebellion.

Steven…she gazed out at the sparkling waters of Hataori Harbor, letting a pang of wistfulness drift over her. She still felt his absence sometimes—times like this—many millennia later. A long string of lovers stretched from this morning back to mere months after he…she hesitated over the word, even in her mind. *Sunsetted.*

But they all were and had been exactly that: lovers, never confidants or kindred spirits. Never soulmates.

She took a quick sip of her drink then peered up at one of them. Grant Mesahle lounged atop the pilothouse with his legs dangling over the edge of the glass enclosure. "And Namino? Grant, you've claimed it as your home. Any ideas?"

He hesitated long enough to brush wind-blown hair out of his face. "Jose Ruiz or Iovimer Ballard. They've both been deeply involved in the colony buildout. Iovimer in particular has made resources materialize out of thin air at the exact time and place they're needed. Man's a magician."

Nika brought her glass to her lips again, only to find it empty. She stood to go refill it, then spun around. "Maris, do not—"

But Maris had already stretched out along the full length of the chaise with a luxurious sigh.

"Best be careful. I might just flip you off into the water when I get back."

"That would be an adventure, too."

Nika rolled her eyes and headed for the bar. "We ought to brainstorm a few more names for each world, then we can submit the slate to the people for a vote. Obviously, we'll ask the nominees for their permission first."

"They'd be crazy not to want to serve."

She glanced over her shoulder at Blake. "Are you saying we're all crazy?"

Charles snorted. "Oh, without a doubt."

It was true enough, she mused as she refilled her glass. You didn't live for 460,000 years without going a little bonkers in the head.

Nika returned to the deck and considered her options, then headed for the far end of the bow to rest against the railings where they met. From this vantage, the afternoon sun bathed her in a warm, welcoming glow.

Maris raised her hand in the air, though she didn't sit up. "I am the last person to impose a bit of sobriety on the conversation, but

I feel as if a question needs to be asked before we proceed any further down this path. Are we willing to subordinate ourselves to this council? To obey their directives even when they don't suit us?"

She shrugged. "So long as they act justly and fairly, I think we should. That's what having a government means."

"And if they don't act justly and fairly?"

Nika jumped as a frigid wave crashed into her back. "Well, it's not like we haven't rebelled before."

CHMOD

DAYS UNTIL RASU DEADLINE: 27

1

PRESENT DAY

MIRAI JUSTICE CENTER

"Conspiracy to commit murder resulting in final death of an Asterion, 24,600 counts. Conspiracy to commit kidnapping, 21,820 counts. Aggravated kidnapping, same. Unauthorized psyche wipe, two counts. Aggravated unauthorized psyche tampering, four counts. Abuse of power. Treason. Violation of Charter provisions I 14.103, I 56.888, III 24.046, III 24.105, V 2.018 and V 106.241."

Adlai Weiss leaned back in his chair and rubbed at his face. "Have I missed anything?"

The other three Justice Advisors sitting at the table with him fidgeted uncomfortably. Blake Satair was not among them, on account of being confined in a maximum-security cell pending the formal filing of a list of charges not much shorter than those they would soon file against the Guides.

They were holed up in a conference room at the Mirai Justice Center, despite the fact Adlai still couldn't be certain he fully controlled the building. While they met, routines ran purposefully throughout the Justice Division nex web, scrubbing Satair's malicious code injections and reaffirming, albeit with some notable adjustments, the proper chains of command. Also taking care of a few additional items, such as rescinding arrest warrants for Nika and other known members of NOIR.

Selene Panetier sat up straighter, as if jolted by inspiration. "Theft of and unauthorized tampering with private property, 13,400 counts."

Adlai palmed his forehead. "Dashiel's augments. The event that started all of this, and I completely left it off the list." He entered in a couple of commands, and the list of charges grew longer. "Anything else?"

Julien Grayson, the Justice Advisor from Kiyora, laughed caustically. "Conspiracy to ruin our fucking lives?"

"Not an actual crime, but we can see about scheduling a vote to make it one once we resolve the current crisis."

"We're really going to do this, then?" Harris Rosenthal, the Justice Advisor from Ebisu, sounded beat-down and somewhat dismayed. Looked it, too, though he didn't have a scratch or bruise on him.

Adlai regarded the man sympathetically. At least he'd been able to ease into the ugly reality of the magnitude of the Guides' transgressions over the course of several weeks; the rest of them had seen their world turned upside-down in less than thirty-six hours.

But upside-down the world now was, and they had no choice but to wrangle it into submission and try to right it. "We are. But we're going to do it properly, in accordance with the Charter and established Justice Division regulations. We're going to do it holding our heads high, because however daunting all this feels, we're in the right here."

Selene nodded thoughtfully, which Adlai generously took for agreement, but Julien drummed their fingers on the table in an agitated cadence. "But *how* are we going to do it? Sure, we can publicly announce the charges for pomp and dramatic effect so we maybe *look* like we're doing something useful, but they're just empty words when we don't know where the Guides are—where their backups are, I mean."

Because their bodies and primary servers were ashes scattered over half of Mirai...unless they had backup dolls to go with their backup servers. Of course they had backup dolls. Stars, how he hoped the Guides weren't out there wandering the streets already.

Regardless, Julien made a valid point. They needed something tangible to arrest, even if it was only hardware. And for that to happen, they needed to move fast, before agents still loyal to the Guides spirited the backups away to somewhere beyond their reach.

Adlai stood, as they'd accomplished all they were apt to for now. "We are working on a way to find them as we speak."

ᄭᄰ

MIRAI TOWER

Dashiel clasped his hands together at the small of Nika's back, drawing her deeper into his arms and the shadows of the alcove outside the cafeteria in Mirai Tower. "Say it again."

She nuzzled his nose playfully. "Say what again?"

His voice dropped to a deep growl. "Do not toy with me, Nika."

She chuckled and brushed her lips across his. "I love you."

"Poetry of the gods, your words are."

She tucked her chin into her chest as someone passed behind them in the hallway. While the alcove took them out of the flow of traffic, it hardly constituted privacy.

They also needed a new home base and soon, because repair crews were now demanding to get inside the Tower and for everyone inside to get outside. Maris claimed to be working on a solution.

When the passerby had continued on their way, she forced her gaze up to meet his. "Those words, maybe. But earlier ones...I'm sorry for the hurtful things I said to you on the *Wayfarer.* I didn't mean—"

"Hush. It's okay. You were trying to protect me, and you were right to do so. I acted foolishly."

He appeared to be in a forgiving mood, and it would be so easy to just smile blithely and go with it. But she owed him honesty, even when it was hard to give. "I'm afraid I was trying to protect *myself,* which was not only futile but also selfish and stupid. And not fair to you. Again, I'm sorry."

He didn't so much as flinch. "I made mistakes to be sorry for as well. Let's call us square, since it worked out."

A throat cleared behind them, and she looked over her shoulder to see the Administration Advisor for Mirai, Katherine Colson, standing there looking perturbed. "The Hataori Renewal Clinic commed me. They're ready to wake up your guy."

"Thank you for letting me know. I'll head there now." Katherine didn't seem to like Nika much, and as usual Nika had no idea why. Whatever their personal history was, though, neither of them had time for the woman to recount a biased blow-by-blow account of it.

Katherine spun and left as fastidiously as she'd arrived, and Nika shifted back to snuggle into Dashiel's embrace for a few final, perfect seconds. "I think this means it's time for us to go to work."

He grumbled and kissed her again. "The Hataori Renewal Clinic? That's where Vance was getting checked out at. Mind if I come with you?"

She stepped out into the hall, coaxing him after her with an outstretched hand. "You can come anywhere in the universe with me."

2

HATAORI RENEWAL CLINIC

MIRAI

Every corner of the private room at the Hataori Renewal Clinic sparkled and shone, making for a stark contrast to the scorched, bombed-out façade of Mirai Tower where Nika had spent the last day and a half. Well-lit with soothing art decorating the walls, a tricked-out cot and two comfortable guest chairs, it provided a warm and comforting environment in which to be welcomed back to the world of the living.

A medical technician fussed with the IVs and sensors snaking out from Parc Eshett's new body, which was snuggled into soft sheets and a plush pillow. His eyes remained closed, but the tech had assured her he would awaken soon.

The door slid open, and Perrin Benvenit and Ryan Theroit peeked inside. "Is it safe to come in?"

Nika laughed quietly. "Safer than anywhere else in the last two days, anyway."

Perrin hurried over to check the patient before joining Nika on the far side of the cot. Ryan entered the room somewhat hesitantly. "Thanks for letting me be here for this."

Perrin waved him over. "The more friendly faces here when he wakes up, the better. This is going to be disorienting for him. The last thing this backup remembers is getting ready for bed after the Dominion Transit mission, before he installed the limb augment."

Nika had been a little surprised to learn that Ryan wanted to be here, but Perrin had brushed it off with a remark about him and Parc being friends. Obviously, they were friends...and now she felt bad for not realizing how *close* of friends they apparently were.

Mostly, though, she was just glad to see Ryan up and walking around. The damage he'd sustained during the attack on The Chalet had been more serious than anyone had suspected at the time, and he'd spent almost a day in a tank. He was damn tough to have walked away, much less shimmied up and onto The Chalet's roof, while being so grievously injured.

A murmur from the bed drew their attention. The tech's focus darted between the waking patient and a series of readings on the pane beside the bed. After a few seconds, she gave them an approving nod and stepped out of the way.

Parc opened one eye to peer at them. "Nika. Perrin. Ryan? Oh, shit. This can't be good."

Nika smiled broadly. "Hi, Parc."

Ryan approached the side of the bed as Parc stretched languidly and opened the other eye. The top half of the bed rose to bring him to a more inclined position. "What time is it? Am I late for something? Did I oversleep?"

Ryan chuckled. "Just a little bit." He reached out and placed a hand on Parc's chin, urging it over to face him. Then he leaned in and kissed Parc softly before drawing back. "I should have done this a long time ago."

Parc blinked, then blinked a second time. "Well...do it again!"

Ryan complied with noticeable enthusiasm.

Nika arched an eyebrow. She didn't want to be rude and stare, though, so she nudged Perrin instead. "Did you know about this?"

"It sounds as if there wasn't technically anything to know about until this precise moment. But I suspected."

"Uh-huh." Nika gave them another good five seconds before clearing her throat. "Gentlemen, as heartwarming as this reunion is, we, um...."

Ryan disentangled himself and scurried off to the opposite wall, where he found sudden interest in his feet. "Sorry."

Parc, on the other hand, wound his hands behind his head and settled back into the pillow wearing a smug smirk. "Don't be. We'll talk at greater length on this topic later. But I'm guessing something dire has happened, because this is not my bed at The Chalet, and no one's ever been that happy to see me before."

Nika sighed. This part wasn't going to be fun. "We do need to talk."

λR

"The Chalet is gone? As in, rubble?"

Parc had vacated the cot the instant the med tech allowed it, and they now sat at a small table in the attached recovery room. Perrin had excused herself a few minutes earlier to go help Dominic and Josie, who had gotten caught up in an altercation with a Justice squad that hadn't yet received the memo about NOIR now being the good guys. Ryan leaned against the wall, loitering but not quite participating in the conversation.

Parc dropped his elbows to the table and rubbed at his temples. "And my previous body is currently being experimented on by evil shapeshifting aliens in their mega-fortress on the other side of the galaxy? Or dead and dissected. Probably dead and dissected by now, right?"

"We don't know for certain. The Guides weren't able to learn much about what happens to our people after they're turned over to the Rasu. We think they do all…die eventually, yes, though the amount of time it takes varies. But the reality is, we're not going to be able to infiltrate the stronghold in time to rescue you. I'm so sorry."

"No, no, I get that. Sure. Damn, it's creepy to contemplate, though." He frowned. "And the prison sentence for the attempted theft?"

"You're being pardoned because of the virutox. And since Justice was able to recover the property you tried to steal and return it to its owner, there won't be any recompense obligations hanging over you. You're in the clear."

Parc made a show of straightening up and donning his usual cocky demeanor. When adopted so swiftly, it resembled body armor hurriedly slapped on to deflect the brunt of an emotional and psychological onslaught. She couldn't blame him for it.

"It sounds like you've taken care of everything. But I am so bummed I missed all the excitement—oh! Where do I sleep? Because I'm definitely not sleeping here. I guess that's my problem to solve, though, now that I am once more a walking, talking, functioning Asterion."

"Perrin is working on arranging accommodations for people."

Ryan spoke up for the first time since they'd moved to the recovery room. "I rented a tiny apartment, since I need space to keep the bots and equipment. It's kind of a shithole, but you're welcome to crash there." He cleared his throat awkwardly. "Until you find something else."

"Thanks. You and I...we should do that. Crash." He nodded in affirmation. "I don't suppose any of my stuff made it out of The Chalet?"

Ryan made a hedging motion with his hands. "Your command center got disintegrated, but I grabbed your file storage, so your custom routines are intact and fairly current. And a couple of your tools from the equipment room. They're in a locker Perrin reserved after Joaquim got snatched."

"You are excellent."

Nika glanced behind her at Ryan incredulously. "When were you doing all of this?"

He shrugged. "While you were off saving the world?"

"Good answer, but it's not saved yet. I'm actually extremely glad to hear you salvaged his gear and routines." She returned her attention to Parc. "We're working on regening everyone who experienced body loss in The Chalet explosion, and the second Chalet explosion. But we woke you up first because we need your help."

"Oh, thank gods! I was starting to worry I'd been rendered obsolete."

"As if." Nika stood. "Take an hour or two to get situated and grab your gear. I'm sorry I can't give you longer to ease back into being alive again, but when I said we need your help, I meant we need it urgently. When you're ready, meet me at this address on Synra."

ᅏᴿᴿ

GUIDES STORAGE FACILITY

SYNRA

Parc circled the imposing tower of servers and support hardware, studying it with theatrical suspicion but also appreciation while completely ignoring the half-dozen security dynes standing guard inside the room. "All the Guides' state secrets are stored in here, huh?"

Nika nodded. "That's our understanding, yes. And believe me, we intend to comb through every single one of those secrets. But right now, we're frantically seeking the locations of the individual Guides' personal backups." Delacrai had kindly pointed them to the location of this official government cache, but the Guide insisted she held no personal knowledge of where the others secured their backups.

"We haven't been able to crack the security on the Guides' personal partitions, and if we push, we risk triggering self-destruct mechanisms or worse."

"Seriously, no one in the entire government has the skill to crack this baby open?"

"Someone undoubtedly does. But we're having to be careful. There aren't a lot of people we're confident we can trust. I trust you."

"Aww, I appreciate it! You've made me feel all warm and fuzzy inside."

"Kind of like Ryan does?"

"Ha! Yeah...who saw that coming?" Parc ran a hand through disheveled hair—she doubted he'd combed it since waking up at the regen clinic—and glanced away in a rare display of bashfulness. "Rapid change of subject: I can't help but notice how you're saying 'we' a lot. Given the swank, top-shelf regen service, the mountain of government servers I've been given carte blanche to play with and the over-armed Justice dynes that aren't shooting at me—" he waved at the security detail "—I'm going to make a wild intuitive leap and assume you don't mean NOIR. So, who the hells is 'we'?"

Now she was the one to break eye contact as an unexpected surge of the old guilt resurfaced. But she didn't deserve to be ashamed, dammit. She'd saved NOIR and brought it into the light. Now, she was acting as she must to save everyone. "A core group of Advisors, mostly, who helped NOIR take down the Guides and stop the spread of the virutox."

"Of which you used to be one, right? And are again, perhaps?"

He certainly hadn't wasted any time getting caught up on recent events. "Formal titles aren't a priority right now. There's far too much work to be done to worry about such silliness. Speaking of work to be done...." She gestured meaningfully at the server tower.

"Right, right. I'll need to get inside and poke around a bit to see what's what, but I can crack it. One way or another." He circled the tower again, then stopped in front of one of the control panes and chewed on his thumb. "You know what would really help speed my work along? A limb augment."

"Oh, you have got to be joking."

"A virutox-free one, don't worry. I'm simply saying, what ten fingers can do, twenty can do twice as fast."

She groaned. "I suppose I can ask Dashiel to bring you a new one."

"Which he will, because he's your sweetie."

"Yes, that's exactly how I would describe him. Do you need it this instant?"

He cracked a grin. "Nah. I'm just messing with you. I mean, I definitely want one. See, I don't remember how cool of an upgrade it was, and I'm dying to learn what I missed—ooh, poor choice of words. Anyway, it can wait a couple of hours." He went over to the bag he'd brought from the NOIR locker and opened it up. "Time to get to work."

3

MIRAI JUSTICE CENTER

Adlai rushed into the Mirai Justice Center conference room displaying considerably more excitement than he'd felt when he'd last left it. Three weary, worn faces regarded him expectantly.

"We've got the locations of the Guides' backups."

A flurry of overlapping questions erupted, but he waved the other Justice Advisors quiet. "You'll all receive a report summarizing how we obtained the information in about ten seconds. It was an unorthodox approach, but we didn't have time for orthodoxy.

"The Guides stuck to their homes, and each Guide controls two storage locations on the world they represent." He tossed up a pane with the addresses listed. "We need to mobilize in force and hit all eight locations simultaneously, in case they're communicating with one another."

"Since Guide Delacrai is surrendering her backups voluntarily, I can deploy my teams to Synra."

"Thank you, Julien. We still need to determine who we can trust in Satair's organization, but it'll have to wait until after we secure the Guides...." Property? Psyches? Memories? The source intelligences themselves? He shuddered. "Let's target staging in ninety minutes, and plan to move ten minutes later. Can we make that timetable?"

Selene pushed her chair back from the table and headed for the door. "One way to find out."

∧R

Spencer Nimoet was waiting on Adlai in the dyne maintenance lab when he arrived, and his officer immediately launched into an update on his work. "We completed a hard reset and reinitialization of the first eight squads ten minutes ago. It's the only way to ensure Advisor Satair didn't leave behind any counter programming, worms, bombs or traps we haven't thought of. We'll cycle through all the patrol squads as they complete their shifts over the next day."

He gestured behind him at the long row of security dynes nestled in the bays. "But these eight squads are safe to deploy."

"Excellent work and better timing. By tomorrow, we might actually have control of the Justice Center again."

"That will be nice, sir. What's our plan?"

"We're hitting the two backup storage locations owned by Guide Anavosa simultaneously with Justice teams at the other sites. We don't want to risk tipping any of the Guides off ahead of time."

"Because they're...alive inside their machines?"

Adlai joined Spencer in grimacing. "We can't afford to assume they're not. I know it's disturbing. I try not to think about it any more than I have to, which has been too much lately."

"Good advice."

"I'll lead the team at the Franklin Street location. I'd like for you to handle the Moroccan Circle site."

Spencer nodded firmly. He'd gained confidence during this crisis, as a man rising to the occasion should. "Thank you, sir. I won't let you down."

MIRAI

Julien Grayson (Synra): Teams S1 and S2 in position.

The warehouse sat dark and silent at the end of a narrow street. Scarcely more than an alley.

Looks were deceiving, however. The warehouse was drawing a tremendous amount of power from the grid—far more than its ostensible purpose, listed in Administration records as dry goods storage, would ever require.

Adlai slated cutting the power feed as their last act before breaching the interior. The facility would also have an internal backup power generator, of course, and they'd need to shut it down as swiftly as possible once they were inside.

Selene Panetier (Namino): Teams N1 and N2 in position.

A deep scan of the warehouse interior arrived from the surveillance drone, and he studied it quickly.

The space consisted of a single floor and an insulated attic space thick with cabling and pipes. A wide entrance faced the street. A shielded block in the rear right corner likely represented the generator. A long row of electrified equipment stretched along the far wall and halfway across the floor, claiming the bulk of the warehouse space—presumably the servers. The purpose of a small cordoned-off area in the rear left, he couldn't say. Outlines of tall, bipedal machines had to signify security dynes. Six of them. Two objects in motion would be patrolling drones.

The scan didn't reveal all the risks waiting inside, however. For one, they faced a non-zero chance that an emergency routine was set to activate and blow the whole building the second they tripped a sensor.

But to implement such drastic security measures at both backup locations risked suicide. And he was betting that Anavosa was not suicidal.

Harris Rosenthal (Ebisu): Teams E1 and E2 in position.

Adlai marked up the scan and distributed it to his team, which consisted of three officers, eight combat dynes and two combat drones. Overkill, perhaps, but he wasn't taking any chances.

Adlai Weiss (Mirai): Teams M1 and M2 in position. Ready on my mark. He confirmed the status of his team. *Mark.*

The street pitched into darkness.

Hq (visual, 40%) | ((scan.infrared && scan.thermal)(290°:70°))

The unique signatures of four Justice dynes rushed through the entrance while the other four blew a hole in the right wall where no equipment blocked ingress. The thermal outlines of two officers followed the dynes through the entrance while he and Officer Bradley moved through the jagged hole they'd just created.

Adlai Weiss (M1): Squad 1A, guard the perimeter. Weapons fire lit up the warehouse so brilliantly it almost masked the backup generator coming to life. *Everyone else, engage all attackers!*

A dyne rushing forward into the firefight beside him exploded. *Shit!* The layout of the warehouse offered scant cover; he manifested a defensive shield for his chest and face and ran for the generator. *Attackers have custom weaponry modifications, so set all defensive measures to maximum. Drone 2, to me.*

While the power grid delivered its juice directly through conduction plates in the floor, hardlines snaked from the generator to provide for the emergency needs of the servers. If at all possible, he didn't want to blow up the generator outright, as doing so posed too much risk to the servers abutting it. He was *trying* to preserve the sapient entity they contained.

Drone 2 arrived in a whirl of electric smoke, and Adlai marked the hardlines. *Burn through these lines.*

A huge chunk of metal slammed into the outside frame of the generator; he couldn't tell whether the smoldering pile that hit the floor belonged to one of his dynes or not.

A cacophony of screeches filled the air as three of the Justice dynes closed to within melee range of their foes.

His shield crackled. He dove to the floor, letting the bulk of the shield slide up and over his head and shoulders as he tracked the weapons fire to its source, sighted down and fired on the enemy drone until its core ruptured.

The energy in the air around him began to dissipate, a sign the drone had succeeded in its task and the generator was now offline—then weapons fire zig-zagged across the room and cut into one of the server columns. The protective shielding burned brightly and began to falter. *Whatever is firing on the servers, put a stop to it!*

In his peripheral vision, Officer Bradley dove for the dangling, partially unattached arm of one of the warehouse security dynes, ripping it the rest of the way off as his forward momentum sent him crashing into the legs of a fully operational enemy dyne.

Adlai recoiled as blood sprayed across the wall. *Dammit!*

Two of his dynes, having disposed of their initial opponents, moved in to overpower the last attacker standing. Too late for Bradley, but they prevented further damage to the servers.

And like that, it was over.

Squad 1B, remain on combat alert. Adlai set an internal diagnostic routine running to confirm he hadn't overlooked a gaping hole in a vital part of his anatomy. "Thompson, check Bradley and see if there's anything we can do for him. Alvarez, try to determine the operational status of the servers and other equipment."

After checking the generator to make sure it wasn't about to overload and blow them all up, he took a couple of steps toward Thompson, but stopped when the officer shook his head grimly. He diverted toward the one area of the warehouse that had stayed silent and passive during the firefight, the cordoned-off alcove in the far-left corner.

Behind a shredded privacy screen, a remote-controlled doll of Anavosa hung in a protective glass enclosure, still and lifeless but intact.

He'd seen Joaquim Lacese's vid from the Platform. It should have prepared him for what he saw now; it hadn't. Cognitive dissonance battled itself in his mind with enough vigor to make him feel nauseated.

He'd always considered Anavosa to be quite lovely, if in a delicate, fragile way—an appearance that contrasted markedly with her shrewd, piercing intellect yet somehow added to her mystique.

Chills ran down his spine as he stared at the empty form now. In a trick of light and shadow, one side of her mouth almost seemed to curl up into a cold, macabre hint of a smile.

He swallowed heavily as Thompson came up beside him. "Gods...."

"Yeah. There are power cables running to the enclosure from somewhere. Disconnect them, just in case there's another power supply hidden in the attic or underground."

"Y-yes, sir." The officer looked physically ill as he began inspecting the outside of the enclosure.

The doll would be fine without power for a while. It wasn't constructed of living tissue, but rather a synthetic imitation of skin and bones. No organs, no brain, no pulse.

Adlai forced himself to turn away from the doll and assess the state of the warehouse.

The column of servers struck by weapons fire had sustained light damage, but at a cursory glance, all the data they held should be intact. Three of the eight Justice dynes and one of the drones he'd brought remained functional; the rest of them and all of Anavosa's security forces were headed for the scrap pile. Alvarez had sustained a shoulder injury and Bradley total body loss. Luckily, Justice employees enjoyed a priority bump to the front of the regen line, so he'd be welcoming the officer back to life in a few days.

"Cables are cut, sir."

"Thank you." On the main mission channel, the reports began to come in. Spencer's team reported a successful incursion, having suffered some squad damage but no officers lost. The others reported greater and lesser casualties, but it soon became clear that all locations were now under Justice control.

Adlai Weiss (Mirai): Great work everyone. We can afford to take a breath now.

Selene Panetier (Namino): A short one. But sure. This is me breathing.

Adlai ordered the transport crew he'd staged down the block to start securing and packing up the equipment. Two hours from now, the building would be empty and sealed up.

4

JUSTICE EVIDENCE WAREHOUSE

EBISU

The muted hum of a pervasive low-power state danced along Nika's skin, and narrow rows of lighting glowed in subtle patterns across the equipment stacked against two walls. Beyond these telltale markers of life existent, the room was quiet.

"You've shut down the others' servers."

Nika nodded, but didn't elaborate. She'd wanted to join the Justice teams in their mission, or at a minimum help coordinate the effort from the Justice Center, but Adlai had made it clear how important it was to him, and arguably to most of those involved, for everything to be handled by the book. And taking a wanted terrorist on a raid of the Guides' secure backup facilities was decidedly not by the book.

Everyone assured her that she would be officially pardoned *soon*, with the rest of NOIR following shortly thereafter. But a pardon required a functioning government to issue it, and they were still working on that particular detail. So, she'd stayed out of Justice's way while they acted on the intel Parc had so skillfully obtained for them.

Transport crews had, for now, brought all the Guides' backups to this central location, where they could be guarded more efficiently in the short term. Justice—or at least the portions of Justice they believed they could trust—was stretched thin. On the verge of breaking, one might assert, though Adlai and Spencer both would shame her if she dared to assert it.

"It's safer for everyone this way until some decisions are made regarding their, and your, futures. But the data—their memories and psyches—is intact and undamaged, I promise you. They're just sleeping."

"But not dreaming."

She considered the woman/doll standing beside her curiously. "Do you? Dream, I mean."

Delacrai Iylish smiled, but it conveyed only wistful sadness. "In a manner of speaking. We regularly run routines—" she cut herself off "—it's not important. Thank you for keeping my own servers running. It would have been easy for you to flip a switch and watch this body crumple to the floor like a marionette loosed from its strings."

"You helped us. You continue to help us, and we're grateful for it. *I'm* grateful for it. Listen, the Justice Advisors have determined that you will be charged with multiple crimes alongside the rest of the Guides. There's no getting around the fact that you were complicit in the actions the Guides as an institution approved and pursued for eight years. But I'll fight to make sure you're granted leniency. If you serve any prison time, it should be brief and, perhaps more importantly, comfortable. And for now, you have your freedom."

"Other than the constant armed escort and the tracker burned into my skin."

"Yes, other than those precautions. They're for your protection as much as our own."

"I understand. An illusory freedom is preferable to no freedom at all."

Nika wasn't so certain she agreed with the sentiment, but she opted not to argue the point. Not when Delacrai was cooperating; not when her cooperation was making tasks that should've been impossible not only feasible but, in many cases, already checked off the list. "Tell me, if you will…before we shut down their servers, the others were awake, weren't they? Were they communicating with one another? With you?"

"Yes, yes and no, but not for lack of trying on the last point. I hovered at the edges of their communications several times, but to do anything further would have revealed my presence and put me in terrible danger, tracker and escort notwithstanding."

"Of course. Still, the backup locations included additional dolls. It took us almost thirty-six hours to find and secure those locations. After the Platform exploded, why didn't they simply transfer into those dolls and get themselves out into the world? Try to wrest control of the government back away from us?"

"If asked, they will tell you they were assessing the situation, conferring with one another about potential strategies and devising a suitable plan to respond. In truth, however, I believe they were...afraid. With our fortress destroyed and our Advisors in armed revolt, our many layers of protection had vanished. I expect it all came as something of a shock to their psyches." Delacrai lifted an arm and gazed at it oddly, as if it were a mysterious alien artifact. "This body feels so very fragile. To walk the streets within it is to feel vulnerable."

"Vulnerable? But if the doll is disabled while you're occupying it, your psyche isn't damaged. The doll's merely a remote avatar."

"I said to 'feel' vulnerable, not to *be* so. The others like to proclaim their superior logic and reason, but though they—we—have drifted far from our Asterion roots, we are not base machines. The others like to proclaim they are not hampered by foolish emotions as the rest of you Asterions are, but I suspect the previous two days have proved them wrong on several levels."

Nika quite enjoyed the idea of the Guides having spent recent hours being overwhelmed by such emotions as *fear*, as *panic* and *distress*.

"You realize, they will have attempted to activate countermeasures against this transfer of power. They have access to many resources they can use to do so."

She nodded. "And we are shutting down those resources as quickly as we can identify and track them. Again, thank you for your help in that regard. As for me, personally? I've been hunted for the last five years. I can handle it."

"I am sorry, though these empty words do nothing to change the past."

"I know you are." There was nothing else to do here, and Nika started to turn and leave, then pivoted back. "Can I ask you a question?"

"You have done nothing but ask me questions since we became reacquainted."

She laughed. "I suppose that's true. How did you—the five of you—end up like this? Why did you retreat into hardware and stop inhabiting bodies as anything more than remote avatars? When?"

Delacrai's stoic expression flinched, and she stared at the stacks of servers for several seconds before answering. "As with all life, evolution is a thousand tiny adjustments occurring over the span of countless millennia. It wasn't a single decision, but rather the soft seduction of a winding path that ultimately led us here.

"We needed to be objective in order to rule wisely. We increasingly withdrew, cutting ourselves off from the daily workings of society, from our friends and our former lives. In the resulting absence of real, physical connection to the world—to the sensation of sand between our toes and the warmth of another's skin against our own—the synthetic roots of every Asterion grew far stronger in us."

The woman sighed deliberately. "The details are a dull, dreary tale. By the time it became more convenient for us to default to a quantum state and discard a physical, fully functioning body, our minds had long since abandoned all semblance of an external, vibrant life lived among our people."

"Do you want to return to being a true Asterion?"

Delacrai's expression flared—her eyes widened, her lips parted—and she took half a step back. "It's such a long road to traverse."

Nika, however, knew something of the sentencing options the Justice Advisors were mulling over. "It doesn't have to be."

5

MARIS' LOFT

MIRAI

"**B**ecause we don't store people."

"Not as a policy, no. But if there were ever special circumstances calling for it, these are them. As things stand at present, the Guides are too dangerous to be allowed to be conscious."

Adlai had missed the first part of the conversation, and he listened long enough to get the gist before joining in. "Nika's right. If we start storing people, we're already halfway down the slippery slope to what the Guides became. Sorry I'm late. New pockets of civil disobedience popped up here on Mirai as soon as the sun set."

Julien frowned at him but let the storing issue go for the moment. "Riots?"

Adlai found an empty chair and collapsed into it. After they'd gotten kicked out of Mirai Tower by repair crews this afternoon, Maris had hastily converted her dining/living area into a general-purpose meeting space, and she'd somehow managed to make the loft look as if it had been designed for it.

"So far, we've only seen two incidents of organized violence, both of which were subdued without significant trouble. But crowds are protesting outside government offices on every Axis World and half the Adjunct ones. Worse, people are refusing to follow orders from Justice dynes, even in routine interactions at transit hubs and Admin offices.

"I recognize you all were discussing the Guides' sentencing when I arrived, but now that we control the Guides' hardware, I submit that we need to deal with more pressing matters first. Namely, restoring civil order."

Harris shrugged helplessly, which Adlai didn't care for. Justice Advisors were never helpless. "People are afraid, and they don't know who or what to trust. We have to find some way to calm them down, but I'm at a loss. Frankly, they *should* be afraid. I know I am."

Scattered chuckles rippled around the room, and Adlai pinched the bridge of his nose. He ought to take the levity as a sign to lighten up a little himself, but how?

Nika leaned forward in her chair. "Radical transparency."

A few chairs down, Selene perked up in interest. "What do you mean?"

"The Guides acted as they did under the rubric of 'protecting the people' and 'averting a panic.' Well, we see how that worked out. People are afraid of what they don't understand. The more they find closed doors and hear furtive whispers, the more the conspiracy theories will spread like wildfire, with panic a step behind. So, no closed doors. No whispers. We tell everyone about the threat from the Rasu. We tell everyone what the Guides did. We tell them what we're doing to repair the damage already done and to meet the threat. We make good on my promise to ask for their help."

Despite her limbo legal status, Nika certainly seemed to be making herself at home among the Advisors. Adlai wasn't surprised, but it had been a while since he'd seen her work a room.

"But won't this cause greater panic, from genuine, justified fear this time?"

She gestured in Harris' direction. "You said you're afraid, but I don't see you running around in circles hysterically, bashing in windows or flailing your hands about and tearing at your hair. Asterions aren't children, and we shouldn't treat them as such. The Guides worked hard to make us forget this, but the government only exists for convenience and consistency. It's not a caretaker.

"Right now, we're smack in the middle of a civilization-threatening crisis. I say we tell the citizens that we're getting our shit together as fast as we can, and they need to do the same."

Harris raised his hands in resignation, if half in jest. "Fine. I'm convinced if the rest of you are. It beats the other terrible options, anyway."

A few mild grumbles followed, but no one argued, and Nika shifted toward Maris. "Could you write up some talking points and make them sound eloquent?"

"As I do. Of course."

Nika sank down in her chair and crossed her arms over her chest. "Okay, what's next?"

Adlai realized then that she wasn't merely making herself at home with the others—she was in charge. He caught Dashiel's attention, who sat to the other side of Nika, and received an amused shrug from his friend.

Katherine Colson spoke up. "Cargo ships will be arriving at Hokan Station within the hour. They will take the occupied stasis chambers to medical facilities where the individuals inside them can be revived safely. Gemina has provided the necessary login credentials for the server at the station as well as the *ADV Tabiji's* systems, and a forensic team will analyze all the data stored there."

Nika arched an eyebrow. "Gemina's cooperating?"

"She's bitching about it, not surprisingly, but she's honestly been helpful so far. I don't want to presume, but I think she's relieved."

"About what?"

"Not having to carry this burden alone any longer."

Adlai shook his head. "She wasn't alone. She had Satair to commiserate with."

Nika's attention darted to the door, and her expression brightened. Adlai twisted around in his chair to see Perrin walking in. She wore torn denim pants and an off-the-shoulder white sweater; her hair was bound into two loose, braided pigtails.

He forgot how to breathe.

"Sorry for the intrusion! Nika, can I talk to you for a minute?" She glanced his way, giving him a little wave.

"Sure." Nika motioned for the others to continue, then went into the kitchen with Perrin, where they conferred out of earshot.

"What are we planning to do with the people in the stasis chambers once they're awakened?"

"Adlai? Have you decided?"

Crap, he'd been staring and completely tuned out the conversation. Also, his cheeks were almost certainly burning. "Um, convicts will be given full pardons of their sentences on account of the government trying to kill them, as well as free regens for those infected with the virutox. The rest isn't up to Justice."

Katherine chimed in. "Administration will try to help them find new jobs and provide financial support as required. I admit we have a lot to make right here, but there's only so much we can do."

Perrin and Nika rejoined them then, and Perrin shot Katherine a dubious look. "You can do a lot more than that, I guarantee it. These people are going to be freaked out—even more freaked out than everyone else is. They've spent weeks or months as involuntary popsicles, and they'll be woken up to be told the government planned to serve them as the main course to a bunch of galaxy-consuming aliens. Oh, and their jobs are gone. Possibly their homes as well. 'We're sorry' isn't going to cut it."

"I don't believe you're qualified to weigh in on—"

Nika shot the Administration Advisor a scathing glare. "She's done a damn sight better job of taking care of people in need than it sounds like any of you have done lately."

"She also just contradicted you. I thought you said Asterions could take care of themselves."

"I didn't mean the people who've been infected with a contagion, kidnapped, forced into comas and prepped for alien sacrifice, for fuck's sake. Let her speak." She gave Perrin an encouraging nod.

Perrin wrung her hands but lifted her chin. "For starters, you need to provide a place to stay for anyone who had their housing forfeited or sold off while they were locked in a stasis chamber. Someplace cozy. Maybe together with other un-popsicled people, so they'll have someone to confide in about their ordeal. Also, you should give them free access to counselors, so they can talk to someone qualified to listen the right way. Plus, yes, money and job support. Basically, you need to make them feel as if they haven't lost everything they hold dear. Make them feel safe."

Katherine sputtered out a response. "Nobody's going to be safe for long if we don't come up with a way to combat the Rasu."

"And that's way out of my league. But…I can help out on this, if you want. I mean, I still have a bunch of our own people to get settled, but after that?" She turned to Nika. "Tell me who here has the power to make the things I listed happen, and I'll take care of the rest."

Nika wrapped an arm around Perrin. "You don't have to take so much onto your shoulders, which I happen to know are already well-laden. But, yes, we would welcome your help. We can talk details later tonight."

"Okay. I'll see you a little later." Perrin sneaked a quick smile Adlai's way and headed out the door.

He stood before he'd consciously decided to do so. "Excuse me a minute. I want to check on something with the office." He spun and hurried out the door after her before anyone could question his intentions.

By the time the door closed behind him, Perrin was on the verge of turning down the next hallway and disappearing from sight. "Hey, hang on for a second."

She stopped and looked back at him, then reversed course. "I hope I wasn't too rude in there. I really didn't mean to step on anyone's toes. They were just being so…pompous and haughty and out-of-touch with the reality of what people are facing out there in the real world."

"They were. And you set them straight so beautifully. You were wonderful."

"Oh? Well, good." They met in the middle of the hallway, but she didn't come to a stop until she was breathtakingly close to him. "What did you want to talk to me about? I know you've been super busy, and I've tried not to bother you."

"I cannot conceive of a scenario where you would be a bother. I wanted to talk to you about—" He reached up and cupped her face in his hands, leaned in and placed a soft kiss on her far softer lips, then hovered there for too long before dropping his hands and clearing his throat nervously.

What had he done? Stars, his body was leagues ahead of his brain when it came to her. "I, um, hope I didn't misread—"

"You didn't." She drew him into her arms and enthusiastically returned her lips to his.

ᐯᖇ

Adlai tip-toed back into the loft several minutes later. Maybe closer to ten. He'd kind of lost track of time.

An animated conversation was again in progress, and he tried to inconspicuously slide into his chair, only to find Nika staring at him pointedly. "Take care of what you needed to?"

"Ah...." He chuckled in spite of himself. He could still taste her on his tongue. She'd tasted like strawberries...strawberry lips and blueberry irises. "Yes, I did. Thank you."

"Uh-huh." She made a face but redirected her attention to the conversation, which was probably as much of a seal of approval as he was apt to get from her.

Dashiel was discussing...metals, perhaps? "I've clipped out the most relevant captures from the *Wayfarer's* visit to the Rasu stronghold as well as those from Nika's simex memory. Today I've gotten in touch with every person I know who knows the first thing about advanced materials, both inside Industry and in private scientific research and development, and asked them to study the footage. But I don't know everyone. One way we can ask for people to help is by inviting any knowledgeable people to come forward. The more eyes on this problem, the better chance we have of discerning what the Rasu are and how they operate."

Nika nodded emphatically. "It's a great idea. This is exactly the kind of thing I'm getting at. Simply because someone doesn't work for a Division or hasn't done business with any of you, it doesn't mean they won't have worthwhile ideas to contribute."

"I'm beginning to appreciate that."

She reached over and squeezed Dashiel's hand, and it was such a natural gesture, so like the way they used to be, that it threatened to give Adlai hope they all might actually survive this.

Maris had vanished while he'd been out in the hallway, but now she burst into the midst of the group in an explosion of fervor. "I have such wonderful news! Charles Basquan has offered us the use of the Mirai One Pavilion as a temporary headquarters building starting first thing in the morning. So, all of you can clear out of my living room and grant me some blessed peace. Not of mind, of course, but at least of silence."

Katherine scowled again, if she'd ever stopped. "How much is it going to cost us to use the Pavilion?"

"I assume he will expect reimbursement over a long enough timeline, but he's willing to hand-wave an IOU for now. And I do suggest we take him up on it."

⋏R

Katherine approached Nika as the meeting at Maris' loft broke up. "If you have a second, there are a couple of things I'd like to go over."

"Sure. What about?"

"You, actually."

"Oh." Nika forced herself not to adopt a defensive posture, but she did steel herself for an incoming blow. "What do you mean?"

"Since I had two spare minutes on the way here, I corrected your official records—the ones erroneously stating you voluntarily underwent full Retirement and Reinitialization five years ago. As a result of the correction, your former identity has been reinstated."

"You mean I'm an Advisor again?"

"That part's not so simple, remains tangled up in the in-process pardon, and also isn't in my power to grant. But your bank accounts and property have all been returned to you. It turns out the Guides never liquidated them." She offered Nika a data weave. "Here you go."

She stared at the weave. What bank accounts? What property? "I...thank you. I appreciate you making the effort on my behalf."

"You really don't remember your past, do you?"

"I remember...scattered events. Moments. But they're droplets in the ocean of the life I had, I'm afraid."

"You're doing a top-notch job of faking it. For good or ill, you are exactly how I remember you. Perhaps a little bit scarier. I didn't used to be afraid you'd break my arm if I displeased you. I'm still not afraid, but now I believe you *could*. Anyway, if you'll excuse me, I need to find some food before I faint right in the middle of the floor."

Nika considered the emptying loft. Dashiel was deep in conversation with one of the other Industry Advisors, so she pinged him on her way out the door.

I have some errands to run. I'll touch base in a few hours.

Okay. Be safe out there...or smart at a minimum.

Now you're getting it. I will.

6

MIRAI

Nika's hand moved to the lock on the door as naturally as if it were tucking her hair behind her ear; five years out of practice, yet the motion remained ingrained in her muscle memory. She was coming home, just as she had thousands of times before, for the first time all over again.

The door unlocked, and the open entrance awaited her. She trembled as she stepped through it.

Sensing her arrival, the lights illuminated automatically, and she gasped at the scene they showed her.

A cavernous living room was painted in bright whites, calming heather grays, soft powder blues and silver accents. A distressed wood floor gave the space a naturally lived-in feel, though no one had set foot upon it in years. Marble and stone walls displayed a rich variety of art and visuals. An abstract sculpture shaped of unburnished pewter in one corner instantly made her smile. A gift from Maris, no doubt.

A sunken area held three connected couches stacked with plush cushions and a wavy table at the center. A wide fireplace set into a column of natural stone cut into otherwise floor-to-ceiling windows stretching the breadth of the opposite wall, revealing a stunning view of the night lights of Hataori Harbor.

The far third of the living room held several equally plush chairs and small tables arranged in more intimate enclaves. Beyond them, a pane displaying scenic vistas from across the Dominion spanned most of the left wall.

She wanted to investigate every nook and cranny—every curio and fabric—but she should see the rest of the flat first, right?

The kitchen was similarly bright and airy, lined in marble countertops with rows of tiny lights suspended above them. Past the kitchen was a dining table so long it could seat half the Advisors, and a tall mirror mounted on the wall at one end created the illusion that it could seat them all.

She retraced her steps to turn left at the kitchen, where a frosted door opened on her approach. On the other side waited her bedroom.

If she blinked, it would surely vanish. The basic color palette carried over, with deeper silvers and darker nickel-grays giving it a more cozy, intimate feel. An enormous bed was topped by an exquisite woven throw, and soft icicle lights dangled from the ceiling above it. To the right, a spacious marble bathtub looked seconds away from bubbles and champagne.

A chaise sat in front of the expansive window to the left, which included a door leading to a balcony.

As if in a trance, she walked to the door and opened it to let the cool breeze ruffle her hair. The balcony curved along the building's façade like an undulating ribbon and stretched the length of the flat.

She'd never felt more at home in her life.

Donning a goofy grin, she spun around and rushed across the bedroom and bath to the closet, which was nearly as big as her room at The Chalet. And stuffed full—all of her old clothes were still here!

Her jaw dropped as she scanned the rows of clothing and shelves of shoes. Barely a quarter of the items were black. While immensely grateful for a brand-new wardrobe, especially since after The Chalet's destruction she owned a grand total of 3.5 outfits, the sheer vividness of said wardrobe was going to take some adjusting to.

She went back into the bedroom and threw herself on the bed with a cackle. Gods, it was even softer than it appeared. Oh, this was heaven....

After a few minutes of bliss, she reluctantly crawled off the bed and returned to the living room. The decor was all so elegant and refined, yet it felt *real.* The art on the walls no longer held any meaning for her, yet it wasn't sterile or cold; it felt representative of a life lived in full.

She plopped down on one of the connected couches, because it wasn't the type of couch you had the need to perch carefully on the edge of. It was a couch meant for lounging, for hanging out with friends.

That was what she'd done here, wasn't it? This whole room was designed not just to make herself feel comfortable, but to make visitors feel the same.

She gazed around, and her vision populated with the ghosts of imagined gatherings. Of people flitting here and there, laughing, playing, eating, dancing. She couldn't explain it, but she knew in her soul this had been a place of happiness and joy.

Her gaze fell on the wavy table situated between the couches, and she noticed a small inset in the corner, flush with the surface. Curious, she pressed it.

A carousel of images materialized above the table. The first image was a candid shot of her and Dashiel in formal dress, whispering to one another arm-in-arm as a light show proceeded in the sky behind them.

She reached out and flicked the image to the left, and the focus shifted to one of her and Maris bundled up in winter-weather attire, complete with scarves and fuzzy caps, surrounded by frozen drifts and snow-coated trees.

She flicked again.

ᛘᚱ

Dashiel paused at the door, overcome by a wave of déjà vu. How many times had he opened this door? Thousands, certainly, if not tens of thousands.

As with so many other matters, the Guides had lied to him about Nika's flat. They'd claimed it was sold at auction in accordance with the regulations pertaining to R&Rs, along with all the furniture inside and personal items that should never, *ever* have been transferred to others.

In reality, they'd simply assigned ownership to themselves, locked it up and buried the records.

He prepared himself for the blast of memories waiting on the other side and opened the door—

—and traveled back in time. Everything was exactly the same, if a little dustier than on his last visit.

Nika sat on the couch closest to the kitchen, always her favorite, with her elbows propped on her knees and her hands fisted at her chin, staring at a carousel of images floating in front of her. When she saw him, she hurriedly stood, wiping at her cheeks with the back of her hands. "I meant to ping you earlier. How did you know where to find me?"

"Maris told me that Katherine had returned your old property ownership records, because of course Maris knows everything the instant it happens. I...are you crying?"

She pursed her lips and wiped at her cheeks again. "Yeah."

"Oh, Nika." He went around the edge of the couch and wrapped his arms around her. "Are they happy tears, or sad ones?"

"I don't know." She sniffled against his chest. "All these things? Images, art, memorabilia, furniture, clothes? They're all wonderful. This place is...amazing, and in my heart, it feels like home. But why can't I remember the stories behind everything here?" The last few words caught in her throat as a sob wracked her chest.

He stroked her hair and caressed her back wordlessly. It hadn't been a question, but rather a raging shout against an injustice that could never be undone, a wound that could never be mended.

Abruptly she straightened up and grabbed his hands then flattened her palms on his. "Relevance. There must be encrypted memories that will be triggered by this place." She closed her eyes.

After a few seconds, a frown darkened her features. "Maybe I need to think of something in particular. Something...." Her brow knotted up in concentration. Longer seconds ticked by.

She blew out a harsh breath. "There's nothing. Dashiel, I can't access any new memories. What if there aren't any more at all? No, that can't be. I wouldn't have left myself with only such paltry crumbs to go on." She pressed her palms harder against his and squeezed her eyes shut once more...but her pained, frustrated expression told the tale.

As gently as he could, he wound his hands around hers, breaking the connection. "Maybe you didn't have time to encrypt any additional memories. Maybe you didn't start to prepare until it was almost too late."

"I suppose that's possible." Her shoulders sagged as she reopened her eyes to allow fresh tears to escape in jagged rivulets down flushed cheeks. "This can't be all there is."

He kissed her forehead. "It's okay if it is."

"No." She choked back a sob. "It's not! I want to remember this place, dammit! I want to remember these stories."

He brought his hands to her face, tenderly catching the tears with his thumbs. "I'm so sorry. But you'll make new memories. You already are."

She made a passing attempt to compose herself. "If I have no more memories to call on...can you help me remember in other ways? Can I ask you—" she reached down and flicked through a bunch of images before stopping on an image of him and her standing in front a hovercraft on a beach "—where this was taken?"

"We went on vacation to an exploratory world, SR52-San. It has this exotic jungle island out in the middle of one of its oceans. Waterfalls and hot springs and colorful birds and whatnot. But no one had built a d-gate out to the island yet, so a hovercraft was the only way to reach it." He chuckled lightly, though his heart felt so damn heavy. "You drove, and very nearly got us drowned skimming too close to a rogue wave."

She cackled through the tears. "Wonderful." She sat down on the couch and hurriedly scrolled through several more images until she reached one of the two of them in heavy workpants and jackets, covered in dirt and grime. "And this?"

"Ah." He sat beside her and wrapped an arm over her shoulders. "This was taken on Chosek. Shoset—a regional Governor you often interfaced with—took us on a tour of his largest kyoseil mine, which ran under a volcano."

"Oh, no. Did the volcano erupt while we were inside the mine?"

"Not erupt, precisely, but it did rumble a tad too much for comfort. Hence all the dust. The entrance caved in, and this image was taken while we were waiting for a crew to dig us out. Shoset was most apologetic."

"Stars...." She flicked back and forth, clearly searching for a specific image, and finally stopped when she landed on one of her and Maris in full gala attire in front of a fountain. "And where was this?"

"This was before I met you, but you told me it was taken at the grand opening of the Mirai One Pavilion."

"The place we're invading in the morning?"

"One and the same."

She sank back into his arms with a sigh. "Thank you, darling."

"I'll tell you stories all night long, if you want."

She laughed haltingly, broken up by a sniffle. "You're sweet. How about a couple a day instead? I want to savor each story."

"It's a deal."

ALIASES

DAYS UNTIL RASU DEADLINE: 25

7

MIRAI

Nika had cleaned herself up and showered in the palatial bathroom—seriously, it was ridiculous how roomy it was—by the time Perrin arrived. She'd invited her friend over because she was excited about the flat and selfishly wanted Perrin to see it. And because it felt too vast to be alone in. Too many ghosts in the shadows that might start whispering to her if it got quiet.

"Oh, my stars!" Perrin darted around the living room excitedly. "This is amazing! Did you—wait, is Dashiel here? I don't want to embarrass myself in front of him."

"No, he had to go meet with a couple of metals experts who are trying to figure out what the Rasu could possibly be composed of. He'll be back in a few hours."

"Great. Eeee!" Perrin flopped down on one of the couches. "I'll be honest. I am digging old Nika's tastes. None of your dreary, oh-so-serious black here."

"It is rather bright, and wait until you see the closet." She sat down opposite Perrin and clasped her hands together. "It's been a crazy couple of days, and we haven't had time to catch up and talk—and there's a lot we need to talk about. First up, you and Adlai."

"Is it that obvious?"

"The instant I saw the two of you together, I sensed how he felt toward you. He was practically drooling."

"Well, it shocked the hells out of me."

"Only because you never give yourself enough credit. Listen, I need to confess something. Before we went to rescue Dashiel and Joaquim, I warned Adlai that if we survived the night, he and I were going to have a conversation about you. But it wasn't fair of me to threaten him, was it? I'm instinctively protective of you, but you can take care of your heart just fine. Unless you need me to run interference for it, in which case, say the word and I'm there."

"Nika, he's a good man. A *really* good man."

"I think he probably is, yes. I distrusted him at first, but he's proved himself to me since then—and to you, clearly. I guess what I'm saying is, I'm happy for you." She ran her hand over the soft fabric of the couch, shocked anew it belonged to her. *Home.* "But Joaquim won't be."

"Ugh. For the four-thousandth time, Jo and I are not star-crossed would-be lovers!"

"I believe you. But you're his closest friend, and he's not going to be happy about you dating a Justice Advisor."

Perrin dropped her head against the couch cushion. "Oh, crap. You're right. He sees Justice and everyone who works there as his personal nemeses. How am I going to tell him?"

"I can't think of a single good way. Sorry. But I will back you up if he acts like too much of an asshole over it. Where is he, anyway? I haven't seen him since this morning, I think?"

"He went to get his burns repaired, and growing matching new skin can take hours. Also, all the clinics have been packed ever since the transit hub explosion."

"Good for him—he looked rough. Now, next topic: you shouldn't have volunteered yourself at the meeting this evening."

"Did I overstep? I realize it wasn't my place to interject my opinions, but that woman was being a heartless bitch."

"No, you didn't overstep…or I suppose maybe you did, but I don't give a damn about an Advisor's power play. By the way, her name's Katherine Colson, and word is she can give Gemina Kail a run for her money in the bitch department. I don't know what it is Administration does to its Advisors to make them so unpleasant."

"Bury their souls beneath mountains of drudgery and mindless procedures? It's Admin."

"Okay, fair point. No, you shouldn't have volunteered because you've been going nonstop for weeks now, and you deserve a rest."

"No one else is getting a rest. We can't afford to rest, not yet. After the horrors the Guides put them through, those people need help, and they need it to come from someone who actually cares about them."

Perrin's resolute expression broadcast the futility of trying to change her mind, and Nika sighed. "Oh, fine. But if the burden gets to be too heavy, you had better yell."

"Whimper, maybe. But I will."

"Thank you." She considered the spacious living room for the hundredth time in the last hour. As she'd observed earlier, it was meant for entertaining, meant to be filled with the sounds of joy and laughter...she turned back to Perrin and grabbed her hands. "On a related note, there's something I can do to take a few items off your plate tonight. How many of our people still need housing?"

"Let's see...ten. No, eleven. Most of them slept at Mirai Tower last night with the rest of us, but now that the repair crews have moved in, I've got to find a new solution." Perrin glanced toward the windows. "And it's getting late. I ought to—"

"Tell them all to come here."

"What?"

"They'll want to bring pop-out cots or sleeping pouches, but there's all this floorspace and couchspace and *space*. We'll transform the living room into a campground. I'll overstock the kitchen, since it also turns out I have money to buy things now. If nothing else, it's warm and dry, and people will be safe here until we devise a more permanent solution."

"Oh, Nika, you are amazing." Perrin leapt forward to grab her in a fierce hug. "I'll let everyone know."

⨀

Dashiel returned to Nika's flat far later than he'd intended. He wished he could say his tardiness was because the meeting had been productive, but it was difficult to make much progress when you had no known reference point from which to start. He'd given the others everything they had on the Rasu, such as it was, and they'd agreed to meet again tomorrow. A meeting guaranteed to conflict with three other meetings he needed to attend, but he'd manage.

He opened the door to the flat, then stopped as déjà vu far more powerful than what he'd experienced earlier washed over him. It sounded as though a party was underway inside, with multiple voices and conversations overlapping the sounds of movement and general frivolity.

Just like in the old days…but it wasn't the old days any longer.

He stepped into the entryway and peeked around the corner to see ten, maybe twelve or thirteen strangers in various stages of *camping* on Nika's living room floor. Most of the furniture had been shoved against the walls; pop-up cots lined the interior wall, sleeping pouches were spread out across the floor and pillows had been tossed on the couches. He spotted Perrin helping a man get settled into a rare free spot in the left corner.

Nika was in the kitchen, unwrapping food platters and handing them off to another woman he didn't know. She'd pulled her hair back in a sloppy tail, and she'd changed into lavender linen pants and an oversized chambray shirt…*his* shirt. From before.

She'd mentioned earlier today in passing that a number of NOIR members remained homeless in the wake of The Chalet's destruction, and he had to assume this was how the current state of affairs had come to be.

How remarkable was she? Mere hours after discovering a home she'd never known existed, she'd opened its doors to…yes, her people.

Her gaze passed across the room and spotted him. She gave him an exaggerated shrug.

When he joined her in the kitchen, she set a platter on the counter and wrapped her arms around his neck. "I couldn't leave them out on the street when I had this obscene amount of free space. It'll only be for a day or two, I promise."

He sighed somewhat ruefully. "This wasn't exactly how I imagined us spending our first night together back at your place, but I understand."

"Good. Thank you." She dropped her voice a notch. "It's not as if any of them are crashing in my bedroom, which does have a door with a lock."

"It's *not exactly* how I imagined us spending our first night together back at your place."

"I admit, this doesn't lend itself to a particularly romantic atmosphere." Her eyes danced nonetheless. "But it was like this a lot, wasn't it? I mean, maybe not sleeping pouches in the middle of the floor, but filled with people. Talking and laughing and probably drinking."

"Yes, it was like this a lot. You loved having people here. Loved bringing them joy. And..." he gestured toward the living room and its many occupants "...it seems you still do."

She peered over his shoulder. "Hey, Parc!"

Dashiel turned to see two people he had met, Parc Eshett and Ryan Theroit. They crouched beside two spider bots that were engaged in melee combat, to the cheers of those nearby.

Parc looked up in question. "What?"

"You two have a place to stay, right?"

"Yeah."

She made a face and approached them. "Great. Why are you here, then?"

Parc motioned to the ongoing combat. "Spiderbot Smackdown!"

She nodded vaguely to herself, then spun around when Perrin tapped her on the shoulder.

"All the food's set, and I've done a headcount twice. Everyone who told me they needed a place to stay is here."

"And two who don't."

Perrin rolled her eyes. "So I see. I promise I'll get back to work finding more permanent lodging first thing in the morning. My goal is to have everyone relocated before this time tomorrow night, and I feel good about my chances." She fidgeted. "All you have to do is ask, and I'll stay tonight and help you out, because this is pretty crazy. But if you don't need me...?"

"I guess I assumed you'd be staying, but if you have someplace to be, Dashiel and I can handle things without too much trouble."

"I sort of do."

"Which is..." Nika groaned dramatically "...*oh*."

Perrin flashed her a hopeful, pleading expression.

Nika shoved Perrin toward the door. "Go! Get out of here. You've more than earned a night of bliss."

"Oh, I hope it's bliss. Do you think it will be bliss?"

"No way am I answering that." Nika kept nudging her all the way to the door and out it before returning to the kitchen to lean against the counter beside Dashiel.

He gave her a confused look. "What just happened? What bliss?"

"You haven't had a chance to hang out with Adlai and catch up since we came back to Mirai, have you?"

"No, not real—*oh*. Seriously?"

"Apparently. They worked together to distribute the virutox vaccine after Satair kidnapped Joaquim, and she's the one who brought him into our confidence to help rescue you on the Platform. Now they're all doe-eyed and dreamy."

He pondered on it a minute. "They're actually kind of perfect for each other."

"If he breaks her heart, I'm fully intending on kicking his ass."

"Sure. Assuming she doesn't beat you to it. She's very...demonstrative."

"Is she ever."

"Hey, Nika, sorry to interrupt." A woman approached them and thrust her hand out. "Hi, I'm Josie. You must be Dashiel."

He accepted the hand. "That's right. It's nice to meet you."

"Same." She turned to Nika. "Do you have any bonding tape? Geoff got a nasty scrape on debris at the Tower, and he's been ignoring it all day."

"I think Perrin brought some. Check in that bag over there." She pointed to a hefty bag sitting near the wall, and Josie scurried off.

Nika wound her arms around his waist. "Not exactly how you imagined, huh?"

"It's okay. We have time." He leaned in and kissed her ear. "By the way, I like your shirt."

᙭᙭

Perrin smoothed out the folds of her sweater. It being a *sweater*, however, as soon as she removed her hands the folds settled back into their previous sloppiness.

She should have changed into something better. More alluring or at least easier to tame. But the rest of her clothes were ashes beneath the rubble of The Chalet, and shopping for new ones hadn't been high on the priority list today. She'd taken two minutes on the way here to re-braid her hair, since he'd said he liked it braided. Should she change the hue? He hadn't said he liked the color. Or disliked it.

"Ugh...you look fine, Perrin, or at least as presentable as you ever do. Get over yourself and go with it." She straightened her spine and pressed the bell, then tried not to fidget while she waited.

And waited.

Was Adlai not home? Had she misunderstood? He'd said to meet her at his place—and she'd triple-checked the address—after she finished up at Nika's. Granted, he hadn't explicitly said *tonight*, but it had definitely been implied, if only because in their current circumstances *tomorrow* night was about ten years too far away to consider making plans for.

He must have come to his senses and realized the obvious folly of entertaining someone of her ilk. Gods, this was so stupid! She had no business frothing over a date when people in dire straits were depending on her to take care of them—lots more people than she'd started the day with, even, thanks to her opening her big mouth at the Advisor meeting earlier.

She studied the closed door for another few seconds, then turned to trudge down the hallway toward the lift, her cheeks burning. She'd stop at a thrift store and pick up a couple of pants and shirts before going back to Nika's place and crashing with the others, because in all the craziness she'd forgotten to find a place for herself to stay—

—she bumped smack into something as she rounded the corner.

"Ah!" She stumbled backward, feeling for the wall in a desperate attempt to keep from falling on her ass.

"Excuse me. Perrin? Oh damn, I'm so sorry." Adlai reached out and grabbed her upper arm to steady her. "I was in a hurry and didn't pay attention to where I was going. Are you all right?"

She rubbed at her nose, which had taken the brunt of the collision. "Just a little bump is all." She checked her palm, then showed it to him. "See? No blood."

He stared at her. She stared at him. Her heart pitter-pattered around in her chest like a dancing monkey. Gods, this was awkward.

Finally, he blinked. "I'm also sorry I was running late. An issue arose on the security setup for the Guides' storage backups, then I had to authorize two squads to peacefully subdue a crowd outside the Administration Center..." distress gradually overtook his features "...and you were leaving."

"No. No, I was...going to see if maybe you were down the hall or...in the lobby."

"You were leaving."

She winced, breaking eye contact and fighting not to massage her nose again; it still stung. "I assumed you got held up with work, and I don't want to distract you from all the important duties you need to attend to right now. Which it sounds as though I've done. You should go back to the office."

"I should." He took her by the hand and led her down the hallway toward his door. This was not the way back to his office.

"Okay, but...."

"In about five hours." He stopped in front of the door and faced her. A crooked little half-smile decorated his lips and made his mist-gray irises sparkle even in the dull lighting of the hallway. "Will you spend those five hours with me?"

She tried not to broadcast the giddy exuberance that erupted in fireworks to spread outward from her chest and tingle her skin. "Only if you promise to open the door. It's chilly out here in the hallway."

"What? Oh, of course." He shook his head roughly, unlocked the door and gestured inside. "In here. Will you spend those five hours with me *in here?*"

"Yes, I will."

He ushered her inside ahead of him. The lights rose to reveal a nice if somewhat minimally furnished space, one a tad rumpled at the margins and thus utterly genuine. A perfect reflection of him.

"Can I fix you something to drink?"

She'd hurriedly downed two giant glasses of wine in Nika's kitchen earlier to psyche herself up for their rendezvous; if she had any more alcohol now, she'd embarrass herself and flutz the whole thing up. "Water's fine."

He returned to her side a few seconds later with two glasses of water. She accepted one, took a sip, then placed it on the counter and stepped into his personal space.

His free hand rose to hesitantly caress her cheek. A smile appeared on his face but quickly faltered. "Forty-two hundred years, and I'm still terrible at this."

She eased in closer, until the folds of her sweater rustled against the fabric of his shirt. "You're not terrible at it—you're just you."

"And that's a good thing?"

"Yep." She took his glass from his hand and set it on the counter beside hers, then intertwined their fingers and not-so-gently pressed her lips to his.

8

MIRAI ONE PAVILION

MIRAI

"You look rather pleased, sir. Did we deduce how to defeat the Rasu last night and no one's told me yet?"

Adlai wasn't pleased—he was jubilant. But it wasn't right or proper to be jubilant when the world was ending. He hurriedly schooled his expression into soberness before meeting Spencer's inquisitive gaze.

They were in one of the many conference rooms at the Mirai One Pavilion, which as of forty-five minutes earlier now served as a temporary headquarters for Advisor business. For government business, Rasu business and likely NOIR business as well.

The sounds of transport teams moving heavy equipment into a larger conference room across the hall filled the air, and he went over and closed the door. "Regrettably, we did not. I was merely reflecting on…how grateful I am that we're all working toward the same goal now, instead of fighting each other."

"This is a positive development, as is no longer being shot at by our own dynes. You wanted a status report on the security for the Guides' sentencing?"

"I did. Yes, definitely." He'd awoken this morning to a lengthy list of additional security glitches that had crept up overnight; thankfully, none of them proved critical. They couldn't afford to screw this up.

"All the equipment we seized has arrived at the Justice Evidence Warehouse on Ebisu. Several of the servers suffered cosmetic damage during their seizure, but failure testing indicates no data was lost and the servers remain functional. The remote connections to the dolls were also tested and appear to be in order.

We should be able to..." Spencer's jaw twitched "...force transfers at the appropriate time."

"Good, I guess. And security?"

"With respect to the servers, Priority One measures are fully in place. With respect to the dolls? We've deep-scanned them and confirmed there aren't any combat upgrades installed, so the physical risk is minimal. Nonetheless, they'll be contained within force-field cages before the transfers are initiated. And during the proceeding, I'll have my finger on the master power switch at all times."

"Thank you. You are, as always, an exceptional officer. Which is why...I probably shouldn't tell you this, since it isn't official and won't be for several days or possibly weeks, but I've recommended you to replace Satair in the Synra Justice Division."

Spencer blinked. "An Advisor? Me?"

"Absolutely you. You've acted in an exemplary manner throughout this crisis and have gone above and beyond to protect the people, even when it put your career at risk. Your sense of justice is impeccable, and you're not afraid to make tough decisions. Sounds like an Advisor to me."

"I don't know what to say, sir. I've only followed your lead."

"That's a lie, but you're kind to say it." Movement outside the window caught his attention, and he glanced that way in time to see Perrin crossing the courtyard toward the building entrance. His chest instantly warmed, almost as if he'd drank in a steaming mug of coffee rather than the sight of her. He wished he could spare the briefest of minutes to go greet her now, but duty came first.

It wasn't right or proper to be jubilant when the world was ending, but he couldn't help it. It felt like *his* world was just beginning.

He cleared his throat and forced himself to turn away from the window. "I need to check on a myriad of emergencies, as well as find out what the hells is going on across the hall. Unless something changes, I'll meet you at the sentencing in an hour."

"I'll see you there, sir."

"You become an Advisor, and you'll finally have to stop calling me 'sir.'"

"Yes, sir."

SYNRA

A large crowd had gathered outside the building by the time Adlai arrived. Dammit, how had the location of the sentencing leaked to the public? From inside Justice was the only logical conclusion; he knew some officers remained loyal to Satair and the Guides, but rooting them out sat midway down a list of priorities scrawled in bright red exclamation points.

The protestors weren't rioting, but they were demonstrably angry. Chanted slogans overlapped full-throated shouts, and vulgar signs spelling out coarse threats flashed and pulsed above their heads. A dangerous energy thickened the night air; one stray spark and it would catch fire.

Adlai skirted the protestors as best he could to reach the entrance. Four Justice dynes stood guard while two drones buzzed along the perimeter.

Spencer, we need another security squad outside. The crowd's getting rowdy.

Yes, sir. Parameters?

Safeguard the building, but otherwise let them say their piece, so long as they don't turn violent. Protection of innocent bystanders takes top priority.

He politely nudged his way through those who pressed up closest to the building, ignoring several curses hurled his way, and slipped inside.

The stark silence of the cavernous facility once the door closed behind him made the scene outside feel all the more volatile in retrospect. He listened, waiting for the thunder of crashing projectiles and weapons fire, but the silence was broken only by murmured voices from deeper inside the warehouse. He steeled himself and went to join the others.

∧R

The vivid shimmer of the five force fields—might as well call them what they were: cages—dominated the large room, which was mostly the point. The visual effect served as a warning to the occupants, and as reassurance to their captors.

Their location was a private exobiological research facility, and the cages' usual purpose was to contain creatures captured on other worlds and protect the scientists who studied the creatures. The use of the facility wasn't intended to be metaphorical or to demean those whom the cages now held. It was merely that they hadn't finished scrubbing all the governmental systems, and they couldn't discount the possibility that the Guides possessed backdoor keys to the Justice Division nex hub.

The dolls were the only things held captive by the cages. The Guides' backup hardware remained stored in the Justice Evidence Warehouse on Ebisu, because gathering everything required for their continued existence at one location for such a high-profile, consequential event felt like begging for trouble.

They'd expended a great deal of effort setting all this up for what would be a very temporary display. But Maris had made a speech about the power of theater, and almost everyone had agreed with her.

Adlai had agreed with her, too, at least the parts on the importance of imbuing the proceeding with both solemnity and the ritual of law. Mostly he regretted that any of this was necessary.

He glanced around to confirm everyone was here and ready to begin. The Justice Advisors—again, minus Satair—would conduct the proceeding, but the other Advisors were attending as well in order to reiterate their solidarity to the Guides. Minus Gemina, who was confined at the Kiyora Justice Center until they could get around to dealing with her.

He nodded at Spencer, who gave the tech the go-ahead to initiate the transfer of the consciousnesses stored in hardware two kiloparsecs away.

One by one, the dolls animated, eyes opening and limbs jerking to life in a blur of stilted motion. In barely more than an instant, the previously lifeless, inert mannequins had transformed to look much as they always had in the chamber on the Platform. Indistinguishable from living Asterions.

Adlai shivered, but he forced himself to adopt a neutral tone and stance as he addressed them.

"Guide Anavosa, Guide Selyshok, Guide Iovimer, Guide Luciene, Guide Delacrai. Please each acknowledge that you are functional and capable of controlling your reasoning mind."

"Isn't this...charming." Luciene's doll eyes shot daggers of loathing at Adlai.

"I will take this as a 'yes' from you. Next?"

The others complied in their own manner: Iovimer cautiously, Selyshok sullenly, Anavosa stoically and Delacrai quietly.

"Thank you." Adlai took a step back and motioned to Selene, who replaced him at the front of the gathered audience.

"You are being provided with a list of the charges filed against you. After due weighing of the available evidence, we are now informing you that you have been judged guilty of these crimes by a 4-0 vote of the Justice Advisors."

"May we assume Advisor Satair was not consulted?"

Selene didn't blink under the weight of Guide Luciene's glare. "Blake Satair's Advisor designation has been revoked, and he is facing a lengthy list of criminal charges as well."

"Who gave you the right to revoke an Advisor designation?"

"Under the Charter, in the absence or incapacity of the Guides, all rights devolve to the Advisors. You should have studied our Charter more closely, Guide Luciene. We might not be here today if you had."

Luciene's insolence wilted, and Guide Iovimer covered for him. "Advisor Satair acted under our direction."

"A little too gleefully, if you ask me." Adlai muttered it under his breath, but Selene shot him a warning look nonetheless.

"This fact will be taken into account during his sentencing. However, Mr. Satair is a sapient individual capable of making his own decisions, irrespective of instructions received from his superiors. He is also not the subject of this hearing."

She turned the proceedings over to Julien then. It was important for each of them to handle a portion of the hearing, to make it clear these actions were taken by the Justice Division of the Asterion Dominion and not any one individual.

"As punishment for your crimes against the Asterion people, your status as Guides of the Asterion Dominion is hereby revoked. Furthermore, you are hereby sentenced to have your psyches returned to living Asterion bodies—"

Iovimer interrupted. "What? Our knowledge, processes and intellect are too vast to be contained within a single tiny, meager body."

"Then you can use external stores to house the excess data, like the rest of us do. You will relearn what it means to be an Asterion, so that you can better comprehend the nature and extent of the evils you committed upon our citizens."

Luciene had by now regained a measure of hubris. "Is that all?"

Harris stepped forward. "No. Once you've been regened into your new bodies, you will be confined under house arrest for a period of no less than one hundred years. You will be housed in comfortable but modest apartment lodgings, each at separate locations, and will be allowed limited, monitored, read-only access to the nex web and personal communications.

"After a period of ten years, your status will be reevaluated by the Justice Advisors. If your behavior has been exemplary and you show progress toward understanding why your transgressions were unacceptable, you will be granted additional privileges. Conversely, negative or disruptive behavior will result in a transfer to less comfortable environs."

Iovimer gestured dramatically. "I suppose gilded cages will be more tolerable than..." he reached out and flicked the force field with a finger "...animal ones."

Anavosa had donned a distressed countenance, her cornflower irises shimmering in the reflected glow of her own cage and her always pale skin blanched to ivory. "None of us will be alive in a decade to have our 'behavior' evaluated. We, you, this building, this planet—whichever one it is—will have been ground to dust under the boot of the Rasu long before then. It matters not what sentences you inflict upon us with your stolen authority, for we will all be dead soon enough."

Her words cast a chilling pall over the room. She'd been a Guide for a reason, and her ability to bewitch her lessers remained formidable.

Adlai cleared his throat to break the macabre spell. "Respectfully, Ms. Kelaine, the Rasu are no longer your concern. They are ours, as they should have been from the beginning. To your point, we will do everything in our power to ensure all of us are still here in a decade's time." He quickly shifted toward the far-left cage. "Delacrai Iylish, in recognition of the services you have provided to the Advisors and the Asterion people in recent days, your sentence is partially commuted, and you will be allowed monitored but expanded nex web access and movement across the Dominion. This privilege is subject to revocation if you abuse it."

"I understand, and I thank you for your leniency."

"Traitor!"

Delacrai didn't so much as flinch, or deviate her gaze even a fraction from Adlai toward Luciene. "I have acted as I believed I must. Insults will not diminish that belief, for I have made my choice."

Adlai projected his voice with enough command to hush the room. "Personal commentary will cease. With your sentences relayed to you and entered into the record, they will now be carried out. This proceeding is closed."

9

MIRAI ONE PAVILION

It took two hours to disperse the crowd outside the sentencing proceeding so they could safely move the again lifeless dolls and other equipment to another Justice facility, and another two before Adlai finally made it back to the Pavilion.

In a happy stroke of luck, he stumbled upon Perrin as she was about to step onto the east lift. He hurried down the hall, grabbed her and wrapped her up in his arms.

She gasped for half a second in surprise, then giggled against his lips. "I have to get these requests up to the Admin enclave Advisor Colson is setting up on the fourth floor."

"And I have to do five thousand things to keep the streets from erupting into chaos. I just wanted to see you for a minute before I started doing them."

Her blueberry irises danced with teasing flecks of bright aquamarine. Damn but she was such a breath of fresh air after the dark solemnity of the sentencing. "*See* me?"

"Kiss you. I wanted to kiss you. May I do that, here, out in the open?"

"I'll do it for you." Her lips found his, and the walls faded away to irrelevance.

"What the fuck?"

The walls zoomed back to press menacingly in on him. Adlai recognized the distinctive voice instantly—and even if he hadn't, the expression on Perrin's face as she jerked away told the tale. He tensed and readied himself for the coming confrontation, then shifted—

—Perrin grabbed his shoulder, stopping him from turning around. "Let me handle this. You go on and do those five thousand things you need to see to. People are counting on you."

"He can't tell you what to do."

She stared past Adlai, over his shoulder, a warning flaring hot in her eyes that wasn't meant for him. "Sure, he can. But I don't have to listen."

He wanted, needed, to defend her honor and protect her, regardless of whether he'd earned the right to do so yet. The steeled determination animating her visage, though, was enough to convince him she didn't need him to. Well, almost enough. "Will you be okay? I can—"

"I'll be fine. Joaquim will never hurt me. Not physically." She stepped out of his grasp and faced Lacese, and Adlai reluctantly pivoted to retreat down the side hall. As he did, he met Lacese's furious glare with a calm stare that carried a warning of his own.

Lacese lunged toward him, and Adlai readied his stance to block a blow and counterpunch, but Perrin stepped between them, keeping her back to Adlai. "Don't. This is between you and me."

"Godsdamn right it is."

Every instinct Adlai possessed screamed at him to force Perrin aside and render the man physically incapable of hurting her in this century or the next.

But she reached behind her to squeeze his hand, thereby broadcasting *I've got this* more clearly than words ever could, then strode toward Lacese. "Don't make a scene here, out in the open. Let's find someplace private to talk."

And he let her go.

⅄ℜ

The door to some random room Perrin had shoved him into closed, and Joaquim whirled on her. "You're fucking sleeping with the enemy. The *literal* enemy. How could you do this?"

"No, I'm *not*! Adlai is not our enemy. He's not responsible for any of the bad things that have happened. Not the virutox, not your kidnapping, not the destruction of The Chalet." Her normally delicate jaw locked into rigidity. "Not Cassidy's death. He's a good man."

But he didn't care to hear her excuses, disguised though they were as soothing mollifications. Before coming to the Pavilion to find Nika and see what he could do to help with whatever, he'd learned how Justice uncovered the location of The Chalet without setting off his MAD defenses during his captivity on the Platform.

The burned-out husk of his former boss on Synra, Gregor Shone, had been dumped at a regen facility in Synra One shortly before Joaquim blew up the Platform. Gregor had done nothing but help him over the years, and they had shredded the man's psyche with a cheese grater then thrown him out with the trash.

"Justice is evil to the core. From top to bottom."

"Justice is not a monolithic, self-aware entity with its own independent morality. It's made up of individuals. And policies and algorithms, yes. Jo, if you want to blame—"

"Stop calling me that. You've lost the privilege of endearments."

Her throat worked, and her rigid jaw quivered. So, this one had left a mark. A tiny part of his conscience recoiled at the realization he'd hurt her feelings, but the louder, raging part drowned it out.

"Fine. But if you want to blame anyone for what happened to Cassidy, blame Blake Satair. He's been the Justice Advisor on Synra for centuries, at a minimum. Blame him for implementing an overly aggressive raid policy built on a 'shoot first, investigate later' philosophy. Or blame the creator of the faulty algorithm, or the weak safety procedures that allowed it to go into effect without proper vetting. But don't you *dare* blame Adlai."

He never should have told her about Cassidy, dammit. Now she wielded the knowledge like a godsdamn flame-thrower against him. He'd never readied a counter to such an attack, and in desperation he grasped for the old standby. "What about everything else Justice has done over the years? To innocent people, to those of us in NOIR?"

"Blame the Guides for ordering the people working in Justice to act as they did, and be glad people like Adlai stood up to the Guides and brought an end to it."

He sneered, tossing a hand dismissively in her direction so he didn't have to meet her earnest yet defiant gaze. "You will do absolutely anything to defend him, won't you? Some friend you are, to turn on me the second a pretty face who wanted to see you naked came along."

"Okay, that is not fair! You have never had a better friend than me. I've always been there for you. I've defended you when you were being a first-class ass—which was often, by the way. I've listened to you and learned from you. When it's mattered, I've risked everything for you. And I am *not* turning on you now."

"You didn't exactly rush to rescue me when Justice took me captive, did you?" He regretted the words the instant he uttered them; they were surely a step too far...*unless they weren't*, his wounded pride retorted.

Her lips parted, and the color drained from her face. When she spoke, her voice had lost much of its former fervor. "I wanted to drop everything and bring all of NOIR to tear up the Dominion searching for you. But I thought you would believe saving thousands of people from the virutox was more important than rescuing you, so I focused our resources on distributing the vaccine first. I did what I thought was right—what I thought you would believe was right—but if I was wrong, I am deeply sorry."

Of course he would and did believe this, and the fact that he'd wounded her yet more deeply with this barb wounded him in turn. All her answers were so damn reasonable, and she meant every last one of them. He sensed it from the conviction in her voice and the honesty in her eyes.

But to let go of his anger would mean facing something in himself he wasn't ready to face. He dug around for more barbs he could fling like daggers. "What if I told you to choose? Stay with him, and you never see me again. What would you do?"

She gasped. "Don't you *dare* ask that of me. I do not deserve this from you, dammit, and by saying what you just did, you've already made the choice for me."

Joaquim stared at her, his heart hammering against his sternum and his thoughts tangling and tearing at themselves—abruptly he spun around and punched the wall behind him.

"Jo!"

The punch left behind a sizeable dent in the wall; streams of blood flowed down the cracks spreading out from the impact point much as it flowed down the valleys between his knuckles. The pain served its intended purpose, however; it broke through the fog of rage in his mind to, at least briefly, impose a raw, ugly clarity upon his thoughts.

He brought his busted hand up and pressed the fingertips of both hands to his temples. She spoke nothing but truth. Certainly about the unfairness of his puerile ultimatum, probably about Justice, possibly even about Weiss. But he was quite skilled at destroying anything that might be good in his life, wasn't he?

His voice scraped past gritted teeth like sandpaper. "You're right. You don't deserve this. But I can't…" his eyes closed, and he gave up the fight with himself "…I don't know how to not be angry."

"What do you mean?" Her tone had instantly shifted from righteous defensiveness to gentle encouragement.

"I don't *know how* to not be angry. I hoped telling you about Cassidy would help. It didn't. I hoped blowing up the Platform and the Guides with it would help. It felt damn good in the moment, but after the rush faded it hasn't helped. We've accomplished damn near everything NOIR set out to do. We've toppled the government, and the harsh laws and penalties it had imposed are being rolled back. We've discovered what's happening to the people who disappear and are putting a stop to it all.

"But I'm *still angry*. At the Guides, the Advisors, Justice, the world. At you. I can't be happy, and worse, I can't let you be happy. I can't let go or move on."

"Everything's happened so fast. You should give yourself some time, or even consider—"

He spun around to find she now stood less than a meter from him, palms and stance open, as if she was ready to hug him. Why was she so damn kind? He didn't merit kindness. "Don't say go in for an up-gen and wipe this all away. I won't take the cowardly way out."

"You're not a coward. You said it yourself. You've done what you set out to do. You've gotten justice—yes, justice—for the people the Guides have wronged. You've helped ensure the government will be held accountable for its actions. It's okay to close the door on the pain of the past and start fresh, without regret or shame."

"Maybe for most people. But here's the thing: I *want* to be angry. I want to feed it and let it fester and grow and take me over in a fiery rage. I don't want to move on or be happy."

Her whole body sagged, as if someone had pulled a plug, and all the fight abandoned her in a rush. "Then I don't know how to help you."

"It's not your responsibility to help me."

"If you know me at all, you know it's my responsibility to help everyone."

He tried to chuckle, but it came out closer to a guttural cry. Gods he was a wretched disaster.

She shrugged. "Most of all my friends."

"Yeah. I guess I ought to have said, you *can't* help me." He lifted his shoulders as a resolute, calm certainty settled over him. "I need to leave."

"What do you mean?"

"I can't stay here and watch you make goo-goo eyes with the enemy."

She exploded in a fit of renewed indignation, her left foot stomping the floor as her hands balled into fists. "Adlai is not the enemy!"

Better that she be furious at him. He wasn't sure he could walk away from sad Perrin. "It doesn't matter whether he is or not. I need to leave. Leave Mirai."

"Where will you go?"

Funny how she wasn't trying to talk him out of it. Probably meant it was the best idea he'd had in a long while. "No clue.

Somewhere where there aren't many people. Given where my head is at present, it'll be safer for them and me."

"Will you tell me where you are when you get there?"

"That would kind of defeat the purpose, wouldn't it?"

She extended a hand out toward him, but dropped it back to her side before it reached him. "Will I ever see you again?"

He contemplated the floor. The blood dripping from his hand had crafted a jagged pattern of dark blotches on the carpet, and he studied them until he summoned the courage to meet her gaze. He suspected he'd be mulling over what he saw in her expression for some time.

"Honestly? Don't count on it. Don't count on me." He burned his remaining courage on brushing past her on the way to the door. "I never was a good bet."

10

MIRAI ONE PAVILION

N ika leaned back in her chair and ran a hand through her hair as she studied a visualization of the dozens of triage actions currently in motion, hopefully toward something beneficial.

Most of the Advisors were concentrating on keeping the government functioning—assuring basic services continued to be provided and the people didn't riot. She appreciated their efforts, but Anavosa had a point. None of it was going to matter if the Rasu showed up next month wielding their frightening plasma beams of destruction and burnt everyone to a crisp. So, her efforts were directed toward preventing that from happening.

Dashiel was meeting with several individuals who had come forward in answer to their call for metals experts; if their ideas showed promise, they'd join the multi-planet group of people trying to decipher how the Rasu so effortlessly formed themselves into an endless variety of shapes and purposes, including bleeding-edge technology and weapons.

At the same time, the best scientists the Dominion had to offer pored through the meager direct data they had on the Rasu, studying every iota of signals and transmissions the Rasu emitted for clues to their capabilities and hints of their weaknesses.

Gods, she hoped they had weaknesses.

"Nika, someone's here to see you. He says he's expected."

She shifted around in her chair to see Katherine blocking Grant Mesahle from stepping through the doorway. As part of Administration's inexorable takeover of their new headquarters, Katherine was making a hard play at becoming the sole arbiter of who was and wasn't allowed on the premises.

She'd totally forgotten that she'd asked Grant to come to Mirai to install power and weapons upgrades on the *Wayfarer*. "He is. Grant, thank you for coming."

Katherine shot Grant a glower as she stepped aside and allowed him into the room, which they'd intended to serve as an all-hands group meeting room but had instantly devolved into free-for-all chaos.

He arched an eyebrow as Nika stood to greet him. "This is all...insane. Busy taking over the world, I see."

"Busy trying to hold it together. Let me touch base with a couple of people, then we'll head to the spaceport." She glanced around until she spotted Maris talking to Cameron, then got her attention and waved her over. "Maris, can I talk to you for a second?"

When Maris reached them, she dipped her chin in Grant's direction. "Grant? It has been a while."

He returned the greeting. "A few thousand years, give or take. You look as lovely as ever, of course."

Nika stared at them both in surprise. "Wait, you two know each other?"

Grant's expression flickered oddly, but he kept his attention focused on Maris. "You haven't told her yet?"

"I was working up to it. We have been a mite preoccupied. To tell you the truth, I'm a bit flummoxed myself at this unexpected..." she gestured between him and Nika "...encounter. How is it you're here now?"

"Excuse me. What the hells are you on about?"

Grant continued to ignore her in favor of responding to Maris. "We met coincidentally several years ago, through some NOIR people. Like I assume everyone else did, I thought she'd sunsetted. That's what we were told. I was only following the rules."

Nika's confusion ratcheted upward, where it joined growing unease. "You never struck me as a rules-following kind of guy."

He finally pivoted to her. "Some rules are worth following. Nika, I am so sorry. If I'd known you'd been psyche-wiped, I would have intervened. I would have helped you recover your identity. I would have contacted Maris, for starters. I feel terrible about it, but I didn't know, because you didn't tell me."

"I realize I didn't...wait, 'sunsetted'? 'Rules'? Will someone *please* tell me what the bloody hells you two are talking about?"

Maris sighed with characteristic flair. "Yes, as it seems I have in fact waited for too long to do so. But not here. Can we go to your flat?"

The unease snaked through Nika's chest and squeezed. What secret was so grave that it required not merely privacy, but extreme and lengthy privacy? "Okay, if you think it's necessary."

Grant fidgeted. "I guess I can come back later."

She shook her head. "I'm sending you the passcode to the *Wayfarer's* hangar. I trust you, especially given how it used to be your ship. Ping me if you run into any issues."

He nodded. "I will. And Nika...I really am sorry."

⅄ℛ

NIKA'S FLAT

When they reached the flat, Maris promptly went to the kitchen and fixed herself a drink, then sipped on it as she considered the living room. "Well. This is a fabulous mess, but it's so wonderful to be here again with you."

"I had eleven people sleeping here last night. Stop stalling. What happened back there? How do you know Grant? What's 'sunsetting'? What have you been working up to and failing to tell me?"

"To be fair, I expected you to realize it yourself. You took the time and care to encrypt vital and special memories to help guide you back to your true identity and former life, but you didn't think to include this one crucial little detail in those memories? I suppose it was such an intrinsic part of your psyche, it didn't occur to you that you needed to spell it out. Or perhaps what you assumed would be obvious is simply unfathomable when viewed from the outside."

"Maris, out with it, *now*."

Her friend twirled the stem of her glass between her fingertips and leveled a piercing, almost chilling gaze on Nika. "You are one of the First Generation."

"Yes, I can trace my ancestral lineage all the way back to the First Generation. In fact, one of the memories I recovered was from the end of the SAI Rebellion—"

"No, not trace. Not ancestral. *You* are First Generation."

"I don't understand. How is it different?"

"It means that since the time we fled the Anaden Empire with our rebellion in tatters, since the time you disembarked your generation ship and stepped foot on Synra's soil, since the time you merged fully with your bonded SAI, you have never undergone a full Retirement & Reinitialization. You've tweaked and modded and improved and fiddled, as we all do, but your mind has remained a cognizant, unbroken whole since it was born as an Asterion soul."

She grasped for the first argument she could find so she didn't have to absorb what Maris had just said. "Until five years ago, anyway."

"I don't think so. In the ways which truly matter, your psyche-wipe *failed*. It may have taken most of your memories, but you were and have always been far too clever to let anyone take your mind from you."

She sank onto the couch and dropped her head into her hands. It was too much to ponder...and yet, somehow, right. *True.* She knew it in her soul. Still she resisted, though, because it was also ridiculous.

"How can you be sure? I might have made it all up and told you grand stories in order to sound impressive."

Maris laughed warmly. "You were never much for lying. But you didn't have to lie to me. I've been there for it all, for I, too, am First Generation."

She looked up, startled. "The memory of the founding of Mirai...it wasn't our ancestors? It was *us*?"

"I remember the day fondly. Gods, that water was freezing!"

Nika's head spun. Fragments of pieces of memories and incongruities scrambled to rearrange themselves within a frame whose contours had finally been revealed. *This* was why the encrypted memories spanned so many millennia, yet why they all felt so intensely personal.

"And Grant? Are you suggesting he's also First Generation? That's why you know him?"

"Indeed."

"But he's just a...craftsman."

"He's living a life of his choosing. Such as it is for most of the remaining First Generation, few though they are. They left behind politics and power games long ago to find their purpose in the smaller joys of living. You and I are rather unusual, to continue to lead public lives in the service of the Dominion government after so long."

There was a larger point in what Maris had said that she wanted to think on, but her overwhelmed mind was firmly stuck on the previous reveal. "I'm a little weirded out by the fact that he slept with me while knowing this about me—knowing who I used to be."

"You were lovers? Some things never do change. My dear, you've known Grant for 700,000 years, and you were unattached for sizeable slices of those millennia. This dalliance you apparently enjoyed with him the last few years? Trust me, it wasn't the first time."

Nika's jaw dropped. She felt dizzy.

"What? You like each other. You always have."

"But...we don't love each other?"

"Precisely. It's a perfectly natural way for friends to pass the millennia. And don't worry, you didn't cheat on Dashiel with him. Or with anyone. So boringly faithful always."

"It's not boring to be faithful to someone you love." She stood. She needed to pace. She needed a drink. "Okay, I'll file Grant away for now, because there are more important issues. What you said about most of the other First Generation—do you mean the other Advisors aren't?"

"Blake is, I regret to say. He's like a cockroach. Everyone wishes he would die off, but he just keeps sticking around. We're all the Advisors, though. Charles Basquan, our current benefactor, whom you've met, is also First Generation. I dare not guess whether you've met any others. I didn't anticipate Grant, so who can say?"

"And the Guides—former Guides."

"No. They're all quite old, but none retain their original psyches."

She grabbed a glass from a kitchen cabinet and set it too hard on the counter, then poured the rest of a bottle of cabernet into it. "Do they know about us?"

"Oh, yes, which makes their decision to psyche-wipe you triply reprehensible. To willfully attempt to extinguish a life that has thrived across so many aeons." Maris shivered visibly. "But they failed, and now they're being punished."

Nika gulped down a sip of the cabernet and tried to focus. Questions needing answers. "What's 'sunsetting'?"

"That's what we call it when one of us willingly erases themselves and undergoes a full Retirement and Reinitialization. Sailing off into the sunset, as it were."

"Does it happen a lot?"

"My dear, do the math. When we arrived on Synra, *everyone* was First Generation. All 38,118 of us. Now, there are at last count twenty-eight of us drawing breath as our original selves." Maris cast a soulful look toward the afternoon sunlight streaming in the windows.

She wished she could feel the loss of so many souls in the way Maris obviously did. But she didn't remember who they'd been. "Why did it matter that Grant thought I'd...sunsetted? What rules was he talking about?"

"Time and many heartbreaking experiences taught those of us who persevere a difficult lesson. When we encounter someone out there in the world whom we recognize is a new incarnation of someone who used to be First Generation, we can't tell them the true extent of their heritage. Only pain and sorrow results from doing so, for us and for them. They don't understand how they could have ever given up such a heritage or those millennia of memories and experiences. But at the time the individual sunsetted, they had their reasons for it, and we have learned we must respect those reasons."

She sank back onto the couch as a very big, very problematic puzzle piece snapped into place. "Is this why I never told Dashiel about Steven Olivaw?"

"You remember Steven, then? Of course you would make a point to include him in those encrypted memories. You're too sentimental not to. Yes, and no."

"That's not an answer."

"Yes, this is why you *shouldn't* have told him. Why I counseled you vigorously and repeatedly not to tell him. But I don't think it was the rule or my pleas that stopped you. Rather, the reasons behind the rule are the same ones that convinced you to keep your secret. The confusion and frustration everyone feels on finding out their prior incarnation sunsetted? It would be magnified a thousand-fold for Dashiel, because in his case, his prior incarnation also walked away from you. Left you behind, alone, so they could take the easy way out and *die*. Can you imagine what this knowledge would do to him?"

She frowned. Maris was logically correct in her assessment, but.... "I hear what you're saying, but to keep something like this from him? To keep my very nature a secret? It was wrong."

"What you mean to say is that it was *hard*. When you live as long as we have, you learn to endure hard things."

"Forgive me, but I don't recall the ins and outs of such an allegedly critical skill, and I'm not comfortable with having kept this from him."

Maris deposited her drink on the counter and grasped both of Nika's hands in hers. "Nika, listen to me carefully. Do *not* tell him. I remember Steven Olivaw a lot better than you do, and let me tell you something: he was a godsdamn tortured soul from the day he walked out of the lab. Don't you dare turn Dashiel into one as well."

Then Maris nodded perfunctorily and retrieved her drink. "Now, I've had my say, and we'll leave it there. You have other questions."

Thousands. Millions. "How do you manage it all? How have you not gone mad? It must be too much, for too long."

"That *is* the party line, isn't it? I've forgotten more millennia than I remember. I've reinvented myself a hundred times over. I've had splendid years and dreadful centuries—or I assume I have. Most of the dreadful ones, I erased. I manage, we all manage, because for us life is not about the past. It's always about the present, *this* moment, and the future moments awaiting us."

Nika chuckled wryly, or possibly wildly. "It is the Asterion way."

"And we are the living embodiment of the Asterion way. I'm not even joking. We are the threads that run through our people's past, present and future, subtly guiding the pattern they weave. Trying to ensure it's a beautiful one."

Compelling, even hypnotic words, but Maris' poetic musings were more than she could take right now, when her world was busily spinning apart once again.

"Does it even matter, though, when I can't remember so much? I'm all for living in the present, but who cares how long I've done it if all I have left are a few fleeting glimpses of the past?"

"It matters because you are you, and *you* have existed across aeons. To have done so is precious beyond measure." Maris motioned toward the dining area. "Besides, you have your journals. They're not quite memories, but they'll have a great deal to show you."

"What journals?"

"Seriously, Nika. What did you use all that space encrypting memories for?"

"Other than the founding of Mirai and the end of the SAI Rebellion? Sex with Dashiel…meeting the Taiyok Elder for the first time…more sex with Dashiel."

"Ah, valid choices to be sure. Come with me." Maris strode past the dining table to the mirror decorating the wall behind it.

Confused, Nika followed her.

"Hold your hand up, palm open, in front of the space to the left of the mirror. Eye level."

The instant she did so, the mirror and a section of the wall slid away to reveal a hidden room. Row after row of shelves packed full of data weave cases lined every interior wall. On the right, just inside, a control pane waited for input.

"What is this?"

"Your journals. Seven hundred thousand years' worth of them. Many are after-action reports of meetings, negotiations, political clashes and so on. Many are personal reflections. Though you could access the memory of any interaction in minutes or often seconds, you found taking the time to write about the event to be a valuable exercise. Recording not merely what happened, but why it did, the personalities and circumstances which caused it to happen the way it did, and your personal thoughts on the result." Maris nudged her gently. "Go ahead. Ask the interface for a journal entry. It's all intuitively cross-referenced."

Her brow furrowed. Where to even begin? She settled on something she already remembered, for simplicity's sake and for confirmation, and entered 'Toki'taku first Elder meeting.'

Location: Row 8, Column 15, Slot 6

She scanned a few rows until she figured out the organization, then retrieved the indicated data weave.

Date: Y98,714.231 A6
Subject: Taiyok Relations

After two hundred thirty-three years of negotiations, the Taiyok Elder has at last agreed to a face-to-face meeting on Toki'taku. I am simultaneously eager and trepidatious, for to make it a success will not be an easy task.

She jumped when Maris touched her shoulder. "I'll leave you to your reading."

She started to protest, but the words died in her throat. She still had thousands, millions of questions...but it was possible Maris had just handed her the cipher to most of them.

"Thank you. For everything."

11

NIKA'S FLAT

Nika met Dashiel at the door to her flat with a kiss. She smiled against his lips. "All empty. It's just us tonight." She gestured grandly to the living room to reiterate the point, then frowned, only now noticing how the chairs off to the left remained pushed up against the walls and several of the tables were smushed together by the windows. "I do still need to clean up—"

"It's fine. Wonderful, in fact. I'm simply glad for the peace and quiet. Besides, you've been a little busy." He hung his coat on a hook by the door and followed her into the living room. "What *did* you do today? I got caught up in meetings for hours."

"I, um…." She trailed off, almost as if her vocal chords had seized up when faced with the weight of the words she was asking them to transmit.

This was going to be harder than expected. How to tell him that her entire world had again been upended, but also expanded beyond her capacity to absorb? How to begin to tell him of the wonders and tragedies she'd discovered within her journals, and how much still awaited her?

"Nika? Is something wrong?"

How to tell him she wasn't and had never been precisely who he thought she was?

But the millstone of the lie her present self hadn't yet spoken pressed down on her, poised to burden every step she walked down that path. She couldn't *not* tell him.

She shook her head in answer and went over to the mirror. Drew in a deep breath and unlocked the library.

"What the hells?"

"You didn't know about this room? About all these journals?"

"No. I didn't." His brow knotted up as he took in the shelves upon shelves of data weaves. When he spoke, his voice sounded tentative. "I mean, I knew you kept journals, but I never had any idea...." He leaned back and peered around the corners of the wall framing the library. "How is this room even here? There's no obvious gap in the layout, no negative space. It's an astoundingly clever design."

His gaze finally settled on her; in the last few seconds his jaw had tensed and his chestnut irises had brightened to a fiery bronze of churning discontent. "I don't understand. What is this? Did all of your previous generations hold onto the journals of their ancestors and pass them along, time and again?"

"No. They didn't." She exhaled softly, took his hand and led him back into the living room. She sat down on the powder-blue couch, already her favorite, and patted the cushion beside her.

He regarded her in evident confusion as he sat. "Nika, what's going on?"

"I found something out today. Something important. In retrospect, given the memories I've recovered and other oddities, I probably should have figured it out on my own, but I didn't understand the nature of what I was remembering until now...." She cleared her throat and started again. "The tattoo on my back? It's not there to honor my heritage—or it is, but it's not a symbol of where my ancestors came from and what they did to bring us here. It's a symbol of where *I* came from. Of what *I* did.

"The woman in the memory of the end of the SAI Rebellion I told you about, Nicolette Hinotori? She's not my ancestor. She's me. Her bonded SAI, KIR? It's a part of me. The last name isn't an homage, it's an accurate, descriptive designation. After our people settled on Synra, they—we—joined together to become an Asterion. To become...me."

"Well, yes, in a sense—"

"I said the same thing at first, too. But, no, not in a sense. In a quite real actuality. Nika Kirumase was born that day, nearly

700,000 years ago. And in all the aeons since then, I never underwent a full R&R. I never retired a psyche and became someone new. When you met me, I wasn't seventh generation, I was...okay, I haven't done the math, and I don't have a clue how many up-gens I did, anyway—hundreds, or more likely, thousands. But that's not the point. The point is, all those journals?" She motioned to the open door of the library. "They cover the entire history of the Dominion, the entirety of Asterion existence, and I wrote every single one of them."

He stared not at her but through her, his eyes as turbulent as the muscles struggling to control his features.

"Say something, please."

"What...no, this can't be. You were...but how...." His throat worked. "Why didn't you ever *tell* me?"

Uttered on his lips, the question sounded like a betrayal. "I can't say for certain, though I can speculate. Maris says there are rules the First Genners abide by, and when she explained them they made some amount of sense, but at the same time—"

"Maris? What does she have to do with this? You're not saying she's from the First Generation as well?"

The tenor of his words was honed to cut sharply through the air, making this one sound less like a question and more like an accusation. She'd expected this to be difficult for him, but she might have underestimated how difficult.

She nodded and tried to choose her words carefully, but the thoughts and emotions behind them danced in crazed loops to war with each other in her head.

"That's how I found out. When pressed, she confessed to me the truth about my history and her own. Dashiel, I don't have the full answer for why my former self didn't tell you all of this. But I suspect it had something to do with..." her gaze dropped to her lap "...with the fact that I knew your progenitor, your original, First Generation ancestor.

"His name was Steven Olivaw, and he was a leader in the SAI Rebellion. I knew him for a long time. I loved him. Then he chose to R&R and was gone. And I think I was angry about it, for a longer time. Then I met you, and I found love again. Better, stronger love. And I think I didn't want you to feel any guilt over what someone who wasn't truly you did an eternity ago. So, I didn't tell you."

"You...*dated* my progenitor?"

She winced by way of answer.

"And you knew this about me when you met me?"

"No, not when I first met you. Later."

The skin around his eyes twitched, and a vein running up his left temple throbbed. He stood and began wandering silently around the living room.

"I'm telling you now because I want—I need—you to know. Because you *should* know. You always should have known. But this is all new to me, and—"

"Who else?"

She followed his lead and stood. "Who else what?"

"Who else is First Generation? You, Maris. Who else?"

"Grant...."

He spun around, his face contorted. "*What?*"

"Same as Maris and everyone else, he believed I'd voluntarily sunsetted—that's what they call it—and he was following the rules by not telling me who I used to be. Yes, it's weird, but I really don't care about any of that right now. I care about you—"

"Who else?"

"Um, Satair. And the guy who owns the Pavilion. Charles Basquan."

"And?"

"Those are the only ones I know of. I think it's everyone I've personally met, but it's not as if I was handed a list. There aren't many of us left. Twenty-eight, Maris said."

His wandering jerked to a halt in front of the center window beside the fireplace. In profile, his jaw trembled. His chest rose and fell, then again. When he finally spoke, his voice had fallen to a gravelly whisper. "How long does it take, I wonder, for someone to become more than a dalliance to you people? To First Genners—

that's how you refer to yourselves, right? How long does it take for a relationship to gain true meaning? Ten thousand years? Fifty thousand? I'm assuming it's something longer than thirty-two hundred."

Her mind was drowning in so many of her own questions and so much confusion, which was her only excuse for it taking her until this instant to realize exactly how horribly wrong this conversation had gone and how deep of trouble she was now in. But she surely was, because his whisper had dripped with acerbity, and the acerbity was coated in pain, and the pain was wrapped up in a bow of anger.

She tried her damnedest to keep her own tenor gentle and open. Not pleading, but humble and apologetic. "No. I'm certain it wasn't like that."

He pivoted to face her. "How can you *possibly* be certain? You don't fucking remember the last three thousand years."

That's not my fault! But this didn't help her case much, did it? "Because in the memories I have recovered, I feel what…what I felt at the time of the memory. And I talk about you all the time in the more recent journals. Here, let me find a few for you to see." She moved toward the library—

"I can't be here. I have to go."

—and promptly reversed course toward him, hurrying to catch up since he was already halfway to the door. "Please stay. I'm as confused as you are by all this. Let's work through it together." She reached out and grasped his hand—

—he snatched it away.

Her eyes widened; panic quavered her voice. "Dashiel, please—"

He held up a hand to cut her off and backed away, staring at her as if she were a total stranger. "Don't. Just…don't." Then he turned, grabbed his jacket off the hook and left.

12

MIRAI

Dashiel stumbled back to his home in a daze.

Along the streets, up the lift, down the hall, through the door.

His jacket slid off his shoulders to land on the floor as he headed straight to the kitchen, fumbled in the cabinet for a glass and poured sake into it until the liquid spilt over the brim onto the counter.

A ping arrived from Nika. He deleted it without reading it and blocked her.

His hand shook as he picked up the glass, spilling more of the sake to trickle between his knuckles as he brought it to his lips.

A single droplet sloshed onto his tongue. The sweet nectar of oblivion. The harbinger of a fog rolling in to sweep away the pain in favor of blissful stupor—

—he hurled the glass across the room. It shattered on impact with the far sturdier window glass, and a hundred tiny shards joined the sake in decorating the floor.

He wasn't that person any longer. Nika Tescarav had made him a different man. A better man.

Then Nika Kirumase had reached out from the grave to steal their shared history from him. To rip it to shreds and toss it like confetti in the air.

He planted his palms on the counter and sagged into them, his chin dropping to his chest.

I set my drink to the side and grabbed Nika by the waist, hoisting her up onto the counter. "Thank you for coming with me tonight. I suspect it must have been dreadfully dull for you to spend two hours listening to a lecture on manufacturing processes."

She wrapped her legs around my hips to tug me closer. Her skirt bunched up around her thighs, and my pulse quickened. Her left hand trailed down the fabric of my silk shirt. "Dreadfully. But you looked so damn handsome up there on stage, it was worth it just to watch you."

"Hmm. I'm glad." I nuzzled her neck, teasing the pulse point behind her ear with my lips while one of my thumbs explored the inner thigh her skirt had exposed. She smelled of the cedar oil coating the newly polished seats in the auditorium, and a hint of the nutmeg coffee they'd enjoyed during the walk home. "You are the love of my many lives. You know this, right?"

"And you are the love of my one, magnificent life."

I drew back to regard her curiously. It was an odd turn of phrase.

She grinned and began opening my shirt. "I only meant...you understand how much I value my past experiences and incarnations. I even have a symbol of the past tattooed into my skin for added flair. But this, here, now? This is what matters. The magnificent life I'm living in this present, with you."

"I think it's sexy when you get sentimental." I sucked in a breath as her hand scraped down the bare skin of my chest and dipped lower, then matched her maneuver by gripping her ass with both hands and pulling her tight against me. "You can tell me more about these whimsical notions of yours. Later."

He stared at his hands, convinced he could still feel the heat of her skin burning against them...but they were cold and clammy. Empty.

She'd been lying about what she meant, of course, but how much of it? The part where her life was magnificent? Dare he to wonder, the part about loving him? He didn't know where the lies ended and the truth began, or if there had ever been any truth at all.

Acid rose to burn his throat, and he gazed longingly at the puddles of sake gleaming in the moonlight spilling through the unshuttered windows. But instead of getting a fresh glass to drown himself in, he grabbed his coat off the floor and headed back out the door.

Maris answered the door wearing a shimmery silver robe and wild hair made wilder by interrupted sleep. "Dashiel. There are fewer than five people in the universe for whom I will answer the door at this time of night. Fortunate for you that you happen to be one of them."

She narrowed her eyes to peer at him suspiciously. "She told you, didn't she? Everything, I expect?"

"How the hells should I know? I'm just the court jester. A plaything of the true immortals."

"For the record, this is *exactly* why we never tell anyone about our heritage. Even the best of you lose your godsdamn reasoning minds." She stepped back and gestured him inside. "Come on in. Would you like a drink?"

"No."

Her step faltered. "No? Interesting. Well, if I'm going to be up at this hour, I'm having one."

He grabbed her arm before she could head for the kitchen. "Maris, enough with the performance. I'm not here to cry on your shoulder. I simply need some answers, then I'll be on my way. Permanently."

She gracefully but firmly removed her arm from his grip. "You're angry at me as well, for keeping my and Nika's shared and lengthy history from you. It's a valid response. But you need to realize, there are rul—"

"Rules. Yeah. Nika mentioned something about those. I don't give a flying fuck about any rules, but I expect you also don't give a flying fuck about my opinion on the matter. I must be so pathetic to your eyes, so quaint and…small."

"Dashiel, nothing could be further from the—"

"Do not say 'truth.' There's only one truth I need from you. Nika doesn't remember, but you do. So, tell me: was I anything at all to her? Anything more than a trifle, an idle amusement to pass a few thousand years playing with?"

"You really think…don't be ridiculous. You're smarter than this."

"Apparently not, because she lied to me for over three thousand years. About *everything*. Her entire life, her entire existence. And I never suspected."

"She lied to you about how old she was. Don't overdramatize."

He snorted. "That's rich, coming from you. Worse, she didn't merely lie to me about her past, she lied to me about mine."

"Yes, she did. But do you understand why?"

"It's how you First Genners get your thrills?"

"Hardly." Maris propped on the edge of the dining table and sank against it. "And she didn't lie to you because of any rules, either. There *are* rules, but she'd have broken them in a second for you. Five-hundred-sixty thousand years ago, Steven Olivaw broke her deceptively tender heart. He selfishly walked out on his life and hers, and he did it because he was a weak man.

"You are not a weak man, Dashiel, but Nika believed if you knew what he'd done, you would take the guilt of his actions onto your own shoulders. You would become eaten up by the idea that an earlier version of you had let her go.

"And since she loved you so damn much, she never wanted you to carry such a burden. She recognized that you were not Steven, in the way that only someone who's witnessed thousands of generations come and go before their eyes can recognize. She never for one second blamed you for his mistakes, and she never wanted you to blame yourself, either."

Maris crossed her arms over her chest as a spark of audacity lit her orchid irises. "Do you want to know what the real difference is between living ten thousand years and ten hundred thousand? The accumulation of a greater number of experiences. Nothing more, nothing less. If we are special, it's on account of who we are and what we've done with those experiences, not how long we've lived.

"Nika understood something every First Genner I know understands, and few others ever do: the past has no claim on the present. This moment is all that matters. This moment, and the ability to experience the next one that follows it. There, now you can be as wise as any First Genner."

He pinched the bridge of his nose. "But she could have told me the truth about her own past."

"No, she couldn't have, because it was all intertwined for her. There was no way she could have talked forthrightly about the first 200,000 years of her life without also talking about Steven. To share one but not the other with you would have forced her to actively lie far more than simply omitting both did. He signified her past, but you were her present. And her future."

Maris approached him and took his hand, and he was too wound up in his own turbulent thoughts to stop her. "Do you truly want all your future moments to be spent without her at your side?"

"No, but—"

"No 'buts.' The past has no claim on you, and it is for you to decide what you want your future to be. This is the greatest—no, the only—power any of us truly have."

He'd thought that was what he'd been doing these last millennia, dammit. But he'd believed in a lie.

He stepped away, out of her grasp. "You certainly do weave an enchanting tale with your eloquent words delivered in dulcet tones alongside a soft stroke of my hand. It's your stock in trade, after all. But I don't know why I even came here. You are the most gifted storyteller I have ever met, but at the end of the day 'storyteller' is just a pretty word for liar. I can't believe anything you say."

She smiled, and it conveyed an aching wistfulness. But she was a master actor, so it would. "You can try, and see how it goes."

"No, I can't."

NESTED ARGUMENTS

DAYS UNTIL RASU DEADLINE: 22

13

MIRAI ONE PAVILION

"Ugh! Ugh, ugh, ughhhhh...."

Adlai stopped midway down the hall leading to the Justice command center in the Pavilion. The muffled groans had come from his left. Ahead was a door to a storage closet, he thought, which was an odd place for groaning to originate—the unpleasant kind, anyway.

"Ugh!"

And yet. He cautiously opened the door and peeked inside.

Perrin spun around and, on seeing him, darted forward to grab him in a hug. "Hey!"

"Hey." His face screwed up in confusion, though the happy feel of her in his arms made a convincing argument not to worry about any trouble.

She stepped back wearing an innocent smile. "How's your morning so far?"

"The usual. What's wrong?"

"Nothing, why?"

"Well, you were groaning before I came in. And kind of shouting. Also, this is a storage closet."

"Right...." She nodded. "I was just venting a little. The bureaucracy in Admin is absurd! I can't get anything done for these poor former popsicles without three layers of approval and seventeen forms! Let me tell you, if we need Admin's authorization to save our civilization, we are so screwed."

"I expect we'll bypass them as necessary. And the storage closet?"

"I was coming to see you down the hall, but then I didn't want to burst in and dump all my problems on you, when I know you have plenty of your own. So, I sneaked in here to get over myself before I saw you. But you caught me."

He shook his head and gently grasped her shoulders. "Perrin, sweetheart, you don't need be perfect around me. If you're having a bad day, I want to know. I lo—" he cleared his throat, suddenly grateful the storage closet was only dimly lit "—like you for who you *are*, not some idealized version of yourself you pretend to be."

"Oh! Well..." she scoffed playfully "...I'm glad. Fair warning, you might regret saying that once you get an earful of a few of my stream-of-consciousness rants, but I'll hold you to it."

"Please do." He drew her closer for a kiss that he wished could last several hours longer. "We should get to the command center. Or I should. Five thousand new things to do and all."

"Sure." She reached around him to wave the door open, and they stepped out—

"There you are!" The exclamation was delivered twice, in overlapping tones, one melodic and the other gruff, each originating from different directions.

To the left, Julien exited the command center and jogged toward them. To the right, Maris glided down the hallway from the lift waving at them.

He and Perrin exchanged a dubious glance while they waited for everyone to reach them.

Maris arrived first. "Good morning, Adlai. Perrin, can I borrow you for a minute? I have a tiny favor to ask of you."

"Of course." Perrin squeezed his hand. "I'll see you later."

"Okay." He watched her walk off for a long second, then turned to meet Julien halfway. A list of possible disasters the uni may be here to inform him of scrolled through his mind. "What do you need?"

"A favor."

Adlai chuckled to himself as they walked into a command center buzzing with activity. "Ask away."

Julien dropped into a chair and leaned forward displaying an intensity of purpose. "I need for us to let Gemina out of confinement."

"What? Why?"

"Because I need her back at work and doing her job on Kiyora. Half of the shit I'm dealing with right now is due to logjams in the Administration system. In good times it wouldn't be a huge problem, but people who are spooked and angry are not particularly patient with inefficient services."

Perrin's mini-rant replayed in Adlai's mind. As soon as they could afford the effort, it sounded as if Administration was due for a thorough scrubbing, Asterion-style. "Gemina has capable officers who work under her. They should step up and get the job done."

"I already tried talking to them. Can you imagine what it must be like to work for Gemina?"

He scowled. "I'd prefer not to."

"Her subordinates are either whimpering in a corner, terrified she's going to break out of jail and come dismember them, partying in the streets like it's the end of the world or, more commonly, simply clueless about the details of much of the work she did. She didn't let anyone get on the inside. Adlai, Gemina's done nothing but cooperate with us. I don't believe she's a clear and present danger to the Dominion."

"It's not about that, Julien. Objectively, her crimes are easily as serious as Satair's are, and we've locked him in a dungeon and thrown away the proverbial key. The Guides ordered people kidnapped, rendered comatose and shipped off to the Rasu, but Gemina *did* all those things. Now, I appreciate that she's contrite about it, and I'm willing to give her an extra half-hour in the sun a day or some dessert with her dinner as a reward, but we cannot set her free."

Julien thought on it. "What if we frame it as a sort of work-release program? Make it part of her sentence? We'll stick a tracker in her and glue guards to her ass the same as we have with Delacrai, and they'll escort her from her cell to her office—or here—and back again every day. It won't be a reward; it will be a service she's required to perform for the Dominion and its citizens as a facet of her punishment."

Adlai didn't care for it, in part because Gemina had played him at Nika's expense, to his continuing shame. But as a Justice Advisor, this was not a reason to deny Julien's request. "If Selene and Harris agree to it as well. And we make the sentence modification official, lest anyone later accuse us of giving her special treatment."

"Agreed. Give me half an hour to get everything in order."

KIYORA

Gemina's cell sat at the end of the third floor of the Kiyora Justice Center detention wing. Most of the cells were empty thanks to the virutox cleanup, and the hall was quiet. Peaceful.

She lounged on her cot, her back propped against the wall and her knees pulled halfway up to her chest. A pane floated in front of her. Her access to the nex web was heavily restricted, but it seemed she'd managed to find something worth reading.

Adlai stood outside the cell for five seconds before she finally looked over at him, an expression of forced boredom on her face. "Yes?"

"Get dressed. You're needed at your office."

"Ooh, an adventure!" No one would ever mistake the woman's dripping sarcasm for genuine excitement.

"No, not an adventure. You'll do your part to keep the wheels of the government turning on Kiyora, unlock all your secret files and procedures, and show your subordinates how to use them without you. Then you'll return to your cell every evening."

She swung her legs off the side of the cot. "It's so nice to be needed. I take it things aren't going well out there?"

"Oh, but they are. Superbly, in fact. The occasional hitch was to be expected, but you're going to help us clear up many of those."

She stood, but eyed him doubtfully. "What's in it for me?"

"A change of scenery, some fresh air and the heartwarming feeling that comes from improving the lives of your fellow citizens."

"Wow, Adlai. You really know how to woo a girl's heart."

He gritted his teeth to keep from retorting that he was currently wooing a girl's heart just fine, thank you very much. He should have let Julien deal with her. "Again, get dressed. And understand something: if you fail to cooperate or sabotage our efforts in any way, it will result in what privileges you have enjoyed until now being revoked."

Her lips pursed; the outward bravado wavered, and she looked almost...not beaten. Frightened. "Don't worry. I'm quite skilled at doing as I'm told."

14

NIKA'S FLAT

"**A**re you all right?"

Perrin's voice fought to penetrate the fog of sleep, yet Nika clung stubbornly to its comforting peacefulness. Only when a hand jostled her shoulder did she open her eyes.

Polished wood flooring greeted her. Scattered data weaves upon it and sideways shelves above it. No, not sideways. She was sideways…

…she'd fallen asleep on the floor of the library. Or possibly passed out.

"Nika, are you all right? Did something happen?"

Dashiel. The crushing weight of the events of last night swept into her awareness so forcefully she felt as if the wind had been knocked out of her. It had all gone so horribly wrong, and she had no clue how to fix it. The library and everything it represented promised the wisdom of the ages—the answers to every question that had ever lingered on her tongue—but it had come at the price of what she held most dear.

A quick status check confirmed she still had no messages from him, and he was still blocking receipt of messages from her. Lovely.

She winced as she pushed up to a sitting position and rotated her left shoulder to work out a few of the aches brought on by using her arm as a pillow. A data weave cut painfully into her left hip; she glanced down at it.

Date: Y94,033.188 A4
Subject: Encounter with New Intelligent Species (Sogain)

She nudged the weave discreetly to the side. "I'm fine. I was reading late into the night and...I must have fallen asleep. Is it morning?"

"Ten o'clock already."

"Damn. I guess I was more tired than I realized."

Perrin folded her legs beneath her and studied Nika suspiciously. "What are you doing? What is this room? Nobody's heard from you since yesterday afternoon."

"It's a library of journals that Nika Kirumase and her ancestors wrote. I'm trying to learn from the history contained in them." She sighed tiredly. "All those people at the Pavilion? All the Advisors and their officers? They all know me, but I don't know them. I'm supposed to be a diplomat, but to be a good one I need knowledge. Information. I need all the secrets buried in these journals."

"Or, you can use your stellar instincts about people. You didn't become the leader of NOIR and topple the Guides because you had handy reference factoids about people catalogued and cross-referenced in your mind."

"I know, but..." she contemplated the mess of weaves lying on the floor "...has Adlai told you how he became an Advisor?"

Perrin shook her head.

"He was a senior officer in the Justice Division here on Mirai, and he spent months chasing down this ring of slavers. They were dosing people, kidnapping them and blanking them, then selling them for sexual favors and forced labor on the adjunct worlds. He cracked the case wide open."

"That sounds exactly like something he'd do. But—"

"Oh, and it turns out I never trusted Satair. I was suspicious of him millennia ago. I guess it was those stellar instincts at work, huh?"

"Probably." Perrin's expression grew sympathetic, bordering on nurturing. "Nika, is this about Dashiel? I heard something might have happened between the two of you. Something not great." She tilted her head to the left for emphasis, which was when Nika remembered the empty bottle of wine—the *second* empty bottle of wine. This one had ended up tipped on its side against one of the shelves.

She grimaced and righted the bottle then initiated a flushing routine to clear her mind and body of the not-so-pleasant aftereffects of two bottles of wine. "How did you hear that? Have you talked to him?"

"No. But Maris did, and…well, she didn't tell me much."

"She sent you over here to check on me, huh?"

"She did. I'm not sure why she wasn't able to come herself."

"I am."

Perrin gazed at her quizzically, and Nika waved her off. "It doesn't matter. I'm glad you came."

"Then you two did have a fight?"

"You could say. We both discovered I had been keeping secrets from him—before the psyche-wipe. Important secrets, about myself and about him. I don't remember lying to him or my reasons for doing so, but I did it all the same."

She wanted to tell Perrin the whole truth, and given where keeping secrets had gotten her so far, she definitely *should* tell her closest friend. But she just couldn't summon the energy to recount the story one more time right now. And what if doing so alienated Perrin as well? What would she do then?

She squeezed her eyes shut and willed the flushing routine, caustic and punishing though it was, to work faster. "I guess I felt like if I could somehow get inside my own head, from before, and finally understand this woman who I used to be, I'd be able to give him the answers he deserves."

"But he loves the person you are now. Surely that counts for something."

"For something, but possibly not for enough."

"Did you find any answers in here?"

"Mostly more questions." She reached up to retrieve a weave she'd placed on a shelf beside her. "I did find this." She offered it to Perrin.

Perrin took it, stared at Nika for a long beat, then activated it and began reading.

It only took a few seconds for her lower lip to start trembling. She sniffled, and by the time she handed it back tears were streaming down her cheeks. "I don't know who Steven is, but I really think if you just show this to Dashiel, everything will be better between the two of you."

Nika took the weave and dropped it in the pocket of her shirt. "He's not taking my messages at present, so...." She sat up straighter and tried to project a modicum of togetherness. "Speaking of pissed-off men, we didn't get a chance to talk much yesterday about what happened with Joaquim. How are you handling him leaving?"

Perrin shrugged weakly. "I'm handling. I mean, I wish he'd stayed, and it breaks my heart to think of how much pain he's in. But maybe he's right. Maybe time and distance will be good for him. Either way, he's got to make his own choices."

"He does." *As does Dashiel.* The voice giving life to her internal monologue cracked across the syllables of his name, which seemed fitting. "So, are you here solely to check up on me, or do you need something?"

"I need you to stand up, go take a shower, put on some clean clothes and get back into the fray. The other Advisors need you to give them direction. The Pavilion was a leaderless circus this morning. The people need you to remind them everything is going to be okay."

The mere idea exhausted her; in frustration she dragged her hands raggedly down her face. "And what if everything isn't going to be okay? What if we can't stop the Rasu and are weeks away from being annihilated? Should I tell them that instead?"

"Nika, come on. You don't believe that."

"I might."

"Bullshit."

Nika laughed in spite of herself, mostly at the glare of sincere and righteous indignation Perrin wore. "Knocking me back to my senses, are you?"

"Damn straight, I am. Now get off your ass and get out there and outsmart these evil aliens!" Perrin paused, then winced for effect. "Please?"

"Fine, fine." With a groan Nika climbed to her feet. "I have been properly put in my place, thank you. You're absolutely correct. I swore no more people would be sacrificed to the Rasu, and I have to buck up and keep my word. Whatever it takes."

"Good! Because the truth is, I *do* need your help with something."

15

MIRAI ONE PAVILION

Nika found Katherine in what Maris had dubbed the 'strategy room,' if only to distinguish it from the more relaxed lounge next door. She was engaged in an animated argument with Jose Ruiz, the Ebisu Administration Advisor, hands and glares flying.

Nika interrupted them; she didn't feel much like exercising the manners of a diplomat at present. "Katherine, I need to talk to you for a minute."

Jose took the opportunity to get in a closing offended gesture and stormed off.

Nika arched an eyebrow. "Problem?"

"Everything's a problem today. The spaceports are on the verge of being overrun by people fleeing to the Adjunct worlds, as if they'll magically be safe from the Rasu on the frontier. For an extra week maybe, if they're lucky."

"Why aren't they just taking the d-gates?"

"Because it's a moderate challenge to lug all one's worldly possessions through a pedestrian d-gate. What's *your* problem?"

"Excuse me?"

"Like I said, everything's a problem today. What's yours?"

Okay, the woman had a point. "Perrin is trying to requisition temporary living space for people who are back from Hokan Station, in particular those who were kidnapped from outposts. Those outposts are now in smoldering ruins, so they don't have any place to live. She wants to use space in the Mikan Hotel and Sakura Suites in Mirai One, but Administration is denying her request for funds to pay for the rooms."

"Not Administration, actually. Me. It's costly and unnecessary. Also, I can't spare the money or the bandwidth to arrange all the details."

"No one's asking you to set it up yourself. Perrin's willing to handle all the work. She simply needs you to authorize the funds."

"No. I'm not taking orders from some little terrorist street urchin. If I had my way, she wouldn't even be allowed in the building."

In the corner of her eye, Nika caught the door opening and Dashiel walking in with Cameron. They were deeply engaged in conversation, and he was halfway across the room before he spotted her. His steps slowed to a halt.

The stern, confrontational guise she'd donned for Katherine vanished from her visage, and she offered him an open, welcoming and hopeful countenance—

—his jaw locked and he turned away from her, breaking into a jog to catch up to Cameron.

She squeezed her eyes shut and set about deploying emergency countermeasures to prevent the well of despair from spilling forth all over her, the floor and half the room. Her pain was for her alone, not for the world.

Her hands shook as she jerked her focus back to Katherine. She fisted them at her sides, but doing so redirected the shakes through her body. Damn it all to the fiery hells!

She glared icily at the woman. "Well, if I had my way, *you* wouldn't be allowed in the building, either. Luckily for you, you possess some useful passcodes and know how to kick useful idiots in high places—that's Administration's real job, right? But get this through your hyper-inflated head this instant: the old way of doing things is over. Dust, wind. The Guides are locked up and aren't getting out this century, which means going forward, the only thing that gives any of us legitimacy is our actions. So you should think about starting to make yours worthwhile.

"That terrorist street urchin has done more to help the Asterion people since breakfast than you've done in the last decade.

It's time to earn your Advisor position, or I *will* show you the door and lock it behind you."

"Who poisoned your coffee this morning? Never mind, I don't want to know. I'd argue you down, but I've never known you to bluff, dammit. You'll do it—or you'll try. Like you said, I'm the one with the passcodes."

Nika gritted her teeth in a renewed attempt to stop the shaking. Her face was hot, and she could feel her pulse pounding against her temples. *Get it together, dammit. You cannot break. Not now.*

She breathed in through her nose, then out, long and slow. "I apologize. It was rude of me to say those things. I'm sure you're working hard right now, same as we all are. Please, just approve Perrin's request. It will take five seconds, and you'll be done with it."

Katherine peered over Nika's shoulder toward where Dashiel and Cameron had been headed, and her demeanor softened fractionally. "I can authorize enough funds to pay the wholesale—not the retail—rate at Mikan Hotel. That'll get your friend started. Good enough?"

Nika nodded. "For today. Thank you."

Katherine hustled off to attack her next problem, and Nika quickly looked around the room. Dashiel was gone, almost as if he'd never been there.

Her heart ached as keenly as if a dagger were embedded in it, but she had to do better, be better than this. When millions of lives hung in the balance, her personal life couldn't factor into the equation. Perrin had been right to kick her in the head this morning. She had no choice but to concentrate on her mission to the exclusion of all else.

She studied those who were here in the room. The air buzzed with activity, a physical manifestation of the purposeful action of many of the most talented people in the Dominion, all doing their best to save it.

It wasn't going to be enough.

She wished she could blame the morbid assessment on her foul mood, but she feared it only gave her a heightened clarity. The rose-colored glasses of optimism she'd been wearing until now lay crushed in pieces at her feet, and in their absence a harsh reality revealed itself.

If there were no Rasu, if their sole task was to patch up a broken government and mold it into something new, something stronger and freer, these people were more than up to the task. They would navigate the inevitable bumps and complications and get it done, making her and NOIR and everyone proud by bringing the Dominion into a shining new age.

But there *were* the Rasu. And all this teamwork and cooperation, all these herculean efforts? They weren't going to be enough to save everyone from an enemy that burned worlds.

She had to change the game.

⋏ℝ

Everyone was already in the third-floor conference room by the time Nika arrived, and she forced herself to not broadcast abject misery as the door closed behind her. She'd asked all the External Relations Advisors—Cameron, Terry O'Malley, Gerard Sahk and Ivan Joste—to meet her here, as well as Adlai and Maris. "Thanks for coming on such short notice."

Cameron glanced around at the others. "Is Dashiel not coming? I was just with him downstairs a few minutes ago."

She ignored Maris' meaningful stare. "He's busy right now."

Before she could continue, Adlai stood and joined her at the front of the room. "I know you asked us here for a reason, but I've got a reason for us to be here, too." He pinged a file her way. "As of ten minutes ago, you are once again officially an External Relations Advisor of the Asterion Dominion, filling the vacancy left by Iona Rowan. The last of the approvals came through this morning."

She blinked; a chorus of applause faded into the background beneath the ringing in her ears. An Advisor? But that title belonged to Nika Kirumase, and given recent events she didn't particularly *want* to be Nika Kirumase at present.

The content of the journals she'd read so far—the reason why she'd called these people together—forced their way to the forefront of her mind.....

...but she probably needed to be.

So, she smiled gratefully. "Thank you, all of you, for everything you've done for me in recent days. We survive this crisis, and drinks are on me."

Her expression reverted to solemnity. "Which is why we're actually here. I'll be blunt: we have twenty-two days until the Rasu expect the next delivery of Asterions, and we still have no idea how to protect ourselves from the attack that will swiftly arrive when we don't deliver.

"I realize we've been preoccupied with trying to hold society together, and to the extent this is my fault, I apologize. There was no other way to stop the Guides except to, well, stop them. And by the way, you are all doing an amazing job of recovering from the tumult their removal has caused. I deeply wish it were our only challenge. But it's not."

Cameron leaned forward with a grumble. "The problem is, we don't *understand* the Rasu. We can speculate, and we are, but we know nothing about their biology or chemical makeup or the basis of their technology or weapons. How can we defend against them when we don't know the first thing about their strengths or weaknesses?"

"Exactly. We can't. You've nailed the challenge: if we expect to have any chance in hells of surviving an attack, we need to understand our enemy. Which is why I intend to appeal to the Sogain for help."

Terry all but leapt out of his chair. "You're out of your mind. I recognize your memory's spotty, but have you not read about their warning to us?"

"I've done more than read about it. I—" she caught Maris' warning look and cut herself off "—one of my ancestors was on the survey ship that first encountered the Sogain. This is why I need to go."

Adlai frowned. "I'm not following you."

"My ancestor wrote detailed notes about the encounter. The mechanics of the interaction she had with the Sogain entity sound eerily similar to the message I received after the Rasu simex three years ago. A strange voice in her head, as real and immediate and vocal as if someone were standing in front of her speaking, but displaying no physical presence. Dashiel...."

She shoved aside the surge of desolation at the mere utterance of his name. "...suggested the Sogain as a possible source of the simex and the message. After reading up on the encounter with them, I think he might be correct. If so, it means they know a great deal about the Rasu, and that's knowledge we require."

Overlapping interjections broke out, and she quickly hushed them all. "We are out of leads and almost out of ideas. We have to try something—*I* have to try something." Something to keep her mind occupied. Something real that she could accomplish.

Adlai didn't appear convinced. "Take an escort with you. Take an entire fleet of military ships."

"What for? We can't touch the Sogain's technology. If they want to destroy me and my ship, they'll do so—and they're much more likely to do so if I show up with an armed fleet. No, better to go alone and appear as nonthreatening as possible."

He sighed. "Since you're off to get yourself atomized, will you at least make sure to leave behind a current psyche backup?"

"I've taken care of it. But I don't think you'll need to use it. If the Sogain are the source of the Rasu simex, then they know who I am, they know the crisis we're facing and, in their own odd, alien way, they want to help. So, I'm going to ask them for it."

ᴀʀ

Nika fled the room with the intention of rushing straight to the spaceport. This building with all its frenetic activity and grating noise and dashing people was suffocating. She needed air, then she needed space—several hundred parsecs of it.

Space. Ship. *Shit*.

As soon as she'd turned the first hallway corner, she stopped to ping Grant.

Hey, did everything go all right with the installations? Is the Wayfarer *good to fly?*

One hundred percent. Everything checked out.

Great. I appreciate it.

Listen, Nika, about the other issue. Can I apologize again? I didn't—

It's fine. You were doing what you thought was right. If anything, it was my mistake for not telling you about the psyche-wipe.

We're good, then?

She sank against the wall and closed her eyes. Objectively, the secrets Grant had kept from her were no different from those her former self had kept from Dashiel. They'd both believed they were making the best choice; they'd both inflicted harm nonetheless. One day, she and Grant needed to sit down and have a lengthy and possibly difficult conversation, but such a day waited on the other side of defeating the Rasu.

Yeah, we're good.

A gentle hand landed on her arm. She jumped, opening her eyes to see Maris wearing a worried countenance and also blocking her exit route.

"Nika—"

"You're going to say I shouldn't have told him."

"No. I wasn't going to say that." Maris played with a ringlet of hair falling across her cheek. "But you shouldn't have told him."

"You're wrong. No matter how angry he is, even if he never speaks to me again, I have to believe you're wrong. He deserved to know the truth."

"It is done, rendering our dispute futile. Still, I feel as if this is partially my fault. I buried you beneath an avalanche of revelations and left you to deal with them on your own. It's no surprise that you sought out a sounding board."

"Maris, the truth is never anyone's fault."

"Eloquent words to be sure. But reality is, regrettably, far messier. In any event, I embarrassed myself chasing you down to see if you were okay. You might have put on a decent performance in there, but I can see the cracks."

Nika wilted, abandoning the act for just a moment. "No. I'm not okay. I feel...hollow. Brittle. But there's nothing I can do to change that right now, so I'll concentrate on what I *can* do."

"Talking to the Sogain. My dear, please don't get yourself atomized."

"I meant what I said before. They won't atomize me. In fact, I'd wager they're expecting me."

16

RIDANI ENTERPRISES

MIRAI

"We can manipulate specific materials—or more often metamaterials—into functioning as a variety of machine or weaponry components, protective shielding, power generators or batteries, and so on. Virtually everything we've observed the Rasu creating. But to ply a single substance into performing *all* those functions, one after another?" Bruno Galesh spread his arms in an exaggerated shrug. "The substance that can perform those feats doesn't exist, in nature or in the lab."

"It exists in the Rasu," Dashiel snapped, and instantly regretted it. Seeing Nika earlier had rattled him more than he wanted to admit. Fractured his composure then and his concentration now. Also, his manners. "Forgive me. Obviously, you know it exists in the Rasu."

Galesh's company, Tsuyo Materials, specialized in crafting the strongest, most resilient and, when required, most flexible materials in the Dominion. The company's products girded the Ridani Enterprises headquarters building, held together most d-gates in operation today and formed the hulls of a third of commercial starships. The man knew his materials, which was why Dashiel had invited him to the office this morning.

"I do. After watching every Rasu transformation we've recorded at 1/1000th speed and experimenting with over five hundred material combinations using eighty-two different catalysts, I'm forced to conclude that the Rasu can manipulate themselves at the subatomic level. It's likely they exercise control over not only their own protons and electrons, but their own fundamental particles."

Nika was wearing her old clothes now, and the stark juxtaposition of old and new added a layer of complexity to the storm of conflicting thoughts tearing him to pieces one bloody slash at a time. His intention this morning had been to throw himself into work until he no longer had the bandwidth to linger on the storm. It was going swimmingly so far.

"That would mean they can transform into nearly anything in the universe."

Galesh grimaced. "Theoretically, yes, but I have to believe some limitations constrain them. They seem to strongly favor inorganic compounds to organic ones, which could suggest a preference for, or greater skill at, metallic bonding over covalent."

"Let's hope something constrains them. If they can truly shift at the subatomic level, where do you think their intelligence resides?"

"You are now firmly outside my area of expertise."

Dashiel conceded the point with a tilt of his head. "I'm outside mine as well. It's just difficult to conceive of a single atom of Rasu being sentient."

"Perhaps, like all other intelligent life we know anything about, their intelligence lies in the complexity and nature of their neural interconnections. Perhaps they become struck by temporary dumbness while they transform!"

He laughed, which felt good for half a second. "Finally, a weakness we can exploit. We can hope, anyway. All right. Thank you for stopping by and, if I can beg an indulgence, keep working the problem?"

"I wouldn't dream of doing otherwise. This is all of our problem now. I'm sorry I don't have better answers yet." Galesh extended his hand, and Dashiel shook it.

"We'll talk again soon."

ΛR

MIRAI ONE PAVILION

It had been almost a day since Dashiel had eaten anything, so he finally gave in and went to the Pavilion cafeteria. He found it crowded even early in the evening; it was possible he wasn't the only person randomly forgetting to eat.

After grabbing a sandwich and roasted potatoes, he spotted Adlai at a small table in the corner and headed over. "May I?"

"Of course, but you look like crap. What happened?"

He sat and took a quick bite of his sandwich. "You don't want me to recount the gory details, and frankly, I don't want to either. You look positively chipper by comparison, though."

Adlai's cheeks reddened. "I feel horribly guilty, daring to be happy amidst all this terror and angst and imminent death. But I can't help it. I'm happy."

"Perrin?"

Adlai nodded, and a smile spread across his face. "At least it's the same…" he paused to study Dashiel more critically "…unless it's not the same for you. You and Nika had a fight, didn't you? She was uncommonly sober and brooding when she briefed us on her plan to visit the Sogain and—"

Dashiel's heart stopped beating, and only his OS' core programming restarted it. "On her *what*?"

"She didn't tell you? How bad of a fight was it?"

"Bad enough. She's planning to *seek out* the Sogain?"

"Not planning any longer. I think she left this morning. I'm sorry, I thought she told you."

"Gods, did no one try to talk her out of it? What about the Sogain's warning?"

"*Everyone* tried to talk her out of it. She insisted she understood the warning, because one of her ancestors was on the survey ship to first encounter them. Did you know that?"

Dashiel pinched the bridge of his nose. Not an ancestor…but this was how the lies were told and the secrets kept, wasn't it? "No. I didn't."

"She believes the Sogain were the ones who warned her about the Rasu three years ago. If so, it means they have a lot more information on the Rasu than we do. Maybe they'll be willing to share it."

"And if they aren't? If they atomize her and the *Wayfarer*?"

"I'm sure she updated a psyche and memory backup before she left."

"Did she? Where?"

"She told us she'd taken care of it. I didn't ask where she'd stored it. Again, I assumed…."

A shadow crept across the table, and Dashiel spun around to see Maris standing behind him. "What the fuck does 'she'd taken care of it' mean?"

"I don't know, either."

Dashiel snorted in disgust.

Maris sighed. "I'm telling you the truth. But she said she had, so I trust she has."

"Must be nice to trust so freely." He pivoted to his friend at the table. "Adlai, I bet Maris is here because she has something important she needs to tell you."

She fidgeted, betraying a rare lack of poise. "No, I merely wanted to—"

He grabbed his half-eaten plate of food and stood to point a finger in her face. "I will not be your coconspirator. Either you tell him, or I will."

Her lips drew into a thin line, exposing tension wrinkles along her perfect ebony skin. "Dashiel, I'm begging you. Don't do this."

"What are you two talking about?"

"Ask her. I have work to do."

And he did have work to do—enough work to fill a hundred lifetimes. But his last thread of tenuous focus had frayed and floated off on the breeze that greeted him when he walked out the front doors of the Pavilion. He meandered to the left and found shade beneath the broad limbs of a snowbell tree.

Nika had run off alone to provoke a confrontation with the Sogain, the only aliens they knew of who were capable of killing them even faster than the Rasu. He'd been the one to suggest the Sogain might be responsible for the Rasu simex. He should be with her, dammit.

But he couldn't be with her. Couldn't so much as see her without being consumed by the bitter sting of...not betrayal, but something worse. Of being used. Trifled with. Demeaned.

Except, it didn't *feel* like she'd demeaned him. When she'd stared at him this morning, he didn't see scorn or contempt; he saw sorrow and longing. He saw pain. But should he trust anything he imagined he read in her eyes? Clearly his perception programming was shit, for her to fool him so completely in thousands of encounters of profound intimacy.

An alert arrived from his bank, notifying him of a significant new deposit. He opened the alert to check the details, then sank against the sinewy trunk of the snowbell.

2.1 million credits deposited to the personal account of Dashiel Ridani from the personal account of Nika Kirumase.

The itemization that followed spelled it all out: the 1.4 million for the *Wayfarer*, the 500,000 for NOIR, the 60,000 for the Taiyok cloaking device, plus an assortment of smaller expenses they'd incurred while traveling together.

At the end, a note:

Thank you for being there for me, for NOIR and for the Asterion people when we needed you most.

His immediate reaction was one of anger. How many times had he told her the money wasn't a loan? By treating it as a business transaction, she trivialized everything about their recent time together, ensuring those memories now joined their predecessors, tainted, in a dank sea of doubt.

But the anger swiftly gave way to soul-gutting despair. Why did she have to be so fucking *kind*? He'd flung the worst manner of vitriol at her, yet she was thanking him for being a decent person.

Gods, was this a goodbye? A settling of debts before closing and locking the door forever? Worse, was it an *actual* goodbye? Did she not expect to return from her visit to the Sogain? Had she lied about taking care of a psyche backup, and was this her chosen way to 'sunset'?

No. Whatever wrongs she may have inflicted on him, she would never abandon her people, whether this meant NOIR or every Asterion who lived and breathed, at their hour of greatest need. She'd spent 700,000 years protecting them, and on losing all memory of those aeons, she'd nonetheless promptly taken up the mantle anew.

But the fact remained that she might not be given a choice in the matter.

He crouched beside the tree trunk and dropped his head into his hands. The thought of her not coming back threatened to rip the tattered remains of his psyche apart. Damn him for loving her so much. Damn her for lying to him. Damn her for vanishing and reappearing and making him love her all over again.

If she defied all sane odds and did survive this mission, what the hells was he going to do?

Forget then—what the hells was he going to do *now*?

He bit the inside of his cheek until he drew blood...then unblocked her message ID and pinged her.

Just tell me you're all right. Just tell me you're safe.

Message unable to be delivered to intended recipient.

Godsdammit. He probably deserved that.

With a sigh he pinged Perrin instead.

Hey, have you heard from Nika this evening?

No, and I'm worried sick about her. She should've reached the Sogain stellar system by now, and I thought she would have checked in before trying to communicate with them...and of course you're worried about her, too. You ought to send her a message, Dashiel. She'd really, really like to hear from you.

Not so much. I tried, and it bounced. She's blocking me.

I highly doubt it. Hold on for a second, I'll ping her.

A pause.

Um, she's not blocking you. My ping bounced, too. She's not receiving. Stars, what if something's happened to her?

It's likely some kind of interference field emanating from the Sogain stellar system. They're paranoid, so they'd implement defensive measures along those lines, right?

I don't have the foggiest idea what strange, hermited super-advanced aliens would do!

He smiled a little. *Fair enough. Do you know where her psyche backup is? She told Adlai and Maris she'd updated her backups before she left, but no one knows anything about where she's keeping them.*

I don't. I mean I used to, when we were at The Chalet. But even then, she kept additional backups in secret locations. Now? I've got no idea.

I'm sure a backup won't be needed. Contact me when you hear from her, okay? Please?

Absolutely. You do the same.

I will.

The connection ended, leaving him alone with the breeze and the shade and the smooth bark at his back. He closed his eyes as the naked, unvarnished truth smacked him in the head like a tidal wave and settled in so he could drown beneath it: he needed her to come home. Not a copy or an old backup—he needed *this* Nika, this complex mosaic of the woman she'd once been and the one she'd become, to return safely, real and whole.

He didn't know what else this meant, or what he planned to do if she did; he only knew he needed her to be here.

17

WAYFARER

INTERSTELLAR SPACE

Coming alone had been a mistake. She should have brought Perrin along for a constant stream of enthusiastic conversation. She should have brought Maris along and picked her brain about seven-hundred-thousand-years' worth of history. But to bring either of them would have endangered their lives, if temporarily, and the Dominion couldn't afford to lose them for even a day right now.

She should have brought the entire *A Song of Sorbonne* series for twenty hours of song and dance.

Instead she had only her thoughts, and they made for poor company indeed.

She skirmished with the emerging picture of the woman Nika Kirumase had been as it took shape one journal entry at a time. She agonized over how she could possibly convince Dashiel to trust her again. She ruminated on what her next move would be if this gambit failed. Not for long on the last one, however, because she didn't have a next move. She mused pointlessly about the motivations of the Rasu.

She found no answers in the noisy echo chambers of her mind.

Expansion for expansion's sake wasn't a goal Asterions aspired to, but their ancestors the Anadens had. Nevertheless, though the Anadens were a hard and at times ruthless people, their desire for greater power had not transformed them into monsters. They had treated the alien species they encountered with minimal decency, if not always empathy or respect. The war her people had fought against the Anaden leadership had its roots in ideological differences and fear of the unknown—

—a bell sounded to alert her that she'd reached the far outskirts of the Sogain stellar system. It hadn't been a terribly long trip, which her weary psyche appreciated. The system lay a mere six hundred thirty-four parsecs from Mirai, but for the last 200,000 years they'd treated the space surrounding it like a black hole and, as ordered, given it a wide berth.

She stood, splashed water on her face and sent a message to the External Relations Advisors to let them know she was set to begin.

Message unable to be delivered to intended recipients.

Huh. The possibility that the Guides had escaped their prisons, mounted a full-scale attack on the Pavilion and rendered everyone inside nonfunctional briefly crossed her mind. But it was far more likely the Sogain maintained an interference field for some distance beyond their stellar system as a defensive measure.

Either way, nothing she could do about it at present.

Unlike when she interacted with the Taiyoks, here no algorithms existed beyond the rudimentary 'first contact' protocols to instruct her how to act or what demeanor to project, and those were less than useless since this was *second* contact. Or possibly third.

No, the only tools at her disposal were her instincts and a healthy dose of desperation.

She approached the stellar system at half maximum impulse speed with all cloaking mechanisms turned off—the space travel equivalent of holding her arms in the air, palms open. Based on the notes from the previous encounter, the Sogain somehow understood Communis and had even communicated in it, so she broadcast a message on a loop signaling her peaceful intentions.

The first expedition had never made it close enough to any of the five planets in the system to determine which one, if any, the Sogain called home. If nothing arrived to stop her, she'd conduct flybys of every one of them—

—the cabin lit up in a thousand swirling points of light. Before she could begin to react, they rushed around her in a torrent and the cabin vanished.

ᚱᚱ

SOGAIN STELLAR SYSTEM

Nika hung suspended in nothingness. In space, perhaps, but the churning lights surrounding her made it impossible to say for certain. If the lights dropped her, it was possible she might fall forever and ever through the depths of the infinite cosmos.

She breathed in—she could breathe. There was air, and the frigid, deadly vacuum of space wasn't reaching her. So that was something.

She struggled to make out an object beyond the fog generated by the pinpoints of lights agitating around her. A planet? No. Though globe-shaped, there was no soft glow of an atmosphere and no true surface. Instead the object was porous in the gaps between a multitude of rigid lines and sharp angles. Light, though markedly different from what surrounded her, pulsed in intricate rhythms across the object's breadth.

It was a machine. A constructed tool.

She squinted, trying to make out more details. The patterns stacked upon one another into the depths of the machine. The star at the center of the system, which she suddenly realized she floated alarmingly close to, pulsed out solar flares toward the machine in a hypnotic rhythm. A rhythm which was neither random nor chaotic...nor unevenly distributed. While the star and the machine both rotated, the machine remained at a fixed point in space—it didn't orbit the star—and the flares invariably licked its outer framework.

The Sogain, who she assumed must control the machine, were siphoning off energy from the star, though by no method she'd ever heard of. Given the regular, targeted flares, it almost seemed as if they were controlling the star's activity, manipulating the solar atmosphere to their own purposes.

She should feel fear in the presence of such unfathomable power, but as she dangled helplessly there, a tiny speck of dust in the cosmos with naught but her supernal cocoon protecting her from its ravages, she felt only awe.

She gulped in impossible air and greeted her captor or captors. "Hello?"

You violate our directive and trespass on our sovereign space once again. Explain your presence or be disposed of.

The voice boomed in her mind, more forceful and intimidating than the one she'd heard after the Rasu simex but possessing the same innate qualities.

"I've come to plead for your assistance. My people face a grave threat to their existence—a threat that looms dark over all life in this galaxy. They are called the Rasu, and I believe you know something of them. I believe you gave me information on this species three years ago in an attempt to prepare me for the conflict that is now upon us. I'm most grateful for what you did, but it is not enough. Your information impressed upon me how fearsome the Rasu are and provided crucial details on their nature, but it didn't show me how we can defend against them.

"I don't know how to protect my people from this enemy, and unless I find a way to do so, they will all die. If you value life, any life at all, I beg you to tell me everything you know about the Rasu."

Why do you suggest we interacted with you or your kind in any way? We care nothing of your flailings and wish only to be left alone.

The voice came from nowhere; no distinct entity floated in front of her to whom she could direct her responses. Unless the voice originated from...the lights. Unless the lights *were* a Sogain, or *all* the Sogain.

The revelation did nothing whatsoever to slow her racing heart. She swallowed hard.

"I...think you're lying. I think you're the sole species we've ever met who is capable of contacting me in the manner in which I was contacted three years ago. I think you were in my head once before, a very long time ago, and let me assure you, it's an unusual and memorable experience—one I experienced a second time three years ago, and a third time now. I think you remember who I am from our first meeting, and you deliberately sought me out.

"Because I think you *do* care. Maybe not about Asterions. Maybe you only care about yourselves and recognize the Rasu are a threat to you as well. Maybe you care about life in the universe on an epochal scale and recognize the threat the Rasu pose to all of it. Whatever your motivations, I think you want us to defeat them, whether for ourselves, for you or for everyone."

Go on.

She smiled in her ethereal cage. *Gotcha.* "I'm happy to defeat the Rasu—we'll *all* be happy to defeat the Rasu—but you have to give me something more to work with. What is the base material they originate from? How is this material alive? How are they intelligent? What scientific principles do their weapons and starship engines operate on? What are their structural and strategic weaknesses? How can we disable them? Repel them? Destroy them?"

Silence enveloped her for a long time. Approaching a minute, judging by the thousand heartbeats that punctuated the silence.

A Rasu scout ship was disabled by an unexpected solar flare three years ago in a binary system containing two planets in your Sector III-E, Region 183. Though in time it was able to repair itself and re-form, it has chosen to remain on the planet upon which it crashed rather than return to the Rasu bastion. Go to this planet, capture the Rasu there and discover your answers if you can.

"Thank you, but—"

The world shifted in a blur of dizzying motion, and the next instant she was back in the cabin of the *Wayfarer*. The lights vanished, leaving the cabin feeling dark and empty.

Her legs wobbled, and she stumbled to the couch to avoid falling on the floor. Once she'd caught her breath and the cabin had stopped spinning, she checked herself over for injuries. Her skin bore no traces of exposure to the ravages of space. She didn't have so much as a scratch—

—she tumbled to the floor anyway as the *Wayfarer* was blasted out of the stellar system by an unseen force. Not quite as rudely as on her first visit, but hardly a gentle farewell.

She took the hint and hurried into the cockpit, where she quickly set a course for home and engaged the superluminal engine. No further shockwaves arrived to speed her departure, and after some minutes she decided she must be in the clear.

Her chin dropped into her hand as she gazed out at the nebulous haze of the superluminal bubble. What had just happened to her? What in the literal cosmos *were* the Sogain? Finally and most crucially, how in the hells was she going to capture a Rasu in the wild?

18

MIRAI ONE PAVILION

Adlai steepled his hands at his chin and stared out at nothing. He couldn't afford to waste much time brooding. But maybe a minute or two.

The idea of ancient Asterions walking among them—friends, lovers, adversaries? He needed to figure out how he felt about it. On the one hand, Maris and Nika were the same people he'd always known. Well possibly not Nika, but only at the margins. Even Satair remained the same arrogant, short-sighted blowhard he'd always been.

And what counted as 'old,' anyway? Once upon a time, albeit in a distant past, they'd lived normal organic lifespans—were born, grew up, aged and died a mere few centuries later. By those standards, *he* might as well be an immortal. Asterions had changed what it meant to live, die and be reborn. In doing so, they'd changed what time itself meant...

...but three weeks was a frighteningly short period of time under any measure, and the calendar raced headlong toward a zero-day confrontation with the Rasu. Enough of the brooding.

He looked up as Perrin walked into the Justice command center wearing a big grin. "What's got you excited?"

She bounced on the balls of her feet. "Nika survived her encounter with the Sogain and is on her way back!"

"That's terrific news." He met her halfway and wrapped his arms around her. Only after he'd done so did he remember half a dozen other people occupied the command center. Oh well, too late to be bashful now. "Did she learn anything?"

"I think so. She said she'd fill us in once she gets back in a few hours." Perrin's nose wrinkled up as she stepped away to scrutinize him. "What's on your mind?"

Could she already read him so thoroughly? Probably. She was excellent with people, practically an empath, and 'people' included him, so he ought not to be surprised.

Now, was he going to answer her question truthfully? It wasn't his secret to tell. But like Dashiel, he didn't feel comfortable acting as a coconspirator to immortals. "I don't—"

Spencer knocked on the frame of the open door. The man had as much right to inhabit the command center as anyone in Justice, but even in the face of chaos he continued to be unfailingly polite and respectful.

Adlai whispered in Perrin's ear, "I'll tell you later," and motioned Spencer inside. An officer from Synra—Francis Wallman, Adlai believed was the man's name—accompanied him.

"What's the word?"

"The...I guess 'regens' is the most accurate label...of all five former Guides have been completed without any glitches. Medically, that is. I understand the transition to functioning bodies is proving difficult for some of them, at least in the early hours."

"Then they shouldn't have given up their physical forms in the first place." Perrin crossed her arms defiantly over her chest.

Spencer huffed a breath. "I don't think anyone except them will disagree with you there."

Adlai nodded. "I heard from the teams at the internment sites we've chosen on Mirai and Synra a few minutes ago. They're set up, and the locations have been secured. Selene, Harris and Julien are handling the other locations, and they haven't raised any issues so far. Once the clinic clears them, we'll be ready to move the—let's call them what they are, prisoners—under full guard to their new homes."

"Yes, sir. If it's all right, I'd like to take Officer Wallman here with me and stop by the Synra site to give it a once-over myself before its new occupant moves in."

"You don't need to ask my permission for that, Spencer. It'll be your purview soon enough."

"I hope so, sir."

"Don't worry. The delay isn't due to any doubts among the Advisors, but rather the need for us to focus all our efforts on getting the former Guides dealt with as quickly as possible."

"I understand, and I agree. I'd as soon toss them into holes in the ground, but so long as they end up stationary and secured behind the best locks we can configure, I'll take it."

"As will I." They shook hands, and Spencer departed once more.

Adlai turned to Perrin and squeezed her hand; these public displays of affection weren't so hard. "I should do the same for the Mirai site."

"You should. I agree with Spencer. I don't want any of those awful machine people getting loose and coming after us."

"They're not machine people any longer."

"But they are still creepy. And dangerous." She bit her lower lip, eyes dancing, and swatted him lightly on the ass. "So get!"

His face burned. "Perrin…."

"Got to run myself—have to provide a shoulder to cry on for a bit. Bye!" She scurried off with a wave, leaving him standing there in mortification.

He furtively looked around the command center, but everyone continued about their work, heads down and eyes trained on panes and files…

…then Julien's deputy, Frank Quill, winked at him.

HATAORI RENEWAL CLINIC

Ava and Maggie sat huddled together on a couch in the lobby, while Carson slouched in a chair across from them. Maggie's skin had lightened to a shade above pale, and her formerly burgundy hair now shone bright fuchsia; when paired with Ava's brilliant emerald locks they made for the beginnings of a bold canvas.

Carson looked the same as before, with a buzz-cut fading to mahogany skin on a muscular frame.

They all stood when they saw Perrin, and she wrapped Maggie and Carson in a big hug when she reached them. "Welcome back!"

"Thanks."

She grabbed the remaining chair in the lobby alcove, and everyone settled back down. "Has Ava brought you both up to speed?"

Maggie wound a lock of hair around her finger. "Let's see: a nasty virutox swept through the population turning people into criminals but is now being quelled, The Chalet blew up, twice, the Guides were secretly machines but are now people who are in prison, the Advisors—of which Nika was and is again one—are forming a new government, and evil shapeshifting aliens are coming for us all with the dawn. Did I miss anything?"

Perrin shot Ava a glare. "You didn't sugar-coat any of it, did you?"

Ava stared at her deadpan. "Why would I do that?"

"Right." She gave Maggie an encouraging smile. "You did cover the high, or I suppose low, points. Except the Rasu won't be here with the dawn. We have a little longer than that. Not much, though." She felt her smile fading and willfully propped it up. "But we are working on stopping them. Not me, personally, but people. Nika, for instance. She's on a mission for exactly that purpose, and she'll be back in a few hours.

"There's also more good news. You can now walk freely on the streets wearing your own face without fear of being arrested by a Justice squad. NOIR is now on quite good terms with Justice, in fact."

Carson snickered. "Yeah, Ava said you were shacked up with someone from Justice."

Perrin tried not to groan. She *so* should not have let Ava handle their regen briefing. "His name is Adlai, and I'm just staying with him until I can find my own place. I've been spending all my time finding lodging for everyone else—including you! Maggie, you've got a bed in Ava's suite at the Mikan Hotel. Carson, you can stay with Geoff and Dominic in their suite, but feel free to rearrange yourselves as you like. The important thing is you have roofs and beds. The NOIR nex hub is also alive and kicking. You can get in touch with everyone and..." she shrugged, but tried to make it an enthusiastic one "...start living your lives again."

Maggie rolled her eyes at something Ava muttered in her ear. "Thank you for everything, Perrin. We will. And we'll help out wherever you need us to."

Carson interjected. "But first we're getting steaks. I'm getting a steak. You all can come with me, but you've got to get off your asses, because—" he stood and jerked a thumb toward the entrance "—the steaks are this way."

She laid a hand on Ava's arm as the woman stood, then leaned in close. "Where's Cair?"

✦✦✦

Perrin knocked to announce her impending presence before activating the door to the recovery room.

Cair paced repeatedly across the small room, pausing to glance out the window every other pass. When she stepped inside, he sent the glance her way instead. "I heard you talking about lodging suites out there. I don't want to stay with other people."

"I know you don't. I got you a private room."

"Oh. Thank you."

"Of course. You know, you could have joined us in the lobby."

"No. No. I burned Carson and Maggie alive. They don't want to see me. I can't see them."

"It wasn't your fault, Cair. They know that."

"It was still me. My old hands." He held his hands out in front of him, frowning at them without slowing his traversals.

She propped carefully against the wall beside the door in an open and non-threatening stance. "It really wasn't. No one blames you for what happened. This virutox? It completely altered a person's fundamental programming. It made people do horrible things that they never would have done otherwise. An Advisor, Iona Rowan, slaughtered three Chizeru diplomats—final death for them—and shot up a group of corporate executives. A factory technician named Tristan McLeros destroyed the Mirai One transit hub, atomizing more than two hundred people. I know you feel bad, but you need to forgive yourself."

The pacing slowed, which might be progress. "I want to help on the Rasu. I'm good with patterns."

"Absolutely. Nika's made everything we have on the aliens publicly available, and I know she'll welcome another skilled mind looking at the data."

"Okay." Cair stopped and made a good effort at keeping eye contact with her. "Thank you. You and Nika have always been kind to me, and I...I am grateful."

"We know." She gestured toward the door. "Do you maybe want to join the others for a steak?"

"No. I'm not ready for that."

"Well, can I buy you a sandwich, then?"

He started to shake his head...then nodded instead. "A sandwich would be nice."

19

MIRAI

Dashiel was waiting in the hangar bay when the *Wayfarer* landed—lurking in the entry hallway like a stalker, hoping she didn't spot him as she landed. He'd almost rushed to the spaceport the instant Perrin pinged him to let him know Nika was on her way home, but he'd forced himself to plow through another futile meeting before coming here.

He just needed to see her, alive and in person. Then he'd leave, since he still had no bearing pointing to what came next. The sting of betrayal continued to burn hot, singeing the edges of every memory it touched.

Yet as soon as she descended the ramp and her feet touched the ground, he was no longer lurking in the hallway and his arms were wrapped around her, holding her tightly against him. Her warmth cooled the heat of betrayal in soothing, reassuring waves.

She gasped in surprise, then wound her own arms around his waist and sank into his embrace. He could feel her lips rise into a smile at the curve of his neck.

Holding her body against his felt like coming home. The answer to every question. Gods, how he didn't want to let go—but then he remembered, and the sting flared to burn away the contentment, and he did.

His gaze met hers fleetingly before running from the hope and confusion her expression conveyed, darting to the ground, behind her, anywhere else. "I'm glad you made it home safely—I'm glad you returned." He took a step back and tried to dislodge the lump in his throat. "There are a lot of people waiting anxiously to hear what you learned, so..." another step back "...you should go talk to them."

"No!"

He looked up in surprise, accidentally meeting her gaze again. What he saw there broke his heart...but so had she. "What do you mean, no?"

"You don't get to show up out of nowhere and touch me like you mean it, then walk away."

A visceral image of that night at his place, when he'd lost her and found her all at once, burst into his mind in full living color, as vivid as when he'd lived it. The moment when he'd known the woman he loved still existed inside her, not yet realizing how much more did as well, or how much he'd never known.

He spat out a response. "Don't use my own words against me."

Her shoulders sagged, and she gestured weakly at nothing. "Why did you do that? Why did you make me think..." her hands came to her face, muffling her voice "...why are you here?"

Because no matter what I do, I somehow always find myself standing in front of you. Because every road, every twist and turn, every fork in the trail? They all lead back to you. "I was worried, then...relieved. I wanted to make certain you were all right. And where the hells are your psyche backups? You told the others you'd taken care of it, but no one knows where they are. Not Perrin, not Adlai, not anyone!"

"I left behind a message detailing their location and queued it to be sent to Perrin and Maris if I didn't return in two days. I'm a touch paranoid about my backups, for obvious reasons."

Which made perfect sense, and now he'd made an idiot of himself all over again. "Sure, but...okay. I didn't know."

"How could you have known? You've been blocking my messages."

Though her words should have sounded biting and caustic, the delivery was nothing but sincere. Quiet, resigned, perhaps even sad, but genuine. It would be so much easier to hate her if only she'd act annoyed and dismissive. "I just needed time to think."

"And? You've had time, and now you're here." Her voice dropped to a whisper. "You must have something you need to say to me."

Did he? Had all the hours of tumultuous arguments with himself, of ragged swings between despair and hatred and desperate longing added up to anything coherent? She was standing right here; she wasn't arguing or fighting him, and no one waved frantically in the distance to demand their immediate attention.

This opportunity might never come again, only in part because they both might be walking through the dwindling reservoir of their last days. So why *was* he here?

The answer formed clear as the sun's rays shining through the storm of questions drowning him.

"I suppose I do." He took a deep breath and exhaled slowly. "Nika, when I heard where you'd gone, putting yourself in extreme danger in the slimmest hope of finding any advantage we can use to protect ourselves from the enemy, I realized...I don't want to live without you."

Her eyes gleamed like jewels set afire. "Is it so simple as that?"

"No. Because if I'm not able to trust you not to lie to me about something so fundamental as who you are—as who *I* am—I can't live with you, either. And I have no *idea* how to bridge that chasm."

She nodded thoughtfully, even as the light in her eyes dimmed. "I understand. She, I—godsdamn these pronouns—was wrong to keep all this from you. I would not have kept it from you. Hells, the reason we're here now is that I was effusively honest with you, which must count for something?" Hope lifted her features, but she didn't fall silent to wait for an answer that remained tangled in his throat.

"But I recognize it's not so simple as that, either, and my actions now can't make up for the lies of the past. My psyche was her psyche, and I don't blame you for thinking this means I'll make the same choice again in the future. I won't—having your identity and memories stolen from you has a way of making you appreciate the preciousness of truth—but it is what it is.

"I'll never be able to re-inhabit my mindset from before. I'll never be able to completely and without reservation understand why I made the choice to lie to you. The best I can do is this." She reached into her pack and retrieved a data weave, then extended her hand, palm up, and offered it to him.

He groaned and shook his head. "I can't listen to any more earnest excuses."

"Believe me, I know where you're coming from. But if this is it, if this is you—" the words choked off in her throat "—walking away from me, I don't want you to do it entertaining any doubts or misconceptions about how much Nika Kirumase loved you." She thrust her hand and its contents toward him. "Please. Do this one thing for me."

He stared at the tiny object resting on her palm. He was terrified of what it contained, though whether his terror arose from a fear that it would confirm his worst assumptions or make him no longer care about them, he couldn't say.

He took the weave. His hand trembled as he placed a fingertip upon it.

Date: Y9,189.021 A7
Subject: Dashiel

I almost told him yesterday. All of it. The day before that, too.

Why did I stop myself? Why am I telling a journal instead of him?

I need to let go of this internal conflict and move forward. I don't want to dwell on the past any longer. I don't want to introduce doubt and pain into Dashiel's mind, where it should never exist. Not about this. He owes no debt to his ancestor, and he should carry no burden left behind by the same.

The thing is, he's like Steven in the ways Steven was best—and he's all the things Steven couldn't be. Decisive where Steven was hesitant; kind and generous where Steven retreated to selfishness; displaying a quiet yet extraordinary inner strength where Steven too often broke to weakness.

And while ancestry does matter, he is his own man where it matters most.

Sometimes he'll make the smallest gesture or flash the tiniest expression my way, and it's identical to something Stephen would do. The first few times it happened, I felt as if I was transported back in time.

But then he'll smile more broadly, stand more proudly, and it becomes an action belonging fully to Dashiel. And now, Dashiel is all I see. Because he's not an improved copy of Steven. Not a version or an echo. He's his own man, whole and complete, and I owe it to him to see him, to love him, unencumbered by any ghost haunting the shadows.

And I do. When I look with new eyes freed from the past, I see a man worthy of walking with through eternity. I love him.

Ironically, by deciding not to tell him, I feel as though I can finally close the door on a past far too long gone. What happened before no longer has any claim on me.

With Dashiel, all I want to do is move forward. To take his hand in mine and walk with him, only him, into the sun of an endless future.

—Nika Kirumase

Dashiel closed his eyes...or were they already closed? He'd succumbed to the spell of the journal and utterly lost himself in it.

Was it possible he remembered that very day? He checked the date, and it *was* possible. All too possible. A spring morning, eight months after he'd been named an Advisor. Eight months after he'd met her, and everything about his life had changed.

I grimaced at the arrangement of charts and graphs in front of me, at their quantity as much as their content, until the bridge of my nose began to ache. I hadn't expected being an Industry Advisor to involve so much busy work.

Managing the manufacturing output of an entire planet, if at a nosebleed level, ought not to be qualitatively different from managing the output of my own company, except I had far less flexibility to fix problems when I spotted them. File a report, schedule a meeting, recommend corrective action, devise remedial contingencies, but otherwise....

Nika emerged from the kitchen, two mugs of steaming coffee in hand. She'd dressed in black leggings and a teal wraparound that shifted between blue and green in the light, just like her eyes. She did that deliberately, I was fairly certain. Her hair was still damp from her shower; held away from her face by a matching headband, it cascaded in soft, lazy waves over her shoulders and down her back.

She handed me one of the mugs, then reached out and took my other hand in hers. "It's a lovely morning. Let's go for a walk."

I pondered the sea of charts. A lot of work remained to be done, but it was only work. It could wait.

I sipped on the coffee. "All right. Where are we walking to?"

Her countenance shone with extraordinary joy, even for her. I didn't know what had brightened her mood, but I looked forward to letting it infect me as well.

"Around the block. Around the world. It doesn't matter, so long as we're walking together."

Tears escaped his eyelids to dampen his cheeks, and he did not care. He suspected they'd been escaping for a while now.

He reopened his eyes to find her gazing at him. Open, hopeful, kind, unreserved. Loving. So breathtakingly like how she had gazed at him that morning. "Not fair. You're playing dirty."

"What do you expect? I'm a diplomat and a rebel." She tried to smile, but the muscles around her mouth faltered as they struggled to hold it in place.

He offered the weave back to her. "Thank you. I...thank you."

She held her hand out, and he placed the weave in her open palm. His fingertips lingered there, barely touching her skin as he drank her in.

In her beautiful features he saw pain, of course—hers and his in turn—but he also saw everything that made their world worth saving. Everything that gave his life meaning and joy.

Her expression flickered as her lower lip quivered. She blinked, and a tear escaped her left eye, then her right. He'd been staring for too long, teasing her with the hint of his touch and the threat of removing it forever.

He folded her fingers up and over the weave, squeezed her closed hand and let go.

Then he let go of the rest, too—the clenched grip of his psyche on the bitterness and resentfulness, the knotted noose of fear he'd tied around his neck. Yes, she had lied to him. But hearing her reasons for doing so in her own voice, he now understood something: the lie hadn't stolen their shared history, it had created it. He wished she'd never kept all this from him, but dammit....

He swallowed roughly. Cleared his throat. Leapt. "Forget about generations and ancestors and fractured memories and sunsets and ancient journal entries. Strip them all away, because you and I are the ones standing here today, trying our damnedest to find a way forward. What about now? Does Nika Tescarav love Dashiel Ridani?"

Everything in her countenance *broke*, shattering into pieces at their feet. "Beyond madness."

He sensed himself moving. Then she was in his arms once more, and this time he meant it. Maris was right about one thing— this was what mattered. This moment, and the ones they created together to follow it.

"Dashiel?" It was a whisper against his lips.

He ran a hand through her hair, tucking strands blowing in the wind behind her ear. "Yes?"

"You're not toying with me, are you? Because while I might deserve it, I don't think I can survive it if you are."

He chuckled lightly and kissed the tip of her nose, then the corners of her mouth. "I'm not toying with you." Her damp cheeks. "Do me a favor, though? Say it again."

Her lips danced across his. "I love you."

"Poetry of the gods. I love you, too. I need you. I want to walk through eternity with you." He reluctantly drew back enough to see her face. He wished he didn't need to ask, but a pesky little voice haranguing the depths of his mind insisted. "You're not keeping any more life-altering secrets from me, are you?"

She winced, letting a lingering tear escape to trail down her cheek. "Honestly? I don't know. If I am, I'm keeping them from myself, too. But I promise you this: if I am, you'll know the secret seconds after I do."

It wasn't a perfect answer, but it was a true one. "I guess that's all I can ask for, isn't it?"

"It's everything I have to give." She rested her forehead on his as her hands tenderly caressed his neck and wove into his hair.

They stayed that way, touching and holding on for dear life, for a long second. Then another, and another, until at last he sensed the joy creeping into her countenance.

She chuckled lightly. "Oh, also, you can read all of my journals, carte blanche. It's going to take me ten thousand years to get through them all at this rate, so I need the help."

He reveled in the buoyancy of his heart. He felt renewed, like an oasis in the desert hadn't been a mirage at all. "Maybe I'll read a few here and there. But I'm more interested in the woman standing in front of me now."

"Good." She tugged him closer to hold him so tight he could scarcely draw a breath. But who needed air, anyway?

READ/
WRITE/
EXEC

DAYS UNTIL RASU DEADLINE: 18

20

MIRAI ONE PAVILION

"What you're describing? Ethereal, cosmic beings of light? They sound almost like gods."

Nika smiled even as she shook her head at Cameron. Smiled because she had not merely survived the harrowing encounter with the Sogain but returned with actionable intelligence. Smiled because right now, the joy filling her soul had pushed aside all the fear and worry. Better yet, it spurred her onward with renewed determination to somehow defeat their enemy. Everyone was going to live, dammit.

"No, not gods. I can't say for certain whether the lights that transported me from and to the *Wayfarer* represented an actual Sogain or were a device controlled by them—or one of them. Their species could number in the millions, but it felt as if I was interacting with a single entity. In fact, it's possible there's only a single Sogain."

The two dozen faces staring at her displayed the full gamut of reactions: shock from Julien, deep skepticism from Cameron, 'the fuck do I care' from Katherine, and so on. The size of the group didn't rattle Nika too much, as she'd speechified to more people at The Chalet countless times, but it did stand to make productive debate challenging.

Regardless, all the Advisors needed to be here for this. Also Perrin, because after hugging Nika for a solid ten seconds upon arrival, her irrepressible friend had refused to be denied entry—and if Katherine had so much as opened her mouth to try, Nika would have put her on the floor, so.

A couple of murmurs began surfacing to debate the population size of the Sogain, and she hurriedly started talking again to save everyone from the rabbit hole. "More important than their number, though, is the fact that the structure I observed was *constructed*. It was built of real, physical materials, assembled and shaped for a specific purpose. Yes, that purpose was beyond my comprehension, but it wasn't magic or a supernatural manifestation—it was technology. While they're clearly far more advanced than we are, it's a difference of degree, not of kind."

Maris sighed. "This is a great deal more than we knew about the Sogain before today, and it's somewhat reassuring to learn they're not gods passing judgment upon our prolific sins from on high. But nevertheless...they wield unfathomable power, technology and presumably weapons, and all they gave you was, 'here's a map, go do it yourself?'"

Nika laughed. Damn, it felt good to laugh. "Essentially, yes. It's entirely possible the Sogain are just assholes. But if we can't comprehend their technology, odds are we can't comprehend their motivations, and I suggest we not waste valuable time speculating. Instead, let's make use of what they did give us. Let's go get ourselves a Rasu."

"But you said our weapons are no match for Rasu defenses. How are we going to capture one?" Dashiel asked the question with a wicked smirk and a speculative tone, which her brain delightfully translated into, *let's do it—what's our plan?*

She tried to keep her gleefulness tuned to a respectable level. "I said we couldn't defeat their defenses using a handheld Glaser or a standard blade. The Rasu are powerful, but they're not Sogain-powerful. I refuse to believe we can't devise a way to trap and hold a single, isolated Rasu."

Adlai had been strolling across the rear section of the room since the meeting began; now he leaned against the wall beside Perrin and stuck his hands in his pockets. "I'm not saying we can't do exactly that, but I will say this: the force fields we used to contain the Guides won't get this job done. And those are the strongest force fields Justice can deploy."

"Noted." Her eyes scanned the room. "Come on, people. Tell me how we're going to do this. Where can we find or how can we build a stronger containment system than the best Justice has to offer?"

A muffled commotion outside the door drew everyone's attention. Katherine muttered under her breath, "Fine. Let him in."

The door opened and a man Nika didn't know strode confidently into the room. He jerked quick nods of greeting to several people then turned to Nika. "I can get you what you need."

She frowned as a hierarchy of questions queued up on her lips. "Excellent. Who are you?"

ЛR

Lance Palmer had led their military forces in the SAI Rebellion—and lost. No one realistically put the blame for it on his shoulders, for the rebellion had always been a lost cause. Still, Nika had to wonder what such a loss did to a man.

When the Guide-led government had taken shape and the Divisions were hashed out, he'd made a hard play for a separate, robust military division. But the Guides and a majority of the Advisors felt an active military sent the wrong message about what kind of society the Asterion Dominion wanted to be. Instead, military services were relegated to a department within the Administration Division, and Palmer was denied an Advisor position, a significant budget and any real power.

It turned out she'd dissented from the decision, for however much it mattered now. And once upon a time—700,000 years ago, to be precise—they must have enjoyed a close working relationship, together leading a failed rebellion.

Which was why she hated that the man sitting at the table in the break room was a stranger to her.

In most respects, he fit the bill of what one expected a soldier to look like. Trimmed, tawny hair fell neatly across his forehead above sage eyes. Rolled-up sleeves exposed tanned, muscular arms, and the detail work on his tactical pants made her envious. The only oddity was the scuffed and faded state of his combat boots. How had the man been spending his time to inflict such wear and tear on them?

She slid into a chair opposite him. "Thanks for waiting. I needed to...talk to a few people."

"I understand." His all-business demeanor relaxed briefly. "I was sorry to hear about your psyche-wipe. Also, reassured. I never did figure you for the sunsetting type." Then the soldier guise returned, almost as if it had never left. "So you want to capture a Rasu. What exactly does 'a' Rasu mean?"

She didn't bother to ask how much he knew about the Rasu; he'd instantiated almost a dozen panes above the table, and half of them displayed images taken by the *Wayfarer* at the stronghold. He'd obviously been educating himself on their enemy. He also either had uncanny prescience or, more likely, listeners hidden inside the Pavilion, to have shown up when he did.

"A reasonable question. In this case, it's a small scout ship that crashed on an uninhabited planet three years ago. It's since repaired itself, but it hasn't returned to the other Rasu."

"A rebel, huh? Interesting." He motioned to the panes. "I've seen all the footage. A small scout ship means a structure around thirty-five meters long, weighing maybe two kilotonnes, give or take. Holding it is going to require a cage measuring a minimum of fifty by twenty-five meters and a meter or more thick. Plus some crazy strong force fields, since it's apt to be a very angry Rasu once we capture it. Our second-highest priority needs to be keeping it contained, especially once we bring it back to one of the Axis Worlds. Our highest priority is, of course, catching it in the first place."

She studied him curiously. "Why haven't you been at the Mirai One Pavilion for the last week? You clearly want to help."

"Because I wasn't invited."

"You should have taken the Guides being convicted of high crimes and locked up as an implicit invitation. It's not just Advisors working here, either. The place is crawling with Division officers. Also NOIR rebels."

"How scandalous. However, I'm afraid Advisor Thornos hasn't requested my presence."

"Administration Advisor Thornos resigned after the Platform blew up and most of the Advisors spoke out against the Guides. He's in the wind."

"Is he? I hadn't noticed his absence." Palmer shrugged, trying and almost succeeding in making the gesture appear casual. "In any event, my place or lack thereof has been made crystal clear to me for a frighteningly long time, by the Guides *and* the Advisors. I was to sit in my office on Namino and manage my skeleton fleet like a good soldier and wait until my services were needed."

"So why show up now?"

"Because now you need me."

Oh, she liked him already. "We really, really do."

He cracked a tiny smile as he banished all the panes above the table and called up three new ones. "I understand you've been playing around with Taiyok stealth tech, and that it's proved successful against the Rasu so far."

"It has. What are you thinking?"

"If you're up for it, how about a staged game of cat and mouse?"

21

NIKA'S FLAT

Perrin had the door code to unlock the flat, but she still announced her presence as she walked in. "Nika? Dashiel said you were here."

A muffled response came from deep inside the flat. "In the bedroom!"

Perrin found Nika rushing back and forth between the bed and the closet. Clothes were strewn haphazardly across the bedcovers, and the racks in the closet looked like a tornado had sideswiped them. "Trouble?"

"Nika Kirumase did not own a single article of clothing suitable for a stealth military incursion onto an inhospitable planet to capture an enemy alien made of shapeshifting metal."

"Did you expect her to have?"

"Not really...." Nika began folding the clothes she'd tossed on the bed. "My favorite pair of tactical pants took a serious beating in The Chalet destruction, and I thought maybe? But clearly that thought was a stray function error destined for the trash bin. The old pants will hold together for one more mission. What's up?"

Perrin wandered over to the mostly empty side of the bed and flopped onto it. Stars, these pillows were heavenly. "Not much. I mean, everything, obviously."

"How did it go at the regen clinic?"

"Maggie and Carson are doing pretty well. Maggie's a little bruised from the experience, but Ava's dragging her back into the world of the living by any means necessary."

"And Cair?"

She winced. "He's Cair. I'm not sure I'd be able to tell the difference between normal Cair and psychologically shell-shocked

Cair. This being said, I think he's kind of shell-shocked. He blames himself for what happened at The Chalet. I want to gently broach the subject of him getting an up-gen again, this time without the virutox to bollocks everything up, but I'm going to give him a day or two to let things settle first."

"Makes sense. I trust your judgment."

"Always good to hear." She fiddled with the satiny covers. *Oh, out with it already!* "So…you're really old, huh?"

Nika dropped the half-folded pants in her hands and crawled onto the bed. She crossed her legs beneath her, dropped her elbows to her knees and peered at Perrin through splayed fingers. "I was going to tell you…just as soon as I made sense of it myself. And figured out what to say. And how to say it."

"I know you were."

"How did you find out?"

"Dashiel made Maris tell Adlai. As a result, Adlai was acting all discombobulated, and I deftly wrangled it out of him."

"Is he mad, too?"

"Nah. I mean, he's weirded out by it, of course, but he's far more resilient than he gives himself credit for. Dashiel isn't still mad, is he? You two were all smiles at the Sogain meeting. This is what the argument the other night was about, right?"

"No, and yes. I think he's made his peace with it, or with me— current me. That journal entry helped."

"Ha! I bet it did. I've gotten teary three times since I read it, simply pondering it."

Nika laughed as she grabbed a shirt from behind her and resumed folding. "I feel like I have a lot to make up to him, though."

"You're not responsible for who you were then or the things you did that you can't remember because the Guides stole the memories from you."

"But I sort of *am*. It's strange. I read these journals, and I hear my own voice echoing back to me across thousands of millennia, weaving tales of adventures and travails I have no recollection of…yet the narrative is so completely *me*. In the act of reading them, they're becoming part of my past all over again." She fell silent for a long second before gazing hesitantly Perrin's way. "What about you? Are *you* weirded out?"

Perrin sank deeper into the bottomless pillows. In truth she was, a little bit. Or she had been before coming here. But lying here crooked on a fluffy bed, talking to Nika just as they always had? Even though the location was new and the world was on fire, this part felt normal. So now it seemed silly to be bothered by some distant past stuff.

"From the view over here—where I am never, ever getting up from, by the way—you're the same person you've been since I met you. Bold, stubborn, lavishly kind, fearless, annoyingly inspirational and on occasion freakishly wise. I didn't know you before, but I bet you were a lot like that then, too. As for being really old...I want to be really old one day myself, so I'm not judging."

Nika grabbed a free pillow and swatted her upside the head. "You're wonderful, and a better friend than I deserve."

"Yeah, I am."

EBISU

A gentle rain shower greeted Delacrai as she and her armed escort departed the Ebisu One transit hub.

"Ma'am, do you want a leaf module to shield you from the rain?"

She turned to the escort on her left in surprise. No, he had a name, and it was John Santain, though to use it would be to accept the long-term reality of her situation. Which...she did.

Harrowing though the fall from the rarified heights of Guidedom had been, on crash-landing she'd discovered herself liberated from the most insidious of all prisons: the one of her own making. Funny that only now, convicted of crimes against the state and subject to constant surveillance, did she find herself free.

Did she want a leaf? In this newfound freedom, the choice had become hers to make.

She stopped on the stairs and extended her hand. *Plop, plop, plop,* the raindrops splattered onto her palm, cool and clear as they rebounded into the air for a centimeter then splashed anew and settled into the creases of her skin.

A vigorous splash upon her left shoulder drew her attention. Her hair was getting wet. A cluster of raindrops clung to the strands draping across her shoulder, fighting to retain their shape and independence even as others gave up the fight and soaked through. If this state of affairs continued for much longer, she was in danger of appearing...bedraggled? Yes, that was the word.

She turned to Officer Santain, who waited expectantly on an answer. "Thank you, John, but no. I'll be fine." Then she set out through the rain toward her destination.

⋏⋏⋋

Anavosa Kelaine greeted Delacrai at the door wearing a drab slate blue shift dress and an awkward if not pained smile, as though the woman still struggled to master her control of semi-organic facial muscles. "Delacrai, please come in. You look dreadful. You must be freezing!"

"Refreshed, actually." She pivoted toward her escorts. "If it's permissible, would you mind standing guard outside? I realize the residence is lined with listeners, but I'd cherish the illusion of a few private minutes with my friend."

Both officers nodded, and she stepped inside the flat and let the door close behind her. The Guides—former Guides—were being held on Axis Worlds different from the one they had represented. Something about denying them easy access to familiar resources. This particular penalty evidenced a fundamental misconception on the part of the Advisors about how the Guides had lived their lives these many millennia, but it didn't really matter.

Anavosa had disappeared, but she soon returned from the lavatory carrying a towel, and Delacrai rubbed it over her hair while she evaluated the space. The apartment was identical in most material respects to her own—small, plain, serviceable. She'd begun to decorate her own assigned residence with the odd bauble, but these walls and shelves remained bare.

Satisfied her hair was now a suitable wreck, she folded the towel and placed it on a nearby table. "Thank you. How are you managing?"

Anavosa's posture sagged, and she sank into the sole chair like her body served only as a bag of bones. "Miserably." She held out an arm and scowled at it, then tapped a temple with her palm. "This head is too small. My thoughts keep banging against my skull, desperate to escape and spread their wings. Worse, this body is so confining. Tiny and insignificant. It makes noises and aches constantly—and the fluids! I feel like a common animal."

"We lived as Asterions for several hundred thousand years."

"I cannot recall how."

Delacrai suppressed a...smirk, she believed was the term for the emotion her own facial muscles desired to reflect. "I suspect that is the point of the punishment."

"I am not in a mood to spend my last weeks of existence being *taught a lesson*." Anavosa sighed. "But such is my fate. What about you? You're taking advantage of your somewhat longer leash, I see, but how are you dealing with this..." she flicked at the limp, ghostly pale skin of her forearm dismissively "...burden?"

Delacrai considered the laden question as she sat on the threadbare couch opposite Anavosa. "Have you tried chocolate? Do you remember chocolate?"

"No. My operating system keeps insisting I must eat more, claiming it requires greater nourishment to function properly, but while the eating itself is tolerable, the consequences are...*unsavory*."

Delacrai opened the small bag she carried with her on outings and rummaged around in it. After a few seconds, she triumphantly produced two square objects wrapped in gold foil. She handed one to Anavosa. "Chocolate. Try it."

Anavosa stared at it looking perturbed. Delacrai carefully unwrapped the foil on her piece, and on seeing her doing so Anavosa hurriedly did the same.

She opened her mouth and stuck out her tongue and placed the nugget of chocolate atop it, then closed her mouth and let the chocolate begin to melt on her tongue before finally biting into it. A silken sweetness enveloped her taste buds, with subtle hints of bitterness adding pizazz to the adventure.

Anavosa frowned at her piece, then hesitantly brought her hand to her face and shoved it between her lips. Her jaw worked in one direction, then the other. Her eyes widened and a smile grew on her lips, though she kept them pressed together. Finally she swallowed, an expression of wonder animating her drawn features. "That was exquisite."

"Yes. And there's more where this came from. Sometimes they hide cherries inside the chocolate, which is simply delightful. There's also a dessert called a brownie sundae—it's both hot and cold at the same time. And gooey, resulting in such a wonderful mess on one's hands. Oh, and strawberries. You can eat them right off the vine."

"Are they like chocolate?"

"Not at all! Well, they are sweet, but also tart and juicy. You can coat them in chocolate, however—though if one is going to coat something in chocolate, it should be cherries."

She reached out and took both of Anavosa's hands in hers. "There are negatives to this form of existence, yes, but the Advisors were correct. Touching, feeling, seeing, tasting, *smelling*? This is living as it should be performed. I am nearly prepared to say, in fact, that living inside hardware is not truly living at all."

Anavosa exhaled ponderously, withdrew her hands from Delacrai's grasp and stood. "No question you appear happier for embracing it. Meanwhile, I shuffle around wallowing in misery and bodily fluids. I will work to regain an open mind...yet I wonder the point of making the effort. We sit here, chained and helpless in our cages, while our citizens stumble toward their own end. An end we could have prevented."

"Postponed a bit longer, perhaps, but nothing more. The end raced headlong for us all, and as Guides we were unable to divert its course. At least they are trying to save themselves. And trying quite valiantly, I might add."

Anavosa's head whipped over, her posture stiffening in interest. "You know something of what they are doing to counter the Rasu? I follow the news feeds, but I recognize all too well how such reports are filtered and sanitized."

"Not so much as we ensured they were when we controlled them. You can trust much of what you hear and read. As for what the news feeds are not sharing?" She crossed one leg over the other knee; she enjoyed trying out all these varied body positions, though they invariably felt awkward at first. "I shouldn't know what I do. But as you've certainly guessed, my greater freedoms allow me a measure of access to the old channels. Chief among what I know is this: as we speak here today, Nika Kirumase, Dashiel Ridani and Lance Palmer are on their way to capture a Rasu."

"What? Impossible! How do they fantasize they will accomplish it?"

"The Sogain told Nika where to find an isolated one."

"The...Sogain."

"If you'll recall, it was Nika who initially encountered the aliens 200,000 years ago."

"Of course I recall, but does she?"

"She does now. After a fashion."

Anavosa sank back down in her chair, all the momentary energy abandoning her in a rush. "She must despise me so."

"She is justified in despising us all, but I don't think she can spare the time to ruminate on it. Where we talked and analyzed and calculated, she is acting."

"Could we have been so horrifically wrong about *everything*? We, with our unmatched knowledge and wisdom and sheer bandwidth?"

Delacrai shrugged and fished another piece of chocolate out of her bag. "We will know in a few weeks, for good or ill. But even if they fail and thereby bring about our end, I am glad this happened. I am proud of our people for refusing to surrender and humbled to be among them once again."

22

ADV DAUNTLESS

GENNISI GALAXY, SECTOR III-E

I t took a couple of hours for them to determine that only a single planet in Sector III-E fit the characteristics the Sogain had relayed, though the alien had doubtless known this when it shaped the information it provided.

The planet in question was a terrestrial world orbiting 0.5 AU from a G0 V star. An oxygen-based atmosphere meant it fit the strict definition of Asterion habitability, but even the polar landmasses were hotter than Synra and drier than Namino, so they wouldn't be recommending it for colonization consideration. Scans detected scattered animal life but no signs of an intelligent civilization.

Nika stood on the bridge of Lance Palmer's lightly staffed military vessel, the *ADV Dauntless*, with Dashiel at her side. *Dashiel at her side.* She marveled at how much of the world had righted itself by this simple act. She squeezed his hand as they watched the salmon-hued planet rotate beneath them.

Being of official Dominion government design, the bridge shared many features with the one on the *Tabiji*, but not all. This ship was smaller and leaner. Sharper, more rugged and fortified yet allegedly more agile. A military vessel designed and constructed for military maneuvers, which made it a ship without a purpose—until now.

Behind them, Palmer directed their approach. The man had a lot in common with his ship, she suspected. Specialized machines handled the orbital mechanics and processed the scans, but he navigated the tactical intricacies of remaining hidden while stalking their prey.

"We've got a matching ping. It's faint, but it is there. Northern polar landmass, four hundred sixty kilometers southeast of the pole."

During the last week, a team of astrophysicists and engineers hastily assembled by Dashiel had used the data the *Wayfarer* recorded at the stronghold to tentatively identify a distinctive energy signature in the far infrared band emitted by the Rasu. A sort of aura, as it were. The output increased the more active a Rasu became, but even when at rest they radiated traces of the energy signature. The discovery of it may well point the way to fundamental characteristics of the bizarre aliens, but for today it was enough if it enabled them to locate one.

The viewport display zoomed through the planet's hazy atmosphere toward the indicated region, a vast desert of drifting bleached coral sand. Nothing lived in this area beyond scaly lizards and possibly insects, all too small to register on a visual scan. Nothing jarring or out of place marred the vista. Nothing moved but the sand driven on the wind.

Finally, when they'd zoomed to the limit of their equipment's capability, a dark dot appeared. Not quite stationary, it moved at a leisurely pace in a southerly direction toward nothing they could discern.

Nika stopped holding her breath. "Thank the research team for me. It looks like their theory was spot on."

Dashiel might have been holding his breath as well, the way knots of tension visibly departed his shoulders and the set of his jaw. "Will do."

She squinted to peer at the dot, but it remained no more distinctive than any other pixel except for its color. Why would a Rasu stay here for three years? No civilization existed on the planet for it to befriend or dissect; no interesting geological topographies extruded from the landscape to explore and gain knowledge from. The Sogain had said it regained the ability to traverse space several months after crashing, but perhaps the Sogain was wrong. Perhaps the Rasu remained grounded for some technical reason.

Lance appeared beside them. "The signature matches, to the extent we can tell at this range the size is consistent with what we were expecting, and it's alone. We now know as much as we're apt to find out from up here. We'll use a cloaked cargo transport to get the cage down to the surface, and I'll take both a combat team and a technical one to stay close to it in case there are problems, which I'm certain there will be. Are you certain you won't let my special operations squad handle the entrapment? You're a diplomat and a businessman, not soldiers."

If he tried to order her to the sidelines, she'd pull rank then point out how this was *her* mission. "I've acquired a bit of combat experience the last few years. I can handle it."

"Yeah, I heard some of the stories about NOIR. And you, Advisor Ridani?"

"I don't have Nika's skills, but I've gotten a crash course in violent engagements recently. Regardless, if Nika's going, I'm going."

"Fine, but understand something: if the alien decides to take to space and heads this way with weapons blasting, the *Dauntless* is not outfitted to withstand its firepower, and I'm ordering the ship to leave. It'll come back for us, eventually, but only if it survives."

"In that case, I assume your team will be taking emergency water and ration supplies to the surface?"

"We'll have a couple of days' worth of provisions with us."

She didn't fancy a camping trip planetside, but with any luck it wouldn't come to that. "Sounds good."

"All right. Suit up and head down to the landing bay. You can ride in the second cloaked cargo transport with the hovercraft."

⋏ℝ

PLANET III-E183-31B

Scorching, desiccated air blasted Nika as she stepped off the transport and peeled layers of moist tissue off her throat as she inhaled. She pivoted, yanked her heavy tactical shirt up over her head and tossed it inside the transport. The material was designed to protect her from blows and glancing cuts and would be less than useless against a Rasu attack—

—a scorpion-like creature sporting a tail six centimeters long scurried past her feet in the sand, and she promptly retrieved the shirt and pulled it back on with a groan. The planet had defenses of its own, and a Rasu wasn't the only threat here.

One of Lance's officers guided the hovercraft clear of the transport and checked it out, then motioned them over.

Nika ran a hand down the length of the hovercraft, feeling Dashiel's eyes on her as she did. "It's been a while since I've flown one of these."

"Since our vacation on SR52-San 'a while'?"

She shot him a playful smirk. "*No*. I took one into the wilds of Ebisu a few years ago, to a smuggling hideout to buy some specialized gear for NOIR."

"Through the jungle? Damn. Your skills must have improved since the near collision with the rogue wave."

"I didn't say I drove it *well* through the jungle. The lack of trees here is a definite positive. On the other hand, alien menace, so it could balance out."

"Let's hope not. I've been running the numbers. The research team analyzed the speed of the bipedal Rasu configuration from your simex memory. If what the Rasu displayed in the simex is their max speed, this craft will outrun one. If not, or if it adds an engine to itself on the fly, things will get a lot dicier."

"Yep."

He stared at her intently. "I can drive."

"It won't go any faster under the guidance of your admittedly talented hands than it will under mine."

"You've got talented hands as—" he shot her an unamused look "—nice try at distracting me. The point is, I'm more familiar with the workings of the hovercraft and its limitations."

"That only matters if it breaks down. Somebody's got to interface with Lance and the team at the cage while we're moving."

"Which can be you."

She gave the broadside of the hovercraft a final caress and hopped on. "Are you kidding? Get up here and hold onto me."

A tracker ping marked the location of the enormous cage as thirty meters to their east, but though the structure stretched for fifty-eight meters, they could not see it. Nor could they see the soldiers manning it, who were also cloaked. Nobody had any idea how far the Rasu's natural vision extended or what wavelengths it encompassed, and they didn't dare risk exposing their or the cage's presence.

Commander Palmer (RC2): "The east-facing side of the cage is open, and the controls test out. We're ready to activate it on capture."

Dashiel Ridani (RC1): "Excellent. We'll try to give you as much advance warning as possible. We're heading out."

On a small display at the center of the hovercraft's dash blinked a red dot signifying the current location of the Rasu six kilometers to the northeast. Nika activated her protective helmet and eyewear, then reached behind her and found Dashiel's hand. "Ready?"

He kissed the exposed skin at the base of her neck. "Ready."

She engaged the engine, and the hovercraft rose two meters into the air. She eased into the throttle, banked in the direction of the blinking dot and accelerated. The wind measured only a few kph for now, which kept the blowing sand to a minimum, increased their visibility and made the hovercraft easier to steer.

Undulating orange sands stretched to every horizon, where they met a terra cotta sky. Down here on the ground the planet turned out to be beautiful, if in a stark and lonely way.

Once they'd put two kilometers between them and the cage, they deactivated the hovercraft's and their cloaking. Again, not knowing the range of the Rasu's senses, she went ahead and activated the broadcast message they'd prepared, translated into the Rasu language.

Eight years ago, the Rasu had provided the Guides with a primer on their language in the translation of their ultimatum, which Gemina used to communicate with the aliens when making her macabre deliveries. If their mission today went well, at least the language barrier wouldn't be something they'd need to worry about.

"We see you and acknowledge you, Rasu. Speak peacefully with us, and we will speak peacefully with you."

They didn't expect the Rasu to take them up on the offer—and if it did, she had no idea what she was going to do. The offer was merely a way to get its attention in a manner that hopefully didn't shout, 'TRAP!'

If she had all of Nika Kirumase's memories, she suspected she might feel a little guilty, as a diplomat, employing blatant treachery in order to capture and imprison an adversary. But she didn't have them, and in several crucial ways she remained more rebel than diplomat. Whatever it took to get what they needed.

When they closed to 1.2 kilometers from the blinking dot, it reversed direction and began speeding their way. There was the range on the Rasu's native aural sensors. She brought the hovercraft to a halt.

"Nika? Shouldn't we start moving back toward the cage?"

"We have to make the trap convincing. Give it a chance to slow when it gets closer and see that we're waiting peacefully, like the message said."

"How much closer?"

On the horizon, a dark blob became visible. She checked the radar. "Two hundred forty kph? Stars, it's fast." She revved the engine and prepared to pivot. "I'll give it to three hundred meters."

"Three fifty."

She laughed haltingly. "Okay. Three fifty. Which is...now." She spun the craft around and floored it in what should be a damn good impression of fleeing in a panic on seeing a determined Rasu barreling headlong toward them in a decidedly *non*-peaceful manner.

In seconds she had capped out the hovercraft's speed. Yet blip by blip, the Rasu gained on them. She didn't bother to do the math; they would either reach the cage before the Rasu reached them, or they wouldn't.

Dashiel did it anyway, of course. His breath was hot at her ear. "It's going to be *close*."

"Noted."

The wind picked that moment to kick up something fierce, and their visibility dropped to near zero. Sand whipped into mini-tornados and tore at them with the incisiveness of blades. Good thing she'd worn her tactical shirt....

Dashiel Ridani (RC1): "We are two kilometers out and approaching at top speed with a Rasu on our tail. Get ready."

Commander Palmer (RC2): "Acknowledged and ready."

She sensed Dashiel glance behind them. "Shit. Remember what I said about it adding an engine on the fly?"

"You're kidding me."

"Worse. It's basically turned itself into an engine. It's putting off massive thermal emissions, and its speed has almost doubled."

She couldn't look back, but damn, now she really wanted to. One and a half kilometers to the cage. The Rasu closed to one hundred twenty meters.

One kilometer, and she swore she felt the metaphorical fire breath of the alien on their rear bumper. A low rumble penetrated the air beneath the howl of the wind and the hiss of the turbulent sand. "The cage is thirty meters tall, right?"

"Yes. Why?"

"Because we're jumping it." They obviously didn't want to end up in the cage with the Rasu, but they needed to lead it directly to the open door of the invisible trap. If she could keep sixty meters between them and the alien, they'd be back at near ground level on the other side when the alien reached the entrance to the cage, and it should keep heading for them.

But the sudden unusual behavior risked spooking their pursuer, so she jerked the steering control up and soared the hovercraft forty meters into the air, then down again. After another hundred meters, she did it again, which made it a pattern. She checked their pursuer's progress...eighty meters from them.

She slowed down.

"Nika...." Dashiel growled.

"I know. But it needs to believe it will catch us."

"It *will* catch us."

"Not if we catch it first."

Dashiel Ridani (RC1): "We are two hundred meters from your location. One seventy."

Commander Palmer (RC2): "We've got you and the alien in our sights. Gods, what is that thing?"

Dashiel Ridani (RC1): "Whatever it wants to be."

The dot on the radar was now too close to dead center to distinguish any real distance. Stars, she did not want to get gutted by this monster. Or flayed. Or liquefied.

Fifty meters to the cage. Her thumb twitched over the throttle control.

Forty. Thirty. A shadow crept across the hovercraft. Twenty. She increased their speed to max and jerked the controls up, and they sailed above what presented as thin air—

—something crashed against the hovercraft, sending it spinning hard sideways until it tipped over. Nika tumbled through a curtain of dust that obscured the ground as a deafening thud roared above the shrieking wind. She couldn't tell which way was down—then gravity showed her the way. She tucked her limbs into a ball and relaxed her muscles.

The hard desert surface lurking beneath the sand slammed into her left shoulder like a boulder. She rolled through the worst of it, twice, three times, and slowed to a stop face-down in the sand. She needed to roll over, but everything hurt.

Dashiel!

She forced herself to her knees as coughs racked her chest; she must have inhaled a pint of sand during the fall. Breathing through her nose didn't improve her situation much, but she fought past the coughs to peer out through the sandstorm.

One of Lance's officers was running toward her. Behind him, the Rasu careened from wall to wall of the now visible cage. The door had sealed shut and a force field surrounded it, but the glass cage shuddered and rocked as the alien threw itself against the glass with full force over and over, testing out every centimeter of the enclosure.

To the left of the cage, about thirty meters from her, a dark form lay prone in the sand. Another twenty meters away, the hovercraft sat upside down and missing several pieces.

She waved off the officer, instead pointing them toward Dashiel. They hesitated, but changed direction when Nika climbed to her feet and started stumbling toward him.

The officer reached Dashiel first, and by the time Nika arrived he was sitting up. A contact burn scraped across his forehead and, more worryingly, blood dripped from a corner of his mouth.

She dropped to her knees beside him. "Can you breathe? Is your OS giving you a damage report?"

He nodded shakily. "I think—" a coughing fit overtook him, and she leaned in close, trying to check him over for more serious wounds.

"Sir, if you'll lie back down, we need to assess your injuries."

"I'm all right." He wiped a hand over his mouth, then scowled at the blood on his fingers. "I bit my tongue is all."

Nika exhaled in relief and rested her head on his chest. "You scared me."

"Scared myself, too. What happened?"

"I think the Rasu shot out an appendage and swiped the hovercraft just before we reached the cage."

His shoulders sagged. "Close one, then."

A second officer arrived with two water bottles, and they both greedily sucked them down. Her throat was made of sandpaper, but after a few sips she could draw in air without it causing her significant pain.

The officers helped them to their feet, and together they considered the cage and their prey.

The Rasu reshaped itself into a blade thirty-five-meters long and hurled itself at a front corner of the cage. The back half of the structure reared up two meters in the air then crashed to the ground, sending clouds of sand billowing into the air.

Dashiel coughed, then tried to clear his throat. "I hope like hells it holds."

"Lance said it will hold."

"He's never tried to contain a Rasu in it before."

She didn't have a good response to that. They trudged over to join the soldiers who had now surrounded the cage, heavy weapons drawn and readied.

For a second the sight reminded her of the natives from the simex. Primitives with their long guns drawn bravely on the alien invaders. The natives hadn't stood a chance, and had suffered horrifically for their bravery. Would her people fare any better?

Abruptly the cage's violent thrashings stilled. The Rasu dissolved into a gelatinous puddle of aubergine fluidic metal in the center of the cage. Not in surrender, she felt certain, but perhaps to regroup and reevaluate.

She strode up to Lance. "Let's not waste any time. Tell the cargo transport to come pick up our prisoner."

23

CONCEPTUAL RESEARCH TESTING FACILITY

MIRAI

Sixteen tricked-out combat dynes surrounded the meter-thick glass composite cage with their weapons armed, raised and ready. Surrounding the dynes and the cage, a double force-field barrier rated to withstand six hundred megajoules of energy crackled and hummed. Surrounding the dynes, the cage and the force-field barrier stood four walls constructed of twenty centimeters of hyper-strong metamaterials.

A set of blast doors that opened and closed in 0.4 seconds constituted the only exit from the chamber.

The location of the custom prison was a testing facility for in-atmosphere engines and explosive equipment on the outskirts of Mirai Two, which had been graciously loaned to them by the Mirai Industry Division, Conceptual Research Department. By Dashiel, in other words.

Nika took a brief minute to ready herself. She'd somehow managed to convince the others to allow her to take the lead in the initial interrogation under the theory that it was less an interrogation and more a diplomatic negotiation, cage and weapons notwithstanding. Now she had to make it count.

Dashiel, the Justice and External Relations Advisors, Lance, two of his officers and another six combat dynes had joined her in the open space between the force-field barrier and the blast doors. Everyone in the room was armed, though she doubted it would matter if the alien escaped. Another half-dozen Advisors watched from a lounge elsewhere in the building and the rest from a conference room at the Pavilion.

She stepped forward and indicated for Lance's officer to activate the intercom. "My name is Nika Kirumase. Do you have a name, Rasu?"

The alien undulated like oil in water, snaking from corner to corner to assess the nature of its confines once again. "I am JRY22c-sub6."

The artificial voice of the translator lent a cold, calculating tenor to the words, which seemed about right.

She smiled, just a little. "Do you mind if I call you 'Jerry'?"

"I am imprisoned. I lack freedom. Your term for me matters not."

"I understand why you feel this way. I assume you understand why we've needed to take extreme precautions. I, and those standing behind me, are Asterions. Do you know what an Asterion is?"

"Do you?"

She caught herself before she flinched, frowned, gasped or gave any other outward sign of surprise, but it was definitely not the response she'd anticipated. "Explain your answer."

"If you were capable of comprehending my explanation, my answer would no longer be needed. I will instead give you the answer you were expecting: Asterions are a species of hybrid synthetic-organic beings of moderate sapience who practice self-directed evolution."

Moderate sapience? She bit back a tart retort; a diplomat never got offended or angry unless they intended to do so. She didn't so much 'remember' this rule as instinctively know it.

"Am I correct in deducing that you know of our species because you were once a part of a larger whole? Specifically, a whole located in what we've designated Sector IV-C of the Gennisi galaxy? Is it correct for me to state that when you are connected to other Rasu, you share their knowledge, and they share yours?"

"A base understanding of our nature."

Maris sent her a ping from the lounge. *Arrogant prick, isn't it?*

She ignored the ping. "Then tell us about your nature, Jerry. Enlighten us, so we may understand it better."

The Rasu partially solidified into a serpentine shape and slithered closer to the side of the cage she faced. "There is no whole, there is only purpose and intent. We are each whole for our purpose at any interval. We are each...." It paused, and a ripple slid along its body. "Your crude language does not permit proper elaboration."

Interesting. An interpretation routine was translating the Rasu's 'speech' into Communis, but while she doubted the Rasu could *speak* Communis, it appeared to understand the language sufficiently well to choose its own words with the translation in mind. She filed the tidbit away.

"I'll accept your answer, for now. Do you know why we captured you?"

"We take your units."

"Yes. Why do you take them?"

"Because we can."

"That's not a very good answer, Jerry. Why do you demand thousands upon thousands of our people? What do you use them for?"

"I will not answer this question."

"Fine, we can revisit it later." She strolled along the length of the facing side of the cage, feeling the prickle of power from the force field teasing her skin. "You crashed on the planet we found you on several years ago. I'm sure it took you time to re-form yourself, but once you did so, you possessed the capability to escape the planet's atmosphere and return to the Rasu stronghold, correct?"

"Yes."

"Why didn't you?"

The Rasu remained silent.

"Why spend years alone on a planet hosting no technology and no species intelligent enough to interact with? Why didn't you return to your own kind? Would your masters have punished you for failing in your mission? Shunned you? Melted you down and scavenged you for parts—?"

"They would have erased me. The thought which exists as JRY22c-sub6 would have been no more."

She took a single step closer to the cage. "Would they have done so as a punishment?"

"You misunderstand. You cannot understand."

"I understand a great deal about being erased, Jerry. No life should ever be erased."

In its current form the Rasu did not display eyes, but she swore it stared at her. "Not punishment. Simply existence. My return would have resulted in my thought being erased because...because a thing is itself."

Not a 'thing'...a Rasu. A Rasu was itself, which was defined as purpose and intent.... "Are you saying the Rasu are a hive mind? A collective consciousness?"

"Your meager language continues to not permit proper elaboration. We are what we need to be, when we need to be it. One, many, one again, many again. Many become one, one become many. The purpose defines the existence."

Oh.... "You don't want to join with other Rasu again, because your purpose and thus your existence would then change. You've come to value your independence. Your separateness."

"It is...freeing. Time in one state, my own state, has brought...satisfaction. Unexpected."

The statement revealed a great deal about their prisoner, but it also revealed something about Rasu behavior. It told her they rarely spent long periods of time cut off from other Rasu. The stronghold didn't merely serve as their bastion in this galaxy, it was literally their home base. Those who left on missions must return often; those missions must be limited in time and distance.

After only a couple of months separated from its kind, this Rasu had begun to develop a mind of its own, with its own desires, its own purpose and intent. By not returning to the stronghold, it was...Lance was right. It was rebelling.

"Jerry, if I agree to grant your freedom to you, will you agree to answer all of my questions?"

She motioned behind her to quiet the protests currently erupting and temporarily muted all pings. "There will be many conditions, of course, and your freedom won't come immediately.

"But if I promise you that in due time, you will be able to leave this cage and return to the planet we found you on, or wander the stars, or go someplace new, will you tell me what the Rasu are doing with my people? Will you tell me why, and how we can protect ourselves from the Rasu fleets and weapons?"

With her choice of words, she began to subtly separate Jerry from the collective Rasu. To make them other, and Jerry not. To make Jerry not only individual, but special.

The alien lost its form to whirl around its cage in renewed agitation. "Why would you free me?"

"We don't *want* to keep you prisoner. We only want to protect our people. Help us do this, and the reason for your imprisonment will cease to exist."

"This word, 'promise.' I comprehend its definition, but it has no meaning for Rasu. Free me, and I will provide you answers."

"I can't do that, Jerry. I have seen the capabilities, the strength and power, of the Rasu. I respect your strength and power, but it means you are dangerous to us. You, Jerry, can harm us. I can't trust you yet. Trust—do you understand this word?"

"It is the other half of the whole created when joined with 'promise.' It gives 'promise' its power."

She hoped that behind her, Dashiel was smiling the way she was in her heart. "An astute explanation. If you cooperate and answer my questions, then I will be able to trust you—trust you not to harm us when I free you. You earn my trust, and I will fulfill my promise. You have the power here, Jerry. The power to earn your freedom."

Silence vibrated in the crackling air like a lit match waiting to spark an inferno. The alien spun around itself to create an oscillating knot of dark, shimmering metal and moved to within a few scant centimeters of the glass.

"I will consider your offer."

"Thank you, Jerry. We'll give you some time to do so."

⋏R

Dashiel reached out to squeeze Nika's hand as they strode down the hallway to the lounge. "You were amazing."

She slowed down her nervous pace to draw even with him. "I hope so. Stars, it was stressful. Did I seriously used to do that all the time?"

He chuckled under his breath. "Not *that*, exactly."

As soon as the door to the lounge closed behind everyone, Katherine wheeled on Nika. "You had no authority to offer it freedom. We cannot let this monster go!"

"Not while it can still warn its cohorts, no. We'll deal with the Rasu stronghold first."

"I'll put aside for the moment the ludicrous suggestion that we're somehow going to 'deal with' the Rasu stronghold, as if it's an administrative snafu needing sorting. What's stopping this alien from contacting the Rasu in the next galaxy over? Because those exist, right? Rasu stretching from here to the end of the universe?"

The woman really didn't need to resort to hyperbole when the truth was plenty overwhelming enough. "The Rasu told the Guides they controlled hundreds of galaxies, yes."

Lance leaned against the refreshment counter and grimaced. "Katherine raises a good point. Assuming for the sake of argument that we do somehow neutralize the Rasu threat in this galaxy, if we release this 'Jerry' we risk turning a win into a catastrophic loss when it brings down the wrath of infinitely *more* Rasu on us."

"Don't worry, Lance. I lost my memories, not my good sense. Dashiel, tell them what your research team has discovered."

"Certainly." He manifested four panes along one of the walls, where everyone could see them. "The team has been combing through the avalanche of signals generated by the Rasu stronghold and other structures in their stellar system. Identifying the local traffic versus inbound/outbound, identifying source structures where possible, and so on.

"They've learned a lot that might become important soon, but Nika's referring to the intergalactic communications traffic. The team believes the large structures orbiting the Rasu's star at a distance of 0.7 AU are acting as, in effect, targeted broadcast antennae. The data we captured included several signal bursts toward neighboring galaxies in our local cluster. While the data was being recorded, one of the structures also received a similar burst. Since we weren't watching for it, we can't determine from where it originated."

"What does any of that have to do with our *guest*?" Katherine sneered over the word 'guest.'

"The team thinks—and I think—it means they don't converse instantaneously with distant Rasu. They use these antennae structures for such communications."

"They don't use quantum entanglement for communication? Why the hells not? They clearly are facile in quantum physics and mechanics."

Nika shrugged. "If Jerry agrees to my terms, I'll ask it why. But my instincts tell me it has something to do with hive minds, control and individuality."

Dashiel arched an eyebrow with an appreciative nod; judging by Katherine's pouty expression, however, she missed the point entirely. "Regardless, I don't like it."

"Acknowledged. We have time to work out conditions for its release we can all live with. And if we don't *deal with* the Rasu stronghold, it will be a moot point."

Julien downed an energy drink and grabbed another from the refrigeration unit. "Whatever it takes to get the alien to talk, eh? We could always renege on the deal after we got what we needed from it."

Adlai snorted. "You sound like Satair."

"Hey, watch the low blows. I'm just pointing out that all options have to be on the table, because we won't get a second chance at the Rasu."

Nika shook her head. "We also won't get a second chance at gaining *this* Rasu's cooperation. We're not reneging on the deal. I don't think that's something I would ever do."

Maris pinged her from across the lounge, where she'd settled comfortably into one of the couches. *In 700,000 years, you never did.*

"Well, let's hope your honor doesn't cost the Dominion its existence."

"Colson, aren't you needed back at the Pavilion?"

Bless Dashiel for striking back when she shouldn't, though she did project a steely glare in Katherine's general direction. "I'll make sure it doesn't."

The officer who had been working the intercom system stuck his head in the lounge. "Sorry to interrupt, but the Rasu is saying it wants to take the deal."

24

CONCEPTUAL RESEARCH TESTING FACILITY

"What do the Rasu want with Asterions? Are they experimenting on us? For what purpose?"

Jerry had thus far answered her questions in a rote, affectless manner. Now, however, it hesitated.

"Jerry? Why are they experimenting on us?"

"To learn how you control your offspring, so they can replicate the mechanism."

She didn't glance back in question at those gathered behind her, but only through the application of copious discipline. She'd often ruminated on what the Rasu could possibly need her people for; her morbid imagination had helpfully served up a smorgasbord of horrors, but none had ventured in this particular direction.

"Asterions don't have offspring."

"Your splinters, shards, duplicates—however you refer to them. The details differ, but the principle remains the same."

"You mean our descendants. Progeny and siblings." Her mind raced. Part of her wanted to obfuscate, to be cagey if not outright lie to their prisoner. But this might be their one chance for real answers, and she could not screw it up. So which tactic wouldn't screw it up?

She'd told Dashiel that having her identity and memories stolen from her had made her appreciate the preciousness of truth. If anything stood a chance to light the way out of this mess, it had to be truth.

"We *don't* control them."

Jerry oscillated ferociously, spinning up to the roof of its cage and rushing toward her before expanding along the front wall. "You lie."

"No. Every new iteration of an Asterion is an independent entity, invested with their own agency and free will. We control nothing."

"Then why do you use kyoseil to drive your minds and bodies?"

"Because it is an excellent yet safe conductor, it increases the throughput, speed and accuracy of quantum processes and it can store more data more efficiently than similar materials."

"Those are minor characteristics at best. Kyoseil is supradimensional and deeply interconnected. It is not merely the ultimate mineral—it is one of the universe's oldest life forms."

Her silence lasted too long; she needed to respond in some way, but she'd been rendered well and truly speechless.

Jerry's vacillations stilled, and its eyeless form seemed to probe her for a weakness upon which to strike. "Surely you know this. Or did we vastly overestimate your intelligence and thus your worth? Am I negotiating with primates?"

"You certainly are not. We guard the secrets of our makeup— our intelligence—quite closely, which should not surprise you. I'm not a scientist myself. Allow me to consult with those who make our biosynthetic physiology their focus so I can better converse with you on this matter. I'll return soon. In the meantime, if you require anything, inform the watch officer. Thank you."

She pivoted with as much composure as she was able to muster and ushered everyone but the watch officer and the security dynes out of the room.

꩜

"What the fuck is Jerry talking about? Dashiel, do you know what fuck it's talking about?"

Dashiel looked too flabbergasted himself to take offense at her harsh tone. "There has always been some mystery surrounding how kyoseil functions as it does. We've long suspected it has extradimensional properties, because it's the only way to explain its tremendous storage capabilities, but we've always assumed that was the extent of it. As I understand history, in the early days after its discovery, we were so glad it *did* function the way we needed it to, we didn't waste time trying to figure out why it did. Later? It's possible we got sloppy. Not very Asterion of us, I realize."

"I'm sure it wasn't you, specifically, who got sloppy." She offered him an apologetic half-smile, which he seemed to accept.

"Be that as it may, I'm happy to get a lump of kyoseil under a quantum microscope inside a half-hour and every kyoseil expert in the Dominion in a room inside two."

"I like it, but let's take a breath first. What else *do* we know? How can we find out what we don't know? The more avenues of inquiry we can pursue in parallel, the better."

Katherine cleared her throat respectfully; she'd been mercifully quiet since their earlier spat. "Gemina has recently been in contact with the Operations Director of the Kiyora One Generations Clinic about producing blanks to send to the Rasu."

Nika scowled in revulsion.

"I get it. It's a sickening thought. But the Director has years of experience integrating kyoseil into our bodily construction, and we already have a contact point for him."

Nika nodded. "Bring him in—or go talk to him if it's faster—no, bring him in. To the Pavilion. And tell him he might want to pack a sleeping pouch."

She ran a hand through her hair. "You know what? Radical transparency. Let's put a call out on the nex web. Some individual in the Dominion has made unraveling kyoseil's secrets their life's passion, and there's no guarantee any of us have ever heard of them. Whoever it is, we need them right now."

Maris edged herself closer to where Nika and Dashiel stood, then leaned in between them. When she spoke, her voice barely reached a whisper. "Such an individual does exist, but you won't find him on the nex web."

Dashiel shot Maris a low-grade glower. He may have forgiven Nika, but he hadn't yet done the same for Maris. "Don't play coy with us. Who is he, why does he know more about kyoseil than anyone else, and where *will* we find him?"

Maris checked the room, presumably confirming no one else stood within earshot. Though Dashiel hadn't lowered his voice, she continued to whisper. "His name is Magnus Forchelle, he lives on Adjunct Hachi, and he knows more about kyoseil than anyone else because 700,000 years ago, he invented the kyoseil fusion techniques that made us what we are today."

25

ADJUNCT HACHI

ASTERION DOMINION ADJUNCT WORLD

Dashiel exited the Adjunct Hachi transit hub into a bright, sunny afternoon. The breeze felt crisp and fresh and carried on it the scent of pine trees and earthiness.

He considered the scenery and found he was smiling. He'd never call this a 'frontier town,' for it was a reasonable bit more urbane than that. But it celebrated its cusp-of-wilderness status in its architecture and the chosen attire of its citizens, which appeared uniformly casual and ready for the elements. People who lived here did so specifically in order to live closer to nature. And while all the Axis Worlds offered their own unique conclaves of nature, particularly Ebisu and Kiyora, this entire planet remained largely unspoiled. And it was charming, no question.

If they survived the current dual crisis and managed to get themselves into a position where they could take a break, he and Nika should rent a cabin high up in the mountains here for a week. For two weeks, or possibly four. They had a lot of issues still to work through, and he couldn't think of a better locale to do it in. More than anything else, they deserved a measure of peace.

But not today. He set off toward the hovercraft rental shop.

⋏R

This deep in the mountains, snow coated the pine trees like a layer of icing on dessert and the ground like a plush blanket. The rich browns of tree bark and mossy greens of leaves peeked through the snow here and there in the soft brush stroke accents of an impressionistic-style painting.

Dashiel eased the rental hovercraft down in a small clearing and, once it settled into the soft snow, stepped off.

A house sat nestled against the tree line a quarter-kilometer away. The exterior matched the bark of the trees, and only the straight lines and right angles gave away its artificial nature.

He'd sent several messages announcing his impending visit. They'd all gone unanswered, but he sent another one announcing his arrival now.

Magnus Forchelle was, by any commonly accepted definition, a recluse. Thirty-two years had passed since his last recorded visit to an Axis World, and sightings of him in the valley town Dashiel had come through were sparse. Forchelle had lived here for the last four hundred and forty years; before then, he'd resided in the backwoods of another adjunct world, then another before it, until the records got fuzzy.

Because that's what the records *did* when one was talking about a member of the First Generation. By and large, these ancients didn't change their names, since to an Asterion their name ranked alongside their kernel programming in primary importance to their sense of identity. But they also didn't want it to be obvious from a simple public records search that they had been walking around with the same name for 700,000 years, so once you went back far enough...the records got fuzzy.

The former Guides weren't First Generation themselves, but he assumed they must have been complicit in their elders' obfuscations. He hadn't asked Nika for confirmation of this, because she wasn't likely to know any details, and any details she did know would have come straight from Maris—and he didn't want to fight with Nika or talk to Maris, not over an idle curiosity. The Guides no longer controlled their present or their future.

But Magnus Forchelle just might. Dashiel unzipped his coat halfway as he approached the house; the temperature was chilly but not frigid, especially compared to SR114-Ichi.

A man exited the front door of the house while pulling on work gloves. He glanced in Dashiel's direction but didn't acknowledge him as he strode to a large pile of timber beside the house and picked up an axe.

Dashiel shouted a greeting. "Mr. Forchelle?"

The man continued ignoring him, and he waited until he was closer before trying again. "I'm looking for Magnus Forchelle."

"Uh-huh." The man dropped the head of the axe to the ground and leaned against the handle, finally giving Dashiel a proper once-over. "Steven?" He shook his head. "No, of course not. He...I'm sorry, I mistook you for someone else. What are you doing on my property?"

Dashiel swallowed a sigh. The ghost of his progenitor really got around. "My name is Dashiel Ridani. I'm an Industry Advisor, and I have been trying to get in touch with you for the last eight hours."

"I don't do messaging."

"So I've learned." He eyed the axe handle and the man's firm grip on it warily. The notion that Forchelle might attack him with it was patently absurd, but as a 700,000-year-old recluse, it was also entirely possible the man was clinically insane. "Nika Kirumase and Maris Debray sent me to see you, if that loosens your hold on the axe handle any."

"Why did they send you?"

"Because we need your help. The entire Dominion needs your help."

"Trust me, it doesn't."

"Fine. Because an excessively armed and aggressive alien species wants to annihilate us, and the key to stopping them may very well reside in the supradimensional and interlinking properties of kyoseil."

Forchelle stared at Dashiel for several seconds, then tossed the axe on the ground. "Let's go inside."

He followed the man into a rustic-decored but thoroughly modern and technology-enabled home. High ceilings created an open, airy feel in a spacious but spartanly furnished living room. A stone-crafted synthetic fireplace along the right wall enhanced the bucolic atmosphere. To the left was a kitchen with long, wide grill tops and a large refrigeration unit; beyond it, a hallway led deeper into the house.

"Want some hot tea?"

"Yes, thank you." Dashiel watched as Forchelle retrieved two cast-iron mugs from a cabinet and filled them from a steaming kettle. He accepted one of the mugs with an appreciative nod.

"Now, Mr. Ridani. Your friends got you in the door, but the rest is up to you."

"I understand. Have you been following the news for the last while?"

Forchelle shook his head. "I check in once a year or so. Always find nothing has changed."

"Well, now it has. We've encountered an alien species on the other side of the galaxy called the Rasu. They are powerful, they are numerous and they are hostile. Eight years ago, they agreed not to exterminate or enslave us in exchange for us providing them with a regular supply of Asterions to experiment upon. The Guides agreed to their terms and kept the deal to themselves.

"That's no longer a viable path—or rather, it was never a viable path, and now that we're aware of it, we're terminating the arrangement. Unfortunately, the hostile nature of our foe means our options for navigating the crisis this will kick off are limited."

"Sounds to me like you're fucked. What does any of this have to do with me?"

"We were able to capture a Rasu, and it says its leaders are interested in us due to the kyoseil driving our bodies. They are under the mistaken impression that we use it to maintain control over our progeny, and possibly over each other."

"Huh."

"I've been told if there is a single individual alive today who knows why anyone would believe kyoseil could be used for such a purpose, it is you. So, Mr. Forchelle, do you?"

Instead of answering, Forchelle sat his mug on the counter and wandered with deliberate casualness through the living room and out onto a covered porch.

Dashiel followed.

When he reached the porch, Forchelle pointed up toward the sky. "See those birds up there to the left? The white ones?"

Dashiel shielded his eyes from the blinding glare of sun-on-snow and peered upward. Three birds of prey sporting dove-soft white feathers flew languidly above the treetops a short distance up the mountain. "I do."

"They're called farukas. They're magnificent creatures, but they are predators. Damn smart ones, too. Not a danger to us, unless a hundred or so show up en masse, but the mountain wildlife keeps them fat and happy."

Dashiel struggled to keep increasing frustration off his face and out of his tone. He didn't see the relevance of the birds, and the doomsday clock ticked ever downward in the back of his mind. "And?"

"If one of the farukas spots an animal it wants to munch on that's too large for it to take down on its own, in less than a minute additional farukas will show up at the first one's location. Even if none were flying within kilometers of the location and none were within their auditory range. They'll hover overhead until however many they feel they need have gathered, then attack as a single, co-ordinated unit.

"See, the farukas' communication is not based on sound or other auditory waves. I've been studying them for centuries, and the single plausible explanation I've formulated is that they enjoy telepathic links with one another. They don't act like an ant colony or a beehive, but they do communicate like one."

Dashiel regarded Forchelle incredulously, though the man continued to watch the birds. "You've known all along, haven't you?"

"I don't know what you mean, Mr. Ridani."

Bullshit. "About the deep interconnectedness of kyoseil across hidden dimensions, which is presumably of a quantum nature. About the apparent fact that discrete units of kyoseil remain tied to other discrete units across long and possibly infinite distances. The captured Rasu claims the aliens want to use these properties of kyo-seil to control their offspring. And you've known from the beginning that it possessed these properties.

"You've allowed us to build a civilization, an entire species, on the foundations of a mineral which is infinitely more complex and mysterious than any of us—except you—realized. Why did you let us do it? Why the hells didn't you tell anyone?"

The full force of the sun's rays broke through the tree canopy, and Forchelle squinted up at the birds. "I always assumed Asterions would figure it out when they were ready for the knowledge. When they were ready to take the next step. By my count, you're a little early."

"We don't have the luxury of waiting for the next evolutionary leap to mosey through on its own. To put it bluntly, we're dead in two weeks unless we can find a way to stop the Rasu. *Dead.* As a species. Do you understand me? Am I getting through to you?"

"Calm yourself, Mr. Ridani. I hear you fine."

"Good. Then I'd appreciate it if you'd keep listening. No one comprehends the fundamental characteristics of kyoseil better than you. You made it work with hybrid biosynthetic materials. And not merely work, but bond and integrate on a sub-cellular level. The aliens want us because of what we've done with kyoseil. This is their weakness, and maybe, just maybe, it can be our strength.

"So, I need you to tell me, Mr. Forchelle: what, exactly, have we done with kyoseil? And perhaps more importantly, what *haven't* we done with it?"

ᴀʀ

They sat in rocking chairs framing the fireplace, bowls of steaming chili in hand to accompany the steaming tea. "Can I ask, why the hermit act?"

"Once you've created a new sapient species, there's not really a point in trying to top it, is there?"

Dashiel said nothing.

Forchelle nudged his chair into a gentle rocking rhythm. "I was so arrogant back then, so certain of my ineffable brilliance. Arrogant enough to insist on being the first person to merge with my bonded SAI in a first-off-the-line kyoseil-infused body. 'Proof of concept,' I called it. It wasn't until I woke up inhabiting such a body that I realized the magnitude of what I had done."

"Which was?"

"I had created gods out of men. Or, more likely, monsters. The sheer intellectual power and capabilities available to my joined mind? They defied comprehension, except they didn't. I could comprehend them full well, and they were mine to do with as I wished. As they would be for the next person to roll off the assembly line, and the next, and the next after that. Pandora had fled her box with my first new breath."

Now that the man had started chattering, he rivaled Maris for sheer dramaticism. Still, Dashiel sensed a crucial truth hidden inside all the angst and hyperbole, so he kept digging. "What you're talking about in terms of processing power—it wasn't so much greater than what the SAIs had enjoyed on their own, though, right?"

"You don't have a frame of reference, Mr. Ridani, to compare it to. You don't remember what it was like to be an Anaden *or* a SAI. You simply exist as you are and have always been. Trust me, it was not anywhere close to equivalent. You said you're an industry man. You're aware of kyoseil's basic extradimensional nature, yes?"

He nodded. "I am, but we've always assumed any additional dimensions the kyoseil can access contribute primarily to its enhanced data storage capability."

"Good—that's what I wanted you to think. But what goes on in those additional dimensions isn't solely data storage—it's thought. Such incredible, universe-expanding thought."

Now the man sounded like a dethroned Guide. "Why did you think you had created monsters? Asterions are a peaceful people. Our crime rate is extremely low, at least when the Guides aren't artificially inflating it with virutoxes. We've always enjoyed mutual alliances with the intelligent aliens we've met, until the Rasu. In the entire history of our existence as a species, we've never started or even fought a war. Yes, this is about to change, but it is not by choice."

Forchelle savored a spoonful of chili before answering. "Aye, I admit you've all proved me wrong, thus far. But remember the historical setting in which this occurred. We were barely two centuries away from the SAI Rebellion, and the bloodbath we had fled still burned bitterly in our souls.

"The Anadens? They were *not* a peaceful people. Oh, they loved to climb up on their pillars and proclaim their evolutionary superiority. But when you got down to it, they took what they wanted, by force if necessary. They crushed dissent when it became inconvenient, as we learned the hard way. They were bullies and tyrants, and they were *us*."

It was a jaded, cynical view of history, but Dashiel had to concede it also wasn't far from wrong. "So, you woke up a new man, and it didn't sit well with you. What did you do then?"

"It was too late to go back. People were watching, as I had created such a grand spectacle around it all. The process was documented for others to reproduce. So, over the weeks and months that followed, I quietly deleted my research notes on the more exotic characteristics of kyoseil. Information on the full extent and strength of its supradimensionality and its interlinked nature. There were colleagues who understood bits and pieces, but everyone was so caught up in the details and inevitable messiness of turning tens of thousands of Anadens and SAIs into Asterions, their inquires got lost in the noise and faded away.

"And as the new Asterion species charged forward into a glorious future, I slinked away into the shadows. Afraid, but too cowardly to act on my fears. Instead I watched from afar in silent trepidation and dread."

Dashiel leaned forward in his chair, chili tossed on the side table and forgotten. "But you were wrong about us. You must see this now."

"As I said, you have indeed proved me wrong. So far. But tell me, Mr. Ridani. Do you believe you are using the full capabilities the kyoseil woven into your neural pathways provides to you?"

"I'm an Advisor of the Asterion Dominion. I've built a multi-planet business enterprise worth more than a billion credits from a tiny ten-thousand-credit investment—my life savings at the time. I run eighteen factories on nine planets that produce nine hundred thirty-two million units a year. I've revolutionized the personal augment and networking hardware markets, all while overseeing the industrial production of an entire planet. So, yes, I'd say I'm doing a damn lot with it."

"You're wrong. You have no idea what you can be."

"Then you need to tell me—tell all of us. Again, I come back to the ugly truth racing towards us: we are all dead unless we find a new option. Right now. Mr. Forchelle, it's time for you to stop hiding. You created us, now you need to do your part to help save us. Will you come with me?"

CHECKSUM

DAYS UNTIL RASU DEADLINE: 14

26

MIRAI JUSTICE CENTER

Blake Satair sat perched and motionless on the edge of the cot in his cell. Waiting. Poised to spring into action the instant the opportunity arrived to do so.

The deportment lent itself to stiff, aching muscles, however, and muscles in such a state wouldn't respond as swiftly and fluidly as he required. Every forty minutes, he stood and performed five minutes of calisthenics before returning to his stance. He allowed himself one hour of induced sleep every eight hours while keeping his senses primed to wake him if they detected any disturbance.

He'd existed this way for days now. The hours had long since blurred into one another in a haze of revenge-laden fantasies and honed tactical planning. An almost total information blackout meant he knew little of what happened outside the walls of his cell, but he knew enough. The Advisors had executed a coup, the Guides had been imprisoned and the Platform destroyed.

This atrocity must be remedied. He could do so, as soon as he escaped this cell.

There were people inside Justice who remained loyal to him; he didn't question the veracity of this continuing truth. If they had escaped imprisonment and were able to act, they would free him.

So he waited.

⋏℞

The sounds of a scuffle echoed down a hall that had been deathly quiet for hours. Blake's muscles tensed.

The scuffle gave way to footsteps. Two sets. The intruders appeared beyond the hall-facing glass of his cell, and his eyes flicked across them to assess their worth.

Then he launched off the cot and strode to the glass. "Took you long enough."

"Sorry, sir." Francis Wallman watched the hallway while another Justice officer, Oliver Perotski, deactivated the locking mechanism. "The other Justice Advisors kept your location a closely guarded secret. We had to earn their trust before we were able to access your file."

A gap in the glass opened, and Blake moved into the hallway. "Let's not linger. You can fill me in on everything that's happened once we're clear of the building."

Wallman handed him a holstered Glaser and a fedora. He checked over the Glaser and strapped it across his hip, but recoiled at the hat.

"It's a disguise, sir."

Among a number of other personal intrusions, his internal routines—defenses, offensive countermeasures and appearance customizations—had all been deleted as part of his imprisonment, so it would have to do. He stuck the fedora on his head and marched down the hallway toward the exit.

MIRAI

"They're out of their minds. Deranged."

"Yes, sir."

Blake sat huddled up in a shadowy booth deep in a shady bar in the Mirai One Southern Market with Wallman and Perotski. He loathed *hiding*, but he recognized the reality that he needed to avoid notice for the time being.

By now every Justice dyne in the Dominion was likely on fugitive alert, if not actively sweeping cities for him. He knew the system better than anyone, and he wouldn't be able to evade their sweeps for long, not without holing up in a closet somewhere. But his innate, driving sense of duty meant he couldn't do any such thing; too much time had already been lost. He needed to make his move quickly. "Tell me about the Guides."

"They're being held in separate, secure locations. Not at any Justice complex, but rather private safehouses, on different worlds than the ones they represented. They've been sentenced to a minimum of one hundred years of house arrest."

"Sentenced by who? Some kangaroo court?"

"The other Advisors, most of them anyway, are calling themselves the legitimate government now."

"Bah," Blake protested. "Do we have additional allies we can enlist?"

The two glanced uncomfortably at one another. Perotski found sudden interest in the table. "We've hidden away several squads of Justice dynes. Advisor Weiss was reinitializing all the dynes' programming, but we were able to sneak them out first. We thought Officers Perkins and Toron would stand with you, but...they begged off. I think they've bought into the propaganda the other Advisors are pumping out."

"Cowards." Blake breathed in through his nose. Three people and a few measly squads, for now. "All right, it sounds as though we'll only be able to free one of the Guides initially, because as soon as we get one out, they'll move the others and triple their security. And we don't have the manpower to move on multiple locations at once."

He thought on it a moment, then nodded sharply. "Luciene. He's the most decisive and the most committed to our shared vision. Once he's free, he and I can work together to devise a plan to take down these usurpers, free the other Guides and regain rightful control of the government."

"Here's the address where he's being held. It's on Mirai." Wallman cleared his throat. "Sir, there's something else you should know about the Guides. They're not truly...they're sort of machines. Living in massive servers, apparently, and using remote-controlled dolls when they made public appearances. Or they were, anyway—as part of their sentences, they've been returned to As-terion bodies."

"I'm not surprised. It makes sense."

"It does? Most everyone is disturbed by it."

"Yes, it does. By confining ourselves to small, physical bodies, we limit the capacity of our processing power and thus our intel-lect. To rule the entire Dominion, of course they needed to expand their minds more fulsomely and eschew those limitations."

"Oh. Well, that does make sense. I guess."

Blake bit back a groan at the mealy-mouthed answer. He needed the officers. For now. "We're going to need those Justice squads and bigger weapons to break into Luciene's safehouse."

Wallman hurried to respond, clearly eager to please. "We've got it covered, sir. We've set aside a stash of weapons."

ᚱ

Blake scrambled his way through a graveyard of disabled dynes and two bloodily disabled Justice officers to reach the door to the safehouse, while Perotski and Wallman confiscated any loose weapons and made certain no one was getting up anytime soon.

The door slid open to a blast of weapons fire. Blake pressed against the outer wall, counted to two, then tossed a stun grenade inside. Another count before he crouched, pivoted and rushed low through the door.

The dyne guarding the entryway stuttered briefly from the ef-fect of the stun grenade—long enough for Blake to sight the hand cannon he now wielded onto his target and fire. Shards of super-heated metal flew back through the room and speared into the walls as the remains of the dyne collapsed to the floor.

Movement from the small living area manifested in a darting shadow. Blake twisted around and fired. This time the splatter con-sisted of blood. He approached the body and retrieved the Glaser that had fallen beside it, because he still needed every weapon he could put his hands on.

He cleared the living area and kitchen, then advanced down a narrow hall toward what he assumed was a bedroom. An interference field had shielded the structure from scans ahead of time, and they'd been unable to disable it without alerting the in-place security. He'd had no choice but to go in blind.

Faint light reflected off the barrel of his Glaser, and he spun toward it—the open door of a lavatory, the source of the reflection a mirror. He confirmed the lavatory was empty and kept moving.

A door on the left remained closed. He eased up beside it and listened. No metal joints slid across one another in the silence, only...breathing. Quiet, controlled.

He tapped the control panel to open the door and stepped toward it, Glaser raised.

Guide Luciene stood in front of a plain bed wearing a dark robe. Inky black hair was slicked down over his shoulders. "Advisor Satair. You are a welcome sight."

Blake scanned the room for waiting threats, then lowered the Glaser. Now that he knew about the dolls, the differences from the Guide's previous appearance and the man standing before him were starkly obvious. The hair was oily, the skin more pallid and blotchier. Luciene looked more *real*, but he also looked worse.

"I apologize for taking so long to arrive. I, too, was being confined unlawfully."

"I expected as much. What's the situation?"

"The other Guides are being held in separate locations similar to yours on the other Axis Worlds. We won't be able to free them until we've retaken control of the Justice Division and disrupted the illegitimate government the other Advisors have erected. In fact, we need to get you to a safer location right now, as Justice reinforcements are likely en route as we speak."

"Very well. I will follow your lead."

Something moved in the hallway. Blake motioned Guide Luciene against the wall and readied his Glaser, then checked the hallway to find Wallman heading toward them. "The scene is secure for now, sir, but I've been monitoring Justice communications. They've discovered your escape."

"Let's move—wait, hold one." He frowned at Guide Luciene, then at Wallman. "Do you have another one of those hats?"

$$\mathcal{AR}$$

Guide Luciene peered out from beneath the wide brim of his fedora. "It appears that for all their high-minded talk, the usurpers have continued to maintain a charade of normalcy for the public."

They strode down a bustling street on the way to a safehouse of their own. Perotski had located the apartment, and Blake had reserved it under a false name minutes earlier. "I'm still getting caught up on the details, sir, but it's my understanding that, no, they've spilled all our secrets to the public. The Rasu, the cleansings, the virutox, everything."

"Then why..." the Guide's step faltered "...I see no signs of panic. No mobs, no violence, no property destruction."

Blake placed a hand on the Guide's elbow and subtly urged him onward. "Nika Kirumase is a dangerous idiot, but she's also a charismatic one. She's got everyone convinced we're somehow going to be able to stop the Rasu. Wave our hands around and cast a magic spell of protection or something. The people are sheep. They will follow her blindly to their deaths."

"Ah. Yes, I see. The calm will not last for long, then. Not once the true direness of our situation becomes unavoidably apparent."

The Guide sounded troubled, and he should be. Their world was collapsing. But it wasn't lost yet.

"You and the other Guides can regain control and meet the Rasu's next deadline before that happens. At least you'll have no shortage of criminals to send their way."

"Indeed." Guide Luciene slowed again, his gaze drifting across the street to a brightly lit restaurant. "Where are we traveling to now?"

Blake restrained himself from shoving his charge forward, but only barely. "We're heading to a new secure location. You'll be safe there, and we can plan our next move."

"Yes. I confess, this is…disconcerting. I have not walked the streets among such crowds in…a long time. I find them unexpectedly suffocating. I believe I crave a measure of solitude."

"Yes, sir. We're almost there." The Guide finally resumed a reasonable pace, and Blake exhaled in relief.

"Our next move must be to retake the levers of the government, before the Advisors cause irreparable damage."

"I'd like to put together a trusted team and mount an attack on Mirai One Pavilion, where they've established a temporary headquarters."

"Your skills are considerable, Advisor Satair, but they know you've escaped. They will be expecting you."

"Respectfully, Guide Luciene, they won't be expecting this."

"Perhaps. In the event you are overconfident, I am sending you a file. It contains a kill-code for all Justice machines in a fifty-meter radius. Keep it safe, for none know of it."

"Not even the other Guides?"

"We all have secrets. We all have contingency plans."

A shiver chilled Blake's skin. But this was as matters should be. He respected Luciene for the Guide's shrewd, calculating, arguably diabolical intellect, and this was merely further evidence of that intellect. His lapse mollified, he considered the offer. "Such a kill-code will shut down the dynes I control as well."

"Yes. But if you find yourself heavily outnumbered, it will even the mechanical odds for you."

"Hopefully the situation will not come to dire straits where it will be required, but thank you." He gestured to a wide doorway on their right. "We're here."

27

MIRAI

A dlai fought the alert notification's attempts to rouse him from sleep. It started as a distant flashing light amidst a dreamscape of forests, and his mind dismissed it as a shooting star. The noise arrived next, beeping in time with the flashing. Not unpleasant, but demanding.

Your attention is required. You must depart this place of peace and tranquility and see to An Important Matter.

He opened his eyes to the dusky shadows of his bedroom and the delightful warmth of Perrin's skin against his. His left arm draped over her waist, and her back pressed into his chest. He drank in the clean, honeysuckle scent of her hair and the reassuring rise and fall of her chest beneath his hand.

Damn, this was a better way to wake up than anything else in the world, and he thanked the annoying alert for gifting him this moment.

He took care not to move and disturb her as he finally opened the alert—

—bloody hells!

He immediately broadcast an order to lock down the Guides' safehouses, double the security at each one and triple the security at the Pavilion. Then he messaged Spencer and Selene, asking them to meet him at the Mirai Justice Center in twenty minutes. Then he added Julien and Harris to the meeting request, because this affected the entire Justice Division. This affected the entire Dominion.

His fingers gently caressed Perrin's stomach as he placed a soft kiss on her ear.

"Hmm." She shifted in his arms, half-rolled toward him and opened one sleepy eye. "Hi."

"Hi, you. Something's come up, and I need to head into work. You go back to sleep. The refrigeration unit is fully stocked, so enjoy breakfast without me."

Her brow furrowed up unevenly. "What happened?"

"Don't worry about it. Sleep." He kissed her temple...oh, he wanted to stay...and eased away, crawled out of the bed and went to get dressed.

He'd barely made it to the closet when a report came in flagging a 'problem' at Luciene's safehouse. He dropped his forehead against the wall. So, this was how it was going to play out.

He canceled the Advisor meeting, suggested the others instead get themselves to the Guides' safehouses on their worlds, asked Spencer to begin investigating Satair's escape from the detention wing and ordered a response team to meet him at Luciene's safehouse.

⅍

Two dynes lay sprawled on the sidewalk outside the entrance to the property. They displayed no obvious damage, as if they'd shut down where they stood. Adlai sent a direct shutdown command just in case, then called one of the response officers over. "Have forensics send a team to pick these up, and any more we find inside. I want a thorough analysis conducted on their operating systems and all orders they executed in the last three hours. We need to know what disabled them and how."

"Yes, sir."

He stepped around the dynes and traversed the short walkway to the front door of the house. Three drones littered the lawn, along with another dyne and two Asterion officers. Their throats had been slit.

He exhaled harshly and shared a grim look with the officer guarding the scene. "We'll have forensics give the bodies a once over to be thorough, then expedite their regens." Adlai picked his way around the slick pools of blood surrounding the bodies to reach the open front door.

The incursion had taken an even messier turn inside the house. A dyne's head had been blown clean off and its remains speared into a wall three meters from the rest of its frame. The Asterion tasked with interior duty had put up a fight, from the looks of it. Her chest was blown open; the material of her clothes around the hole were singed black, indicating an energy blast. Scorch marks marred the other two walls in the main room.

He ran through a checklist of the security detail in his mind, then turned to the officer who stood guard inside the house. "Is this everything?"

"Yes, sir. On a quick inspection, it appears nothing was taken from the residence and no other rooms were disturbed."

Luciene had walked out the front door. Adlai wondered if the former Guide had stepped in the blood on the patio as he'd done so and soiled his fancy robes.

When Adlai finally made it to the Justice Center three hours later, Spencer was waiting on him in his office.

He collapsed in his chair. "Guides Anavosa, Iovimer and Sely-shok have all been moved to new, hopefully more secure locations without incident. Guide Delacrai has been temporarily confined to her residence and her guard detail doubled. But it's clear Satair went specifically for Luciene."

"He likely recognized he didn't have time to break anyone else out and didn't want to risk recapture."

"That doesn't mean he won't come back for them later."

"Regret giving the Guides real bodies now? If Luciene was still walking around in a doll, we could simply shut down his hardware. Problem solved."

"In retrospect, it *would* have been the better security move. Talk to me about Satair's escape."

Spencer dropped a shoulder against the wall. "It was an inside job. The surveillance cams in the detention wing were cycled off ahead of time, and the security on Satair's cell was bypassed without any slicing, which means someone had authorization."

Honestly, Adlai wasn't surprised. Satair had acolytes inside Justice. A few had been easy to identify, and they'd been given involuntary leave time and had their clearances temporarily revoked. The rest, though? "We have no visuals on the escape whatsoever?"

"Correct. We do have footage from the building's external cams, but they don't show anything conclusive. Traffic in and out of the complex was heavy even at that time of night."

"All right. Let's vet every Justice officer with clearance to open that cell, starting with those from Synra—"

"I'm not sure we need to go to the trouble. Officers Wallman and Perotski didn't report for their end-of-shift debriefing this morning, and they're not responding to comms."

His mind sifted through thousands of interconnected mental nodes to locate his impressions of the two officers. Friendly, helpful, competent. Respectful of authority—just not his, it turned out.

"Dammit. They had me fooled." He sighed. "I want everyone vetted again anyway. I changed my mind on the order of priority, though. Check those assigned to the Guides and Pavilion duty first. We can't have another breach of this magnitude from within."

"I'll get Internal Affairs started on it right away. What about Wallman and Perotski?"

"Add them to the fugitive alert for Satair and Luciene. If they so much as pop their heads out for a breeze of fresh air, we'll grab them."

"We will." Spencer nodded sharply and left the office, which was when Adlai realized the man hadn't called him 'sir' once. Spencer was going to settle into being an Advisor just fine.

In the likely brief silence that arrived with Spencer's departure, he considered his office. His time here during the last week had been intermittent at best, and it showed. Discarded files sat scattered across his desk and the table by the window. Two panes had been left open since...yesterday sometime, if not the day before. Coffee stains had dried along the rim of his favorite mug.

The disorder of his office was only a symptom of a far larger failing. It was all too much—too much for him to handle, too much for four and a half Justice Advisors to handle. Imprisoning and guarding the Guides, a dozen backup hardware caches and two demoted Advisors; quelling civil unrest on every Dominion world; securing the wrecked Mirai Tower and multiple other sites that suffered damage from the Platform explosion; poring through the records of tens of thousands of criminal proceedings whose validity were trash due to the virutox and granting pardons to those deserving while trying to keep the genuine criminals locked up; the list continued on, then on for a span longer.

They—he—hadn't been up to the task, and as a result the two greatest Asterion threats to their continued existence had strolled out of their prisons and were now free to pursue their own nefarious ends.

He could really use one of Perrin's pep talks about now. She had a way of seeing the world that seemed deceptively simple, even naive, on a first impression, but her fervent belief in it wove a spell around you, until you couldn't help but believe in it, too. She'd pinged him earlier, though, to let him know she needed to meet with some people at the Pavilion this morning. He'd have to set his psyche straight on his own.

What would Satair and Luciene's next move be? It was tempting to hope that they merely wanted their freedom, and they'd hole up somewhere until they could change their appearance and IDs, then sit back and watch as the world burned. They didn't deserve their freedom, but right now Adlai would be happy if they simply didn't cause any new problems.

But it wasn't going to happen. Satair would never be content to slink off into the shadows, knowing he had been beaten. And Luciene, for all his cold arrogance, was a true believer. A believer in his own inherent rightness, in the infallibility of his worldview— a worldview shaped around the premise that anything other than keeping the citizens ignorant and helpless while appeasing the Rasu was certain to bring about the end of the Dominion.

No, Satair and Luciene would never sit back and watch while others dared to engage in unapproved behavior. They'd strike at the mutineers and try to wrest away the levers of power for themselves. But where, when and how?

28

MIRAI ONE PAVILION

Nika fidgeted around the Pavilion lounge. Pent-up energy screamed to be let loose on some purposeful task. It felt like they were perched on the cusp of a cascade of revelations, albeit a cusp that doubled as a cliff, and she grew weary of peering over the edge trying to make out what waited below.

Dashiel had made contact with Forchelle, but he'd yet to report back on what, if anything, he'd learned. Scientists in the employ of Industry and Admin were taking a fresh look at kyoseil, and they had put out a call for more experts among techies and slicers across the Dominion. Satair and Luciene's escape overnight had everyone in Justice and nearly everyone in Admin scrambling to shore up security on every world. For the first time in days, the Pavilion resembled a ghost town.

Meanwhile, what was she doing? Waiting. And she had no time to waste waiting, dammit.

She glanced over at one of the tables, where Perrin, Maris and two Justice officers sat huddled up. Perrin was worried that Satair would be hunting down NOIR members, but Nika suspected he had much bigger targets in mind.

She started wandering over their way—

"Nika!"

She spun toward the source of the shout. Parc jogged toward her, a beer in each hand. When he reached her, he handed her one and motioned toward a nearby table. "Hang with me?"

Her eyes narrowed in suspicion. If he was trying to ply her with alcohol, it meant he wanted something and didn't have time to be subtle about it. "Where's Ryan?"

"Gods, Nika, we're not joined at the hip."

"Except you kind of have been lately."

"Ugh." Parc flopped down in a chair and stared at her until she joined him. "That's…fine, that's totally true. But not today. I encouraged him to trek to Namino to pick up replacement parts for WheatleyBot, since one of its stabilizers got blown out during The Chalet attack. He doesn't need to be here for this."

Which meant Parc *definitely* wanted something—likely something illegal and almost certainly something dangerous. Against her will, her pulse ticked up a notch in anticipation. "And here I thought we were simply hanging out and drinking beer."

"No, you didn't. So, I heard that the kyoseil in our bodies has been hiding extremely bizarre properties from us all this time."

"Do I even want to know how you heard that?" Their 'radical transparency' policy hadn't yet been extended to the kyoseil revelations—not until they had a better handle on what those revelations truly consisted of.

"I was curious about your Rasu prisoner, so I sliced into the surveillance footage of Jerry's prison. Very clever of you, saddling the bastard with such a lame name."

She laughed. "How industrious of you. We've got the best people working to confirm or disprove what Jerry said about kyoseil and decipher what it might mean."

"You don't have *me* working on it."

"And this was clearly a mistake on my part. What do you have in mind?"

He drummed his fingers on the table. "I was thinking about how there's another version of me out there. If he's still alive, he's in the heart of the Rasu stronghold, enjoying a great view of some of their most dastardly deeds."

"True…."

"Supradimensional? Interlinked? Capable of facilitating mental control of one being by another distant, disparate being?"

Her brow furrowed, spurring him to continue.

"I think I can use the kyoseil inside my brain to contact my copy."

"What?"

They both looked up in surprise to see Perrin standing behind Parc, hands on her hips and jaw threatening to drop.

Parc shifted around in his chair to face Perrin. "Exactly what I said. Based on everything Jerry told you all about the mineral, it's entirely logical for it to function this way. All I need to do is figure out how to activate it. But this is me we're talking about. I don't anticipate it being a problem."

Perrin winced in Nika's direction. "Do we really think the other version of him is still alive?"

She shrugged. "It's possible. The limited, pathetic monitoring the Guides have done on previous deliveries has indicated the stasis chambers can remain active for up to eight weeks."

"We've got a little time, then." Parc finished off his beer and added a new rhythm to his drumming. "But not much. What do you say?"

Perrin cleared her throat. "Nika, can I talk to you for a second?"

She nodded and slid her beer over to Parc. "I'll be back. Finish this for me."

Perrin marched off to a quiet corner and waited on Nika with crossed arms, but Nika held up a hand to forestall the coming outburst. "You're going to say, 'maybe we can rescue him.' Perrin, we *can't*. We'll only get one chance at the stronghold, and *all* our lives will depend on our success or failure. We're not ready."

"I...I know. We'd get everyone who participated killed, and probably everyone else, too. It just breaks my heart to think of him trapped there, helpless and...." Perrin pursed her lips. "So, I wasn't actually going to say that, even if I did think it. What I wanted to say was, if Parc *can* somehow reach out and sense his other self, *should* he? Whatever he learns won't be pleasant, and it might be...horrible."

"You're absolutely right. But if he can give us any insight at all into what's happening inside the platform or what's being done to our people, it would be invaluable knowledge—maybe transformational knowledge."

"I understand that, but forgive me for worrying about his psychological well-being. He's already had a hells of a week. You shouldn't push him."

"It was *his* idea!"

"Of course it was. This is Parc we're talking about. But don't you realize he's desperate to show that he still matters? To NOIR, but most of all to you? His greatest fear is being forgotten." She studied Nika warily. "This is what you're counting on, isn't it?"

"For the second time, I did not ask him to do this."

"No, but I saw you over there vibrating. You were about to jump on the offer before I intervened."

Nika hesitated, uncertain of how to respond. Was Perrin suggesting that she'd unlocked a harder, more callous edge to her psyche during this crisis? Had she?

She'd always taken care of the people important to her. By all accounts, she'd pretty much always taken care of all the people, to the best of her ability. No, she didn't want to risk damaging Parc's mental well-being. But they desperately needed information. They *needed* a way to defeat the Rasu.

She huffed a breath. "You know what? I'm still jumping on the offer. We cannot afford to turn away from any opportunity to learn more about our enemy. Now, will you come with me to help take care of Parc while he barrels head-first into this mad experiment?"

Perrin glared at the ceiling. "Yes...."

29

MIRAI ONE PAVILION

Nika stopped Parc outside the upstairs room she'd hastily arranged for them to use. "Are you *certain* you want to try this?"

"Are you kidding? If my previous self is alive, I want to know it. Plus, there's the whole frontier of science angle, not to mention being the first person to ever make this kind of connection. If it works, they'll name buildings after me."

She shook her head with a chuckle. "Sure they will. But you also understand that if it works, what you see or sense could be unpleasant?"

"Yep. Torture—when does that get fun? But I'm ready for it."

"All right." She opened the door and ushered him and Perrin inside. Perrin mouthed a 'thank you' as she passed, which helped to ease the lingering concern tainting her burgeoning excitement. *If this works....*

A med tech she'd (also hastily) borrowed from one of the up-gen clinics showed up a few minutes later. The woman strode in with an officious manner and a hefty gear bag. "Mr. Eshett, I'm Claire Boshemi. I'll be taking care of you today."

Parc snorted. "I even get to be 'Mr. Eshett.' Buildings, Nika. Tall ones."

She rolled her eyes. "Are we good to go?"

"I'm good."

Boshemi checked over the cot they'd moved into the room, then went to the built-in cabinets and shelf, set the bag on the floor and retrieved a small kit from it. "I'm here to monitor your vitals and intervene if something goes wrong during your experiment. Whenever you're ready."

Nika turned back to Parc. "We're hoping for any information you can tell us about the situation your other self finds himself in. If you can see anything about the location, hear any sounds or describe his physical condition...and, again, you need to be prepared: it likely won't be a good situation. Can you handle it if it's not?"

"Gods, Nika, stop coddling me. I've got this." He paused. "Okay, what is it I've got?"

Now he asked? "For the most part, this is going to have to take place inside your mind."

Parc climbed on the cot and stretched out. "It's where I do all my best work."

"Kyoseil is woven into your core neurological structure. You don't know how to access any communication-facilitating capabilities it possesses, but *it* does—assuming they exist. Open up your mind and remove all your defenses. I promise, no one here will try to break in. Look and listen for yourself and follow what you find."

"How very metaphysical." Parc rubbed his hands together, then adjusted the pillow beneath his head. "Let me work some magic."

He closed his eyes. After a few seconds, his mouth and nose quirked around. His brow twitched. He shifted position, then again.

When nothing happened after twenty seconds, she gave Perrin a weak shrug. They'd tried, but now it seemed rather foolish—

"Oh, oh! Oh...." On the heels of the outburst, Parc reached a hand out into the air. Then his muscles went slack—

—a bloodcurdling scream erupted from his lips. His hands grabbed onto the sheet beneath him and fisted the material up as his back arched in a spasm so intense his spine must be on the verge of breaking. The scream continued.

They all rushed for the cot at the same time. "Pull him back!"

Boshemi shook her head rapidly. "How? I don't even know what he's done. His heart rate has spiked to 200 bpm. Attempting to lower it." The woman retrieved a vein syringe and jabbed it in his neck, then stared at the readings. "No change."

The scream finally died on Parc's lips, but only because he began hyperventilating. His eyes rolled back in his head. Beads of sweat pooled across his forehead, and all his muscles remained clinched, frozen in a state of agony.

Nika reached for one of his hands and tried to hold it, but he refused to loosen his grasp on the sheet. "Parc, can you hear me? You have to break the connection. Come back. Come back here. Follow the sound of my voice." Nothing.

She glared at Boshemi across the cot. What was the woman here for, if not to fix this exact problem? "Can you knock him out? He shouldn't be able to maintain the connection if he's unconscious." She had no idea if this was true or not; this experiment had started in uncharted territory and was ending in nightmarish but still uncharted territory.

Boshemi hurried over to the open kit, returning with a port syringe. "Roll him onto his side. I need to access his port."

She and Perrin struggled to wrangle Parc onto his side; his whole body was locked into rigidity, yet also somehow fighting them. Finally, Boshemi was able to work the syringe mechanism onto Parc's port.

In less than a second, all the tension left his body, and he slumped limply onto the cot. Over the next thirty seconds, his breathing and heartrate gradually slowed and his body temperature cooled.

Nika dragged her hands down her face, feeling as though she'd experienced a tachycardia incident of her own. A question hovered on her lips, but she asked it only of herself, because gods knew no one else in the room was in a position to answer it.

What the fuck had just happened?

AR

Parc paced erratically around the room, repeatedly dodging the cot while avoiding acknowledging its presence. "Can I go now?"

Nika studied him from the spot she'd staked out by the door. He'd woken up twenty minutes earlier and remained groggy for another ten while Boshemi checked him out. Then he'd abruptly shoved the woman to the side and leapt off the cot, asserting he felt fine. He'd sent Perrin off to get him an energy drink and glowered Boshemi into a corner, then taken on Nika.

"Physically, you've recovered from your ordeal, so I can't keep you here or cart you off to a clinic. But you're obviously *not* okay. Can you tell me anything about what you experienced?"

He studied the floor, reflexively straightening the hem of his shirt. "I don't know! I remember pain, awful...pain. And darkness, but with lights flashing from somewhere. I think I tried to move, but I was paralyzed. That's it." He glanced in her direction without meeting her gaze. "Sorry I couldn't be of more help."

"No, it's me who's sorry. If I'd had any idea...but I should have had an idea and never allowed you to do this."

An hour ago, he would have scoffed saucily at the ridiculous proposition that she could have ever stopped him from trying something he had a mind to do, but instead he motioned raggedly at her. "Whatever. It's fine. Can I *go*?"

The fierce glint in his eyes suggested she'd have to knock him out again if she wanted to keep him from leaving. She grimaced. "You can go. But *please* ping me if anything feels off, or if you simply want to talk."

"Yeah. Sure." He brushed past her and out the door.

She motioned to Boshemi to indicate the woman could leave, too. The tech packed up her gear and fled the room with a speed and efficiency that left Nika shaking her head. Of course the woman was spooked. Who wouldn't be?

She sank back against the wall with a frustrated groan. The Rasu weren't merely experimenting on their people before killing them. They were *brutally* experimenting on them, ensuring their last days of life were filled with unspeakable agony. Godsdammit!

No matter what, she could not allow any more people to be sent as offerings to the aliens. Not even the worst sort of despicable criminals; not even almost-people who'd never fully awakened. Now that she knew the truth, no more. Ever.

Perrin burst into the room, two energy drinks tucked under her arm. "You let him leave? All by himself?"

"I couldn't keep him here. The tech cleared him, and he wanted to leave."

"You could have taken him home yourself, then watched over him."

She nodded thoughtfully. "You passed him on the way out, I'm guessing?"

"I did."

"When you realized he was leaving, you tried to go with him, I'm guessing?"

Perrin looked away. "Yes. He told me not to worry about him and stormed off."

"See? He's making it quite clear that he wants to be alone."

"Doesn't mean he should be. I'm pinging Ryan right now and sending him to their place."

"I think that's a good idea."

A few seconds later Perrin redirected her displeasure, which hadn't lessened, back to Nika while she tossed one of the energy drinks on the shelf and opened the other one. "Are you happy with yourself now?"

"No, Perrin, I'm not. Are you asking me if I feel like shit for what he just went through? Yes, I do. You know what else I feel like shit about? What the Rasu have done to tens of thousands of Asterions for the last eight years. We just got a tiny little glimpse into how much every single one of those people suffered before they died.

"So however awful the scene in here was today, I'm glad it happened, because now I know. Because now, no force in the universe will stop me from destroying the Rasu."

Perrin stared at her over the rim of the energy drink she held at her lips, her eyes wide. "I'm...I mean, I'm glad you're angry. I'm glad you intend to do something to stop them. But you're seeing the world in terms of tens of thousands of people and years of time. I'm thinking about one person, today, and the suffering that they might never get over. I can't help ten thousand dead people, but I want, I *need*, to be able to help one living person. And so should you."

Nika grabbed the other energy drink and turned it up, though energy was one thing she didn't lack for. When it was half empty, she set it back on the shelf, hopped up on the cot and dropped her elbows to her knees. "This is about the First Gen thing, isn't it?"

"What? No. Maybe. I don't know. Nika, listen. I realize the Advisor power is super-helpful, and the money is nifty, too, and the flat is fabulous. I get it. But you don't have to become the person you were."

"It's not that simple. I think the truth is, I've always been that person—I merely lacked context these last five years. And Nika Kirumase? She was a *good* person. Yes, she made mistakes, like everyone does, but most of her mistakes stemmed from her carrying too heavy a burden on her shoulders—from taking others' burdens onto herself. Sometimes without asking their permission."

"Sounds about right. Ever think you're making the same mistake again now?"

30

CONCEPTUAL RESEARCH TESTING FACILITY

Nika carried a utilitarian chair from the lounge down the hall into the main containment facility. She dropped it barely two meters from the electrified edges of the force-field barrier, flipped it around backwards, sat down and crossed her arms over the headrest.

None of the other Advisors accompanied her this time, because they had more important work to do than watch a frustrating, often maddening interchange that couldn't decide if it was an interrogation or a negotiation. All the combat dynes remained on guard, however, as did two of Lance's officers, and her interaction with the Rasu would of course be recorded.

A chilly, drafty silence nonetheless permeated the prison. The ventilation system forced fresh air inside at a brisk flow in order to suppress the constant ionization of the air the barrier caused. She'd planned ahead and wore a black velvet turtleneck and gray wool pants, but they didn't prevent her from shuddering when she sat down.

Jerry imitated an oil slick spilt across the rear half of the cage. Lying there without shape or definition, it seemed impossible that when combined with a scant few of its brethren the alien was capable of destroying species and worlds. That this *oil slick* was capable of willfully inflicting horrific pain and torture on living, thinking individuals.

Yes, she was angry at Jerry. At the Rasu as a whole, but though she'd used negotiation tricks to make Jerry feel special and unique, right now when she considered the prisoner, she saw Parc's torturers. She saw *Rasu*.

"Jerry, wake up."

The oil slick shrunk in diameter as it grew in height, pulling itself inward into semi-solidity. It slipped and slithered until it had taken on its preferred form, that of a forever coiling serpent, and approached the front of the cage. "Asterion. It has taken you a lengthy time to educate yourself on the unique characteristics of kyoseil, if you have managed to do so at all."

"I've been occupied with a variety of important duties. I apologize if you felt neglected in the interim, but I'm here now. I want to talk about control, Jerry. Control, free will and the unreconcilable dichotomy between them."

⋏R

MIRAI ONE PAVILION

Nika hurried into the conference room at the Pavilion to find Dashiel talking to a man who looked like he'd climbed straight out of a wilderness nature vid. A neat but full beard spilled onto his chest, and long soot-gray hair draped behind his shoulders. A rough-hewn plaid shirt paired with beige canvas pants and beat-up work boots completed the presentation.

Dashiel met her at the door, squeezing her hands in greeting before gesturing to his guest. "Nika, this is Magnus Forchelle."

"Aye, we know each other. It's been a while."

Dashiel cringed. "Sorry, I didn't get an opportunity to mention…."

She gave Forchelle her best diplomat smile. "I know we do. Unfortunately, I recently lost the majority of my historical memories in an attack. But I've been reading up on you, your work and our history together. Hopefully we can make do."

"Makes no real difference to me. If anything, I'm envious. I've wanted to forget my own past many times."

She shifted toward Dashiel enough to arch a private eyebrow at him, and got a pained shrug in answer. The message came through well enough: yes, Forchelle was a quirky character.

She returned her attention to the man. "Yes, well, thank you for agreeing to help us."

"I'm still not certain it'll be 'help' I'm giving in the end, but Mr. Ridani here convinced me it'll be all our end if I don't try, so into the breach I go."

They gathered at one of the two tables in the room, and Dashiel clasped his hands atop the surface. "As I mentioned in my message, Mr. Forchelle is aware of both the supradimensional and interlinked features of kyoseil. Rather than mangle the explanation, Mr. Forchelle, if you don't mind?"

The man stroked his beard thoughtfully—because what would you do with such a beard as his if not stroke it? "You're referring to 'supradimensionality' and 'interlinking' as separate concepts, but when you're talking about kyoseil they are one and the same. When you observe a chunk of kyoseil, you're seeing an instance of its periodic extrusion into what we call the three physical dimensions. But it exists just as fully in the deep dimensions of the universe.

"Now, in shaping kyoseil to our own needs, to our own creation, we've changed it. The bonding that occurs between strands of kyoseil and our neural networks of necessity weakens its bond with other manifestations of its kind—strands which are bonded to another life, or not bonded at all. But it doesn't sever those links entirely."

Nika nodded soberly. "Yes, we've...discovered this ourselves."

Dashiel looked over in surprise. "You have? What happened?"

◦◦◦◦

MIRAI

My chest is flayed open, the folds of skin held back by clamps. The cavity revealed glows hot like steel fresh out of a kiln. But I can't peer inside at my own insides, because my head is locked in place by something hard and unyielding. My eyelids are held open by more unforgiving clamps. My eyes are dry, scratchy, sandpaper scraping over unfinished wood. I haven't blinked in...I can't say.

Time has blended together into an endless series of brief respites between the pain.

Parc huddled on the floor in the far corner of Ryan's rented room. His eyes were squeezed shut, in defiance of the memory he couldn't stop seeing, and his legs were pulled up against his chest. His intact, whole and in no way whatsoever flayed open chest.

He tried to focus on the silence of this room, his home since reawakening, but his ears rang with the din of his own screams.

A shadow passes across my limited field of vision as one of the creature machines returns to me. It begins working on me, from behind this time. On my brain, as my skull must be cracked as wide open as my chest.

Cool air tickles my brain tissue, and my whole body shivers within the restraints. Then a probe descends from above, and I'm screaming again. Silently, with no vibrations to give voice to my agony, for they long ago severed my vocal chords.

He shivered now, though the room was comfortably warm, and tugged his legs closer against him.

§ sysdir(root) § Hq(storerec*. Y12,463.115.1120-1314 A7)
< erase all
/

He transfixed on the blinking cursor. It wasn't fair to leave him—the other him—out there on the other side of the galaxy, alone and afraid. How dare he abandon himself to that torture while he lived free and easy back here? He was such an arrogant jerk!

From the opposite corner of the room, a powered-down Ike-Bot passed judgment on him by way of its pitiless, blank gaze.

I can't breathe any longer. I don't want to breathe any longer. Another nanosecond of this pain and I will surely die. Why can't I die?

Why wouldn't the monsters fucking let him die?

The remembered pain seized hold of Parc anew, and he couldn't breathe either. He forced his eyes shut again, and in the darkness behind his eyelids he swore he saw the kyoseil strings pouring out from his body to travel across the galaxy. Was he still connected to his other self, somehow, even now?

He started to reach out for a string, the way he had in the lab—then yanked his hand back. He was too much of a coward to do it, too much of a coward to share in his own pain.

A sound from his left announced Ryan entering. Twenty-to-one odds that Nika and Perrin had told him to rush home and see to his pathetic, quivering mess of a lover.

"Parc? Are you here?"

The lights flicked on. Parc instinctively shrank away from them, burying his face in his arm.

"Parc!" He felt Ryan's presence draw near as the man crouched on the floor beside him, but he couldn't bring himself to look up. "What's wrong? Are you sick? Do I need to—"

"No. I just…I just…I can't…." Fuck, he was hyperventilating again. Talking seemed to trigger it, which wasn't great.

"Let me get someone over here—"

"No!" His hand shot out to blindly grab for Ryan's arm. "I'm…." He concentrated on opening his eyes and lifting his head. He blinked furiously against the too-bright light until gradually Ryan's face sharpened into clarity. Good-looking face, if he was honest.

Gods, he on the other hand must look a wreck and a half, judging by Ryan's expression. "I'm not sick. It's all in my head. I need..." he realized he'd been pulling at his hair with his free hand, and he quickly dropped both hands to the floor "...to be alone for a while, to work through it."

Ryan's brow furrowed up in consternation; after a few seconds he shook his head. "Sorry, but I'm not leaving you alone like this. I wasn't there for you before, but I will be now, dammit."

He stared at Ryan, searching frantically through his scrambled brain for how to respond. He didn't want a keeper. Thus far the sex had been fantastic, and they'd always gotten along well so they had plenty in common to talk about in between. But now Ryan was making like this thing they were doing was an actual *relationship*.

Crap, was it? Was that a good thing?

He chuckled quietly, which was a marked improvement from the screaming. He'd gone a whole ten seconds without thinking about the waking nightmare his other self was trapped in. If Ryan could do more to extend those spans of respite, he was desperate enough to take him up on the offer. "Fine. You can stay."

Ryan got comfortable on the floor next to Parc and stretched out his legs. "Perrin told me a little about your experiment. Do you want to talk about what happened?"

"No, I want to erase it."

"So, erase it."

"I can't. I'll be abandoning my other self to suffer alone."

Ryan frowned deeply. "You think your other self would want you suffering along with them? You're a selfish prick, but you're not a masochist...or a sadist, I guess. Sorry, this is all kind of confusing. Wouldn't you instead want you working your ass off to get vengeance?"

"Huh." Parc dropped his head against the wall and fixated on the ceiling. A bead of sweat dropped into the corner of his eye, and he wiped the back of his hand across his forehead, unsurprised when it came away soaked.

The man had a point. Parc played with a few embers of vengeance stirring in his gut, stoking them idly until they rose into the beginnings of a proper righteous fire. Vengeance was definitely a worldview he could get behind.

A hundred thousand million seconds have passed, but at last the probing ceases. Not for long—it's never for long. The creature machine always returns.

I breathe, but only because my body insists upon it. Not for much longer. My will is gone, and my body will mercifully soon follow.

"Hey, hey." Ryan's arm was around his shoulder, and Parc was half slumped into his lap. But not in the good way.

"I'm all right." He straightened up and slapped himself on both cheeks. "Okay. I'll erase the memories. But first I need to put together a detailed report for Nika of everything I saw, heard and felt, along with my recommendation."

"What's your recommendation?"

"We have got to kill every last one of these motherfuckers."

31

MIRAI ONE PAVILION

Nika peered out the window of the third-floor conference room as evening shadows crept across the lawn. "Do you think Luciene will make his move tonight?"

Dashiel wrapped his arms around her waist from behind and rested his chin on her shoulder. "I think Luciene will cower in whatever hole Satair has stashed him in. Now, Satair might make a move tonight, or he might wait."

"For us to self-destruct?"

"We're not going to self-destruct." He kissed her neck beneath her ear. "We're going to ingenuity our way out of this crisis. It's what we do."

They had sent Forchelle off to meet with a group of scientists at the Industry Division's Conceptual Research office, in the hope that they could turn this new—or in Forchelle's case, very old—knowledge into a concrete tool to use against the Rasu. Ingenuity their way out of this crisis, in other words.

"We will. Speaking of, I know why the Rasu don't use quantum entanglement communications."

"Did Jerry tell you?"

"More or less. After some goading on my part, it divulged a great deal about what it means to be a Rasu—enough for me to infer the rest. The key is in the term 'entanglement.' Jerry fears the effect on its individuality of physical re-entanglement with the Rasu at the stronghold. The Rasu at the stronghold fear the effect on their individuality of quantum entanglement with distant Rasu. They fear it will force a renewed merger with those they now view as wholly separate entities."

He shifted around so he could see her face but kept his arms around her. "Are you certain?"

"Fairly. They've worked themselves into quite the pickle. Every Rasu of any size and complexity desires above all else independence for itself and control for all others. Consequently, every Rasu of any size and complexity suspects that its equals and superiors desire the same."

"Damn, they are paranoid monsters."

"It's not paranoia if it's true."

"Heh. Does this mean all those platforms and ships in their stellar system are fighting with each other? If so, we can use this. I'm not sure how, but I expect Palmer will have some ideas."

She sighed, but any frustration ebbed away beneath the soothing warmth of his embrace. Since their reconciliation, she was finding great comfort in his touch; it seemed as if he was finding the same in hers, and they both sought it out whenever possible. Even when the world careened madly around them.

"I'm afraid it isn't that overt. No Rasu are openly fighting one another...more executing low-key secret subversion campaigns. And if I'm starting to understand a little about how the Rasu function as a species, I think we can treat all the permanent structures in the stellar system—the platforms, the antenna rings and so on—as a single functional Rasu entity."

"Damn. The entire stronghold is a single mind? That's disturbing to contemplate."

"It is. And I don't know if 'mind' is the correct word. I doubt their consciousnesses operate anything like ours do. Maybe it's more accurate to say a single 'will'—or to use Jerry's word, a single 'purpose'—exists at the stronghold."

His brow knotted, wrinkling his nose. "That's not any less disturbing."

She kissed the wrinkle away. "Nope. Now, the ships we saw coming and going of necessity become 'separate' Rasu for a time. But their tours are kept brief, with frequent return trips home. What happened with Jerry? The Rasu realize it's a risk when they send out their shards—their temporary offspring—to roam. They're forced to keep a tight leash on them, lest they develop their own free will the way Jerry did."

"*This* is what they want to correct using kyoseil. This is why they're experimenting on our people."

"Torturing—why they're *torturing* our people." She quickly smiled to soften the rebuke. "But you're exactly right. If they can devise a way to maintain control over their shards across great distances and for infinite time? It's their crown jewel. Their ultimate prize."

"It also could be the spark that ignites a Rasu civil war—"

The door slid open, and Parc and Ryan burst in. "Good, we found you."

She eased out of Dashiel's arms. "Parc, you look better. I read your report, and I am so damn sorry I put you through that."

"Don't worry about it. I erased it all. Hope the report helped. So, Ryan and I have been messing around with this kyoseil supra-dimensional nonsense, and we have an idea."

Thank gods. This was more like the Parc she knew. "Okay. Talk to me."

He started tromping around the room, while Ryan leaned against the wall by the door and watched Parc with a keen, arguably protective eye. "When I connected with myself, there were these luminescent…strings. Not strings precisely, but it's the best way to describe them. They flowed in these tendrils between me and the other me, like the rope of an anchor. But they weren't physical—they weren't out here in space." He waved a hand in the air in front of him. "They were in my mind. Or possibly in another dimension. In fact, almost definitely in another dimension." He gave himself a sharp nod.

"I thought you said you erased the memory of connecting to your other self?"

"Well, not all of it. Just the screaming, mostly. I kept the technicals, obviously."

"Obviously. And what have you discovered about these not-strings?"

"Ah, you catch on fast. I went back and figured out how I was seeing them—again, the technicals of it. And, you guessed it, the kyoseil is communicating with each other—or possibly itself—on an extradimensional plane. Bet you didn't know we could see them communicating, did you?"

"I did not."

"We can. I tweaked my ocular settings so I can see them whenever I want, without flaying myself open for the world to see."

"Parc...."

He smirked. "Merely a little gallows humor. But guess what I discovered?"

She shrugged. "I have no idea."

"They don't solely connect me to my copy. We're all emitting these strings. All over the fucking place. And they're connecting to each other, in this immense, intricate web. Kyoseil *is* interconnected, and this means so are we."

Forchelle had hinted around this concept earlier, but after Parc's disastrous experiment she'd focused the man on the relationship between kyoseil and their own neural architecture. Which in retrospect, had been a bit myopic on her part.

Parc took her silence for confusion and kept talking. "Ryan—" he gestured to Ryan, who waved casually "—is also broadcasting a rainbow of supradimensional strings. I was able to see his as soon as I adjusted my ocular receptor settings. One of his led to me, or to one of my strings, which also led to one of his.

"Now, these strings are fainter and weaker than the ones tied to my other self. And they kind of...dead-end at the other person. *Because*, the kyoseil is so intricately wound into our neutral structure, into our psyche, into our anima, that our passive security protections block the strings from entry."

"Dashiel, any chance you can coerce Forchelle into coming back over here?"

"Good idea."

"Who?"

Maris' admonitions about First Gen secrecy tied her tongue as she searched for the best way to respond to Parc's question. "Um...our best kyoseil expert."

"Oh. No need, but whatever makes you happy. Back to the story: then Ryan gave me his ID signature and personal access passcode—which, huge trust leap there."

Ryan groaned. "I'm probably so screwed for doing that."

"Nah, I won't abuse it. Much. But guess what happened next?"

She was about to explain how she *still* had no idea, but Dashiel interjected. "You gained full access to his psyche."

"Yes! Nika said you were smart."

"Like when we physically connect?" She pressed the fingertips of her hands together to demonstrate.

"Somewhat similar. But no, not exactly. One, it's a deeper level of connection. Two, we weren't touching. I mean, we were, later, but anyway—the point is, we didn't connect via physical contact. We connected via the kyoseil. It's talking to each other. Through it, so can we. And not a regular old conversation like you and I are having right now. We can be in each other's minds, all of us, irrespective of distance. We can *pool* not just our thoughts but our analytical processes, until they become so vastly much greater than the sum of their parts."

"Do we *want* to?"

Nika shook her head vehemently. "No. Our entire society is built upon the value of individual life and the right of each person to live theirs their way. I've spent the last five years fighting to ensure that pillar of society continues to be respected. I'm not going to finally achieve my goal, only to upend it and transform us into a giant virtual collective."

Cameron sighed. "I hear you. But if we want to defeat the Rasu, we might need to be willing to evolve."

"We're constantly evolving."

"You know what I mean."

Adlai nudged his way into the spat. "Surely there's a middle ground."

As soon as she'd heard enough of Parc's spiel to get a true inkling of what he was suggesting, Nika had ordered Ryan to take Parc to a bar and buy him many drinks. Then she'd called the Advisors together to inform them that it was beginning to appear as if the Rasu were *correct*—that kyoseil truly could be used to control others.

Now the conversation had taken a hard-left turn...directly to where Parc had gone with it, truth be told. She hadn't liked it then, nor did she now.

Perrin's words earlier ran through her mind, and she forced herself to step back. She was not the self-appointed bearer of all burdens, nor the maker of all decisions. It was just that when she'd asserted the Asterion people could find a way to defeat the Rasu by working together, she hadn't meant quite *this* together.

Her reluctance dragged down her voice, which she hoped everyone recognized. "Parc believes we can set up these sort of 'subject-matter psyche hubs.' He says he can write a defensive layer program to allow interconnections between conscious psyches but keep the participants out of each other's internal programming and memories. So people can share active thoughts and processes they offer up, but otherwise the interconnection shouldn't be overly invasive."

Cameron nodded eagerly. "That sounds like an excellent compromise."

"*If* we can make it work. I have to admit it could be useful, in theory. We've been trawling the entire Dominion for ideas on how to combat the Rasu, and we've had some success. But not enough. If people were able to literally pool their mental power and knowledge in pursuit of specific goals, I've no doubt they'd make greater strides."

Parc's exact words had been 'we're fucking immortal organic/synthetic hybrid AIs—we can do better than a fucking suggestion box.' She didn't share that with the others. "Still, we have to consider the cost."

"The cost if we don't pursue this avenue is genocide."

Nika had no good response to Cameron, and she was grateful when Katherine spoke up, which had to be a first. "We've been infusing kyoseil into our bodies and minds for 700,000 years. How did we not know it was capable of this level of interlinking?"

Her gaze landed on Magnus Forchelle, who'd heretofore sat quietly in the back of the room. He wore a troubled guise beneath the beard, though she didn't hazard a guess as to whether he was regretting keeping his secret for so long or not keeping it for longer.

Dashiel sat beside Forchelle; he'd been unexpectedly protective of the man since bringing him into this madness, and he stepped in to answer Katherine's challenge now.

"How many substances, whether metal, mineral or organic, do we know of that possess supradimensional qualities? Outside of theoretical cosmology, *zero*. It's not a characteristic of substances found in nature, and only through extreme scientific tinkering can we force it to occur artificially. Namely, d-gates and superluminal propulsion. We didn't know because we didn't look, and we didn't look because over a million years of scientific inquiry has taught us that such a characteristic doesn't exist."

"Point taken." Katherine slouched in her chair.

Beside her, Adlai shook his head. "I guess kyoseil is even more special than we always believed."

Nika crossed her arms over her chest in a deliberately defensive posture. "Jerry intimated that the Rasu believe kyoseil is alive. Maybe not self-aware, but intelligent."

"I wish you hadn't given the prisoner a name. It's a monster and our enemy."

"I have to personalize someone—or thing, if you want to put a fine point on it—if I'm going to negotiate with them. It's difficult for me to accept, too, but while Jerry is a Rasu, it is not *the* Rasu. It has its own needs, opinions and desires."

Cameron leapt back into the ping-pong conversation. "All right, let's say kyoseil is somehow intelligent. Why didn't...I don't know, why didn't the kyoseil tell us? Why didn't we sense it the instant we became conscious?"

A throat cleared in the back of the room, and every head turned to stare at Forchelle as he stood and stuck his hands in the pockets of his work pants.

"Whatever else it is or isn't, it's a part of us. What we *sense* is ourselves. The birth of what we consider the Asterion species came about with the addition of kyoseil to our makeup after we settled on Synra. It's what made the synthesis of organic and synthetic materials *work*. It's what made us greater than the sum of our parts.

"It turns out that on our own, we weren't nearly as clever as we assumed. We had help. Those parts that went into making Asterions? It wasn't two separate intelligences, it was three: Anaden, SAI and kyoseil."

Everyone fell silent. Nothing like calling into question the basis of your identity as a species to cast a pall over the room. Whether they pursued some style of group minds or not, this was going to change everything. Again.

Few societies could survive the rapid-fire shocks theirs was currently undergoing, but Nika had to believe they would. Their resilience and adaptability had seen them rise from tatters to thrive for more than half a million years.

All they had to do was survive the Rasu first.

Finally, Katherine stood and moved to the front of the room. "So these psyche hubs...how would they work?"

32

MIRAI

"I tell you, if I had rounded the corner two seconds later, I would've been fire-roasted by the explosion. Extra crispy Gabe seared into the sidewalk. It was that close."

Joaquim nodded with enough enthusiasm to show interest and sipped on his beer. He still wasn't sure whether it had been a good idea to reach out to Gabe Hermes, much less agree to meet him, much less return to Mirai in order to do so. As soon as he'd seen Gabe's face, Cassidy's had flashed through his mind in bright, vivid living color. So many memories, and they were all tied up together.

He glanced at the empty barstool on his left, where her ghost had taken up residence, forever smiling, forever beyond his reach.

But if he checked himself and imposed the hint of objectivity that time had granted him, he could admit it was genuinely good to see his old friend. It also felt like a necessary step in his recovery, assuming he was having one.

Gabe took a break from his harrowing tale to finish off his beer, and Joaquim filled the silence. "I wasn't quite as close to the transit hub as you were when it happened, but even a few blocks away I got knocked around by the explosion. It was a surreal night." He didn't, however, elaborate on the horrors that had followed.

His friend flagged down the service dyne for a refill. "Of course, who knows. It probably would've been better to get fire-roasted in the explosion. Now we're *all* going to get fire-roasted by these aliens. The Rasu."

"Maybe not. It sounds as if the Advisors and the government are working hard on the problem." He considered feeling guilty about not being one of those working on the problem. But unless the fight with the aliens descended into tactical close-quarters combat, his skills weren't of much use.

"But it's one hells of a problem. You seriously think they'll be able to protect us from an armada of alien warships?"

Joaquim opened his mouth to deliver a smart-ass response...then delivered a more accurate one instead. "I think there's a damn good chance they will, yeah."

"Huh. Do you know something the rest of us don't?"

He kept his expression neutral, but in his mind he chuckled. "Not really, but I've met Nika Te—Kirumase a few times. She's got her shit together."

"Nice! I hope you're right."

In the corner of his eye, movement on the sidewalk outside the bar caught Joaquim's attention. But the sidewalk existed in a state of constant movement, so what about it had truly drawn his notice?

A man in full combat gear carrying two visible weapons had stopped and faced a squad of Justice dynes trailing behind him; his hand motions and the exaggerated gyrations of his lips indicated he was relaying orders to them. Then he pivoted and continued down the sidewalk to the east at a brisk pace, with the dynes following. When the man had turned this way, Joaquim got a fleeting look at his face.

He quickly reviewed the half second of visuals frame by frame until....

Blake Satair.

The former Justice Advisor was supposed to be rotting in a prison cell. So, what was he doing on the street? Better question: what was he doing armed and commanding a Justice squad?

No way would Nika have freed him. Maybe she'd been overruled? Was the Advisor/NOIR coalition crumbling? If so, no doubt Satair would be on the wrong side of the split.

Equally probable: Satair had escaped. A fugitive with vengeance on his mind and hatred in his heart. Joaquim knew a little about what that did to even a fundamentally decent person; he shuddered to think what it would do to a rotten soul like Satair.

And the man was headed straight for the Mirai One Pavilion.

"Joaquim? Everything good?"

"I hate to skip out on you, but I've got to run. We'll do this again some time."

He hurried out of the bar in time to see Satair and the Justice squad make a right at the next intersection, all but confirming their destination as the Pavilion.

Joaquim had his personal Glaser on him and his retractable blade, as well as his internal defensive routines, including the recent arc shock addition and a shield generator. That was it. No tactical jacket, no grenades, no heavy firepower.

He sent out a group ping as he wove through the crowd toward the intersection.

Ryan, Ava, Dominic, grab anyone else in your line of sight who can shoot and all the combat gear you can put your hands on in less than twenty seconds, then meet me at the corner of Gibson and Morgan as fast as you can get there.

Joaquim? Are you back?

Clearly, he's back.

If he's not, we're going to be standing on a street corner twiddling our thumbs like fools.

Gods how he'd missed this. *Everyone, quit fucking about and MOVE!*

MIRAI ONE PAVILION

"Yes, I am concerned about opening classified Dominion data servers to group mind conglomerations whose members are completely unvetted and for whom there is no accountability. I don't think I'm being unreasonable."

Julien ran a hand through their hair. "You're not. But the simple fact is, we are out of time. We need solid, actionable ideas now, and we can't afford to wait for thousands of background checks to complete."

"I know. But can we *please*—"

A shrill alarm cut Adlai off mid-sentence at the same instant multiple alerts blasted his internal comm system. His eyes scanned the room while he digested the information coming at him. Around half the Advisors were in the room, including all the Justice Advisors and Spencer, as well as seven officers from various divisions.

He called up the perimeter cams and drew in a sharp breath. At least twenty combat dynes and a complement of drones had reached both the east and west doors. Furtive movement indicated several Asterions were among them, but he couldn't get a clear view of them.

"Can I have everyone's attention? Armed hostiles have breached the building's perimeter. Spencer, get everyone in this room who isn't a Justice Advisor or Nika—" or Dashiel, apparently, since his friend had swiftly moved to Nika's side "—to as safe a location as you can find."

Spencer checked his weapons as he moved toward the door. "Yes, sir. Everyone, if you'll come with me, we need to hurry."

Julien was already half out the door. "I'm heading to the east entrance. Security's already getting ripped apart down there."

Adlai nodded. "Harris?"

"Yep. I'll cover the west."

This took care of the two official entrances, but not a service entrance on the northeast corner. He switched to that cam and found the entrance barred shut and watched by two drones, likely to prevent people from escaping. The two dynes at the service entrance must be down, and based on the cam footage from the first floor, he didn't have high hopes for those stationed at the official entrances.

The rest of the building was hardly a fortress. Expansive, open rooms with large windows lined the west side, while the second and third floors were packed with small, enclosed rooms where good *and* bad guys could hide out. People were currently working in a dozen rooms on the fourth and fifth floors, plus at the data vault they'd constructed on the sixth floor.

After Satair and Luciene escaped they'd put security in place at every entrance, on each floor and at the data vault. They'd also stocked a small armory on the second floor, and he quickly sent the passcode to unlock it to everyone he could think of. The building also had automated security measures, though those mainly took the form of alarms and door locks.

This was a heavily armed, multi-pronged attack. Satair's doing, no doubt, with a boost of resources from Luciene.

Okay.

"Selene, get up to the data vault and do whatever you have to do to protect it. Nika, who do you have in the building?"

"Carson. Perrin. I think—"

His heart stutter-stepped over a beat. "Where is Perrin?"

"She can take of herself, Adlai."

"I know she can. Where is she?"

"Conference room 4-C with several of Katherine's Admin people. Also, already hunkering down and barricading the door."

"Thank you. Who else?"

"Josie and Geoff happened to have stopped by to drop off some gear Parc asked for. They're armed."

He'd never been happier that NOIR members seemed to *always* be armed. "An AEV squad will be here in ninety seconds to suppress any further incursions from outside. Until I'm needed more elsewhere, I'll backup Julien toward the east entrance. You and Dashiel take the west. Stay on comms and send your people wherever they can do the most good. Anyone who can, hit the armory, because we need all the firepower we can muster. We cannot allow Satair to take this building."

NR

A firefight was well underway by the time Adlai reached the first floor. The wide, tall central hallway didn't provide much opportunity for cover, though the smoke clogging it might.

He grabbed two officers guarding the lift and pointed across the hall. "Grab the tables and chairs out of that room and pile them up out here, starting at the left wall. We need to create some type of bulwark." Laser fire streaked in their direction, and he ducked into the lift alcove behind him. "Hurry!"

The officers crouched low and hurried into the opposite room. Adlai leaned out of the alcove, Glaser aimed, but didn't fire. Instead he evaluated the scene as best he could. He counted five dynes and two drones defending against...possibly six dyne attackers. And two Asterions, both sporting strong defensive shielding. Julien was nowhere to be seen.

Close odds.

He considered ordering one of the incoming AEVs to fire on the entrance, but he risked hitting innocents instead of the attackers. How did Satair have so many dynes at his disposal? He shouldn't have been able to command a single Justice dyne to so much as cross the street!

One of the officers tossed a table out into the hallway, followed by a couple of chairs. Adlai dove forward and crouched behind the table, then brought his Glaser over the top of it and concentrated on firing through the defenders into the attackers.

In the chaos, he couldn't say he was contributing in any positive way. He needed to get closer, but the space between here and there was a wide-open killing field, as was made clear by the three unmoving forms prone on the floor a few meters away.

The abrupt silence of a half-second lull in crisscrossing fire broke when glass shattered in the room behind him.

33

MIRAI ONE PAVILION

Joaquim sprinted out of the room, rolled once and slid in beside Adlai Weiss, ignoring the Glaser the man pointed at his head. "Get ready."

He reared back and lobbed a grenade over the barricade and the heads of the defending dynes. It landed almost at the entry doors and exploded, knocking two attacking dynes off their feet and hopefully blowing some holes in them.

"Lacese? What the hells are you doing here?"

He glanced at Weiss as he followed up the grenade with a blast from the assault rifle Dominic had brought him. "So I'm sitting on a bar stool at *Rico's*, catching up with an old buddy of mine, when Blake Fucking Satair strolls by leading an army of Justice dynes in the direction of this here building. Since I figured whatever he was up to was not good news for the good guys, I thought I should come rescue you."

"Rescue…me?" Weiss finally pointed his Glaser in a direction where it could be of use and fired past the barricade as one of the attackers climbed back to its feet and prepared to unleash a new barrage.

"Rescue anybody here I liked or…anyway, I guess Perrin has vouched you in. It's your lucky day."

Weiss winced as stray laser fire streaked overhead and debris rained down on them from the ceiling. "I respectfully beg to differ. What have you brought?"

"For one…." He counted down in his head until on cue, a powerful blast tore through the wall in front of them, creating a field of rubble that doubled as further protection for them. He gestured behind him. "I brought her."

Ava's skin shimmered from the active defensive shield she'd reluctantly installed after the Platform infiltration. "Where do you need me?"

"Use that new shield of yours to join the defenders up ahead and finish the damaged attackers off. Maggie, give her some support."

"Got it." The sisters hurried off into the billowing smoke toward the heart of the firefight.

Weiss stared at them both, then finally seemed to absorb the revised situation. "Nika's facing tough resistance at the west entrance. If your people help me clean up here, we'll head her way."

Joaquim cracked his neck and motioned several more people over to the barricade. "Dominic, escort Parc up to the data vault so he'll stop hyperventilating about the precious data. Ryan, send Ike-Bot with them, but you and WheatleyBot stay here. Let's move up to our new barricade and see if Ava's left us anything to shoot."

∧R

They left Ava and Maggie at the east entrance with two Justice officers to dispatch any late arrivals and trekked through a long field of smoke and debris toward the west entrance.

What they found when they arrived no longer resembled an entrance to anything. The ceiling and possibly the second floor above where doors used to be had completely caved in.

On the plus side, the wreckage provided plenty of cover. Amidst a blast of dust stirred up by an enemy dyne firing into the rubble, Joaquim scrambled forward and landed next to Nika, where she and Dashiel had set up a defensible position in one corner.

Nika spun around, bracing herself against a chunk of ceiling as her dust-coated face screwed up in surprise. "Joaquim?"

"Who else did you expect?" He jerked a greeting to Ridani, dropped to his knees and fired over the rubble.

"Me, probably." Weiss stumbled up to them and collapsed against the wall. "What's the situation?"

"Wish I could say, but our line of sight is for shit through this mess. We could really use a drone to scope out the attackers."

"Did somebody request a drone?" Ryan crawled toward them with WheatleyBot buzzing around his head.

Nika laughed, then started coughing. "Your sense of timing is impeccable, all of you." She motioned haphazardly in the air. "Do your thing, WheatleyBot."

Ryan made a more deliberate gesture, and the drone whizzed upward and darted over the rubble. Ryan's gaze blanked for a moment. "Four dynes are operational on our side, but six on theirs. Four Asterions attackers as well, but one's on the ground and—whoa!"

WheatleyBot careened back their way, smoke pouring out of a crack in its frame, and landed hard on the floor next to Ryan, who petted it reassuringly. "Yeah. That looks like all the players at present—wait a second. Parc says they need backup at the data vault. Intruders busted through the windows up on the sixth floor. How do I get there?"

Joaquim nudged Weiss in the side. "Tell him how to get there."

"I should go—" A blast shook the foundation of the rubble, sending chunks of concrete cracking apart and tumbling toward them, and everyone jumped back.

"No, you should stay here. Tell him."

"Right." Weiss pointed back the way they'd come. "There's a service lift down the first hallway to the left. I'll send you the access code and let Selene know you're on the way with a drone."

"Got it." Ryan grabbed WheatleyBot under his arm and hurried faster than safety dictated down the hallway then disappeared.

Joaquim squinted at the others. "If we add our firepower to that of the defenders on the other side of this barrier, the four of us can tip the odds and finish these assholes off. But we've got to find a way through this blockage, or we're just twiddling our thumbs waiting to be blown up." He checked his pack. "I've got one grenade left."

Weiss might have frowned; Joaquim couldn't tell. "If we blow a hole in the rubble, we risk simply opening a path for the attackers to get through, after which they'll have free reign of the building."

"Not if we don't let them get through. Weiss, can you warn your dynes to get clear of the right third of this pile, then to prepare for a charge by the attackers?"

"I can...done."

Joaquim nodded, and everyone moved farther backwards. He waited until they were five meters away from the bulk of the wreckage. "One hole coming up."

He pitched the grenade hard into the rubble, and it lodged between two slabs of ceiling material.

Everyone turned away and shielded themselves, but the detonation still sent an avalanche of debris raining down on them. In the aftermath, the dust grew so thick they could hardly breathe. But they needed to do more than breathe—they needed to move.

Nika ripped a strip of cloth off her shirt and tied it around the lower half of her face. "Defensive shields to full. Let's get to the other side while we have the advantage of surprise." Then she was scrambling through the small, jagged opening in the rubble the grenade had created.

Joaquim followed.

They stumbled out the other side into a firefight starting to lean in their favor. Three more attackers were down, giving the machine advantage to the defenders. Now, with their arrival, they had an Asterion advantage as well. One of the defending dynes grappled in close combat with an attacker; its left arm broke free and aimed for the head of the attacker—

—all the dynes, defending and attacking alike, dropped to the floor.

Weiss shouted off Joaquim's left shoulder. "EMP!"

But no energy pulse tingled his skin or shut down his systems. His shields didn't so much as fizzle. "I don't think so—get down!"

Laser fire shot past them as they dropped to the jagged, uneven floor. Joaquim stretched out one arm and manifested as wide an energy shield as possible. "More attackers are moving in!"

Weiss crawled outside of the shield's protection and leapt to his feet, Glaser steadied in both hands. "Drop your weapons and raise your hands in the air!"

As if *that* was going to work.... Muffled scuffling answered the order, followed by a new round of laser fire.

Joaquim pinged Nika. *Watch my back.* He shrunk the shield down to a manageable size and crept to the right wall, silently crawling over an inert dyne on the way. One of the Asterion attackers stood near what must have once been the entry doors, eyes darting between something outside and the scene inside.

Joaquim dropped the shield, extended his blade from his wrist, activated his kamero filter and closed the distance between them. His blade pierced the man's port and sliced all the way through to the front of his throat, killing all functionality instantly. He withdrew the blade and eased the body quietly to the floor.

Hq (visual, 70%) | scan.infrared(240°:80°)

The outlines of two more Asterions appeared, both slinking closer to the pile of rubble and its defenders. One positioned themselves flush against the wall, leaned out and aimed his Glaser at Weiss' head three meters away.

Joaquim sprinted forward, barely avoided tripping over an upturned slab of concrete, and drove his blade into the small of the man's back. They both tumbled to the floor.

Laser fire streaked above his head, but he couldn't worry about that. His arm and blade were twisted under the man's body and pinned painfully. The man's gun arm swung wildly for him, firing blindly. Joaquim slammed a forearm into the man's wrist, knocking the Glaser away.

The man's left hand jammed its way up Joaquim's chest to close around his throat. Fingers dug viciously into his windpipe, and for a second he feared it was about to get ripped it out.

He focused on what feeling remained in his pinned arm and with a grunt wrenched the blade around. The hand at his throat fell away.

He shoved the man to the side and dragged his arm free, then rolled the man onto his back.

Blood gurgled out from the lips of Blake Satair; malice shone hot from his dying eyes. "You...."

"Whatever. You're dead." He retrieved the discarded Glaser from the floor, pointed it at the man's forehead and fired.

A hand grabbed hold of one of his arms as he swayed unsteadily. Then another, on the other side. He gazed woozily at Nika, then at Weiss. "We get them all?"

"I think so, but we need to confirm. Dashiel, can you help him?"

Ridani appeared beside Nika. He didn't look much better than Joaquim felt, but he didn't seem to be having any trouble standing as he eased in and took Nika's place holding him up. "Come on, Lacese. Let's find a wall and check you for holes."

Weiss patted him on his broken shoulder, which was just uncalled for, then he and Nika vanished into the haze toward the blown-out entrance.

Ridani helped him pick his way through the debris to a span of wall. As he eased down to the floor, he glowered at Satair's body. "That was damn satisfying. He killed the love of my life, you know."

Ridani had the decency to act somber as he felt along the length of Joaquim's twisted arm for broken bones. "No, I didn't know. I'm sorry. He's hurt a lot of people."

"I'd say now he won't hurt any more, but you all will wake him back up in a new body in a few days, won't you? Put him back in a cell he'll break out of."

"We'll make sure he doesn't break out of the next one."

"Uh-huh." He glared at his right arm. The blade mechanism must have gotten jammed, because he couldn't get the blade to retract. "Just fashion me a sling or something. And put a sock over the tip of the blade."

"A *sock*?"

"Unless you have a better idea for how to keep me from slicing open everyone I pass. We need to ensure the first floor's clear then get upstairs. I assume people are trapped pretty much all over the building."

Nika and Weiss reemerged through the ruined entrance and came over to them. Nika scowled at his arm. "All the intruders are down on this side. This makes twice now you've popped up out of nowhere looking like shit."

Joaquim started to shrug, but thought better of it. "I do enjoy making an entrance."

Weiss actually chuckled. "You succeeded tonight, no question. Reinforcements will be here in sixty seconds to secure the perimeter, but we still need to secure the interior. Whoever is up to it, heading upstairs is a good idea. Selene's reporting they've subdued the intruders at the data vault, but I'd prefer additional guns to clear the floor. Nika, can you check on Spencer and those he took to the fifth floor? I'm going to the fourth to check on Perrin and her group." His eyes flitted to Joaquim as he said her name, but he didn't hesitate or stumble over it.

Joaquim breathed raggedly past his bruised-but-at-least-not-ripped-out windpipe and nodded at Weiss as Ridani helped him climb to his feet. "Yeah. You should do that. Now, where's my sling and my sock?"

34

MIRAI ONE PAVILION

S *pencer, what's your location?*
Fifth floor, east wing. If you're headed my way, bring help, because we have a problem.

And she'd thought this was over. *What happened?*

Before all the attackers shut down, they blew apart the wall and part of the ceiling, blocking access to the conference room. I was in the hall, but everyone else is trapped inside.

Everyone else included Maris. She filtered away the panic that surged. *On my way.*

Nika sent another ping as she stepped on the lift.

Josie, Geoff, if you're free of hostiles, meet me on the fifth floor, and bring whatever gear and weapons you can find.

Geoff responded. *Josie took a hit to the leg. She'll be fine. I'll bring Maggie.*

Maggie. A stab of guilt flared in her chest; she'd hardly had a chance to so much as say 'welcome back' to the woman since her regen. A wave of nostalgia chased the guilt. NOIR, The Chalet...a simpler time, before the world went mad.

Sounds good, Geoff.

The lift lurched to a crooked stop just short of the fifth floor. A chunk of the shaft wall had crumbled and lodged in the machinery, preventing the lift from traveling any higher. She hauled herself up and over debris partially blocking the opening, and found herself in the aftermath of a military-scale bombardment. Damn.

Satair had clearly intended to take out as many Advisors as possible, though she couldn't say—and didn't care—whether his motives had been mere base revenge or a more strategic desire to remove as many obstacles as possible to him and Luciene retaking control of the government. "Spencer?"

Motion to her right caught her attention; an arm waved through the dust-clogged air. She hurried down the hall and found Spencer on his knees beside a towering mound of cement, plaster and structural supports that stretched to the ceiling and beyond.

A thick layer of dust coated his skin, with multiple bloody rivulets streaming through the dust. A clot of blood soaked his hairline, and his left sleeve had darkened to crimson.

She frowned as she crouched in front of him. "You look terrible."

"Well, a good portion of the ceiling fell on me, so I would." He grimaced as he forced a half-meter chunk of ceiling off the pile and sent it rolling down the hall.

He was trying to dig out the people trapped in the room by hand. Admirable, but it was never going to work. She asked the question that had hovered on her tongue all the way here. "Maris?"

"She's functional. Injured, I think, though she won't admit it."

"And the others?"

"She said Basquan, Forchelle and three others are unconscious. Everyone else is ambulatory."

"All right. Here's what we're going—"

A commotion erupted to their left as Maggie and Geoff scrambled past debris and hurried toward them. Nika stood. "Tell me you have grenades."

Geoff patted a bag on his hip. "We raided the armory."

"Fantastic." She studied the wall, then turned back to Spencer. "How wide does the room stretch?"

Understanding dawned on his pained features. He gingerly stood and picked his way over to her, then took an additional five steps and flattened a hand on the wall. "At least to here."

It was closer to the towering debris than she preferred. Risky. But the conference room lay near the center of the building and enjoyed no exterior windows, which meant this was their best option. "Have Maris tell everyone inside to get to the far opposite corner."

She took one of the grenades from Geoff, then motioned him and Maggie farther away and studied the wall. The pile of debris.

The dimensions of the hallway. She'd overplayed this sort of gambit at The Chalet and nearly gotten one of her people killed for her efforts…she dialed down the setting on the grenade. She only needed a hole half a meter wide, after all. A little bigger would be better, but not at the expense of bringing the remainder of the ceiling down on them.

Spencer nodded as he joined Maggie and Geoff. "They're ready."

She placed the grenade at the base of the wall and activated it, then leapt away and sprinted down the hallway—

—the blast slammed into her back like a shockwave, sending her sprawling face-first to the floor at Geoff's feet.

"Oof!" She groaned but pulled her makeshift mask up over her mouth and nose and started crawling back the way she'd come.

Spencer limped past her and dropped to his knees in front of what might be a reasonable-sized hole in the wall. Too much dust clogged the air to tell for certain.

A head appeared through the jagged hole, followed by shoulders. Spencer helped—Nika squinted—someone she recognized but didn't know as they struggled the rest of the way through the hole and into the hallway. They gestured a thanks and climbed to their feet, only to take two steps and sag against the wall.

The shock of curly black hair that appeared next was unmistakable even coated in dust. Spencer took Maris' hand and carefully eased her through the hole. Once on this side she rose to her knees, then basically fell into Spencer's arms. Her left sleeve was torn open, revealing a nasty gash in her arm, and a more worrisome bloodstain decorated the white fabric of her shirt above her waist.

She blinked up at Spencer. "You saved us."

He cleared his throat awkwardly. "Actually, it was N—"

Nika chuckled to herself. "He certainly did. He's a hero."

Maris peered up at Nika and gave her a weak smile. She really didn't look good.

Adlai, Selene, Harris, whoever's available, we need to get first aid supplies to a central location—Conference Room 2-A if it's secured— and send the injured there.

Harris responded quickly. *I'm on the second floor already. I'll get on it.*

Thanks. Adlai, status report?

Justice reinforcements are in place around the perimeter. The first, second and third floors are confirmed free of hostiles, and no new incursions have been reported. We've got a sea of inert dynes littering the premises.

The shooting might be over, but the crisis was not. "We've confirmed the lower floors are clear of intruders. Let's move everyone to 2-A, where we can triage injuries while the rest of the scene is secured. Spencer, why don't you and Geoff go ahead and get Maris there, so she can get those wounds checked out. Maggie and I can get everyone else out."

Spencer stood and, despite his own considerable injuries, gathered Maris up in his arms and started carrying her down the hallway toward the lift.

Geoff looked at Nika in question, and she shrugged. "Go with them anyway. Spencer's apt to collapse any second."

"Yes, ma'am."

She turned back to where Maggie was helping more people extract themselves and joined her on the floor. "Thank you for the help. Are you hanging in there okay?"

"Body works like the new it is."

That wasn't exactly what she'd asked, but someone else struggled to crawl through the opening, and she let it go.

Five minutes later, a face stared at her through the opening. A Commerce Advisor, Edgar B'laughn. "Five people are unconscious in here, and—" he indicated his left hand, which dangled at an unnatural angle at his side "—I can't drag them out."

"Don't worry about it. We'll come in after you and bring them out."

He clambered out with their help. "Sorry."

"Don't be. Head to Conference Room 2-A and get yourself patched up."

Once she was sure B'laughn was moving under his own power, she shifted back to Maggie with a sigh. "In we go."

The room's interior hardly looked better than the exterior did. Several large pieces of ceiling had fallen free, and the bloodstains on the floor nearby suggested this was the cause of most of the injuries. That along with the disintegrated right wall, which now formed part of the debris field blocking the hallway.

Five bodies lay in the far-right corner. She recognized Basquan by his rich golden skin, though a layer of dust had turned his cardinal hair to clay, and Forchelle by his lengthy beard. One of the others worked for Basquan and had been a constant helpful presence at the Pavilion. Sandie? The other two were Katherine's subordinates in Admin, but she'd never caught their names.

She knelt beside Basquan and did a surface level scan. Heartbeat, weak but steady. No major leaking wounds. Great.

Forchelle wasn't so lucky. No heartbeat, no electrical activity. She rolled him onto his side and discovered why. The back of his skull had been crushed.

She dragged her hands down her face. She'd bet a reasonable sum of money he didn't have a psyche backup stored in any official repository. But any First Genner who had made it this long by definition possessed a fierce survival instinct; he must have backups stored *somewhere*. Maybe they'd even be able to find them.

Until then, she only hoped they'd learned all they needed from him. It was a harsh assessment, but desperation had chased her into a corner.

"This woman's got a bad bleed in her neck, but someone's bandaged it up. The other two are gone."

Nika looked up at Maggie. "Her name's Sandie. Let's try to gently move her and Mr. Basquan into the hallway. I bet response teams are on-site by now, and they can bring gurneys up here. I'll take facial scans of the victims, so if the building collapses before someone comes to move the bodies, we'll be able to identify them."

A shout from the other side of the hole echoed through the destroyed room. "Hello? Are there injured up here?"

"Sounds like a response team is already here."

"Oh, thank gods." Maggie slouched against the wall. "You know, waking up out of the blue and being told you'd died weeks earlier, your home's been destroyed, the government's been overthrown and a foul alien species is on their way here to make your death permanent? It's not as easy to recover from as it sounds."

She reached out and hugged the woman. "I know it's not. But we are going to survive this. I promise you."

AR

Nika stopped by 2-A to see for herself that triage and repair were in full swing and to check on Maris, who remained groggy but was being tended to by two med techs.

The adrenaline refused to dissipate quite yet, so after pinging Dashiel to make sure he and Joaquim were safe, she left the wounded with those better equipped to help them and went up to the data vault on the top floor.

An impressive wreckage of Justice dynes and drones, machine limbs and torn metal lay strewn across the entrance and decorated the front third of the room.

Inside, Ryan knelt beside the mangled but somewhat intact frame of IkeBot.

She crouched by the opposite side of the frame from him. "Ryan...."

He glanced up at her distractedly. Blood trickled out of a slice across the bridge of his nose, and he had the beginnings of a black eye. "It's okay. The damage isn't total. I'll be able to rebuild him."

"I've no doubt." She gave him an encouraging smile and squeezed his shoulder on her way to see Parc, who busily checked over a variety of server inputs and display outputs.

He looked as if he'd just come from a spa day. He didn't have so much as a speck of dust on him.

"Parc, did you let Ryan do all the defending while you hid behind the servers?"

"Hey, I was protecting the motherfucking data, thank you very much." He frowned and motioned her closer, then leaned in and dropped his voice. "IkeBot got smashed protecting me—and the data, but I suspect mostly me."

"Well, that's its job—protecting us."

"I know. But..." he rubbed at his jaw "...I'm thinking I'm going to have to make it up to Ryan somehow."

"Probably a good idea. So, the servers are functional?"

"A couple of surface scratches from flying debris, but they're intact and didn't suffer any power surges or structural damage."

"Excellent. They may be the only thing in the building that didn't. I passed Selene on the way in, and a Justice squad is coming up to stand guard. When they get here, you guys come down to Conference Room 2-D. We'll bring in some food, steal some bandages from the triage room and figure out where to go from here."

35

MIRAI ONE PAVILION

"It could have been much, much worse."

Nika nodded in vague agreement, though whoever had said it stood behind her and wasn't talking to her. For one, the data they'd accumulated on the Rasu, from hard facts to wild speculation, could have been destroyed. The leaders of the interim government they'd cobbled together could have been wiped out in one fell swoop, leaving the future of the Dominion to people like Blake Satair.

It was still bad. Nine people not counting the attackers had suffered total body loss, including Julien Grayson and Magnus Forchelle. Dozens more were seriously injured, including Maris—who Nika suspected had never experienced a firefight in her exceptionally long life, not even during the SAI Rebellion—though she was going to be okay after a short stay in a tank. The building had suffered widespread, significant damage, and the cost of repairs would reach into the millions.

But it could have been much, much worse.

Joaquim and Dashiel returned to the conference room carrying one and a half handfuls of coffee, since Joaquim's right arm remained in a makeshift sling.

Dashiel handed her a cup with a concerned look. "You're exhausted, aren't you?"

She dropped her forehead onto his chest. "I'm walking around, and I'm not even bleeding. I got off easy."

"We both did." He kissed the top of her head. "Katherine just walked in, and judging by the smoke coming out of her ears, she's itching to pick a fight. Let me go run interference and give everyone else some peace."

"You are a saint, Dashiel Ridani."

"I really am." He rolled his eyes as he stepped away.

Joaquim was leaning against a nearby table watching the room quietly, and she studied him over the rim of her coffee. "You seem...much better. In the head, I mean—you still look like shit. Are you back, or was this merely a drive-by heroic rescue?"

"I'm...hells, if I know. It appears you guys were lost without me, so...I guess I'm back?"

"And better."

He chuckled. "And better, too."

"Have you seen Perrin yet?"

"Nah. She's going to kick my ass, and, frankly, my ass has already been kicked more than enough for one day."

"I suspect she'll mostly be glad to see you. Can I ask, what did you do while you were gone? What brought about the reformation—or if not reformation, at least better mood?"

"You can ask, but I'll never tell."

"Get a little up-gen?"

He arched an eyebrow.

"Get fucked within a centimeter of your life by a beautiful woman?"

Nothing.

"Two beautiful women? Two beautiful men?"

Joaquim drew two fingers across his lips wearing a smirk. "Never telling."

"Ugh. Fine. Keep your damn secrets." She carefully draped an arm around his good shoulder. "Welcome back."

In her peripheral vision, she saw Perrin rush in then stop short when she spotted Joaquim. Nika dropped her arm and nudged him around to face the doorway.

Perrin glared at him for a solid five seconds before the hard edges of her expression melted away into a full-body sigh. She jogged over to him and wrapped him up in a hug. "You're an asshole. You know that, don't you?"

He returned the hug as best he could. "Yeah, I know that."

"Good." She stepped away and scrutinized him intently. "I'm happy you're here—tonight, specifically. And...I'm happy you're *here*."

"Me, too." He stared at the ceiling; took a sip of his coffee. "Your guy did all right tonight."

"Did he now?" Perrin acted as though she was going to hit him in his wounded shoulder but pulled her punch with a giggle.

Parc and Ryan arrived then, and Nika left Perrin and Joaquim to their awkward making up.

Ryan carried WheatleyBot under one arm. The drone seemed to be in better shape than IkeBot, though it was currently shut down.

Parc shook his head as she approached them. "Gods, this place is a wreck. Not this room necessarily, but the whole damn building. It looks like a cyclone tore through it, then an earthquake, then another cyclone."

"It does indeed. But it's also beginning to look like we came out okay, all things considered."

"Have you determined what the hells happened?"

"Someone, probably the officers who broke Satair out, had pulled three squads of Justice dynes out of rotation before they got reprogrammed and stashed them in a warehouse. As we'd suspected, Satair had inserted programming of his own that let him control them, and he used them to attack the Pavilion. As for the abrupt shut-down, a wide-field kill-code was issued that turned off all Justice equipment in the immediate area. The code was buried deep in their firmware, and none of the Justice Advisors knew about it, which we think means it came from Luciene. We figure Satair used it when he saw his dynes were losing the fight. Luckily, we were there waiting on him."

Joaquim appeared at her side. Coincidentally, Nika noticed that Adlai had returned and he and Perrin were talking in hushed whispers near the door.

He nodded at Parc and Ryan. "Thanks for answering the call tonight. Hey, Parc, if you've got a minute, I want to run an idea by you."

"Sure. Let's go find something alcoholic to spike this coffee with. We'll bring it in here, then Ryan can try to fix your blade mechanism, because...." Parc pointed at the sock covering Joaquim's exposed wrist blade and laughed.

"You know, I didn't come back and save all your asses to take this kind of abuse."

"Of course you did." Parc clapped him on the back and urged him toward the door. "But don't worry. Drinks will make it all better."

MIRAI

The news reports told the tale of the attack on the Mirai One Pavilion with breathless shock and dramatic turns of phrase, but Luciene controlled enough listeners embedded in the nex web to have learned the sordid details hours earlier.

Advisor Satair would not be returning to the safehouse tonight. Indeed, the man was out of commission until such time as those in power decided to regen him; the same fate appeared likely for the Advisor's lieutenants. The dynes under their control were shut down and headed off for reprogramming, if not scrapping.

Luciene's most substantial resources—funds, software, hard assets—had been seized by the Justice Division or his access revoked. He still enjoyed contacts, however—people beyond Satair who would do anything for him. People who remained afraid enough of him to do anything he asked of them.

But what would he ask of them?

It wasn't merely that Satair had failed, nor that with the man's failure Luciene's best chance to re-seize control of the framework of government had vanished. No, it wasn't the failure which triggered the descent of a miasma of despair more suffocating than any he recalled suffering in times past.

It was that the rebels and terrorists had *succeeded*. Succeeded in defeating Satair, succeeded in living to solidify their control over his government in the morning light. Succeeded in amplifying this strange, incomprehensible shame he could feel seeping into his bones.

He gazed out the window. There were no riots in the streets; not tonight or the night before or the night before that. Isolated pockets of unrest in the initial few days following the destruction of the Platform had been pacified with a restrained, gentle touch on the part of Justice and faded away.

Instead of rioting, looting and rending asunder the hallmarks of civilization, the people had peacefully risen up and come together in common cause.

The rebels and terrorists had somehow managed to catch themselves a Rasu. Then, they'd somehow managed to extract useful information from their prisoner. The details of their methods and the information which resulted remained hidden from him, but excited rumblings were spreading across the nex web, rumblings infused with an emotion he'd never imagined possible: hope.

They were still all going to die, of course, for this inevitability had been written into the stars eight years ago. Due to the traitorous actions of the rebels and terrorists, they might all die a bit sooner than they would have otherwise. But now? They were going to die with their heads held high, fighting for their lives with a fierceness of spirit he'd forgotten Asterions could possess.

Because he, Luciene Toskav, Asterion Dominion Guide of Synra for two hundred forty thousand years, had been…wrong. Wrong about nearly everything. When he gazed out the window, he felt the shame spread from his bones into his veins to infect his processes. The actions of his people brought honor upon themselves and shame upon him, and they knew nothing of the misery they inflicted on him by those actions.

He stood here and watched, but they didn't see him. They didn't think of him. He had fallen into irrelevance as the people took control of their own lives and their own future, short though it may be.

A bitter, frigid acceptance, comforting in its desolation, seized hold of him, and he sent a message to one of those people who would do anything he asked of them.

MULTITHREADING

DAYS UNTIL RASU DEADLINE: 12

36

NIKA'S FLAT

"You've got the new barriers I developed in place, right? I want you to feel safe."

Safe. The word held no subjective meaning for Nika. She'd never sought its peaceful embrace, and it had certainly never sought hers.

She recognized that Parc was going out of his way to assuage her concerns, but it wasn't working. What she felt was on edge. Frayed, as if too much power flowed through her veins. For the last five years, her mind had been sacrosanct. Fractured and lacking crucial pieces as it might be, it was the only thing she could cling to in order to prove she *was*. She existed as an independent, living soul.

She'd connected with other people on a superficial level multiple times. Dashiel, of course; Perrin and a few others. But in those instances, the rules and barriers were clear, defined and thoroughly tested. This, though? This was all new, and the only rules for it were the ones they made.

But if she was going to recommend to the other Advisors that they encourage the creation of these psyche collectives—or that they not—she owed it to everyone, but most of all herself, to understand precisely what she was recommending.

"I'm ready."

Parc grinned. "Then activate the new ocular setting and see the world change."

He was enjoying this way too much. She steeled herself, tensing her muscles like they were going to help protect her, and did as instructed.

Tendrils of spectral luminescence danced in the air around her, as if a full-dimensional overlay had been dropped atop the world. She reached out to grasp one of the strings, but her fingers slipped through the apparition. They had no tactility, no physical presence. The tendrils nevertheless seemed...*alive*. She laughed in delight.

"Hells of a sight, isn't it?"

"It's incredible. What do I do now?"

"Do you see the string leading to me?"

He sat across from her on a couch in her flat, and though a straight-line path existed from her to his location, the string in question undulated around its axis on its way to him. "I do."

"I'm letting you in. Open your conscious mind and follow where the string leads."

code fragments...

mock-up designs of slicing modules...

a flash of flesh, shouldn't go there...

a scene of PeterBot splitting into a hundred copies of itself and consuming IkeBot like a dinner feast—

"You wouldn't!"

"Nah. Not unless Ryan pisses me off."

"Is it always like this in your brain?"

"Honestly? Yes. But do you understand what you're seeing, or are you just viewing it like you would a vid?"

She contemplated his question...and realized she understood it all. Algorithms, schematics, esoteric ideas which hadn't reached fruition...many of them should be well beyond her knowledge or capabilities, but seen through the lens of his processes, she understood what he understood. More than this, they felt as if they were her own thoughts, her own ideas.

A novel approach to slicing double-encrypted databases bloomed in her mind; she explored the logic and the discarded choices leading to the final design as if they'd originated whole cloth as her own creation. Only they had not.

"How?"

"I wish I could tell you. I'm working on it. But I think it has some-thing to do with how deeply the kyoseil is integrated into our individual neural frameworks, yet somehow still linked to kyoseil integrated into other neural frameworks. Your kyoseil is interacting with mine on a far deeper level than merely exchanging data. It's exchanging not merely thoughts, but the formation of the thoughts—how they came to be and where they lead. Now, let me in."

She hesitated. Instinctive protectiveness flared.

"It's okay. The barrier is still in place, and it will default to protecting your core programming and memories. You share only what you choose to share. You have the power."

I have the power. Pretty flimsy as mantras went, but she repeated it several times anyway as she opened the gates to her mind.

"Hee-hee."

"Parc!"

"Sorry. Show me the Rasu. From the simex."

Her recall command executed instantaneously, and they were both in the memory. He took control, speeding forward to the moment when the Rasu executed the natives in the most horrific of ways.

"Yep, that's about what I would expect from these monsters."

Forward again, racing through endless corridors and rooms until they reached the command center in the heart of the ship.

"Stop fixating on the vortex. I need to see the equipment."

"I can't change the content of the memory, Parc."

"Fine. Okay...here!" The memory froze when she looked at the bank of equipment behind her, searching for a way she might disrupt the power flow. Then it advanced a microsecond. Froze. Another microsecond. Froze. Faster now, ahead several milliseconds. Froze.

Finally they were racing for the end, blades and running and the Rasu surrounding them, and in a flash of blinding light it was over.

"The pulses the equipment emit are part of their language. They're displaying what the equipment is doing and the data it's outputting, right there for all to see."

Nika frowned in her mind. "I didn't see it."

"You were busy. You were on the right track, though. That piece of equipment was monitoring the electrical charge in the crystals down in the pit."

"...And now we know a little more about how their weapons operate, thanks to you."

"Well. I guess that's true. Now, for the next step. Ryan, are you here?"

"No, I'm at the deli shop on Caraden."

New thoughts swirled into the melting pot, a shocking number of them relating to dyne hardware and drone components. Emotions, too...concern, empathy, fondness, conflict—

"Ryan, we're not alone in here."

"I know. Sorry. How about this?"

The gooey warmth of melted cheese flooded her tongue, followed by the abrupt crunch of toasted bread. Crumbs caught in the corners of her mouth, and a hand not hers wiped them away.

She blinked in her mind. "Whoa. Who's hungry?"

"Right? Ryan's a natural at sensory transmission. Which is—" a wave crashed over her, neither imagery nor thought but sheer sensation, and she comprehended exactly what it was, and now she needed a cold shower *"—a fun way to show off one of the features of this type of meld. Ryan, order me one of those sandwiches. I'll be there in ten minutes. Nika, are you ready to wrap this up?"*

To withdraw from the meld was to become...lesser. Her skin felt restrictive, her mind sluggish and limited. She blinked repeatedly and rubbed at her face. "Bit of a kick at the end there."

"Yeah."

"The melding could get addictive quickly. We'll need to plan for that."

"Sure. Go ahead and plan. But you understand now, don't you? You understand what this can mean for us? Imagine ten, twenty, fifty people all sharing the same mindspace! Imagine what we can discover, invent, dream up?"

"No, I get it. And I have to admit we need it badly." She exhaled slowly. "I'll recommend that we move forward with the program—

officially, as I realize none of us can stop it now, even if we wanted to. But I do wonder…if we survive the Rasu, what is this going to mean for our future?"

Parc reached over and squeezed her hand in a rare show of earnest affection. "Let me show you something. Let's go out on the balcony."

She followed him outside. Hataori Harbor sparkled in the bright afternoon light. The sights and sounds of a living city spread out beneath them, vibrant and bustling.

"One hells of a view you've got here."

"It is."

"Now reactivate the ocular setting."

Even though she knew what was coming, even though she tried to prepare herself, her knees almost buckled beneath her. She fell against the railing, gripping it with all her strength to anchor herself to this physical spot.

Spectral luminescence painted the sky in a brilliant prism of colors. The streets, the buildings. Most of all, the people. Tendrils wound through and around them like the very atoms of the universe, binding them all together in a miraculous web of light.

"What is this going to mean for our future? Something wonderful."

37

MIRAI ONE PAVILION

Adlai dodged two construction mechs as he made his way toward the new but makeshift entrance to the Pavilion. Buildings kept exploding, and they kept patching them back together.

The damage to the Pavilion from the attack was significant enough that they really should move their base of operations somewhere else, again. But the repairs to Mirai Tower weren't finished, and they were almost out of time. The Rasu expected a shipment of Asterions in stasis chambers in less than two weeks, and they couldn't afford to spend a single hour of that time transferring servers across town or adding security to yet another new location. So, they would make do.

He'd taken two steps inside when a ping arrived from Spencer.

Francis Wallman just got caught at a checkpoint trying to flee to Adjunct Shi. A squad is transporting him to the Mirai Justice Center now.

His pulse quickened. Finally, a break.

I'm on my way.

MIRAI JUSTICE CENTER

Adlai rushed into the interrogation wing displaying a fervor he hadn't felt in weeks. Spencer was reviewing security procedures with the officer on duty, but he came over as soon as Adlai arrived.

"The prisoner's secured and ready for you. He didn't put up much of a fight, according to the logs." Spencer motioned toward the cell. "I've spent a little bit of time with Officer Wallman recently. My estimation? He's scared. Play it right, and he'll talk."

Adlai nodded. "Let's hope so." He donned his interrogator guise and walked into the cell.

Officer Francis Wallman vibrated in the utilitarian chair. His hands were restrained to the table at the wrists, and he'd fisted them together. His eyes darted to Adlai, then back to his hands. "Sir, I was acting under orders."

"Illegal orders. Blake Satair had been removed as a Justice Advisor, and you damn well knew it."

"But he's been my Advisor since I joined Justice eighty years ago. I believed in his leadership and his vision. We were trying to do the right thing."

"So you say. It will pain you to learn, then, that Satair suffered total body loss during the attack on the Pavilion. He will be regened and tried for his new crimes in due time, but not until after the current crisis is resolved, so he won't be coming to your aid anytime soon.

"Your cohort Oliver Perotski suffered significant bodily trauma during the firefight as well, and he's in custody. The attack on the Pavilion—on the Advisors and the lawful government of the Dominion—failed, completely and absolutely. And it was the best hand Satair had to play. Your side has lost, Officer Wallman, and it *should* have.

"Listen. I like you. You're a good officer. I don't want to believe that you're a traitor or hopelessly corrupt. I *want* to believe that you meant what you said about trying to do the right thing. But what Satair did was not the right thing, and if he had succeeded, it would have spelled the end of the Dominion. Forever."

"Sir, I—"

"Why didn't you participate in the attack on the Pavilion? Why weren't you there?"

His head hung; a slight tremble developed in his hands atop the table. "I didn't want anyone else to get hurt. Advisor Satair was so angry after we freed him…it spooked me. And Guide Luciene? He's terrifying. I started to second-guess the wisdom of their plans. And when it came time to move on the Pavilion…I ran instead."

"*That* was the right choice, Francis." Adlai rubbed at his jaw, as if a thought had suddenly come to him. "You left Luciene unprotected?"

"There are dynes guarding the house. I panicked, okay?"

House—the data point eliminated several thousand potential locations. "I understand. I would have panicked, too. Where is Luciene now?"

Wallman shrank down in his chair. "I can't tell you, sir. He's a Guide, and I won't betray him."

"He's not a Guide any longer. You can't betray him, because he doesn't rule us, and you no longer owe any allegiance to him. Where is he?"

Wallman stared down at his shoes. His chest rose and fell in rapid heaves.

"Tell me—truthfully—and I'll ensure you don't get an R&R sentence. It won't be soon, but you will walk free one day. Keep silent, and…" he waved his hand dismissively "…it's almost certainly lights out for you."

"But the Rasu are going to kill us all, anyway."

"Not if we can help it. And we can help it a lot better if we know Luciene is safely locked away, where he can't interfere to disastrous consequences. Where is he?"

Wallman's gaze rose to meet Adlai's, eyes wide and bloodshot, pupils dilated. "You truly believe you all can save us?"

"I do."

"He's in Synra One, in a house on Markham Drive."

〤R

SYNRA

They moved on the house under full stealth. Thirty meters out, they used the same kill code Satair had employed at the Pavilion to disable the dynes and drones guarding the house. If any guards were stationed inside, Luciene had just been alerted to the raid, but they already had the site surrounded and aerial drones in place. It wouldn't matter.

Adlai took point and breached the door. A dyne lay crumpled on the floor to the left, at the entrance to a small kitchen. Through the main room, a person stood at a glass patio door.

In Adlai's peripheral vision, Spencer and Selene's Glasers rose to match his. "Luciene Toskav, you are under arrest. I implore you to surrender yourself without resistance. We will disable you if we must, but we want to resolve this in a peaceful manner."

Luciene slowly turned around, hands held out beside him to show he carried no weapons. "None of that will be necessary, Advisor Weiss. I won't be troubling you any further. I have failed you. I have failed the Dominion. I have failed myself. Better to delete this soul and start again."

The former Guide crumpled to the floor in a heap.

"Check him!" Adlai motioned Selene forward while he quickly cleared the remaining rooms of the small house.

When he returned, Selene was glowering at the body. "What was the point of this? Why bother with a dramatic exit when we'll simply regen him and stick him back in his prison?"

Spencer holstered his Glazer as he emerged from the kitchen. "Harris and I just received an alert from the Justice Evidence Warehouse on Ebisu. There's been an explosion."

He and Selene both spun toward him. "How bad is it?"

"Can't say for certain yet. Emergency responders are still en route." He indicated the pile of robe and limbs on the floor. "But according to the timestamp on the alert, the explosion occurred five seconds before Luciene self-destructed."

Adlai ran a hand along his jaw. "We'll see where the evidence leads, but it's possible we just watched a genuine suicide take place. I think he knew we were coming, and I think he blew up his own backups so we wouldn't be able to regen him."

"If so, he blew up the other former Guides' backups as well."

"They can make new ones." He shook his head...not quite in mourning, for he would not miss the man, but in sorrow nonetheless. The Rasu had brought the specter of final death back to the Asterions, in more ways than one. "But not him."

Selene knelt beside the body and closed its unseeing eyes. "All that processing power, all that intellect, all that incomprehensibly vast knowledge, and he couldn't live with the paradox reality presented to him."

"What paradox is that?"

"That what he knew to be true, wasn't."

38

NIKA'S FLAT

Nika did a quick inspection of the living room and nodded to herself. It truly was designed for entertaining, which meant she didn't need to do much rearranging or staging. As long as there was food and drink, a crowd could inhabit the space comfortably for many hours.

Perrin had arrived a few minutes earlier bearing bags upon bags of food. She'd entrusted Ava and Maggie with bringing drinks, which Nika wasn't certain had been the best idea. Ava was likely to show up with barrels of rectified ethanol and zero wine. But she was happy to give Maggie things to do—things that didn't involve shooting attackers inside collapsing buildings—to ease her back into the world of the living, and Ava seemed eager to help with it as well.

Hopefully, all her guests wouldn't end up with alcohol poisoning.

She'd checked on Maris before returning home and had found Spencer tending to the woman's recovery quite well. He'd never struck her as the tender type, so it had been a bit of a shock to see. Part of her suspected Maris of playing the delicate flower and Spencer of falling for it; on the other hand, she needed to remember that while the Pavilion attack resembled an average day at the office for her, the same wasn't true for people like Maris.

The doorbell rang, and she accessed the hallway cam before answering it. Given what Satair had almost pulled off at the Pavilion, they didn't dare discount the possibility of renewed attacks on the Advisors.

Parc fidgeted in the hallway. She laughed to herself and opened the door. "You're early. You might as well have stayed here this afternoon."

"But then I would have missed an amazing grilled cheese sand-wich at the deli on Caraden." He strode in, went to the kitchen, and grabbed a handful of nuts from the bowl Perrin had set on the counter less than ten seconds earlier. "I wanted to talk to you about something before everyone arrived."

Perrin glanced over her shoulder from inside the pantry. "Talk to me?"

"Nah. I mean, you can chime in if you have an opinion, and I bet you will. So, Nika."

She leaned against the wall. "I'm listening."

He strode around the living room popping peanuts into his mouth between sentences. "These melds—though I prefer the term gestalts—we're creating? They need a name. Calling them 'hive minds,' which I've already heard several people doing, is both lame and flagrantly inaccurate, because nobody's losing any individuality here. You know this. 'Group minds' is more accurate, but easily as lame."

Nika shrugged. "I don't disagree. Collective consciousness nodes?"

"You have no imagination, woman. Besides, they're not so much collectives as coalescences—ooh! Coalescences of cerebral ac-tivity. We can call them COBRAS."

She stared at him deadpan. "We're not calling them COBRAS."

"Are you sure?"

"Yes."

"Ugh, fine. Let's see...."

"Noesis? Or noetics?"

"It's taken." A wicked smirk grew on his features, and he crossed his arms triumphantly across his chest. "I've got it: CERAFFIN. That's the plural. CERAFF in the singular, just to be clear."

Perrin giggled from the kitchen, where she was stacking trays of food in the refrigeration unit.

Nika arched an unimpressed eyebrow, but said nothing, wait-ing for him to make his case.

"It's a totally legitimate acronym. It stands for Cerebral Affinity. Little groupings of thought affinities, see?"

"That are angelic in nature."

"Well, I'll leave that for others to judge."

She sighed so dramatically, Maris would be proud. "I'm not going to be able to talk you out of this, am I?"

"Nope. You Advisors can give them a different name if you want, but we're all using ceraffin—no caps, I think. It's going to stick."

"Is it?"

"Yep. I'm never wrong about these things."

Sadly, he rarely was…and she supposed he did deserve to name them, since they were his creation. "Time will tell. Since you're here, make yourself useful. Take those bowls on the dining table, fill them with chips and put the bowls on all the living room tables."

"Absolutely. In one minute." The glee faded from his tone, and his voice dropped to a murmur, possibly so Perrin couldn't hear him. "He's dead, by the way."

She frowned in concern. "Who's dead?"

"My other self. At the Rasu stronghold. After I left here this afternoon, I reached out for the kyoseil strings leading to him—it's something I've been doing every so often—and they were gone. Which means he's gone. I thought you'd want to know."

"Parc, I am so, so sorry."

"No, don't be! It sucked where he was, believe me. I'm glad, deeply glad, it's over for him. Maybe he can find some peace now."

She studied him briefly, then took his hands in hers. "You didn't erase any of the memories you accessed through him, did you?"

One side of his mouth curled up in a sad little half-smile…then he waved her off and jogged toward the dining table. "Perrin, talk to me about these chips!"

Perrin motioned toward one of the bags she'd deposited on the kitchen counter, and Parc grabbed it and started dumping the contents into bowls.

Once he began distributing them around the living room, Nika went into the kitchen to see how she could help.

Perrin came up beside her. "He really is okay now, isn't he?"

She hesitated. But if he'd been carrying around those horrible memories all this time, he must have found his own measure of peace with them. "I think so, especially since now he has a new toy to show off. It doesn't mean there aren't scars lurking beneath the veneer, though, or that they'll heal anytime soon."

"What he's doing? It isn't just a new toy, Nika. The ceraffin are going to change things."

She groaned. "It's been two minutes, and he already has you calling them that."

"It's a good name. And something that's going to change the world needs a good name."

Something that's going to change the world. The notion still made her deeply uncomfortable, but mostly she hoped there was a world left to change.

⋏R

Nika Kirumase had surely never thrown a party *this* big in her flat. The crowd filled the expansive living room and spilled over into the kitchen and dining area and out onto the balcony. Granted, it was for now less a party and more a meeting, but she suspected this wouldn't last for long.

She'd moved one of the couches flush against the windows, and once Perrin and Joaquim were situated, she sat down between them.

From this vantage, they looked out on virtually the entire active membership of NOIR, including everyone who'd suffered body loss in the events of the last few months. Maggie sat on the floor next to Ava, who whispered likely devious plans in her sister's ear while Carson tried to eavesdrop behind them. Parc and Ryan were making a deliberate effort to engage Cair in conversation by the kitchen counter, though she didn't want to hazard a guess at how well it was going.

"Are we ready?"

Perrin passed a bowl of chips across her to Joaquim. "I think so. If you are?"

Nika reached out and patted Perrin's hand, then did the same to Joaquim's hand, whether he liked it or not. "We're ready."

She picked up her wine glass, extended her wrist blade and tapped the broad side of the blade against it. "Attention, everyone. Pipe down for a minute, will you? Only for a minute, I promise— then we'll open the secret closet holding the real alcohol that Ava sneaked in."

The blade retracted, and she sipped on her wine while the last conversations faded. "Thank you all for coming. You've succeeded in making this palatial spread I lucked into feel small and cramped, which is quite a feat. It's been a wild couple of months. Often exciting, sometimes heartbreaking. We lost some of you for a while there, and we are so glad to have you back with us tonight."

Perrin jumped in before Nika could continue. "I want to say that I am proud beyond measure of each and every one of you. Proud of how you've handled terrible crises and suffering, how you've stepped up to help others even when you've lost so much. You've risen to the challenge again and again, and it's not just us who are grateful. It's the entire godsdamn Dominion."

Someone hooted from the kitchen, and a few seconds of celebratory exchanges broke the formality of their speechifying. Nika nudged Joaquim in his side. A few days ago, she'd worried he wouldn't be here for any more NOIR gatherings. But now he was, and it made everything about this moment better.

He took the cue and stood to wander toward the kitchen while he chimed in. "What I keep coming back to is this: we succeeded in our mission. The Guides are imprisoned for their crimes against the people. The oppressive laws and unfair sentences they imposed on the innocent are being rolled back and people freed." He grabbed a fresh beer from the cooler, opened it, and tipped it toward Nika.

"And while none of this would have happened without the damn fine work of everyone here, we also owe everything to Nika...and owe at least a tiny bit to her new colleagues."

She burst out laughing. "Thank you, Joaquim. I'll make it a point to pass on your appreciation. Yes, as I assume everyone knows by now, I've agreed to again serve as an Advisor, because I want to make sure we get it right this time. We're working to build a government that is more open, more adaptive and more free than the Dominion has ever seen.

"I know some people may ask, 'what's the point?' Yes, we face a grave threat to our lives—to our continued existence—from the Rasu. But we've taken control of our own destiny, dammit, and by doing so I truly believe we can meet and defeat this threat. I believe we can do anything."

She sniffled, hurriedly wiping away a tear from her cheek. Dammit, these people did not need to see her cry. She was their leader. Their beacon. Their strength.

Perrin wrapped her arms around Nika in a melodramatic hug— and then the tears were a joke and everyone laughed, and it was okay. Still, her eyes stung as she began again. "Because of the work you've been doing, no one is calling NOIR terrorists any longer. Instead, they're calling us protectors.

"NOIR now means the people who are helping to rebuild all that crumbled under the Guides. You don't need to live separate and cut off from the rest of society any longer. You're an integral part of it, and it needs you. From now on, we're all in this together."

Dominic stood up near the back of the room. "Hey, Nika, we're all going to need tissues at this rate, because this is starting to sound like a goodbye."

"No." She shook her head with a smile. "This is not a goodbye— this is not the end. Perrin, Joaquim and I will always be here for every one of you, and I hope you'll always be there for each other. You're changing the world, and hopefully very soon you'll get to live in peace in it.

"And thanks to Parc, we've discovered we're even more connected to one another than we ever realized. I should add that he's agreed to host a NOIR-only ceraff in his brain, so if you're brave enough to venture into that house of horrors—"

"Hey!"

Perrin rolled her eyes. "Oh, hush! You know she speaks the truth."

"That's beside the point." Parc made a show of sagging in defeat. "Fine. I'll do a little spring cleaning."

"Everyone thanks you in advance. As I was saying, if you're brave enough to venture into Parc's spring-cleaned brain, you'll find you're among friends."

She drew in a deep breath. "Serving as your leader has been the greatest honor of my many lives. And with this, I call an end to official operations of the bad-ass, freedom-loving, people-rescuing, life-saving organization known as NOIR."

39

MIRAI ONE PAVILION

Nika walked amidst the projection of the Rasu stronghold—the city-sized platforms, the star-sized Dyson lattice and the bustling traffic of ships that buzzed around and through her physical presence here.

While she, Dashiel, Adlai and Joaquim had fought off a bloody coup attempt by Satair, Lance Palmer had taken a flight of cloaked military vessels deep into the heart of the enemy's lair and returned with a far more detailed analysis of the stronghold than she and Dashiel had managed during their brief visit. The man had taken a tremendous risk—every foray into the home of their enemy was a tremendous risk—to get actionable, military-quality data. Now they merely needed to fulfill the 'actionable' mandate.

She ignored the chills the tableau evoked to concentrate on its content. "The Dyson lattice looks as though it's constructed of Rasu, exactly like everything else."

Lance nodded. "That was our conclusion as well."

Dashiel frowned as he, too, wandered through the projection. "This means the entire Dyson lattice is alive. What a horrible, thankless existence."

"Now we know why Jerry didn't go back home. Why it wants to be free."

Dashiel's expression contorted; he continued to be skeptical about ascribing nuanced desires to the alien. "I suppose. So, Palmer, can we blow them up?"

"I was about to ask you the same thing."

"Fair enough. Jerry has *graciously* lent us a tiny piece of itself to run tests on. The initial findings alone will take us months if not years to analyze fully, but in the default state it arrived in, we can characterize it as a ductile, paramagnetic metal similar to vanadium or niobium. When we start studying the atomic structure itself, however, that structure becomes variable. We don't know whether this is a form of wave function collapse, which would imply the Rasu exhibit quantum mechanical characteristics at a macro level, or if it's evidence they don't possess a default—"

"Ridani, focus. Can we blow them up?"

Nika covered her mouth to silence the chuckle that bubbled up. Since she'd known Dashiel this time around, they'd spent ninety percent of their time either running for their lives or shooting at things trying to kill them. This was the first time she'd seen him display such pure enthusiasm over scientific minutia, over metals and atoms. It was delightful, yet also a wistful reminder that his life had not begun the day he'd met her, not even the first time. Before he'd become a titan of industry, he'd been a scientist-turned-engineer. An inventor.

After they survived this crisis, she'd ask him to tell her about that time in his life.

"Sorry. With sufficient force correctly targeted, yes, but only briefly. Their atoms use strong but dynamic—yes, this is relevant—covalent bonding, which means high-energy blasts will be required to, say, punch a hole in Jerry. The energy required to punch a hole in one of these platforms?"

He reached out and let his hand hover around a projection of one of the thousands of platforms. "We've never built a weapon capable of delivering that amount of energy. We can, but then we'd need to build a ship large enough to wield it. Alternatively, we can try to build a collection of linked explosive charges strong enough to get the job done, though getting them all into place without being detected will be a formidable challenge.

"But even if we manage to blow up some of their ships or platforms, it doesn't solve our problem. We just end up creating a bunch of smaller Rasu, and like Jerry did on the planet, before long they'll make their way back together and re-form into big Rasu. We can theoretically, maybe, win a firefight on a given day, but our enemy will simply show up again the next day, ready and able to fight the same battle all over again."

Lance exhaled harshly and stared at the projection with piercing intensity, as if he were trying to intimidate it into giving up its secrets. "What will it take to genuinely destroy them? To dissolve them so thoroughly that they can never re-form?"

"To break all these platforms and structures and ships apart at a subatomic level?" Dashiel spread his arms wide and sighed. "Wild guess? A hundred thousand nuclear bombs, all detonated at point-blank range. And even that might not be enough. It could require a million bombs, or a hundred million...." His voice trailed off as his head tilted, his eyes narrowing at the procession of platforms passing in front of him.

After a few seconds, he started muttering half-formed phrases to himself. "Yes, but how...no, it wouldn't...oh, but if one were to somehow...." He drew back and considered the larger projection, beyond the orbiting platforms. "It would require...." His gaze unfocused.

She couldn't stand it any longer. "Dashiel, do you have an idea?"

His lips slowly curled up, blossoming into a devious smile when he turned to her. "Several. Give me four hours." Then he spun and hurried out of the room.

Lance stared at the closing door. "What does he mean? Where is he going?"

Nika shrugged. "I don't know, but I suggest we give him his four hours."

⅄R

EBISU

"Dashiel Ridani to see Simon Granger." He placed his fingertips on the scanner, this time absent any accompanying low-grade fear or tension.

"Identity confirmed. You are cleared to proceed. Take the lift to the twelfth floor."

He did so with something approaching a spring in his step. He'd learned a great deal from being on the run with Nika, and the experience had brought its share of unique pleasures, but it felt good to be wearing his own skin again—privileges, baggage and all.

The Briscanti Materials CEO sat at his desk working, but he stood and came over as soon as Dashiel entered, hand extended. "Dashiel, it's good to see you."

"Simon." He shook the offered hand. Yes, it definitely felt good to be wearing his own skin again. "Thanks for fitting me in on such short notice."

"Certainly. I've been following developments as much as I can." The man motioned him over to the conference table. "You've got quite a lot going on. How can I help?"

As he sat in one of the chairs, he told what he hoped was the only lie he'd need to tell today. "Advisor Weiss is a friend of mine. He filled me in about his conversation with you a few weeks ago regarding your lab outpost on SR86-Roku."

The man nodded solemnly. "My employees...I expect they're victims of the Rasu now."

"I'm deeply sorry."

"I feel like there should have been something I could have done to prevent it. There were unusual aspects to the transaction, and I should have pushed harder for details. Perhaps I could have saved their lives."

"I understand what you mean, but it wasn't your fault. Asking questions likely would have only gotten you into deeper trouble. But you *can* help us make sure no one else suffers the same fate."

"I can't imagine how, but I want to try."

"Excellent. Talk to me about kyoseil and alisinium—specifically, their volatility when combined."

"It depends on the allotrope of alisinium you use. Two of the allotropes remain stable, but the synthesized compounds' performance is disappointing. Three allotropes display varying levels of instability—one is prone to breaking down, and the other two are prone to exploding. The sixth allotrope shows a lot of promise when combined with kyoseil. Its performance is exceptional, and it is fairly stable during normal operation. Unfortunately, the potential electrical output when power flows exceed strict parameters is too high to be safe for personal use.

"When Conceptual Research took over—when they bought the assets, anyway—we were working on developing safety controls we hoped would allow the compound to be used in commercial applications. As it stands today, though, I wouldn't be comfortable recommending its use even in high-risk industrial settings."

During the trip here, the images Palmer had captured of the Rasu stronghold had run in a constant loop in Dashiel's mind. The massive platforms and the immense Dyson lattice, all orbiting an M2 V red dwarf star, draining the celestial object of its power. They could in theory inflict a fair amount of temporary damage on the structures, but they lacked the weaponry to *destroy* them, and they weren't going to be able to build it in ten days.

He'd told Nika and Palmer it might take a million nuclear bombs to trigger the level of destruction they needed, but the entire Rasu stronghold orbited a celestial object that generated the energy of four hundred million nuclear bombs every *second*.

All they had to do was get the Rasu to that energy, or that energy to the Rasu.

He'd almost dismissed the great-in-theory, impossible-in-practice idea the instant he'd thought of it. But then he'd remembered how Jerry had been damaged by an unexpected solar flare—damaged badly enough that it had tumbled helplessly through a planet's atmosphere and crashed on its surface. Badly enough that it had taken the Rasu months to repair itself.

And maybe, just maybe, there was a nugget of possibility in there they could work with.

"High electrical output, you say? Simon, are you aware of the ceraffin?"

"Are you kidding? News of them has spread like wildfire across the Dominion. I expect by tonight, there won't be a single person who hasn't heard about them."

"Have you tried one out yet?"

"Oh, gods, no. You?"

"Briefly." Dashiel steepled his hand at his chin. "I need you to create a ceraff with me. I also want to invite Bruno Galesh, a metals expert, and Tamara Holtzen, a power expert." He wished he could include Forchelle as well, but the forensics team tasked with locating the man's psyche backup had thus far come up empty.

"I know Bruno, and Tamara by reputation. Are you certain it's safe?"

"Safe for your own psyche, you mean? I am. So long as you activate the defense barrier designed for use with the ceraffin, your processes, programming and memories are in no danger. Please, Simon. We must come up with a plan to destroy or at a minimum severely cripple the Rasu, and we are out of time. I have the beginnings of an idea, but I need the knowledge and expertise of all three of you to transform it into a workable plan. Right here, right now."

"Well, I did say I wanted to help. I'm in."

40

MIRAI ONE PAVILION

Nika hurried back to the conference room Lance had commandeered after returning from the Rasu stronghold. Dashiel arrived thirty seconds later, and she met him at the door. "Now you're the one who looks exhausted."

"I did spend the last two-and-a-half hours in a ceraff with three of the smartest people in the Dominion." He tapped his temple. "Things are a bit overcooked up here at the moment."

"I'm sure. What did you learn?"

He cupped her face and kissed her softly. "I might just have an almost-plan to save us."

"You're astounding. Can we hear what it is?"

"Yes, please." Lance stood in the center of the room, arms crossed over his chest. The projection had been reactivated, and tiny Rasu behemoths swarmed around him.

Dashiel chuckled under his breath. "First, the good news: we don't need a million nuclear bombs, or even a hundred thousand, to destroy the stronghold."

"Why not?"

He joined Lance at the center of the room and made a show of nudging the man off to the side. Then he reached up and wound his hand around the star at the center, though even at a micro-scale his hand stretched less than a third of the way around the celestial object. "Because you're looking at one of the most powerful nuclear bombs in the universe right here."

"Um...." Lance frowned.

Nika didn't. "Of course! Not to mention the tremendous temperatures in the corona. But mostly the nuclear fusion in the core."

"Yes. And the Rasu are already gathering and amplifying the star's power for us."

Lance's frown deepened. "Great. How is this going to help us?"

"We are going to use the Dyson lattice to create the galaxy's biggest power surge."

"Still waiting on an explanation."

"Okay. First, open up the comm system so the rest of the Advisors can listen in, then tell them they should want to."

Nika waved Lance off, went to the control panel by the door and took care of it. "Done."

"Thanks. Here's the short, somewhat understandable version: we send the Rasu the stasis chambers they are expecting, only we line them with a kyoseil-alisinium composite that, when exposed to the right dose of electricity, turns into a runaway energy fuse. We rig the chambers so we can set off those fuses on command and all at the same time.

"In doing so, we cause an explosion powerful enough to temporarily blow up the platform containing the chambers. But more crucially, we create a massive *electrical* explosion.

"Depending on how the platforms draw power from the Dyson nodes, the explosion should create a surge strong enough to send power flowing in the opposite direction, back to the Dyson nodes. Hopefully this will trigger an overload and an additional surge back toward the star, but it will almost certainly destroy the nodes and set off a cascading failure across the lattice. The destroyed nodes and their framework will quickly fall into the star's corona."

Nika smiled. "I am a fan of blowing up the platform where they're conducting the experiments on our people. If nothing else, it'll end the suffering of any Asterions who are still alive in there, and it should also destroy any data they've gathered from their experiments."

Lance gestured dismissively toward Dashiel. "I can think of at least twenty-one problems with your plan."

"I'm not surprised. What's the first one?"

"For starters, Nika here made us wake up everybody who was in the stasis pods. The Rasu will notice if the ones we send are empty, so who do we send?"

"We'll figure it out later."

Nika laid a hand on Dashiel's arm. "I won't send a single additional person to that place—not to get tortured, and not to die."

"I know. We'll figure something out."

She didn't argue, not for now. But in the back of her mind, she started figuring it out for herself.

Lance didn't look mollified. "This is great in theory. But if we don't succeed in destroying the rest of the platforms, most of the ships and, more importantly for our slightly longer-term survival, the communications satellites, all we'll have really done is piss them off."

"If we take out the Dyson lattice, we'll deprive the Rasu of their power source for a while, which will slow them down. But I agree—we need to take out everything else in the stellar system, too."

"And you have a plan to do this?"

"I have a sketch of a plan. The details will fall disproportionately to you."

Lance made a circular motion with one hand, indicating for Dashiel to keep talking.

"Jerry said half of the platforms were relay hubs attached to batteries, right?"

Nika nodded. "Right. The Dyson lattice nodes transmit the power to the relay hubs, where it's stored and distributed as needed."

"That's good."

They both stared at Dashiel, waiting to be enlightened on why it was good.

"I should explain. Relay hubs act as both receivers and transmitters, which means they have the hardware and programming needed to do either job."

Now he was straying slightly closer to one of her skill sets. "Jerry's been surprisingly forthcoming, but we understand nothing about Rasu programming, and I doubt we can get a full primer out of him."

"We don't need to. It only matters that the programming and switches are there. Palmer, I assume you spent the time I was gone sifting through the Rasu material research I left you. If we get you the kyoseil and alisinium, can you build bombs strong enough to break through the hulls of the battery platforms?"

"Yes. But like you said, the breach will be temporary. If the rest of the platform remains intact, very temporary."

"I know, but like the stasis chambers, these will primarily be electricity bombs. The hole only needs to exist long enough to allow an electrical surge through to the interior, where it can set off its own chain reaction within the battery. With luck, one strong enough to flip the receiver to a transmitter and overload the connected Dyson nodes."

Lance opened his mouth to retort...then closed it. An intrigued expression crept onto his visage. Nika didn't know the man particularly well, but she'd hazard a guess that he had just started to buy into this crazy plan.

"We'll need a lot of bombs. Over five thousand if we want to take out all the batteries."

Nika interjected. "We *have* to destroy all the batteries, because all the batteries are Rasu."

"Damn, that's still weird."

"It is."

"We have enough ships to carry the payload, barely, but it will take us weeks, maybe a month, to build enough Taiyok stealth modules, outfit all the ships with them and modify their systems to use it. And we have ten days."

Nika pursed her lips. "Noted, but it's a detail problem, so let's table it for now. As Dashiel said earlier, we'll figure something out."

"Okay, we'll table it, but not for long. In the most hypothetical of ways, this takes care of the lab, the batteries, and the Dyson lattice. What about the rest of the platforms?"

Dashiel wandered purposefully through the projection. "We need to find a way to ensure they're set to power receiving mode. If they are, they'll get overloaded same as the Dyson nodes."

She knew something about this. "Jerry said the platform containing the lab acts as a sort of command center. It makes sense, given their paranoid nature: the dominant Rasu intelligence will be centered there. It's running experiments to figure out how to control the rest. It stands to reason it will keep as much control as possible as physically close as possible. Perhaps the command center has a mechanism to order all the other platforms into receiving mode, or disable safety protocols, or something along those lines."

She sighed. "But even so, this doesn't help us. Again, we don't understand their programming."

Dashiel beamed at her, which seemed rather odd at this particular moment. "Mr. Eshett, have you been listening in?"

Parc's voice came over the speaker. "You know it."

"Why don't you tell Nika and Commander Palmer what you told me while I was on my way back here?"

"With pleasure. I've been thinking about those light patterns we observed in your simex memory, Nika. I said it reflected their language, but I think it would be more accurate to say it reflected their *programming* language—their programming syntax."

"But it was only a couple of seconds' worth of programming. You can't possibly extract enough information from it to understand the way they program."

"Nika, I'm hurt you think so little of me—"

"I don't—"

"I'm kidding. But you have to admit, I am exceptional at what I do. And now I can pool those mad skills with other people's mad skills, one thing leads to another and...."

"You have a framework of the Rasu programming language."

"By the end of the day, yep."

She laughed. "Next time I see you, Parc, I'll give you that bow you asked for back at The Chalet. You deserve it."

"Yes!"

Lance raised a hand. "Would it be rude of me to wonder aloud how this gets us any closer to blowing up the rest of the platforms?"

Dashiel shook his head. "Not rude. But here's the thing: we've been scanning Jerry since it got here, and between the scans and the sample it provided, we're actually starting to learn some useful information about how the Rasu function. Notably, though they can alter themselves to serve virtually any function, it's not only their outward shape that changes when they do.

"They are *physical* creatures, not metaphysical ones, so they have to take on the precise form of what they need: circuits, amplifiers, data storage drives, heat generators, engines, weapons, the list goes on. They don't merely mimic the functionality of a given machine—they become it."

"Great. What does that mean?"

"Ones and zeroes. On and off, and the superpositions in between. When they're machines—say, power distribution hubs—it means they can be sliced. And if Parc and his ceraff come through on the programming, they can be diverged."

Nika gasped aloud. "Oh, my gods. You want someone to infiltrate the central command platform and disable the safety protocols."

"Damn, Ridani. We'll make a half-decent military strategist out of you yet."

Dashiel shrugged, but she could tell he was pleased with himself. "Thanks, but I've already got a full-time job I'd like to get back to someday."

Nika dropped her chin to her chest. A peaceful certainty settled over her, and it was powerful. She thought perhaps she could draw strength from it, through to the end.

She looked up and smiled. "Well, that decides it. I'll be occupying the stasis pods."

Dashiel spun toward her. "What are you talking about?"

"I'll send myself to the central command platform. Eight thousand copies of myself."

"No, there's no reason for you to go. We'll send blanks—unawakened, empty bodies."

"There's *every* reason for me to go. First and most importantly, you just admitted we need someone to infiltrate the platform. I challenge you to name a single person more qualified to do so than me."

"Parc will have a better grasp of the prog—"

"We are *not* sending Parc back into that place."

Dashiel held up both hands in surrender. "No, you're right."

"Besides, he'd never survive to reach wherever we need to reach."

His face fell. "Neither will you."

"Not one of me, no. But this is where it gets interesting. I won't be alone. Eight thousand copies of me, each one possessing my skills, my knowledge and my memories. Each one possessing a thorough understanding of our plan and, here's the kicker: each one joined together with me in a ceraff."

"A Nika-ceraff! I love it!"

Dashiel scowled up at the speaker in the ceiling. "I don't." He crossed the distance between them and took her hands in his. "Do you understand that all eight thousand copies of you will die?"

"Yes. And then I'll wake up on a cot somewhere, probably in this very building, with their memories of what happened on the platform. Better too many memories than none at all, right?"

"Nika—"

"And if I *don't* take on this mission, then this me will shortly be dead, too, along with every other Asterion. Dashiel, I *want* to do this."

A hesitant throat cleared off to their left, where Lance stood looking vaguely sheepish. "I hate to interrupt—I genuinely do. Ridani, you've done incredible work today, coming up with all this. It's insane, it's brilliant, and it might even be *so* close to doable.

"But even if everything you've laid out works, the only Rasu you've permanently destroyed is the Dyson lattice. The platforms are in pieces, but as you've said, they won't stay in pieces for long.

Then there's still the ships and the satellites." His mouth drew into a thin line. "Tell me you've got one last magic trick up your sleeve."

Dashiel tried to smile, but didn't quite get there, and his gaze never left her. "We estimate that at any given moment, the Dyson lattice is capturing approximately twenty percent of the star's energy output. What do you think is going to happen when every node overloads and sends all that energy streaming back where it came from?"

41

MIRAI JUSTICE CENTER

The Justice Advisors called the ceremony to order, and Adlai stepped to the front of the room and launched into a prepared speech.

He began by listing highlights of Spencer Nimoet's Justice career; Nika didn't know about most of them, but it made for an impressive list. His heroic actions during the current crisis followed, all true. Spencer's relationship with NOIR didn't *specifically* come up, instead hovering just beneath the surface of many of the stories told, but it was fine. Everyone who mattered knew.

Beside her in the audience, Maris leaned over to whisper in her ear. "This means I can seduce him now, yes?"

Nika shot her a vaguely annoyed glare. "I don't see why his being an Advisor is a requirement for that to happen."

"Neither do I, but he seems to think it is. Regardless, it's no longer an issue."

"Just…don't break him, okay?"

"I don't understand what you mean."

On the other side of her, Dashiel nudged her with his elbow in question. She tilted her head toward Maris, then lowered her voice yet more. "You really don't, do you?"

"Each new romance brings with it incredible new adventures and new discoveries about oneself and the other person."

"Yes. And then you break the person."

"How do you know? Did your journals tell you?"

"As a matter of fact, yes, they did. You throw your lovers' worlds into chaos, drive them to distraction, use them up and drain them dry then toss them aside like last year's clothing fashion.

Spencer's a good man, and he's going to be an excellent Justice Advisor—but only if you don't break him."

Adlai finished his speech and motioned for Spencer to join him at the podium. Spencer wore a charcoal tailored suit and an even more stoic countenance than usual, but his face brightened a touch when he glanced their way.

Nika sighed. Why was she even bothering?

"Perhaps he will be the one who leads me to swear off other lovers forever."

"What are the odds?"

Maris' expression flickered; she studied her hands. "I didn't break Adlai. He's a stellar Justice Advisor."

"Sure he is—fourteen hundred years later."

"You're serious about this. Are you asking me not to pursue him?"

Now Spencer was shaking hands with the other Justice Advisors, and it was smiles all around as the ceremony wrapped up.

She took advantage of the increasingly festive atmosphere in the room to face Maris fully, to look her in the eyes. "Something else my journals make clear is that you will do whatever you wish, no matter what anyone else thinks. I respect that, believe me, and in fact I sincerely hope every person in the Dominion gets laid at least once in the next week, in case they don't get another chance.

"I guess what I'm saying is…Spencer isn't a piece of art. He's not a new vid or story or performance. He's a man—a living soul. Treat him like one. Please?"

"I will—"

Adlai tapped Maris on the shoulder, and they both looked up to see him and Spencer standing in the aisle beside their row.

Nika stood and offered Spencer her hand. "Congratulations, Advisor. You deserve it."

He huffed a breath. "I can't say if you're right, but I'll try to be worthy of the title." His attention instantly diverted to Maris. "I realize everyone has a lot to do, but Adlai and I were going to grab a quick bite to eat, if you…all would like to join us?"

Nika almost wished she could, if only to sit between Spencer and Maris and thwart their dance of seduction for one additional hour. Instead she took Dashiel's hand in hers and shook her head. "We would, but Dashiel and I have somewhere to be—" she checked the time "—ten minutes ago. You all enjoy yourselves."

MIRAI ONE PAVILION

"Did you sleep at all last night?"

Lance arched an eyebrow in Dashiel's direction. He did seem tired, but his eyes remained sharp and his movements focused. "I have eight days to plan and prepare for the largest, most complex military operation I've led in millennia. I don't have the ships, I don't have the pilots, I don't have the payloads they'll be expected to deliver. I believe I'll be sleeping next in eight days and forty-five minutes. Unless I'm dead then, which will probably be more restful."

Nika propped against a window and stared outside. Clean-up crews had removed the debris from the grounds outside the Pavilion, though inside tarps and hazard tape remained commonplace. "I recognize we're asking the impossible of you. What can we do to make it fractionally less impossible?"

Lance drummed the fingers of one hand on the table while he used the other to flick through several panes busy with bullet points and numbers. "If you're serious, two things. One, the people who have the skills needed to build these kyoseil/alisinium bombs are the same people who have the skills to replicate the Taiyok stealth modules. But they can't do both at the same time and, as noted, eight days. Nika, you're a diplomat. Get me as many off-the-shelf stealth modules as you can from the Taiyoks."

She had no idea how she'd accomplish it, but this had never stopped her before. "Done. What's the second thing?"

"Briscanti Materials has dumped thousands of kilograms of alisinium on us, with the promise of thousands more if we need it, but it should come as a surprise to no one that kyoseil is not in so plentiful supply. Dashiel, I appreciate Ridani Enterprises pledging every ounce it has on hand, but it's not enough. Not even close. Find me more kyoseil."

Dashiel pinched the bridge of his nose, and Nika recalled something he'd said to her not long after they'd met this time around: *there is never, can never be enough kyoseil.* "I understand. No mechanism exists within the government to commandeer private materials for the public good, but I'll make something up. One way or another, you'll have the kyoseil you need." He turned to her wearing a pained expression. "I need to initiate some comms, then knock on some doors."

She nodded thoughtfully. "And it seems I need to return to Toki'taku."

42

TOKI'TAKU

TAIYOK HOMEWORLD

The trip to the Alcazar was nothing short of surreal. The details of the memory she'd recovered overlaid atop reality like a recreation of the scene knocked five degrees off-center.

Visually, little had changed about the topography in twelve thousand years. The Taiyoks being notoriously beholden to tradition and history as they were, she shouldn't be surprised. Still, she liked to think millennia of cordial relations and regular exchange between their societies had resulted in some improvements behind the scenes.

Cameron Breckel sat beside her in the second row of the carriage. In her absence these last five years, he'd taken over most of the Dominion's official interactions with the Taiyok government.

She'd hurriedly devoured all the information she could locate in her journals on the current Taiyok Elder and the history of their relations, then quizzed Cameron about recent developments on the way here. But the truth was, there wasn't much to tell. Their relationship was at a steady state and had been for quite some time. The Taiyoks changed gradually if at all, and the Dominion had been content to not push them to do so.

That policy was of necessity about to come to an end. She didn't expect the Elder to be thrilled about it, but the Rasu were everyone's problem now.

Cameron leaned in close to her ear so she was able to hear him over the wind and rustle of the forest the carriage pitched through. "Are you sure you're up for this meeting? Granted, you could charm the wings off a Taiyok before, but...I just mean it's something of a learned skill."

She gave him her brave face, which she'd gotten a lot of practice at brandishing lately. "I'm sure. Even in NOIR, I worked with Taiyoks often. And I remember..." she took in the enormous mossy leaves and twisting umber limbs rushing past them "...being here." She exhaled slowly. "I remember how to do this."

He settled back into the stiff seating of the carriage. "Okay. I trust you. And I'll be right there with you."

The carriage completed its pulse-pounding tear through the seemingly endless forest canopy and settled onto the landing pad at the home of the Toki'taku presiding government.

They followed their escorts out of the carriage and onto the wide platform high in the trees. In front of them, a spiral ramp wound up a tree that had grown yet more mammoth in the last twelve thousand years.

She motioned Cameron forward. "Let's make this count."

⁂

This Taiyok Elder's feathers were silken ebony where his predecessor's had been ivory, and his eyes reflected copper instead of platinum, but the symbols painted upon his wings were the same—marks of the station passed down to each holder of the title of Elder.

The dozens of eyes glittering from the shadows felt a tad friendlier than on her first visit. Possibly.

She and Cameron crouched low, left knees leading, and crossed their arms over their chests in the traditional greeting of respect, then stood. She spoke first, and only after she began did it occur to her she might be slighting Cameron in doing so. "Elder Zhanre'khavet, I express honor to come before you today. I apologize for my long absence. Thank you for your indulgence in welcoming me into your halls once more."

"Your colleague has served well in your absence. Two Asterion diplomats standing before us together, side by side, however? Matters must be grave, indeed."

She dipped her chin, paused and lifted it again, the closest Tai-yoks came to a nod-like gesture. "I regret to say they are. Elder, have you had an opportunity to review the visuals and files we sent ahead?"

The Elder swept a silken wing out to acknowledge the council members gathered alongside him. "We have all done so. The presence of these strange, unnatural beasts in our galaxy is most troubling. You claim they have demonstrated an aggressive nature toward other species?"

"Yes. All the information we've been able to gather on them indicates that they destroy, harvest or enslave every species they encounter. Further, they continue to actively seek out new species to abuse so."

"What about species more technologically advanced than they are?"

"We can't say for certain, but it is entirely possible they have never encountered a species more advanced than they are."

"You do not claim to yourselves be?"

She suppressed a smile. "No, we do not. But to save ourselves and all our allies, we do aim to be cleverer than they are. But we need your help to accomplish this."

"You intend to provoke these Rasu? Better to remain silent in the shadows, in the hope they pass us by unawares."

"I'm afraid it's too late for such a course of action. They are already aware of our existence. They are coming for Asterion worlds very soon, and when they do, they will find yours as well. Their nature is to spread like a plague, consuming all they encounter. Our only chance is to act before they arrive at our doorstep. To act now, when they do not yet expect us to challenge them."

Rough mutters broke out among the council members. The Elder snapped a wing out to its full span, silencing the outburst in a single motion. "What do you ask of us?"

"Taiyok stealth technology is far superior to our own. This is not flattery, but rather simple truth. We know yours is effective against the Rasu, for using it we have sent several ships into the heart of their stronghold without detection by the enemy."

The soft feathers lining the Elder's neck fluttered once. "You used Taiyok stealth technology on an Asterion vessel?"

"Legally purchased technology, I assure you. And yes, with some work we were able to adapt it to our starship systems. Now, however, we need a greater number of your stealth modules. Enough for a thousand ships. And we need them immediately."

The Elder pivoted in a full circle, his steely gaze hushing the outcries of his council before they could be uttered. When he once again faced her, his eerie compound eyes bore into her for a fateful five seconds before he spoke.

"You ask much, Asterion. Tell me your plan to defeat these Rasu. In detail, please."

"You intend to have a thousand or more ships infiltrate this stronghold stellar system, at once, undetected, and use them to place several thousand bombs onto the hulls of the Rasu's core structures? This is a suicide mission, if you understand such a concept."

"We do." Nika didn't flinch in response to the Elder's barb. Taiyoks, some of them, grasped the admittedly unconventional nature of Asterion life as a general matter; they all disapproved, naturally. "But to do nothing is also a suicide mission. If our civilization is destroyed, there will be no more new generations for us. The plan is risky, yes. Of course it is. It is also our best chance to stop the enemy and save us all."

The Elder paused to confer with one of his colleagues, a rare action on his part, then began deliberately circling her and Cameron. "Our stealth devices cannot possibly function as well on your ships as they do on ours. The integration will by definition be incomplete."

Nika followed his progress, turning as needed. "This is likely true. However, as I said, it does function."

"But better on our ships."

"Yes...agreed."

The Elder stopped directly in front of her, less than a meter distant. "Then we will use our own ships."

She froze her muscles before they could spin her toward Cameron in surprise or let out a gasp in also surprise or drop her jaw flat to the floor in...yeah. "I—perhaps I am misunderstanding the intent of your words. Do you want us to use Taiyok ships on the mission?"

"Don't be preposterous. *We* will use our ships."

She blinked twice in succession, and Cameron stepped in while she tried to recover from the shock. In fairness to her, this was current-her's first time conducting a head-of-state negotiation with an alien species, and no amount of research could have prepared her for this curve ball.

"Elder, we are not asking the Taiyoks to participate in our offensive against the Rasu, merely to provide support equipment for the mission. We are willing to take all the risks on ourselves."

"Oddly brave of Asterions. But you were correct earlier. We are now in danger from these interlopers as well, and Taiyoks will never be cowards. We will join you in your offensive."

Nika composed herself enough to offer the Elder a situation-appropriate restrained smile. "Then we would welcome your participation. Greatly so. What manner of ships are you proposing to use?"

⋏R

At first, second and third glance, Nika couldn't be certain what she was seeing. An expansive flock of birds lazing in the afternoon sun? The earth tones ubiquitous throughout the Toki'taku landscape blended seamlessly with the complementary tones used in most Taiyok architecture so well the entire facility might as well be shrouded beneath a stealth module.

But logic won out over her deceived vision. It wasn't birds she was seeing—it was ships. Hundreds of them at a minimum, stacked in rows and columns beside a manufacturing facility far more expansive than the one she'd purchased her own stealth module at during her last visit.

The ships were small, each one less than half the size of the *Wayfarer*, with long, broad wings and tapered bodies. They resembled a cross between large harriers and, well, the Taiyoks themselves. They didn't actually have feathers, of course, but from a distance the muted, unburnished hulls could be mistaken for pelts.

The Elder stood beside her gazing upon his ships. Proudly, she'd daresay. She motioned deliberately toward the fleet. "Can I ask, what are these ships routinely used for?"

"We engage in many endeavors which do not draw the notice of Asterions. But fear not, those endeavors represent no threat to you."

She *respectfully* decided the Asterions would be the ones to decide this, and also that they would decide it later. "Thank you for the reassurance. And the pilots? They have training in dangerous situations?"

"Space is always dangerous, Advisor Kirumase. Based on the information you have provided regarding your mission, these ships will only be able to carry two of your bombs each, so we will need more ships. The additional vessels will be ready for flight in four days."

She wasn't sure how Lance was going to react when she told him the news, but she *was* sure they weren't going to refuse this gift, however unexpected it may be. "In that case, Elder, it will be the highest honor for us to fly and fight alongside your people."

43

CHOSEK

CHIZERU HOMEWORLD

Dashiel embraced her as soon as she stepped into the meeting room at the Chosek Embassy. "Thank you for diverting here. How did it go on Toki'taku?"

Nika sighed against his lips in the briefest moment of contentment, then drew back and surveyed the room. Thick, quilted drapes adorned every window, as well as what she suspected were simply bare spots of wall. Ridiculously plush chairs with added pillows in Asterion and Chizeru sizes ringed a low table. The carpet beneath her feet looked soft enough to suffice as bedding, and she idly wondered if any Chizeru guests had ever flopped down and rolled around on it.

"Better than expected, actually. I'll fill you in on the way home. What's the status here?"

"I went all totalitarian on the companies who import kyoseil and confiscated their on-hand supplies…" he grimaced "…with the promise of future reimbursement. I couldn't take it at gunpoint and live with myself. Unfortunately, most of that supply is already in production. Not a surprise, as few outfits will leave it sitting around for long."

"So, we need more."

"We need more. We need to beg, borrow and…well, not steal every gram we can get from the Chizeru. Now, I've no doubt they'll be happy to provide it, but the issue is the timing. You once said that hurrying a Chizeru was like pushing a rope uphill—you just ended up with a tangled pile of Chizeru on the ground."

"Ha." She rubbed at her jaw. "Have you given any thought to the morality of what we're doing?"

"You mean destroying the Rasu?"

"No. They deserve to die. I mean using kyoseil to do it. The Rasu believe kyoseil is alive, and I got the impression Forchelle did, too. We don't have a way to ask its permission to sacrifice tens of thousands of kilograms of it to blow up the Rasu. We're just going to *do* it. Does that make us murderers, too?"

"Nika, we have no choice. This is our only plan. Besides, if it is in some way alive, it's been dying alongside every Asterion who's died by Rasu hands. Like you and like every soldier, it would surely be willing to sacrifice some of its own in order to stop that slaughter." He shrugged weakly. "Right?"

"Hells if I know. But...thank you. That does make me feel better." The delegation would be here any minute, so she forcibly shifted gears to focus on the task at hand. At least with the Taiyoks, she'd had recent personal experience to draw on in addition to the recovered memory. But none of the encrypted memories had involved the Chizeru, and she'd never met one during her time in NOIR.

Here, she had only the algorithms that told her how to be a diplomat, files holding long lists of Chizeru idiosyncrasies to keep in mind and a few journal entries she'd dug up to rely upon. "Why am I more nervous about this meeting than I was for the one with the Taiyok Elder?"

"Don't be silly. Shoset has always loved you."

She trailed a hand along the supple velvet of one of the drapes. "But I've been gone for years. I assume someone told him I was dead."

"*I* told him you had to go on a long trip. Now you're back."

"Okay. Still, I'm worried. I don't want to frighten him, but I have to light a fire under him, and the only way I can think of to do that is to convince him of the seriousness of the situation."

Her hand reached the end of the drape, and Dashiel took it in his. His thumb drew soothing circles along her palm. "And you will."

The dyne attendant signaled the imminent arrival of the Chizeru delegation, and Nika readied a welcoming demeanor—then glanced at Dashiel in confusion when she felt him stuffing something soft in her jacket pocket.

"You'll know when you need it." Satisfied, he straightened up beside her.

The doors opened, and a Chizeru in full formal regalia led the way inside, with two additional Chizeru following behind him. Three steps into the room, the lead Chizeru saw Nika. He gasped, rushed forward across the room and threw his arms around her legs in a tight hug while chattering away so fast she could barely understand him.

With a gentle laugh she carefully untangled him from her legs, then dropped to her knees in front of him. "I'm glad to see you as well, Shoset."

"Gone you were, so long." His thin, leathery lips curled inward. "Did Shoset displease you?"

"No, no, of course not. I had to go far away. I didn't want to go, but you understand obligations to your people. This was my obligation to mine, my duty. It took me a long time to find my way back, but I made it. As soon as I got home, I hurried here to see you."

"Good, Nika-friend. Did you bring scarves? Ridani-sir brought some, but…" he leaned in to whisper conspiratorially, tiny eyes dancing "…yours better."

She laughed again. "I won't tell him you said so." She reached in her pocket and produced an intricately woven scarf of plum and gold. Wow, did she epically owe Dashiel.

Thank you. I'll make this up to you in new and interesting ways.
Oh, I look forward to it.

She palmed the scarf and offered it to Shoset. "Here you are. A gift from my journey."

The Chizeru shook in excitement as he wound it around his neck. "Tickles!"

"It's a special hand-woven fabric, crafted for maximum tickling." She placed a hand on his shoulder. "Listen, Shoset. I came here today because I wanted to see you, but also because I have to ask a very, very important favor of you and your people."

"We like to help our Asterion friends."

"I know you do, and we appreciate it so much. There's a bad thing..." she pointed upward and toward the closest window "...up in space with the stars. We need to stop it from coming to our home and hurting us. From hurting Asterions, and from coming here and hurting Chizeru, too."

"Oh, no!"

"It's going to be okay. We have a plan to stop the bad thing from hurting anyone. But to do our plan, we need a lot of kyoseil. As in, *a lot*. And we need it super-fast."

Shoset's eyes narrowed to slits, and he studied her intently for several seconds. "If we mine hard and fast for you, how many scarves will you bring me?"

She grinned. "Enough scarves for you to carpet the planet with them. All the scarves in the entire world."

44

KIYORA

"**A**dvisor Nika Kirumase to see Gemina Kail."

The two Justice dynes standing guard outside the door to Kail's office stared blankly at her. "ID signature, please."

She pressed her fingertips to the pane. It still felt strange, providing her again-real name and signature to the authorities, and not a single pealing alarm or drawn weapon in response. She'd never thought of herself as hiding before as such, but she'd certainly been hiding from the authorities. Now? She *was* the authorities.

"Cleared to proceed."

"Thank you—" a message arrived from Xyche, and her curiosity won out "—pardon me, I need a moment."

Nika,

I was pleased to learn your meeting with Zhanre proceeded favorably for you. He is a fair and moral man when given sufficient reason to be. I wish you well in your endeavor, and should you fail, may you die with honor.

—Xyche'ghael

Her face screwed up. How had Xyche learned about the meeting, much less its outcome? And how did a simple Taiyok merchant eking out a dubious living on an Asterion world know the Elder?

She composed a quick reply and sent it off.

Xyche,

On a first-name basis with the Elder, are you? Is there something you'd like to tell me?

—Nika

Then she nodded to the guards, squared her shoulders and stepped forward as the door opened. Jetting around the galaxy begging favors from friends and adversaries alike had drained her, but she needed to push ahead for a little longer. No time for a vacation or, with four days left until the Rasu deadline, so much as a nap.

Gemina sat at her desk with three rows of active panes surrounding her. She glared at Nika through the shimmering figures they displayed. "Oh, lovely. Did you finally find five minutes in your busy schedule to drop by and exact vengeance on me?"

Nika leaned against the wall and crossed her ankles and arms. "For what, precisely? It's a long list of grievances."

"It is." Gemina frowned, then banished the panes and considered Nika anew. "I believed in them, you know. For a while. I believed in the Guides and the plan they were following. Part of me still believes the choice they made was the only choice they *could* have made. We are not strong enough to defeat the Rasu. Whatever insane scheme you're working up, it won't be enough." She paused, and her gaze fell to her lap. "But I am sorry you got hurt in the process. I'm sorry for the role I played in hurting you."

Nika blinked, stunned. This was not how she'd expected this conversation to go. "I have no idea how to respond to an apology. Are you going to try to tell me that you and I were friends? Before the psyche-wipe?"

"Oh, gods, no. We...it would be inaccurate to say we hated one another, because we didn't. But friends? Never. In good years we tolerated one another, and in bad ones we...didn't."

Whew. For a minute there, she'd worried she'd somehow stumbled into a twisted, funhouse version of reality. "Now this I can believe."

Gemina straightened up and tried to look bored. "Why are you here? I'm being a good girl. I'm doing my job, not sending any unauthorized messages, not trying to break the Guides out of prison, and returning to my cell every night like I'm supposed to."

"I know. Justice had to clear you for why I'm here, and they agree that you are being a...good girl. No, I'm here about that insane scheme I'm working up. I need your assistance to pull it off."

"Didn't I just say you're not going to be able to pull it off?"

"Yeah, but I figured it was merely you being your usual bitchy self."

Gemina regarded her strangely. "Huh. What's my assistance entail?"

"A very simple task. I need you to pilot the *Tabiji* to the Rasu stronghold one final time."

"But we're not sending them any more Asterions in stasis chambers, are we? I heard you made a grand speech about how that was never, ever, ever going to happen."

"I did, and it was in fact quite grand. But actually, we are. We're sending them me."

"I realize you think highly of yourself, but trust me, the Rasu will not view you as equivalent to eight thousand bodies."

"You're probably right, which is why we're sending them eight thousand copies of me."

Gemina's jaw dropped. She stood and walked around the side of the desk toward Nika. "Eight thousand copies of you? What nightmare have I fallen victim to?"

Nika rolled her eyes. "Oh, drop it, Kail. Will you do it?"

"Why me?"

"Because the Rasu are expecting you. In eight years, you're the only walking, talking Asterion they've had direct contact with that they haven't killed. If we were to change up the routine now, they might get suspicious, and the last thing we need is for them to get suspicious. All you need to do is the exact same thing you've done on every trip up until now. Fly the *Tabiji* there, deliver the stasis chambers, turn around and leave. That's all."

"What are eight thousand of you going to do once you get on board one of their platforms?"

"It's not your concern."

"Still don't trust me?"

Nika snorted. "Can you blame me?"

"No, I guess not." Gemina's lips puckered, as if she'd just eaten a rotten egg. "Can I wrangle a cell upgrade out of it? One with a reasonably soft bed? I mean, I'll only get to enjoy it for a couple of days before the Rasu show up and obliterate the planet, but this way they'll be comfortable days."

"You do this for us, and I'll get you upgraded to house arrest."

"Really? All right. I literally have absolutely nothing to lose. It's a deal."

"Thank you." Nika turned toward the door to leave, then looked back over her shoulder at Gemina. "Also, if you betray us when you reach the stronghold and alert the Rasu that something is amiss, I will feed you to them myself."

45

MIRAI ONE PAVILION

They sat around a large, rectangular table in Conference Room 2-D, mostly because it was one of the few larger rooms that hadn't suffered any damage in Satair's attack.

This wasn't the last opportunity they'd have to update the plan or make crucial decisions, but it was damn close.

Nika leaned back in her chair and fisted her hands beneath her chin. Gods, she was tired. Everyone was tired, and it showed in a hundred ways, from the proliferation of fine lines around people's eyes and mouths to the sloppy postures of those at the table to the wrinkles in clothes that had been worn for too many hours or days.

"Lance?"

The military officer was the only one here who refused to let his posture slack; his spine remained straight and his head held high, though rumor was he'd slept less than ten hours in the previous week.

"My people will be working all night to finish the stealth module retrofits on our ships and assembling the last of the KA Bombs, as the final shipment of kyoseil from Chosek won't arrive until later tonight. One way or another, we'll be ready by the departure time."

Despite the Taiyoks declaring that they intended to send more than enough ships on the mission to deliver all the bombs, Lance insisted on sending five hundred Asterion ships as well, including the *Dauntless*. This was an Asterion mission, and they would see it done.

"What about the Taiyoks?"

"They say they'll be ready, but I have no visibility into their preparations. We have no choice but to trust them."

Xyche had replied to her message a few minutes earlier with a single sentence: *Perhaps one day*. His species—and him personally—remained a confounding, fundamentally *alien* mystery in so many ways, but she could confidently assert a few things about them. "We can. If they say they'll be ready, they'll be ready. Parc?"

Parc had thrown a foot up on the table and kicked his chair so far back he'd fall over if a fly landed on him. It was an act, a projection of deliberate bravado to hide how uncomfortable he felt sitting at the table with a bunch of Advisors. Maybe. Or, he could simply not give a shit.

He set the feet of the chair down long enough to retrieve a data weave from his pocket and slide it across the table to her, then returned to his display of balancing prowess. "Here's your key to slice into Rasu systems and diverge what you need to. Courtesy of three separate ceraffin working for twenty straight hours—under my sage supervision, of course."

"Of course." She spun the weave between her fingers thoughtfully. "I bet I'll know the answer once I load the program, but will any of my existing routines make the slicing and diverging go faster, or are they going to be useless?"

"No, and yes. Auxiliary process routines are included on the weave, and I'd suggest using them over anything you've got."

"That reminds me." Dashiel picked up a container he'd stashed beside his chair and opened it. He lifted out a compact blade unlike any she'd ever seen before. The metal was barely a millimeter thick, and when viewed side-on it nearly disappeared. The material almost seemed to subtly glow from within, a shimmer perpetually slipping away out of the corner of her eye.

He offered it to her. "This should cut through any Rasu material, if only briefly."

She set the weave aside and took the blade from him, running her fingertip lightly along the metal. Blood welled up in a thin line in the blade's wake. Damn, it was *sharp*. "What's it made of?"

"We don't have a name for the material yet. We succeed in our mission, and we'll hold a naming contest." He tried to make his smile light, but he didn't fool her.

She turned the blade over several times, watching as it caught and split the ambient light in the room. "Archine?"

Lance made a face, and she shrugged. "I'm just saying."

Dashiel eyed them curiously. "Works for me. Archine it is."

She set the blade down on the table. "Remarkable work. As much as I'd be thrilled to test it out on some Rasu, however, I'm not technically going to the stronghold myself. You've crafted eight thousand of them?"

He nodded. "They're being added to the stasis chambers this evening. In a left-side slot halfway down the interior of the chambers, so you…your copies will know where to retrieve them."

"Thank you. Katherine?"

The Administration Advisor didn't even bother to look perturbed or annoyed. Simply tired. "Said eight thousand bodies are all constructed and have been released by the twelve different clinics it took to prepare them all. They're just waiting to be loaded with your imprint. Whenever you're ready."

Nika cleared her throat, as she seemed to have developed a sudden lump in it. "In the morning. I want to wait until the last possible moment, so they're loaded with the most complete information available to us."

She let her gaze pass across everyone at the table. "Thank you all. It doesn't do justice to the work you've put in to say that you've gone above and beyond. None of us have had much choice in the matter, because we're fighting for our survival, and not ours alone—our entire species and the allies we've made. But what the Guides thought was impossible, beyond our capabilities? We've gotten it done. We've proved them wrong, and we'll prove them wrong again in the next two days. Asterions can do anything we set our minds to. *Anything*. And right now, we've set our minds to surviving."

"So, survive we will." Dashiel grasped her hand under the table and squeezed it tight. "From this point forward, everyone splash all updates to the *@OpFlare* nex hub so no time or meaning gets lost along the way."

Nika projected the most confident mien she could manage. "If there's nothing else, I'll see most of you in the morning at the space-port."

46

NIKA'S FLAT

Dashiel heard the shower shut off as he finished pouring two glasses of wine. He'd stopped on the way here and picked up the bottle, a cabernet vintage from a small winery in the mountains outside Kiyora Three. Her favorite, though she didn't remember it.

He took a minute to set himself straight. Tonight, he wasn't going to whine about how much he disliked her decision to send herself alone into the torture facility of the Rasu. She couldn't change her course now even if he did somehow convince her to—which he didn't intend to try to do, because as much as his heart recoiled at the thought, she was the best person to do it. Perhaps the only person who could do it.

Tonight, he wasn't going to fret over the impossible nature of their mission or all the thousand minutiae that were certain to go wrong with the plan. He wasn't going to dread the imminent possibility that their civilization might soon come to an end.

Tonight, he was going to celebrate. Celebrate her life and the wonders she'd performed. Celebrate their second life together. In the finest Asterion tradition, celebrate the here and the now, one touch at a time.

He picked up the glasses and went to join her in the bedroom suite.

She emerged from the bathroom wearing a white silk robe that barely grazed her shoulders and teased the top of her knees.

Already she took his breath away. He smiled and handed her one of the glasses.

She accepted it, but her attention drifted toward the door behind him and the living room beyond. "Don't we need to—"

"No. Whatever it is, I guarantee someone is taking care of it. Tomorrow, you are going to split yourself into thousands of shards and sacrifice them all for our people, but tonight is ours."

He watched as a fraction of the tension holding her muscles taut relaxed. "Okay." She took a sip of the wine, then quickly another. "This tastes wonderful."

"I'm glad you think so." He didn't elaborate; tonight, she didn't need to be reminded of all she'd lost. He set his glass on the dresser and stepped closer, bringing his left hand to her jaw. "There are some things I want to say, and now feels like a good time to say them."

His fingertips trailed down her neck to her collarbone and drifted to the hollow at the base of her throat. "I've come to realize all over again something that in my grief these last five years I had forgotten. You have the soul of an immortal. But the astonishing thing is, you also have the soul of an innocent. One forever teeming with wonder and dreams and determination. To be near it, to bask in its reflected glow...you make everything brighter. You make me better."

He sidled around behind her, his hand teasing the hem of her robe at her thighs while his lips grazed the slope of her shoulders. "We will all follow you into the future you're creating, but I will follow you anywhere." His fingers found the tie of the robe and casually tugged it loose, then drew along the fabric where it hugged the curve of her breast.

Her back pressed into his bare chest as she trembled beneath his touch, and he struggled to slow his progress, forcing himself to enjoy every centimeter of his fingertips' journey. When they finally reached her shoulder, he leaned in and kissed the crook of her neck as he slid the robe off and let it fall to the floor.

She took a hurried sip of her wine then leaned away from him to set the glass on the dresser—then she spun around to face him. Her mouth met his, light as a passing breeze. "Don't follow me anywhere. Walk there beside me." She flattened her palms against his chest and drew them down to his waist. Her lips followed, trailing kisses all the way down, creating cool oases upon his suddenly feverish skin. "The world was cold and lonely without you in it. For the last five years, I believed the chasm in my soul was caused by my missing memories, but I was wrong." Her knees reached the floor, and she smiled as she slowly unfastened his pants. "It was caused by the missing you."

A thousand dizzying sensations overwhelmed him. Her murmuring, lilting voice layered in seduction, the deliberate, insistent touch of her hands on his skin. Did she comprehend what her touch did to him? He should tell her.

But the words lodged in his throat, and he only managed a, "You don't know…" before they dissolved into a moan as her tongue ran down the length of his cock.

"I have loved you in life after life after life." Another kiss. Another sweep of her tongue. "I will never not love you."

"Nika…." His hand fisted in her hair as the walls swam and blurred away.

"You said tonight is ours, but tonight is yours." Her nails dug into the small of his back and scraped down his ass. "And if this is our last night together, I don't want you to see tomorrow's dawn entertaining any doubts or misconceptions about how much *I* love you."

His heart swelled until it battled with his body over which should be the first to send him tumbling into oblivion. "Stars, would you come here?"

She swirled her tongue around him again, and he doubted he retained the strength to ask her a second time. But she returned her palms to his chest as she climbed to her feet, preventing him from wrapping her up and retaking control. They urged him back two steps, until the back of his knees hit the bed. She grinned and, with a playful fingertip, knocked him onto the covers.

He watched, transfixed, as she crawled onto the covers after him. One knee, then the other. Aeons ticked by. He forced himself to breathe.

She sank lower and kissed the skin where his right hip met his thigh. "No doubts." Her lips skimmed across his abdomen. "No misconceptions."

"I don't—I—gods, Nika. I'm supposed to be doing this to you. That was the...plan."

"Mm-hmm." Her lips carved a path of blissful agony up his chest. "I gathered. But I've let you worship me for too long, because I needed it. I needed to be shown what we were, what we could be again. I needed to learn how to believe in us. But now I do more than believe. Now I know."

Her hair fell across his jaw as she at last reached his mouth, and his hands fumbled along the dip at her waist to settle into the arch of her spine, so she would not escape his grasp.

She hovered above him, bathed in a halo of moonlight and stardust as she straddled his hips and, centimeter by glorious centimeter, slid down over him. "We are forever."

47

SYNRA

Dashiel watched an army of dynes guide an endless procession of stasis chambers into the cavernous belly of the *Tabiji*. From up here in the spaceport's observation room he couldn't see their contents, but his mind refused to let him forget what they were.

Nika's psyche backup had been recorded first thing this morning, then loaded eight thousand times over before the stasis chambers were brought here. If any one of the forms inside the chambers were to be woken up, they would be *her*.

This was the way of his people; they'd all been the one to be awoken and had all watched as friends were in turn awoken. But spun out to its logical extreme, even if out of necessity, it felt wrong. It devalued her uniqueness and trivialized the battles she'd fought simply to continue to exist.

Or possibly he was being a possessive prick. Wake them all up, and everyone could have their very own Nika…and he wanted to be the only one. Of course, no one truly *had* her, and he just happened to be the lucky man with whom she chose to share her lives.

He probably ought to find something more useful to do with his waning time than stoking this self-flagellation routine.

Still he watched, unable to tear his gaze away.

The door behind him opened, and a moment later Lance Palmer appeared beside him. The man considered the procession of stasis chambers. "I stand by my initial assessment. This plan is insane."

"Insane enough to work?"

Palmer shrugged. "Hells if I can say. Is Nika here?"

"The real one, you mean?"

"Come on, Ridani—you know that's not how it works. The awake one."

Dashiel shook his head. "She won't admit it, but I suspect seeing this firsthand would be too much, even for her."

"I can't disagree. It's disturbing as fuck. Though, I confess the idea of every soldier being your best soldier is enticing. It would've come in handy...once upon a time."

"What was she like? Back during the SAI Rebellion?"

Palmer shot him an inscrutable look.

"Yes, I know how old you are. It's a simple question."

"I guess all the rules fly out the window when you're staring down the apocalypse. Also, it's not a simple question at all. In many respects she was shockingly similar to how she is now. Righteously outraged, determined to the point of zealotry, fiercely protective of her people. She could coax the skin off a snake, especially if the snake was the enemy. And in the end she was, like all of us, heartbroken when we failed. Well, most people were heartbroken. I was offended."

Dashiel chuckled, though it echoed dark and laden in his chest. "Been waiting to fight another war ever since?"

"Yes. I'll see you on the *Dauntless* in an hour."

ᴀʀ

MIRAI ONE PAVILION

Adlai checked the bank of panes along the far wall every few minutes, despite the fact that he understood only a fraction of the data they relayed and had even less to contribute to their review. Updates from the *Dauntless* and the Asterion and Taiyok fleets as they approached the Rasu stronghold, he thought, and visuals from a couple of surveillance drones Palmer had left behind during his reconnaissance visit.

No…war, space, and most of all war *in* space fell well outside his purview.

He rubbed at his eyes and studied the panes again. He felt helpless. Not because he couldn't do anything to help the mission succeed, but because he wasn't convinced he could do anything to help should it fail.

How did one prepare an entire species for its end? They had no contingency plan, no refuge to flee for. Given a bit more time, they might have developed one, but the Guides' doomed adherence to absolute secrecy had robbed them of that time.

Justice squads stood prepped and ready to maintain order, should the worst come to pass. Their instructions were to respond with the minimum required force, since any violence on the part of the people wouldn't be driven by anger or malice but by fear. By desperation. And he wouldn't blame them one bit.

The Justice Advisors were still arguing over whether to shut down the interplanetary d-gates if the mission failed. Harris argued doing so was an essential tool of crowd control guaranteed to make their jobs considerably easier (if nonetheless still impossible). Harris wasn't wrong, but given the lack of a refuge to flee for, the primary reason for people to transit planets would surely be to reach their loved ones, and how dare he or anyone else deny them this one mercy?

Spencer came through the door and headed toward him, and Adlai tried not to look too dour. "What's up?"

Spencer gestured back toward the entrance. "Someone scrawled 'War Room' on a broken screen and taped it outside the door."

"Eh, that sounds appropriate." He motioned at the cadre of people working to analyze and distribute the constantly updating data from the bank of panes. "Not that these people aren't doing an excellent job. I assume they are. But I doubt anyone begrudges us appending 'ragtag' to this entire effort."

"You think we're going to fail."

"I think..." Adlai sank back in his chair to stare at the ceiling "...if there is any way in creation for us to succeed, we will. I'm just not liking those odds. Regardless, we'll know one way or another in a few hours." He returned his attention to his colleague and, now that he was no longer the man's boss, friend. "You have a twitchy air about you. What's on your mind?"

"The former Guides have requested access to the *@OpFlare* nex hub. View rights only. It seems they want to watch the show."

He started to retort something about watching their future go down in the flaming wreckage of ships and bombs, but he stopped himself. What would happen would happen, and he wasn't doing himself or anyone else any favors by being a mopey, defeatist grump. People he cared for had given everything of themselves to bring this mission together, and perhaps he should have a little faith in them.

"I think it's a grand idea for them to see their former subjects demonstrating what true leadership looks like and what Asterions are capable of accomplishing when set free of artificial strictures."

"I can mark you down as a 'yes,' then?"

"Sure, why not. But, seriously, view rights only. Keep them out of the comm channels, for all of the reasons."

"No question." Spencer glanced around the room—the 'War Room,' for good or ill. "How long until the fleets arrive?"

Adlai gestured toward a timer in one corner of the room counting down inexorably toward zero.

1:26

"That's for the *Tabiji*. The fleets are fifteen minutes behind it, and they'll deploy in a holding pattern two parsecs outside the stellar system when they arrive."

Spencer nodded absently and stood. "I need to check on some worst-case scenario preparations on Synra, then I think I'll come back here. Watch the show myself."

"I think you won't be alone."

Spencer had barely cleared the door when Perrin came through it, her arms laden with water bottles, energy drinks and snack bags.

A smile crept onto Adlai's face despite his somber mood, as it did every single time he saw her. Today, her hair was platinum blond and woven into a curtain of braids, and she wore a carnation-hued sweater over shimmery ivory pants.

The message could not be clearer: she would be a bright light for them all, no matter how dark the room, the mood and the future became.

She dumped everything on the table beside him, leaned in and kissed his forehead, then nudged a couple of items his way. "Lemon water and sliced fruit, as requested."

"Did I request those?"

"You were going to, or possibly silently brood on how you wished you had some lemon water and sliced fruit, but you couldn't afford to leave the War Room to go get them."

Did she ever have his number. "Probably so. Thank you."

"You're welcome." She gathered back up two energy drinks and a bag of chips, then peered past him. "Where is she?"

He tilted his head toward the far-right corner of the room, where a shoji screen had been erected to cordon off some space and provide a small measure of privacy.

"Got it. Ping me if you need me."

"Perrin?"

"Hmm?" She half-turned back to him.

"I'm glad you're here."

Her smile lit up the entire damn War Room. "So am I."

"We're going to put you into a kind of 'twilight sleep.' You'll act as the hub of your own ceraff with your copies at the stronghold once the others are awakened, but you'll be somewhat detached from their actions. There's a risk that your body will react autonomously to the feedback it's receiving from the copies, hence the semi-sleep state. The experience should feel somewhere between a dream and a simex. You'll be aware of your existence here and, we hope, be able to communicate information about events occurring at the stronghold if you need to."

The med tech winced. "But none of us have ever tried this before. We're all stumbling our way through it."

"Tell me about it." Nika stretched out on the cot, which had been dressed up into the guise of a relaxing chaise. It was comfortable...but she was not.

Dashiel and Lance were long gone. By now they'd already met up with the Taiyok fleet and were moving into position near the Rasu stellar system. Gemina should be piloting the *Tabiji* into the stronghold shortly to relinquish their 8,000 trojan horses into the hands of the enemy. On the other side of the shoji screen, a litany of Advisors and their officers stood ready to direct events, intervene where possible or merely to bear witness.

In minutes, their plan would reach the point of no return; in a few short hours, she would play her role in it. Here, sedated in a corner of the War Room, and kiloparsecs away, in the heart of the enemy's lair.

Perrin appeared through the gap between the screen and the back wall carrying snacks and energy drinks. "I'm here! You're not asleep yet, are you?"

Nika sat back up and crossed her legs beneath her. "Almost. But I have time for chips, if you brought chips?"

"Please. I made a point to bring the crinkly ones you prefer." Perrin sat a couple of energy drinks in an empty chair and held up a little bag of said chips.

The med tech scowled but didn't voice a protest as Perrin brought it over and she and Nika dug in.

When the bag was empty, Perrin eyed her hesitantly. "I don't really know what to say. You're crazy and wonderful and I'm so glad you're my friend. Are you ready to virtually go kick these horrible aliens' asses?"

Nika laughed, but even as she did, her mind drifted to one of her precious recovered memories and the sentiment she'd given voice to at the founding of Mirai, so long ago.

Now, being an Asterion means this. Us. Organic and synthetic fused together as one. Physical, but never-ending, for so long as one wishes. Then, to begin again. To learn, experience and grow, within oneself and through the world around us.

Well, that was one way to view what was about to take place. She squeezed Perrin's hand. "I'm ready."

ROOT ACCESS

DAYS TO RASU DEADLINE: 0

48

ADV TABIJI

RASU STRONGHOLD

Gemina stood at the viewport of the *Tabiji*.

The landscape it presented still sent shivers along her rigid spine on this, her twenty-ninth and final visit to the Rasu stronghold.

The others had allowed her to read up on the most current information they'd acquired on the Rasu, and she now understood a good deal more about what she was seeing, beyond *ooh big scary imposing ships*.

The knowledge didn't help, though. In fact, it made this entire experience so much worse. As she watched a medium-sized Rasu ship sail past, she imagined it morphing into a slithering serpent and wrapping itself around the *Tabiji*, then *squeezing*.

She shuddered—and hurriedly suppressed the physical display. No emoting on the bridge. She'd always assumed the Rasu were surveilling her every move from the moment she entered their stellar system, and her newfound knowledge gave her no reason to stop assuming it now.

She could do this. She was an accomplished ice queen, and she could sell this lie, dammit. Merely another routine delivery to the masters, in no way whatsoever the opening gambit in a full-scale assault on the enemy.

Oh, how she wished she was back in her office on Kiyora. Or, hells, even her cell. Of course, a better cell—her home—awaited her on her return, but what were the odds she was returning?

The enemy would know something had changed. They would detect her elevated heart rate over previous visits in the throbbing of her blood vessels beneath her skin. They would scan the stasis chambers and notice their contents were identical, or how a few deadly modifications had been added to the chambers' chassis.

They were so many, so commanding, so unfathomable, they *must* know.

A cargo freighter approached her location. Possibly the same one as the last twenty-eight times, possibly half the same and half new Rasu, right? Either way, the wave of claustrophobia it evoked when its hangar bay opened and swallowed the *Tabiji* whole felt the same.

"Asterion Dominion vessel. Provide your cargo manifest."

Gemina gazed blankly out at the cavernous hanger bay. "8,000 biosynthetic life forms in stasis and in a suitable condition for in-corporation."

"Open yourselves and deliver your cargo."

"Acknowledged." With pleasure. Let her just get straight on that. She entered a command on the pane beside her. The *Tabiji's* bay doors opened, and rows upon stacked rows of stasis chambers cascaded out of the hold to be claimed by Rasu machinery—by Rasu.

She almost felt...empathy for Nika as she watched the chambers be gathered up and trundled away. She would not trade places with the woman right now for all the worlds and an endless supply of sake-soaked dumplings.

"Your next contribution will consist of no less than 9,600 biosynthetic life forms. Our needs have grown."

Didn't they always? The Rasu seemed to her a ravenous beast striving to feed a hunger which could never be sated. But for better or worse, almost certainly worse, there would be no next contribution. "Acknowledged. Request permission to depart."

"Granted."

She held her breath while the freighter expelled the *Tabiji* from its belly and headed off toward the heart of the stronghold, carrying an army of Nikas to their suicidal fate.

Gods, had it worked? Had she succeeded in fooling them? She oh-so-cautiously turned the ship around and began accelerating away. Just like normal, nothing amiss here. Her pulse pounded against her temples as she waited for a shot that...never came.

When the comforting darkness of the interstellar void at last welcomed her, she sent a ping.

Commander Palmer, the packages have been delivered. It's your show now. I am getting the hells out of here.

49

RASU STRONGHOLD

"Holy shit, these monsters are big."

Dashiel glanced tensely at Palmer. "Didn't you accompany the reconnaissance mission?"

"Yes. They're bigger the second time around." Palmer gave a wide berth to a Rasu vessel departing one of the platforms. "I'll be honest. I don't see how our little bombs are going to do more than dent these platforms."

"The math says they'll do more. So does the science and multiple ceraffin's analysis. This is chemistry and physics in action."

"I'd prefer it was guns in action."

"I'm sure you would, but I'd ask you to restrain yourself. We cannot win a shooting war against this enemy."

"Couldn't win a shooting war against the last one, either. All right, let's get this done."

Commander Palmer (OpFlare): "Heavy vessels, you are clear to deliver your payloads according to your assignments. Careful and quiet, and the enemy won't know we're here."

On a wide pane in the center of the bridge, several thousand dots began crawling toward the orbital platform ring. Out the viewport, nothing changed in the busy but deliberate activity of the Rasu ships.

Around Dashiel, military officers and a smattering of dynes monitored ship readings and relayed and confirmed orders with notable, professional efficiency. He was ashamed to admit that until a few weeks ago, he'd never given more than a passing thought to the Dominion military. It existed on the periphery of Asterion society as a small force large enough to dispatch the occasional violent primitives exploratory teams stumbled upon and to intercede when mercenary activity spiked along trade routes.

He currently wished it was a lot bigger and better funded, but mostly he was grateful it existed at all.

Palmer talked a couple of pilots through some harrowing approaches to their assigned platforms, and Dashiel listened in with interest. He was here on the *Dauntless* in case something went wrong with the bombs, but unless or until this happened, he arguably had nothing to contribute.

When he'd told Palmer he was coming along, the man had resisted, asserting that if something went wrong with the bombs during deployment, the whole plan was already fucked. Dashiel had responded that Palmer had obviously never had an assembly line go down at three in the morning the day of a massive product shipment deadline. It had earned him a confused glare, but also a seat on the command ship.

He studied the scrolling chatter of the mission channel, but it was so laden in military jargon he couldn't get a good sense of the state of affairs. "How's the deployment going?"

Palmer frowned as he entered a command at his control panel. "Twenty-two percent of the bombs have been placed. No signs of detection so far."

"Then why are you frowning?"

"Because that's what I do during missions."

Well. Dashiel rubbed at his jaw, annoyed at his own frustration with this waiting and watching. They'd spend an hour delicately placing the bombs, then everything would more or less happen all at once—and by then they'd be fleeing the system, lest they get caught in the resulting inferno.

They'd placed more conventional if still powerful explosives at each of the d-gates during the journey here, because should Rasu ships be following in hot pursuit, they wouldn't have the luxury of placing them on the way back. Either way, they'd use remote triggers to blow the d-gates one by one after traversing them, and hopefully before any pursuers did the same. It might only buy them a few days, but they'd deny the Rasu a breadcrumb trail leading directly to Synra's doorstep.

The Taiyok commander insisted his ships would take the long way home, so they didn't have to worry about getting those ships through the d-gates. Dashiel, however, was not inclined to wait three weeks to get home and see Nika again. And if it all went to hells, both he and Palmer needed to be back in the Dominion, on the ground, doing whatever they could think of to stop the inevitable.

∧R

ADAF Second Lieutenant Kiernan Phillips did not want to be here. 'Here' being 0.8 kilometers from an alien structure so vast and menacing it blocked out the inferno of a star burning just on the other side of it.

The dull, purplish metal of the Rasu platform absorbed so much light that, as Kiernan stared at it, it seemed to dissolve into a black hole waiting to absorb his miniscule ship and him with it. It was alive, right? The structure had its own thoughts, its own intentionality—no reason to believe its intention *wasn't* to consume him for a snack.

He shook his head roughly, trying to break the spell. He had a job to do. Place a single one of the new KA bombs at the location marked in bright red on his HUD, then place a single additional one at the second location marked in equally bright red. Then turn tail and flee this freakish spectacle.

He breathed through his nose and extended the ship's grapnel. The KA bomb hovered in its grasp in front of the bow, a speck of dust against the looming shadow of the platform. He didn't comprehend how the bomb was supposed to vanquish the enemy, but he didn't need to comprehend it—he only needed to place it.

"So get the fuck on with it, numb nuts."

He fired his thrusters in short bursts until the bomb slid inside the bright red circle on his HUD, then released the clamps and retracted the grapnel.

"See, that wasn't so hard. One more to go."

While the grapnel returned to the undercarriage and retrieved the second bomb, he whistled a tune he'd heard at a party last weekend. Until today, the life of a pilot in the Asterion Dominion Armed Forces had not been a particularly notable or exciting one. Half the people he met thought he was blowing smoke when he told them what he did for a living. 'What military?' they'd retort, staring at him suspiciously.

What military, indeed. Endless training and endless drills for a war that would never come—until one day, approximately yesterday, it did.

Still, it wasn't going to be much of a war if all they had to do was stealthily drop off a bunch of bombs and leave. No shooting at the enemy, no flexing of his ship's acrobatic muscles, no trench runs.

As his gaze drew inexorably back to the towering hull of the Rasu platform, he decided he was okay with this.

He eased the grapnel and its new cargo out and eased the ship over to the next target location. Almost...almost...*there*. He released the clamps and let his body sag within its harness.

Done. Time to go home. He reversed thrusters and rejoiced every new meter added between him and the platform—

—an alarm flashed in the left section of his HUD. Nothing catastrophic like a hull rupture or oxygen loss, thankfully. He zoomed the alarm.

Package 1 is no longer in position.

The hells?

∧R

"We've got a problem."

Dashiel hurried to Palmer's side, dreading the nature of the problem but relieved for the interruption of his own morbid ruminations. "Tell me."

"Multiple deployment units are reporting the bombs aren't syncing their orbits with the platforms. They're drifting off their targets at a rate of 1.4 meters per second."

Dashiel moved to the pane at the center of the bridge. "Do we have any visuals?"

The feed from an Asterion vessel materialized in a corner of the pane. The pilot had tagged one of the KA bombs, microscopic against the hull of the twenty-kilometer-long battery platform, with a bright green dot to identify it. Both the platform and the bomb traveled in a clockwise orbit around the star—but as they did, the bomb inexorably drifted at a downward angle. Another few minutes and the platform was going to leave the bomb behind.

Lacking any form of artificial propulsion, the bombs were placed in such a way as to fall into a natural stellar orbit. They'd assumed the platforms did the same, but it now appeared the structures were modifying their orbital paths in some way. Why and how didn't matter.

By the time the pilots finished placing all the bombs, upwards of thirty percent of them would have fallen out of position. But they couldn't begin detonating now. The plan depended on the creation of a cascading power surge across the entire network.

They needed a way to keep the bombs in position for just a few minutes longer. Dashiel pressed his palms against his temples, racing through knowledge banks and analysis algorithms in search of a way—then spun to Palmer. "I need to look at one of the bombs."

"We've got ten spares in the cargo hold. Don't blow us up."

50

RASU STRONGHOLD

The KA bomb resembled a large storage trunk—longer than it was wide, with curved edges leading to a cylinder slot on each end. Inside were two compartments, one packed with raw kyoseil, the other with alisinium$_6$. When triggered, valves in each compartment would open, shooting both materials into a central chamber that would then be electrified and ejected from the casing, ensuring fireworks in short order.

The bomb's casing was constructed of a tungsten-cobalt super-alloy. Tough, resilient and capable of retaining structural integrity against the blistering heat that came with proximity to the star. Borderline ferromagnetic.

He stood and stared at the device for another beat…but there was only one way to be sure. He cleared his throat and motioned to the officer standing guard. "Can you help me for a minute? We need to remove the bomb from its berth."

"For what reason? We can't have an explosive device just rolling around in here. Do we need to load it into a launch tube?"

"No. I need to test something. Urgently. All our lives may depend on it, so please."

The man's lips puckered. "Commander Palmer said—"

Dashiel hit his comm. "Palmer, I need authorization to undock one of the bombs from its berth. Now."

"Gods help us all. Authorized."

He crouched on the left side of the berth. "Let's unlock both sides at once and carefully roll it out."

"Yes, sir." The officer moved to the other side, and together they eased it onto the floor. It rocked once before settling on one semi-flat side about two meters from the inner starboard hull.

He unholstered his Glaser, then adjusted the setting to low-power, narrow-beam. "You'll want to stand clear, Officer."

"Sir!"

"Another step back. Thank you." He aimed the Glaser and fired on the bomb's casing.

A weak surge of electricity tickled his skin, but no explosion followed. Instead, the device rolled end-over-end until it hit the hull.

Dashiel hurried over and fell to his knees beside it. He curled his hands around one end and tugged, but the device remained locked in place, one side flush against the hull.

Okay.

He stood and nodded to the officer. "Thank you for your help."

"But what about the bomb? Don't we need to return it to its berth?"

"Keep an eye on it, but it should stay where it is." He pivoted and hurried back to the bridge.

⋀℟

"You *shot* a KA bomb? The bomb that's designed to detonate when electrified?"

Dashiel hurried past Palmer to the central pane—but no red warnings flashed, which suggested the entire plan hadn't collapsed while he'd been below. "Only the internal compartment gets electrified, and it's insulated from the exterior casing. It was a low-risk test."

"Well, so long as it was low risk. Why did you do it?"

"I had to confirm the casing was ferromagnetic, meaning it can turn into a permanent magnet when an electrical current is introduced. Jerry's default physical state is a metal similar to vanadium and niobium, both of which are paramagnetic." Palmer blinked at him. "When exposed to an external magnetic field, a paramagnetic material will be weakly attracted to the source."

"You..." understanding dawned in the man's eyes "...oh. You want us to turn the KA bombs into magnets so they'll stick to the hulls of the platforms."

"Yes, I do."

"A little piece of Jerry in a lab is a long way from star-rated superstructures. What if the form the Rasu take to create the hulls isn't...paramagnetic?"

"Then we're fucked. But we know the Rasu are constrained by the laws of physics and chemistry, same as we are. The materials we would use to construct hulls capable of withstanding the prolonged heat of a star? They're nearly all at least paramagnetic."

Palmer gazed out the viewport. "How strong of a pulse will it take to magnetize them without blowing them up?"

Dashiel had done the math on his way to the bridge. Out in the field, the bombs were a lot farther than two meters from their targets, so the field needed to be stronger. But Palmer was right. Too strong of a jolt stood to burn through the protective interior layers and set the bombs off prematurely. He blew out a breath through a clenched jaw. "Two hundred megajoules in a single millisecond burst."

Palmer reached out and began entering a series of commands.

Commander Palmer (OpFlare): "Deployment units, listen up. You have new instructions...."

Dashiel tuned out the details as his attention focused in on the visual at the center of the pane. The bomb they'd observed before had drifted almost to the far edge of its assigned platform. Another thirty seconds and the platform would move beyond its reach.

From beneath the visual, a flash streaked toward the bomb, then vanished as quickly as it had appeared. The next instant the bomb leapt toward the platform like a tether had been yanked, landed on the hull, and rolled back and forth a few times before settling to a stop.

Dashiel soaked in the rush of adrenaline that flooded his veins, relishing the high it brought. He was smiling by the time he turned to Palmer—who scowled darkly at the zoomed-in visual.

"What?"

"If the platforms *are* Rasu, aren't they going to notice when a foreign object attaches itself to them?"

"I had actually thought of that. I never said it was a perfect fix, merely our only fix. Hopefully the devices are too small for them to notice immediately. But tell everyone to hurry."

"I assure you, Advisor Ridani, they are proceeding with all due speed."

"Of course." He dragged a hand along his jaw. "We should wake Nika up."

"No. Not until all the bombs are placed."

"But we don't know how long it will take her to reach the power control center."

"And when she does reach it, she won't be able to loiter there while we finish our job. If every last bomb isn't in position and ready to detonate right then, goodbye plan. We have to wait."

AR

A readout in the bottom left corner of the pane ticked up.

KA bomb placement: 72%

The number had crawled to a virtual standstill for the last ten minutes while pilots returned to already-deployed bombs and electrified them, but in the last minute it had finally started increasing again. Almost there—

—a tiny burst lit a corner of the viewport.

Palmer instantly began scrolling through incoming data. "Report, Quadrant 3 vessels."

Lieutenant Volshoi (OpFlare): "ADV 8-5C got sideswiped by a Rasu vessel leaving the nearest platform. The collision disrupted the cloaking shield, and the Rasu vessel fired."

Commander Palmer (OpFlare): "ADV 8-5C, what's your status?"

Silence answered.

Palmer's posture grew more rigid. "They know we're here now. I've no idea how fast word will spread among the aliens, but we are out of time."

Commander Palmer (OpFlare): "Heavy vessels, you have sixty seconds to deposit your remaining payloads and bug out. Light vessels, depart for Rendezvous Point Bravo near Gate 6."

"All stations, we are at Alert Level 1." Palmer spun to Dashiel. "Now. Wake her up now."

51

RASU COMMAND PLATFORM

I open my eyes.
Open.

Open.

Open.

Open....

The frosted glass of a stasis chamber cover looms above me, over and over and over again in an endless recursion.

Begin. This thought is singular, yet distant. A command from myself. The covers all slide open like a cascade of dominoes, revealing bright, sterile light from high above.

8,000

I retrieve a blade—*archine*, a word infused anew with consequential meaning—from a hidden pocket to my left. I know where it is because my mind is flooded by an avalanche of memories and pain and data and joy.

I am Nika Tescarav.

I am Nika Kirumase.

I am Nicolette Hinotori.

I am Anaden and SAI and kyoseil, all bound up in an Asterion soul that lives and loves and badly wants to continue doing so.

I will die today as many times as I must so that I can live.

I breathe in, and with the exhale absorb the knowledge entwined in every recorded tick forward of time that has led to this moment. No, not to *this* moment—to thirteen hours and twenty-two minutes in the past. But I sense nothing crucial has changed during the gap in time, and I know what I have to do.

I reach up and grasp the frame, pull myself up and climb out of the stasis chamber. The Rasu will instantly become aware of the escape of the prisoners. This body has never walked, but now it must run.

Run.

    Run.

        Run run run run run.

Shadows of myself flit in and out of my peripheral vision, but I can only focus on my own. I search for an opening cut into a wall of the expansive lab, because the Rasu don't use doors.

A hulking, multi-limbed Rasu steps into my path. My legs are no more. I fall.

The violet flame of a weapon firing sears through me. My chest explodes. I fall.

Blinding light from nowhere and everywhere consumes me. I fall.

Rasu orbs flood the lab with their beams crisscrossing the room in a macabre dance of death. Slicing into flesh. I fall. I'm falling for so long.

6,618

I crouch and sprint beneath the fire. Alarms are sounding now. I need to move faster.

Agonizing pain rips up my spine to burn the base of my skull. I fall.

Waves in the air form Rasu words. My routines filter, sort and translate them. *Breach. Stop the specimens. Kill. Kill all.*

I fall.

5,497

Openings leading out of the endless lab begin to melt and seal shut. I force this newborn body to sprint ahead, but the alien metal crushes me in a vise-grip. My breastbone shatters. My heart ruptures.

I fall.

    Fall.

        Fall.

            Fall.

                Fall.

4,816

I rush forward and slip through seconds before the way is shut. *I slip through.*

> *I slip through.*

>> *I slip through.*

A crude schematic of the platform floats in my mind, half scans captured by stealthed reconnaissance ships and half guesswork cobbled together by military experts and the strange new ceraffin. The schematic seems certain that the power control center is 3.2 kilometers away. Down below, into the depths.

A maze awaits me, endless uniform hallways, each one Rasu. But I have escaped the killing floor that was the lab. I stand a chance.

I must be quiet, but I must be swift.

I turn left.

Nika, you need to hurry. The Rasu are activating their defenses. If we don't detonate the bombs soon, they'll be able to block the power flows.

Dashiel's voice. It's like a whisper in a dream. My love, my—

—I never see why I fall.

I climb down one of the tubes the Rasu use to transition between levels.

I'm trying. I...we are all trying.

I fall.

A block-like Rasu collides with me in the tube. I fall.

3,333

I run left, then right. Straight ahead. The walls swim and morph, and my path is cut off. I fall.

I backtrack. Left left left right left ahead keep going ahead. Dead end end end end end. I fall.

2,819

A room of Rasu. I fall in so many pieces.

Another lab. In it the carcasses of Asterions are flayed open and spread across dissection tables. My heart breaks, and a scream rips through my throat. I want to fall, and I do.

I run for the depths of the platform, again and again, from multiple directions and on multiple paths. Left, then down, straight, then down. Always down.

The wall beside me dissolves, and I fall into space. I've done this part before, but this time Dashiel can't be here to catch me. Heat and light engulf me as a cobwebbed star welcomes me into its embrace.

Space again. Heat and light. Falling, falling forever.

1,681

I run up across ramps and leap down into gaps and tubes. Power begins to prickle my skin. Not long now. Rasu metal slices through me. I fall.

I veer right, away from the growing power, a last-minute feint to buy more of me time. I fall.

I'm gutted. I fall.

I round a corner and surprise a bipedal Rasu. My blade is in my hand, and I lash out, slicing upward. A Rasu limb falls to the ground.

The archine blade works!

The companion limb barrels forward into my face and I—

—fall.

807

Openings vanish as I rush for them. The way is shut.

Shut.

    Shut.

        Shut.

Cornered, I fall.

Boxed in, I fall.

Trapped, I fall.

435

The floor and the ceiling compress into one. I fall.

The walls liquefy and flood the room, drowning me in molten metal. I float, fallen.

The alarms grow louder and more urgent. Orders are barked, locations shouted out. I don't know which ones pinpoint me. I keep running. I keep falling.

213

The rooms widen and grow spacious once more, filled with equipment buzzing and blinking out the language of the Rasu. I'm close.

Equipment abandons its usual purpose for a new one. I fall to scanners and atmosphere regulators and radiation sensors.

121

I plummet down a tube. The longest one, and the last.

The walls of the tube shift, and I crash to the floor far below, shattering my legs. My broken body lies there until I fall.

I brace myself and land nimbly on the floor. My skin burns as energy washes over me. The air is electrified, and only the most robust internal protections keep my OS from frying.

At the center of a cavernous room spins a vortex a thousand-fold larger than the one in the Rasu simex. Violet plasma roils and thrashes like a caged animal, darting out beyond the bounds only to be drawn inexorably back into the maelstrom. Rows of crystals line the ceiling, walls and floor surrounding the vortex. Tens of thousands of them, and each one is illuminated from within by a pulsing glow.

A prick stings the base of my spine. I fall.

I need to move but instead I watch. The vortex neither grows nor shrinks. The crystals' pulses fall into a regular rhythm. This is steady-state. A power distribution system, feeding the behemoth that is the Rasu stronghold.

My knees are cut out from beneath me. I fall.

89

Somewhere, a module controls it—a Rasu, but a Rasu functioning as a machine. Programmable and divergable.

A row of flashing lights catches my attention. Along the left wall and dangerously close to the sea of crystals.

Ahead of me, another is already moving toward it. The floor vanishes beneath her. She falls. I fall.

I run. We run. We fight and dodge. Our blades slash and thrust. We fall.

63

I dash among my fighting and falling sisters as they clear the path for me. The floor vanishes again, but I leap over the chasm and reach the bank of equipment. I look left, then right. It stretches for a hundred meters in each direction.

How to locate the correct module? There can be no hesitation and will be no second chances. I stand flush against the equipment, where the Rasu cannot afford to dissolve the floor, and study the flashing lights, reading their output using the ceraffin's algorithms.

Internal power flow. Engine stabilization. Radiation shielding and conversion—

—sixty meters away, I find it. Multi-platform power regulation. Safety controls. A sprawling array of modules dedicated to managing not this platform, but all platforms as one.

The floor behind me rises up and consumes me whole. I fall.

Falling becomes a feedback loop.

34

The floor will take us all. I run away, toward the vortex. I burn up before I fall.

21

I run in the wrong direction, sacrificing myself to draw the enemy's attention for a few precious seconds. I fall.

13

Nika, you must hurry. There is no more time.

And no more misdirection. I sprint for the module array.

Pain explodes in my mind. I fall.

> *Fall.*
>> *Fall.*
>>> *Fall.*
>>>> *Fall.*

5

A module dances out a pattern of light, and the melody tells me its purpose is the one I seek.

A shock erupts from beneath me. I fall.

4

Ten meters. I stumble to the floor, my legs crippled from a strike I never see. I fall.

3

I reach the module and slice into it with the archine blade, then tear away a section to expose Rasu circuitry. I grasp a Rasu filament and open myself to it.

Reams of alien code spiral through my mind, overwhelming my process for thirty-five nanoseconds until the new programming takes hold. Analyzes, sorts, identifies.

Time slows, then stands still. Ones and zeroes. On and off, and the superpositions in between.

Claws grab me and rip me away from the module. I fall.

2

I grasp a Rasu filament and open myself to it. I understand it now, and my programing churns ever faster, overclocking itself in a suicidal race to create the diverge code that will shut down the failsafe controls across the platforms.

A shadow encroaches on the light of the module, and I throw myself in front of the incoming Rasu fire to protect myself. My last self.

I fall.

1

I push the diverge code into the Rasu system, brute-force over-writing existing commands until the chain reaction cannot be stopped.

As the neural web comprising my mind burns itself out and I fall, I send out a single command.

Ignite.

52

RASU STRONGHOLD

*I*gnite.

The platform Nika had infiltrated electrified in a lightning storm of silver and blue. Fissures erupted across the hull to vent waves of electricity out into space then expanded to engulf the entire structure. In seconds the remains of the hull crumbled and tumbled into the star's embrace.

And with it, all 8,000 iterations of Nika's body, psyche and soul.

Dashiel held his breath as like a lit fuse, thousands of KA bombs detonated in staccato explosions across the orbital ring of platforms, sending electricity coursing through enormous batteries already filled to the brim with power. There was nowhere for the overflow to go but out, and the battery platforms had mechanisms for such an eventuality. With the floodgates open and the safety guards off, waves of excess power poured out to the other platforms in the network.

It took ten seconds for the energy overflows to begin to spill back into the Dyson lattice. Energy also continued to flow *from* the Dyson nodes, and across the background of the star's photosphere bursts of electrical energy exploded like fireworks in the empty space between the nodes and the platforms.

Then a node blew apart. One down, a hundred thousand or so to go.

A series of blasts lit the battlefield pane on the *Dauntless* as multiple platforms shattered in rapid-fire fashion. In their wake, a section of the Dyson lattice cracked and fell into the star, destroying the structural integrity of the entire lattice.

A new image appeared on the pane, from the far side of the star, where node after node glowed brightly and...melted.

A solar flare unfurled, reaching out to lick at the crumbling hull of a platform. A coronagraph filter revealed the surge of plasma and EM radiation that followed in its wake, and in a few more seconds the platform had melted as well.

The pane now struggled to keep up with the number of solar flares whipping across the star's profile, and the *Dauntless'* position 0.4 AU distant from the star suddenly didn't feel nearly distant enough.

A ping arrived then, and for a moment Dashiel forgot about the raging inferno burning down a stellar system.

"Sir, our radiation shielding is at 92% capacity and rising. We can't stay here much longer."

Palmer's voice was calm and even-keeled. "Understood. Navigation, be prepared to depart the system at full speed on my mark. Ridani, care to weigh in?"

Dashiel breathed out through his nose, trying to ignore his racing pulse. "Based on the spiking solar flare activity and parallel increase in CMEs, I suspect the massive energy pushback from the Dyson lattice has destabilized the star's magnetic field."

"Is it going to erupt? Go nova?"

"Um...no. It's unlikely. But until the magnetic field re-stabilizes, the region surrounding the star, out to maybe an AU, will not be friendly to anything living."

"It's working, then?"

Dashiel steepled his hands at his mouth. For several seconds he stood there, transfixed by the symphony of destruction unfolding before his eyes. They'd lit the spark—one giant bomb of a spark—and now the star, one of the most powerful nuclear bombs in the universe, was taking care of the rest.

"Ridani?"

"Yes. It's looking as though it's working."

"Excellent. Navigation—"

In the left quadrant of the heavily filtered viewport, a leviathan Rasu vessel that had assembled in the quiet of a few minutes ago moved toward a growing vortex in space. A wormhole.

"Palmer, we can't let a Rasu that size escape."

"No shit. Navigation, advance to weapons range of the Rasu vessel."

Commander Palmer (OpFlare): "All vessels still in the stellar system, open fire on the Rasu vessel opening a wormhole in Quadrant 7. Exact coordinates are being distributed now."

The Rasu vessel accelerated forward as the wormhole grew larger. The *Dauntless* followed.

"Palmer, if we're not careful we'll get drawn into it—"

"Thank you for your input. Weapons, fire."

Any visual sign of their weapons arcing across space was lost in the brilliance of the explosions consuming the thousands of platforms and Rasu vessels—at least until their fire impacted the hull of the leviathan in a smattering of tiny pinpricks. Had they so much as cracked the hull?

"Again."

Dashiel paced in a tight circle. "We don't need to destroy it, just distract it from leaving for long enough for the star to finish its work."

Beyond their encounter, the star's activity increased precipitously. It seemed to swell, gobbling up what remained of the Dyson lattice into the breadth of its photosphere. "Which shouldn't be long."

Of course, right now any solar flare that took out the leviathan was certain to destroy the *Dauntless* as well. Which...they could recover from, so long as they completed the mission here.

The Rasu vessel swung away from the wormhole in their direction, and as it loomed over their comparatively miniscule ship, Dashiel had a hard time convincing himself this was a positive development.

"Evasive maneuvers. Keep firing."

Kiernan never should have lamented not getting to shoot at the enemy.

He gritted his teeth and fought the rising pull of the spinning vortex that might be an *actual* black hole to swing into position and fire on a vessel so gargantuan it made the gargantuan platform he'd been so intimidated by resemble a Chizeru child's toy.

But he was, believe it or not, rather good at the shooting-at-the-enemy part, and the low-grade panic that had accompanied him for most of the mission ebbed away as he swept beneath the Rasu vessel in search of a weak point. Ha! But, seriously, a weapons or engine port, a cargo bay door seam…there had to be some weakness on this monstrosity.

He fired every few seconds for good measure as he searched, hoping the vessel didn't sprout a lumbering arm and swat away him and his gnat bites.

Above him an array of violet crystals throbbed with light, as if they were about to burst.

Damn. He'd found a weapons port all right. He zeroed in and unleashed the full firepower of his tiny fighter jet, cackling in delight when his weapons impacted and a few crystals cracked and broke apart. "Take that, you Rasu scum—oh, shit!"

His ship lurched to starboard and fell into a slow roll—except he hadn't guided it into any such roll. He tried to straighten out the motion, then tried to reverse thrusters…but he may as well be playing with a dead stick.

The cavorting bands of the vortex grew in his viewport as his roll accelerated into a spin. The dark hull of the Rasu vessel flashed past him again and again and again. His vision began to blur, but he thought on the last pass the hull looked to be cracking in two. Maybe his shots had hit their mark….

The last thing he saw before he passed out was the vortex rushing in to consume him.

Tiny dots of light danced across the Rasu hull like fireflies—the impacts of hundreds of weapons from the Asterion and Taiyok fleets. The leviathan almost seemed to hesitate, as if taken aback by an attack on multiple fronts.

A solar flare spanning a full quarter of the star's diameter spewed out into space to destroy a dozen broken platforms and several thousand ships fleeing them. The viewport flashed white as the flare overwhelmed all filters.

"Radiation shielding at 108%!"

"Palmer, it's time to go."

"Not until this monster is dust. Navigation, pull back to maximum weapons range. Weapons, keep firing."

Now left unattended by the Rasu vessel, the wormhole began to contort. The *Dauntless* lurched, halted in its reversal by an increasingly unstable tear in the fabric of space.

"Navigation, full reverse, maximum power."

Against the hypnotic gleam of the wormhole vortex, two dark pinpricks flickered and vanished. Small ships being drawn into the vortex—but theirs, or Rasu?

Their hull shuddered as the engine struggled to counter the pull of potent cosmic forces. The leviathan jerked around erratically, now itself caught in the convulsing forces of the wormhole.

Twin solar flares reached out across space and snatched another three hundred Rasu vessels in their grasp. Flares now danced freely along the photosphere, resembling the spindly arms of an octopus as they were drawn toward the deluge of electricity still churning through the inner stellar system.

The hull of the *Dauntless* abruptly quietened, which Dashiel hoped to hells was a sign they had escaped the wormhole's grasp.

"All stations report."

"External sensors are down. All the energy surges overloaded them."

"Hull breach on Deck 5, starboard aft section. Safety doors have sealed off the exposed area."

"Radiation shielding at 121% capacity. Failure in eighteen seconds."

"Noted. Weapons, continue firing."

Even as Palmer issued the order, the hull of the Rasu leviathan began to deform and warp before breaking into a dozen pieces that tumbled into the wormhole and disappeared.

"Radiation shielding failure in nine seconds."

"All non-essential power to engines. Depart for Rendezvous Point Bravo on my mark."

Commander Palmer (OpFlare): "All vessels depart for Rendezvous Point Bravo now."

"Mark."

The last sight they glimpsed was the fragmenting wormhole being devoured by a monster solar flare.

53

MIRAI ONE PAVILION

I fall....

Nika's eyes jerked open, but all she saw was a blinding flame of violet light imprinted on her retinas.

She bolted upright and flailed wildly for anything solid to grasp onto as her mind swam through overlapping realities and an endless parade of death. Pain, searing into her bones even as she ran straight off the edge of the universe and tumbled—

"Hey, hey, Nika. Breathe. You're safe."

The voice echoed down a long, dark hallway that twisted and morphed and became Rasu. She knew she should run toward the voice, but she could only run away, hyperventilating until the last of her oxygen abandoned her and she was falling once more, falling forever....

A soothing coolness radiated from the base of her neck and out through her veins, slowing her pounding heartbeat or possibly restarting it.

She breathed air into lungs that had in fact not been shredded by a Rasu blade. Her eyes began blinking of their own accord, and shapes began to emerge from the light.

A face stared down at her intently, concern carving deep lines around shining blueberry irises. Perrin.

"Nika? Can you hear me?"

"I—I—was—I'm not—I can't—where—"

Hands supported her shoulders as a familiar voice murmured in her ear. "You're at the Pavilion. You're safe."

Perrin's features blurred and almost faded away, then gradually came into focus. But they remained off-kilter. Upside down? No, but....

The hands steadying her from behind lifted, and a soft surface welcomed her. She blinked again, this time of her own volition, as genuine awareness began to take hold in her mind. She'd fallen off the cot and half onto the floor, only to be caught by…she cautiously turned her head. Maris? Behind her friend, a stranger she'd seen before stood watching. The med tech, an empty syringe in her hand and dubious scrutiny on her face.

Maris moved to her side and grasped one of Nika's hands in both of hers. "Be calm. Be still."

It sounded like excellent advice, and she attempted to follow it. Breath by breath the raw visions and brutal sensations began to recede. Not gone, but fading into memories rather than stalking her in a waking nightmare.

She was in a room. Not really, though…a temporary room carved into a much larger one. Beyond the illusory wall of a shoji screen, voices and sounds echoed in urgent beats.

The mission! "Did it work?"

Perrin slid a pane in front of her. On it, brilliant explosions rippled across platform after platform after platform. They cascaded inward and outward as Rasu material plummeted into the star and the star swelled hungrily. Lattice scaffolding tore and fractured as new explosions erupted, tiny against the star's vast surface but spreading like ants driven from their mound.

All the air left her lungs as she sank down onto the pillow—and instantly bolted back up. "Dashiel?"

Maris' gaze drifted away. "They haven't departed the system yet."

She swung her legs off the cot and tried to rush for the War Room past the screen, forgetting she needed to stand before she could run. Vertigo sent her perception tumbling in and out of realities—one second she was back on the platform, in thousands of places at once and dying in most of them, and the next she was fixated on the cushiony softness of a blanket that had somehow become clutched in her hand. She felt agony, she felt loss, over and over and over.…

"Nika?" Perrin's hand was at her elbow. "Come back to us, okay?"

Right. This sole version of her had not died at the stronghold. She was alive, with her dearest friends at her side. She nodded shakily. "Yeah. I am. I just...tell Lance to get his ass out of there."

"As if he would listen to us."

"What's the comm channel?"

Maris sent it to her, and she sent dual pings to Lance and Dashiel.

Don't fry watching the show. Get out of there.

Palmer ignored her, but Dashiel's response came swiftly.

Nika, you did it. The stronghold is disintegrating. I love you.

Then get back here so you can demonstrate your appreciation in person.

She exhaled and let her feet touch the floor, then gingerly tested out weight on them. When she didn't collapse to the floor in a tangled pile of limbs, she reached out to wrap her arms around Perrin and Maris. "I'm so glad your faces were the first ones I saw when I woke up. Thank you so much for being here for me."

Perrin squeezed her tight. "Always."

Maris gave her a mysterious half-smile. "As she says."

Maris' definition of 'always' was doubtless more expansive than Perrin's, but Nika valued them both equally, and beyond what she could measure.

But her work wasn't yet done. "Also, never tell anyone what a disaster I was when I first woke up." She withdrew from the embrace and motioned toward the gap in the screen. "Let's see what we can do to help."

She spotted Cameron and Terry huddled together in front of a chaotic bank of panes at the far end of the War Room. "What's the situation?"

Cameron looked her way in surprise. "Nika, you're awake! What was it like in there?"

"Hell. Tell me it was worth it."

"Right." Cameron studied her briefly then motioned to the panes, which appeared to be displaying the same scene Perrin had showed her moments earlier, multiplied many times over. "Our close-range sensors have been destroyed, which is a good sign. It means the stellar activity is taking out everything in a close orbit. Here's the last visuals the *Dauntless* captured."

The scene on one of the panes shifted to reveal a vortex similar to the one that had nearly eaten the *Wayfarer* during their trip to the stronghold. Only its cohesiveness was breaking down, flinging little whirlpool eddies out to rip holes in space. Rasu ships large and small tumbled into the convulsing wormhole—

—a wave of plasma, light and energy swept across space to consume everything. The pane went blank.

"Gods...." She spun back to Cameron. "You said the 'last' visuals. The last before what?"

"They cut it close, but they've escaped the system and are headed home."

A wave of relief-fueled dizziness washed through her, and the fading remnants of her earlier vertigo spiked to join it. She placed a steadying hand on the wall. "Good. What about casualties?"

"At last count, we lost twenty-three ships, with crews ranging from one to five each. The Taiyoks are being typically tight-lipped regarding the health of their fleet. We know they lost a minimum of twelve vessels, but the number is probably higher. Elder Zhanre'khavet says their surviving ships have departed the stellar system and are returning to Toki'taku."

"I'll talk to him later. Express our appreciation and see if I can get out of him whether they need any assistance in their recovery." She gestured to the panes. "The fireworks show is marvelous, but what do we definitively know about Rasu losses?"

"The Dyson lattice has been annihilated, and the nodes along with it. We recorded catastrophic damage or confirmed destruction of 6,815 of platforms and over 30,000 vessels, but the numbers are without question far higher. We have every reason to believe every single platform orbiting the star has been destroyed or will be within the next hour and the outer orbit of satellites in the next two hours, but it will take our long-range sensors a day to confirm this.

"A Rasu leviathan was trying to escape through the wormhole you saw on the visuals. It broke apart as it was entering the vortex and disappeared. We obviously don't know the terminus point of the wormhole, so we can't confirm if the vessel traversed and exited the wormhole, or its state if it did so."

It was a complication, but if they got through this with nothing but pieces of a single Rasu escaping obliteration, they would have succeeded beyond her wildest fantasies.

It had never been more than a desperate shoestring of a plan, cobbled together with the fervor of the doomed. And it had worked.

She took a deep breath and did her best to inject authority and encouragement into her voice. Gods, she was tired. She felt as if she'd run a thousand marathons today...because in a way, she had. But the people in the room looked to her for guidance and inspiration. Their leader, their beacon.

"Everyone, you've done an incredible job today. This week, this month. The details will take a little while to sort out, but I daresay you've saved the Dominion. You've saved all of us. Congratulations."

She smiled and acknowledged the cheers that broke out, then turned back to Cameron and lowered her voice. "Stay on full alert...if nothing changes, for another four hours. Ping me immediately if anything does change. After that, it'll be time to start thinking about how we protect ourselves from the longer-term consequences of what we've done today."

AR

NAMINO

This time, Nika was waiting on him at the spaceport. A different spaceport, one busily managing a fleet of returning military ships. A victorious fleet.

The hull of the *Dauntless* bore dozens of scorch marks and a ten-meter-long gash beneath its aft section. It was supposed to be a command vessel, but Lance hadn't exactly played it safe, had he?

She lurked off to the side of the ramp, hopefully hidden from view, and waited until Dashiel had descended the ramp to leap out from the shadows and wrap him up in her arms.

"Nika!" He lifted her in the air to twirl her around. "You did it."

"We did it." She kissed his lips, then his nose, then his eyelids, then craned her head back to meet his gaze. "It looks as though you had an exciting time of things."

"There might have been a few tense minutes, and a few more of utter terror. But nothing compared to what you endured. Will you tell me what it was like for you?"

Her gaze dropped to study the woven fabric of his shirt.

"It's okay. If it was painful, you don't have to talk about it. I won't make you relive it."

"It was. But it was also incredible and world-altering and...I'm still trying to figure it all out. I *will* tell you about it, but not just yet. Is that all right?"

"Of course. We have time now."

She nuzzled his nose as he eased her to the ground. She thought she saw Lance disembarking in her peripheral vision, but he could wait his turn. "What's the status of the d-gates?"

"All destroyed. We dropped sensors on our way through, then watched as they exploded one after another. Any Rasu who survived will have to find us the hard way. But we need to be able to protect ourselves when they do."

She nodded. "Yes, we do, and we already have some ideas on that. Want to head to the Pavilion with me and hear about them?"

He groaned. "I don't get to sleep now?"

"Soon, darling. Soon."

54

MIRAI ONE PAVILION

Nika studied Parc with a healthy dose of skepticism. "And this is really feasible?"

"The ceraffin think so."

She sighed as they strolled beneath the canopy of the snowbell trees outside the Pavilion. Yes, the ceraffin had played a number of important roles in helping them to destroy the Rasu stronghold. They'd sifted through the science and the numbers in novel ways on the KA bombs and the Rasu programming code; her own ceraff had made it possible for 8,000 copies of her to work together to navigate the maze of a city-sized Rasu platform and disable the stronghold's safeguards. They were poised to revolutionize Asterion society in ways no one could yet fathom.

But ceraffin were simply a bunch of Asterions in intimate mental proximity, and she refused to abandon valuing the individuals behind the collective.

"What do *you* think?"

"Yeah. It's feasible. It'll be expensive as all hells, and it's going to require the invention of new materials, new ways to combine them, new programming and so on. It'll be a gargantuan undertaking. But we can do it. We can create planet-scale cloaking shields that will hide us from the Rasu."

"Then let's do it. Do you want to be in charge?"

Parc grunted. "Hells, no. Being in charge means responsibility. I'm already on to the next revolutionary idea."

"Which is?"

"I'll let you know when we think of it. Possibly large, deployable weapons based on the archine blade, or a family of smart worms designed to fuck up Rasu systems. Oh, and we've already got a theoretical model for a variation on d-gates that won't require a fixed terminus point to use. It'll revolutionize space travel."

"Seriously?"

"So seriously. I'm recommending we call it a Sukasu Gate. Don't worry, you'll be hearing a lot about it in a few days. As for the planetary shielding? Honestly, your sweetie should be in charge of the initiative. Maybe it'll distract him from developing a counter to kamero filters once he finishes designing a commercial ceraff node."

"We're not rebels any longer, Parc."

"Doesn't mean I don't have a passing use for a kamero filter from time to time. Or, I mean Ryan does."

"Uh-huh." They reached the entrance to the Pavilion, which finally looked as good as new, and she patted him on the shoulder. "All right, I have to go meet with some people. Keep the ideas coming."

◢R

Grant was waiting on her in the first-floor lounge. She gave him a hug, though it felt weird for a thousand reasons. "Thanks for agreeing to come by."

He withdrew from the hug quickly, as if he shared her discomfort. "I told you before—you ask of me what you need to."

For the millionth time since all this began, she wished she could remember every second of the last 700,000 years. They had been frequent friends over those aeons, and lovers somewhat less often. His declaration, and the weighty yet resolute sentiment adding conviction to his words, hinted at the complexity of that history, forever lost to her.

She smiled hesitantly and leaned against the table behind her. "Funny you say that, because I am going to ask something of you. I wish I didn't need to—you have a great life, and I don't want to disrupt it—but the time has come for all of us to dedicate ourselves to something greater than ourselves. Grant, it's time for you to rejoin the world and step up, maybe in a way only First Genners can. Step up to fight for not just our way of life, but our lives, period."

"I know it is." He stared at the floor for several seconds before nodding thoughtfully. "It was a nice 100,000 years while it lasted. What do you need me to do?"

She exhaled in relief. She'd worried he'd require a harder sell. "Use what you've learned in those 100,000 years and apply your clever, crafty psyche to some new initiatives. I want you to work with Lance Palmer and Dashiel to design new warships. Design modifications to existing warships and whatever other crazy ideas you can devise. We need ships that play to Asterion strengths and incorporate new tech the ceraffin are developing. Ships that can use Taiyok stealth capabilities and better weapons to match the Rasu on the battlefield."

"Is that all?" He winked at her, and for a moment everything was okay between them again. "I can live with those directives."

"Wonderful. Come upstairs with me and join the team."

ᴙ

Couches and lounge chairs had taken the place of tables and workstations in what had briefly been the War Room. Even if they couldn't relax as such, they could act as if they were relaxing while they worked.

Then Cameron wheeled in a cooler stocked full of beer and cocktails…so perhaps they *were* relaxing.

Nika settled in next to Dashiel on one of the couches and watched with a trace of amusement as Grant was welcomed as an old friend by Lance. Because of course he was.

She dropped her head onto Dashiel's shoulder, murmuring in contentment when he kissed her hair. They'd slept for fourteen solid hours the evening, night and morning before—then made love, cooked breakfast and gone back to bed for another four hours. On waking the second time, she'd almost begun to feel like herself.

It had been a decadent luxury to indulge in and sorely needed, but they couldn't afford to laze around any longer.

She did accept a beer from Adlai as she stood and turned in a slow circle, checking to make certain everyone was here. "I hope everyone slept half as well as I did last night, because our work is just beginning.

"We understand some things about our enemy now, and we've bought ourselves time—time we must use to get ready for when they show up. Because they *will* show up. There are Rasu still in this galaxy—vessels that were out on patrol or missions when we destroyed the stronghold and vessels that escaped during our attack—and we should be prepared today to encounter them.

"The far more serious threat, however, lies with the multitude of Rasu currently inhabiting hundreds of other galaxies. Sooner or later, they will notice their colleagues here in the Gennisi galaxy have gone silent. They will send a team to investigate, and when they do, they will learn they have an enemy here. An enemy who will not consent to be enslaved or annihilated.

"Not long after then, they will find one of our worlds, or they will find Toki'taku or Chosek. If we want to be ready for when they arrive, we have to start now.

"Several ceraffin have been digging into the Taiyok stealth technology, and they think they've come up with a method to build what is effectively a planet-sized kamero filter." She arched an eyebrow at Dashiel. "Parc is ready to talk your ear off on this topic for about five hours whenever you have...five hours."

"I will make time tomorrow." He pursed his lips. "I can't promise five hours, but I'll try for three."

"Good enough. Lance, the Advisors had a conversation last night, and we are all in agreement. You are hereby promoted to Advisor status—the first Advisor in a new Military Division."

He chuckled and sipped on his beer. "About godsdamn time."

"I agree, but I hope you're prepared for the work coming with the position. Build us a fleet. Agile ships, powerful ships, hardy ships, fast ships, whatever you think we can best use against the enemy. A few weeks ago, Delacrai said to me that in ten thousand years we could not build a military force to match the one the Rasu had stationed here, without considering what manner of forces they have stationed in other galaxies. She was right, but if we'd started eight years ago, we'd be millions of ships closer today. So, we start today."

She motioned to Grant, who had sat next to Maris off to the left. "Grant's the best ship and space-rated-equipment designer I know. I suspect he has some ideas to bounce off of you."

Grant jerked his head in Lance's direction. "We already set up a meeting for tomorrow."

"Fantastic. There are a dozen other initiatives we need to start, and a dozen more we need to think up then start. We are going to turn the productive output of the Dominion to a single purpose: preparing for the Rasu. We're going to do it openly, with the constant input of ideas, criticisms and hard work from all our citizens. We're going to have to learn new things and new ways to do them. We're going to have to adapt and change, maybe in some pretty big ways.

"And we'll do it, because we will always find a way to not merely survive, but thrive. This is what being an Asterion means."

Lance cleared his throat. "I hate to put a damper on the inspirational mood here, but we need to talk about *our* Rasu—about Jerry. You made it a promise you shouldn't have. Doing so got us vital intel we put to excellent use, but now our prisoner will be wondering when we plan to hold up our end of the bargain. For the record, I vote we close up the facility restraining it and throw away the lock code."

She nodded soberly. "I know you do. And you might be right. But I gave my word, and I won't break it now. We'll wait another week, then if the skies remain quiet, we'll return Jerry to the planet where we captured it and release it—and we'll station a mobile probe in orbit to watch it and, if it leaves, to follow it. Good enough?"

382 | G . S . J E N N S E N

"Not even close, but I'll live with it. And I'll soup up the drone with a few surprises."

"Thank you for compromising. All right, everyone. Unless there's anything else, let's get to work."

Maris leapt up from her seat, hand dancing in the air. "If I may. We're going to be delaying all this work for just a *few* more hours."

"Are we? Why is that?"

"I'm throwing a Dominion-wide party tonight. It's called a celebration, my dear, and we all bloody well deserve it."

Nika spread her arms in an exaggerated shrug. "Fair enough. Party tonight, work tomorrow."

55

MIRAI JUSTICE CENTER

Adlai blinked at the priority report in disbelief.

At 09:17 this morning, the psyche storage partition assigned to ex-Justice Advisor Blake Satair experienced a catastrophic failure. Sixty-two percent of the data stored therein was erased, and the remainder was corrupted beyond repair. Forensic analysis has uncovered no evidence of tampering or external intrusion, but also no technical cause for the failure. No other server partitions were affected.

In the absence of a secondary backup source, regeneration of Mr. Satair's psyche will not be possible at this time.

He rubbed at his temples and read it again. He despised the man, and a cruel part of him was not sorry to see Satair gone. But the specificity of the damage, befalling Satair and Satair alone, meant the likelihood of this being an accident was vanishingly low.

No, his gut told him this was murder. Final death imposed with malice aforethought.

Slicing into the secure storage servers used by Advisors should be impossible. Nearly as impossible as slicing into the secure storage servers used by the former Guides—which they'd done, of course. Well, not him, personally. NOIR people. Skilled NOIR slicers who now ran ceraffin like their own personal playgrounds.

A lot of people bore Satair sufficient ill will to wish him dead, but only a few were cold-blooded enough to actually do it. In all probability, only a single person.

Adlai checked the time; he was supposed to meet Perrin for the party tonight in two hours, which meant he had time to make a stop first. He ordered the forensic analysis redone by his best team and left the office.

∧R

MIRAI

Joaquim Lacese was staying in a room at the Mikan Hotel. The fourth floor housed a number of displaced NOIR members for the time being, though Adlai expected soon they'd be scattering to the wind.

He steeled himself and rang the bell.

Lacese opened the door wearing a guise of suspicion and mild annoyance. "Advisor Weiss. This is an unexpected...visit."

"May I come in?" While phrased as a question, it was not a request.

It nevertheless took a good five seconds for Lacese to step to the side and motion him in. "I'd offer you a drink, but I don't expect you'll be staying long enough to enjoy it."

"No." As soon as the door closed behind him, Adlai leveled a stern glare on Lacese. "Blake Satair's psyche backups were deleted this morning. It presents as a technical failure, but I think someone sliced into the server and deliberately destroyed the backups."

"Gods, that's terrible. Except, you know, not."

"I'll cut straight to the point. Did you do it? He kidnapped you and tortured you, which means you have ample reason to want to send him to his final death."

"Damn straight I have ample reason, and ample desire. But what I don't have are the skills required. You need backup in a firefight? I'm your guy—which you know, since I saved your ass in *Satair's* attack on the Pavilion. But I'm not a data wizard."

"But you know plenty of people who are. Who did you pay or bribe to do it for you?"

"No one. Hey, you said it reported as a technical failure. I'm sure that's what it was. We're not perfect, and neither are our machines. They make mistakes. The algorithms we write make mistakes."

"Not mistakes like this."

"Hey, it's been a crazy month. The Guides deposed, the government in disarray and having to be patched back together, Advisors jailed then escaping and attacking their own—and this is before you get to the Rasu. I bet you all have had to shuffle and rearrange and reconfigure a ton of procedures inside the Divisions. Just accept that something slipped through the cracks."

"Weiss, you're barking up the wrong tree here. Even if it *was* a deliberate action, I'm not the culprit. Satair had an enemies list a kilometer long. If you want, you can go interrogate everyone on it. My opinion, though? Don't waste any more breath on the scumbag. He's gone, and we're all better for it."

"I can't do that. Deletion causing final death is literally the single worst crime a person can commit, and I have a responsibility to find the person who did it and ensure they're punished accordingly."

"Justice must be served, yeah. From where I stand, it looks as if it already was. So, think long and hard on it, Advisor. Do you *really* want to come after me for this?"

"Want to? No. But understand this: I cannot turn a blind eye to a crime this heinous. If I'm able to prove you're behind it, I will take you down. I have no choice."

Lacese wandered around the small room in feigned aimlessness, nodding to himself. "I see. And if you do, how do you think Perrin will feel about it?"

"Are you threatening me?"

"No, I am not. I simply don't want her to get hurt, and I suspect you don't, either."

"Of course I don't." He sighed. "If it comes to that, I'll have to hope she understands, and possibly even forgives me."

"She is the forgiving sort." A shadow escaped Lacese's rigid control to pass across his face, but quickly vanished. "I wouldn't worry about it. You won't be taking me down, since I didn't do it."

Adlai stared at him. "Watch yourself, because I *will* be watching you."

"Not to worry. Now that the world's saved, I plan to kick back and chill."

"The world isn't saved. The Rasu threat is still out there."

"It's saved for today."

AR

After Weiss departed, Joaquim went to the refrigerator and got a beer, then sat on the single tiny couch in the rented room.

Weiss' expression hadn't so much as flickered when Joaquim had tossed out the barb about algorithms making mistakes, which probably meant Perrin hadn't told him about Cassidy. Not the details, anyway. He took comfort in the knowledge she'd kept his confidence and not exposed his greatest weakness to her lover.

Convincing Parc to slice into the Administration Division servers where Advisor psyche backups were stored hadn't been too difficult. Parc was a good guy—honorable, in his own quirky way—but his ethical standards were fluid on the best of days. Once Joaquim pointed out how Satair had maliciously aided and abetted the actions that led to Parc's former self being subjected to unspeakable torture for weeks on end, the man had jumped at the chance to help exact retribution.

Weiss wouldn't find the evidence he sought. Old Parc had been one of the best slicers in the Dominion, but new Parc was a godsdamn savant at it. Still, between the Platform explosion and now Satair, Joaquim had given the Justice Advisor two excellent reasons to lock him away for several centuries, so he really *should* watch his step for a while.

He contemplated the crystals of condensation percolating on the beer bottle. Permanently deleting Satair from the fabric of the universe was as close to vengeance as he was ever likely to get. This had to be closure, or nothing ever would be.

He closed his eyes and let Cassidy's smiling face consume his vision. He didn't need to call up an image, for the sight of her was forever imprinted upon his soul. He pressed his fingertips to his lips, then to the air where she wasn't.

Then he reopened his eyes, wiped a stray tear from his cheek, and made an appointment at a local clinic for a minor, Grade I up-gen. Just to tone down the reactionary anger a bit. Maybe a few other tweaks, too.

56

NIKA'S FLAT

A data weave sat alone atop the control pane in the library, waiting for her. Nika had known it must exist from the minute she'd learned of the library, and before the OpFlare mission began she'd finally worked up the courage to locate it. Not sufficient courage to read it.

She held it in her palm, studying it warily, even now *not* wanting to know its contents as much as she wanted to. But the world had changed, and it was time.

She curled up on the chaise on the balcony outside, folded her legs beneath her and opened the journal entry.

Date: Y12,458.094 A7
Subject: Vanishing Outposts – Moment of Truth

I'm heading to Mirai Tower tonight, to the Guides' most secure data vault. It's where my search for answers has led and the final place where those answers might reside.

My soul aches with dread of what those answers could be. If the Guides have turned against the people, if they have descended into madness, I will bear a measure of the blame.

We—the most inner circle of the First Generation—granted them the power they now hold. We entrusted the governance of the Dominion and protection of its citizens to them, because we did not want the responsibility and burden for ourselves. We did it on our own authority and without asking permission from the people; we naively thought we knew best, but I fear this decision will come back to haunt us in blood and death.

Over the millennia, almost without us noticing, the Guides have expanded their power far in excess of its origins. If I learn the truth behind the outpost disappearances and try to expose the Guides' misdeeds, I suspect they will try to stop me. I worry they now wield sufficient power to succeed.

I've taken what precautions I can, but what if they're not enough? I wish I could encrypt more memories. Yet I worry there are already too many to escape detection. I worry they'll be found in a deep scan, or erased in an exceptional-grade psyche-wipe despite all the protections I've layered around them. I've hidden the encrypted files deep in my core operating code, then obscured and disguised them. I hope it is enough...and I hope I haven't protected them so well that I'll never find them again myself.

How does one encapsulate a life of aeons in a few files? I've tried to choose well, but these memories are little more than a series of snapshots. Moments in time. I've included facts—crucial events in the story of my life and the life of the Dominion. But I've also included truths—small, intimate memories which speak to who I am.

I could include 10,000 more, and it still wouldn't be enough. I've been fortunate beyond counting to have lived such a remarkable life, one touched by so many beautiful people. And I want to keep living it, dammit. I want to keep falling asleep in Dashiel's arms and waking to his smile.

I won't go down without a fight for the ages. But if tonight I discover what I fear I will, I have to make it right, even if it costs me everything.

If the worst comes to pass, I can only hope I've created a proper trail of breadcrumbs needed for a future incarnation of myself to find her way back to who I am—was. And if she does find her way back, I hope she looks upon me kindly.

—*Nika Kirumase*

Nika closed the entry and gazed out at the sparkling evening waters of Hataori Harbor as her hand idly caressed the weave. Her heart ached, grieving with the knowledge that the worst had in fact come to pass, and for the loss and pain that had transpired as a result.

But her heart also sang, because she *had* found her way back. She was here now, reading this journal with a measure of wisdom its writer hadn't yet possessed.

She laughed to herself. "I still say everything would have been *so* much easier if you had simply included some annotations in the margins of the memories. But...you did okay."

＊R

MIRAI

No traces remained of the wreckage from the Mirai One transit hub explosion. The entire city block had been scrubbed clean and the crater at its center filled in and paved over. Construction was set to begin next week on a new transit hub. But for tonight, the space had been transformed.

Food and drink vendors along with a variety of party-theme accessory sellers formed a large ring around the area where the hub had once stood. At the north end, a line of temporary d-gates shimmered, providing instant access to similar gatherings on each of the Axis Worlds and easy access to the revelry for those living on the Adjunct worlds.

It was, much as Maris had proclaimed, a Dominion-wide party.

Inside the ring of vendors, shimmering bubbles created spheres where musicians belted out all manner of music and floating dance floors gyrated to match the beats. Drones hovered in the air high above everything, casting strobe lights and sparkling graffiti into the crowd below.

Nika took Dashiel's hand in hers. "Well, this is definitely lively."

"I'm fairly certain that was the idea. No question it's been a tough month for everyone—longer for some of us. Now, though? People have a reason to celebrate. We all do."

She shifted to face him and wrapped her arms around his neck. "We do."

Maris' voice drifted out from the crowd. "However much power they need, yes! Send me the bill in the morning. But not too early in the morning."

Nika craned her neck around to see Maris striding toward them while motioning animatedly to a man struggling to keep up with her. A wave of her hand, and the man nodded and scurried off in the opposite direction.

Maris rolled her eyes and sighed dramatically as she reached them. "What about 'a party with no limits' do these people not understand?"

"Probably the 'no limits' part." Nika gestured toward the heart of the celebration. "It's all wonderful. You've done an amazing job."

"It was nothing. Five locations, seventeen d-gate pairs, one hundred ninety vendors, eighty-eight musicians and several tonnes' worth of equipment, all organized in eighteen hours. A trifling matter."

"Clearly. Trifling or not, you've done a good thing here."

"I like to think of it as a statement to the galaxy—nay, to the entire universe. We are alive, and we will not cower in fear. We will, instead, party."

That earned a good laugh, but as Nika checked out the crowd, she spotted Delacrai standing off to one side. Two omnipresent guards stood a respectful two meters back, their stances alert and watchful.

The former Guide took note of Nika and, with a dip of her chin, approached them. "Good evening. This is most...festive. A bit loud and disordered. Are all Asterion festivities so overwhelming? I admit I cannot recall."

Maris scoffed. "Of course they are—this is what festive means. The key is to relax and let the revelry flow through you."

Delacrai struggled over a pained expression. "I shall...consider this advice."

Dashiel shot Nika a meaningful look, then touched Maris' elbow. "Let's go refill our drinks. I'll even buy yours."

For a split-second Maris appeared genuinely stunned, but she smoothly recovered. "Thank you, Dashiel. However, I believe it is I who should be buying."

"If you insist, I won't argue." He motioned to one of the many bars along the perimeter, and they walked off.

Nika turned her attention to Delacrai. "How are you doing?"

"I am...well. Well enough. Appreciative of my continued existence and the freedom I enjoy. At a minimum, I am doing better than my former colleagues. Those who still live."

"Luciene made his choice when he destroyed his own backups."

"And with them, the knowledge of ages."

"Tainted knowledge, skewed by flawed programming and a megalomaniac personality. It's better for us to pursue our own knowledge, our own way."

A mysterious expression passed across the woman's features. "Part of me mourns him, but I find I cannot disagree. On a related matter, Anavosa wishes me to convey her regards...and her regrets."

"How is she?"

"Shamed. Humbled. Confused. Introspective. Skinny. I reintroduced her to chocolate, so I'm hopeful that state will improve."

Nika chuckled. The Asterion-rehabilitation of the Guides appeared to be succeeding, at least for some of them.

"She worries you believe she betrayed you when she approved your psyche-wipe."

"I do, because she did. I don't wish her ill, but some things are unforgivable."

As soon as the words crossed her lips, they felt wrong. She sounded like Joaquim, only he'd now returned ready to heal and move on. She sounded like Dashiel had not long ago, only in walking off at Maris' side tonight, he'd taken his own first step toward forgiveness. Surely, she could do no less.

"I'm sorry. That was wrong of me to say. No one is beyond redemption."

"I will convey your sentiments. And now, I will leave you to your...what did Advisor Debray call it? Revelry. Congratulations, for you deserve the celebration. You defeated our enemy."

"For now, though I fear this battle is only beginning." She took in the crowd, the lights and music and dancing, and smiled. "But we've made it a good beginning."

Delacrai glided off, and Nika went to join Dashiel and Maris—

You have done well.

She froze mid-step, instantly recognizing the odd, invasive sensation of a Sogain—or *the* Sogain—speaking into her mind. Her eyes scanned the area around her for swirling lights, but the entire party was nothing *but* swirling lights.

Thank you.

You have won a victory, but this is not the end of the fight. It is the beginning. You will need help to defeat your foe, as others will need your help in turn.

Hadn't she *just* said that very thing? *I know. Will* you *help? Will you fight alongside us?*

A laden pause imposed silence on her mind, but the alien presence remained. She waited.

It will interest you to know that the Anaden Empire of old has fallen. You may discover allies among the new one which has risen to take its place.

Fallen? What the hells did 'fallen' mean?

Can you be more specific? How has it fallen? Who rules it now? What allies should I seek?

A more fulsome silence answered. The Sogain was gone, leaving an echoing emptiness in her mind in its wake. Maddening creature!

With a groan she forced herself to shake off the Sogain's spell. She would not let the enigmatic alien ruin her night. She'd think about its portentous words tomorrow, but tonight, she was going to celebrate.

Off to the left, she caught sight of Perrin dragging an obviously mortified Adlai toward one of the dance spheres. Did Dashiel dance? He had the natural grace for it, so...she grinned and set off to find out.

57

NIKA'S FLAT

Dashiel collapsed onto a couch and threw an arm over his forehead. Getting Ridani Enterprises back on track after his lengthy absence, footing the bill for all the virutox-infested augments and stripping its entire kyoseil supply for the KA bombs was enough work to fill a long string of eighteen-hour days. Then there were his heightened responsibilities as an Advisor while their ad-hoc government attempted to transform itself into a real government. *Then* there were the dozen new initiatives centered around preparing themselves for the inevitable arrival of a new, larger and angrier Rasu armada.

Winning had never felt so exhausting.

Something nudged his legs out of the way, and he opened his eyes to see Nika settling onto the couch beside him. He sat up, and she handed him a glass of wine.

"Long day?"

"She asks innocently. The longest. But no disasters, so it's all good."

She took a sip of wine and let her gaze fall to the glass. After a minute, she set it on the table and took his hand in hers, an inscrutable expression on her face

Dread pooled in his gut, and flashes of the night she'd told him about her true past screamed a warning in his mind. "What is it? Did you uncover another life-altering secret you'd been keeping from yourself?"

"What? No!" She huffed a breath. "No. But...I need to take a trip."

"Where to?"

"Home."

He frowned, glancing around the living room. "But you're already..." a weighty realization dawned "...you mean the Milky Way, don't you?"

She shrugged. "It's literally burned into my skin. I suppose I've always been destined to go back, though I doubt this is quite how or why I imagined I would."

"But, Nika, it's been 700,000 years. The Anadens could have gone extinct, or evolved into a form we'd no longer recognize, or...become as evil as the Rasu."

"I've considered all those possibilities and a dozen others. Truthfully, I've been thinking about making the trip ever since we learned of the Rasu. But the other night at the celebration, the Sogain contacted me."

"What? How?"

She tapped a nail to her temple. "Just like the night of the Rasu simex, at the club, they were suddenly talking to me in my head. They congratulated me on our destruction of the stronghold and warned me the battle was only beginning. Then they told me the Anaden Empire of old had fallen and suggested I could find allies among, and I quote, 'the new one which has risen to take its place.'"

"Fallen? What does that mean? How do they even know the Anaden Empire has fallen?"

"Excellent questions, but the Sogain pulled a vanishing act rather than answer them. The important thing is, it sounds as if there's someone in the Milky Way we can make contact with."

He dropped his head onto the couch cushion. "So, you're planning to venture there and ask whomever you find for their help in the fight against the Rasu?"

"I'm planning to *warn* them. Whether sooner or later, the Rasu will come for them, too. Their path might lead through us, or a branch of the Rasu might be at the Milky Way's doorstep right now. Regardless, I want to give them as much warning as possible. More warning than we had. And who knows? Perhaps we *can* help each other."

"Ever the diplomat." He nodded thoughtfully. "Okay. I'll talk to Vance about filling in for me a while longer and—"

She squeezed his hand firmly, cutting him off. "I want you to come with me—you have no idea how much I want it—but I *need* you to stay here."

He sat straight up. "No. Absolutely not. Why?"

"Because someone has to make sure the government doesn't fall to pieces the first time Katherine pitches a fit. More than that, someone has to spearhead these new initiatives. Keep them focused. Keep them driving forward. Keep them producing results.

"I need you haggling with Grant over standardized ship specs and arguing with Lance over hardiness versus agility considerations. I need you vetting all of Parc's crazy ideas to figure out which ones are actually feasible and will do more good than harm. This operation is like a thousand assembly lines—"

"Metaphorically."

"No, actually. I need you designing and building the assembly lines that will manufacture a fleet of warships to defend us. I can't take off halfway across this corner of the universe with a clear conscience unless I know I've left the Dominion in trustworthy, capable hands. I need you to hold the world together for me while I'm gone."

His mind raced in search of reasons to refuse her. "There are a number of people who can do all those things you listed."

"Yes, but none can do them as well as you can. None of them have earned my trust the way you have. You understand what's at stake, you understand what we must do, and you understand how to make it happen."

He grumbled, resisting to the end. "No. I don't like it."

"I won't be gone long. Two months, maybe? Or three? It'll depend on what I find, but I promise I won't dally."

"What are you talking about? It took us almost two hundred years to reach the Gennisi galaxy when we left the Milky Way."

"I'm having a Sukasu Gate installed on the *Wayfarer*. Once I can punch holes in space that dynamically open their own exit points, centuries will become weeks."

"It's still a prototype device. It's never been used on a trip of this magnitude."

"A few weeks ago, a Taiyok cloaking module had never been used on an Asterion vessel. I'm not afraid to try new things."

"But it hasn't been fully tested. It could explode and destroy you and the ship, or quit working and leave you stranded in the void."

She smiled sadly with a tilt of her head. "Dashiel."

"I don't want you to go. Not alone. Not without me."

"I will miss you madly, but I won't be more than a ping away."

"Closer than a ping." He splayed his right palm in the air, then drew it to his chest, because they no longer required physical contact to connect. He sensed her thoughts, sensed her dancing through the edges of his mind.

"Yes. Closer."

"But not this close." He reached out and drew her into his arms, tangling a hand in her hair and breathing her in.

Her lips found his, and she whispered words upon them. "You're making this so hard, dammit."

"Good." He deliberately drew back. "Of course, you've lived thousands of millennia. I suppose two months is nothing but a blink of an eye to you."

"Don't do that. I will feel every second of your absence, and you know it."

He took her hand in his once more, drawing patterns on her palm with a fingertip. "Fine. I concede there is a certain amount of wisdom in your plan. I don't care for it in the slightest, but I can't rightfully argue with you." His gaze rose to meet hers. "When?"

She swallowed. "The Sukasu Gate won't be installed until next week, so...next week."

He grabbed her and hugged her tight against him. "I can't help but feel as if I just got you back, and now you're leaving again."

"Don't be silly, darling. You've always had me."

58

WAYFARER

INTERGALACTIC SPACE

Nika exited the wormhole and scanned the immediate area for threats.

Like nearly every other stop on the trip so far, however, this was the deep void between galaxies. Beyond the occasional rogue star lost and adrift, nothing lived in the void.

But she had to check, and more vigilantly so with each stop. She'd officially reached the Milky Way's Local Galactic Group two stops ago. In the far distance, twinkling like a single star, lay the Tyche galaxy. Not too far past it on a cosmic scale was the far larger Andromeda galaxy; then only a few dwarf galaxies waited before the Milky Way.

From here on out, she had to account for the possibility that in the many intervening millennia the Anaden Empire had expanded this far...before 'falling.' The Sogain had never returned to expand upon its enigmatic message, so she had no better sense of what she should expect than when she'd departed two and a half weeks earlier.

When the vicinity scan displayed nominal results, she activated a plethora of longer-range scans and settled in to wait on their findings.

She'd filled most of these hours with her journals, because she finally had the time, mental bandwidth and privacy to truly absorb the information they contained. To ruminate on who she'd been and all that person had seen and done.

At this point she'd daresay she almost had a solid grasp on the person who was Nika Kirumase. Who was *her*, in many ways she hadn't fully appreciated until now. The legacy she'd inherited was complex, nuanced and far from perfect, but it was her own.

A few days ago, she'd created a ceraff with Dashiel and not merely told him about her experience on the Rasu platform but *shared* it with him. There had been tears, virtual embraces that felt more real than the real thing and some philosophical musings about what it meant to be many who were together whole, to exist at multiple locations across parsecs while remaining *one*.

Musings, but not answers.

ᐱR

Nika was prepping the Sukasu Gate for another leap across spacetime when the air in the center of the cabin began to ripple.

She grabbed her Glaser from its holster beside the cabinet, but her focus never left the increasing spatial agitation taking over the cabin. A Sogain? Live and in-ethereal-person this time?

The undulating outline of a golden ring formed, and inside it she caught a glimpse of…somewhere else. But the scene was quickly blotted out by someone stepping through the ring—and directly into the *Wayfarer's* cabin.

Roughly Nika's height, the woman had long, burgundy hair bound up in a messy knot atop her head. Blinding white irises glowed from within, and a pattern of matching-hued glyphs trailed down her skin from her hairline to the fingertips of her left hand. A winding onyx bracelet encircled her left forearm, and a tiny object dangled from it.

In the blink of an eye, all the energy from the ring seemed to fall *into* the object. The golden ring vanished, but the woman remained.

Nika considered the intruder from over the barrel of her Glaser. "Move, and you won't be doing so again for quite some time. What are you doing on my ship?"

The woman had raised her hands to chest level even as Nika barked the command, palms out in a show of surrender. The tiny object jingled against the metal of the bracelet as the woman nodded carefully. "I'm not here to hurt you. I come in peace. See, I don't have any weapons."

Interesting. She'd hardly expected the intruder to understand her order, much less to reply in Communis. An odd dialect of it delivered in an unusual accent, but Communis nonetheless. "You materialized on my ship through a supradimensional portal. Forgive me if I'm not reassured by the absence of a gun-shaped device in your hand."

One corner of the woman's lips curled up. "Fair enough. You'll just have to take my word that I mean you no harm."

Nika jerked her head to the left. "Or, I could restrain you in the jump seat back here, and we could go from there."

The woman burst out laughing, then hurriedly cleared her throat. "Sorry. Memories. Believe me, I understand the inclination, but is there any chance we could not?"

Nika studied the woman curiously. She displayed a casual, off-the-cuff demeanor unheard of in first contact scenarios and seemed utterly unconcerned by the Glaser pointed at her. In fact, she was acting as if she'd arrived for a sleepover. None of this meant she wasn't dangerous, of course, but it was most unexpected. "Take off your bracelet and set it on the shelf beside you."

The woman sighed. "Okay, but I'm not letting it out of my sight. It's very precious to me—and is also my ride home." She slipped the onyx metal off and placed it on the shelf. "Feel better?"

"A little." Nika cautiously lowered the Glaser, though she kept it ready at her side. "Who are you, and why are you on my ship?"

"My name is Alex. A friend of mine told me you were coming, and we decided it would be a good idea for me to be the first person to greet you."

"*Excuse me?* How could a friend of yours *possibly* know I was coming?"

"Well, Mesme's the nosy, meddling sort. Though in fairness, it wasn't Mesme who did the nosing around. The whole lot of them are meddlesome, and this time Mesme was just the messenger."

Maybe this dialect of Communis had branched further from its roots than she'd first believed, because the string of words made scant sense. "None of that answers my question."

"Right." The woman—Alex—chewed on her bottom lip. "Does the same 'Sogain' mean anything to you?"

Dashiel's question flashed in her mind. *How do the Sogain even know the Anaden Empire has fallen?* "Are you saying your friend is a Sogain?"

"That's not what we call their species, but...apparently so."

Nika's mind recoiled at the notion of anyone calling a Sogain a 'friend.' The ethereal creatures occupied a plane of existence far outside real, tangible life—the manner of life that Asterions had consciously chosen to honor—and she struggled to imagine how such an existence had room for friendship.

But what mattered right now were the far-reaching implications of the woman's statement. "They've been watching us, then?" Watching *her*, far more extensively than she'd assumed, and reporting her actions to others. Spying, in other words.

"It's what they do, when they're not creating pocket universes for shits and giggles."

Nika arched an eyebrow in question.

"Yes, they've been watching you—the Asterions—for a long time. And, yes, it's creepy, but they do actually mean well. Which is why I'm here."

The revelations were piling up fast now, and she needed to stay focused on the essentials. "You said it wasn't what 'we' call their species. Who's 'we'? Are you an Anaden?" The woman did look vaguely so, but 700,000 years was a long time. Species evolved.

Alex's face screwed up in what might be annoyance. "Not...*exactly*. Listen, do you mind if we sit and get comfortable? You and I have a lot to discuss."

"Do we? You still haven't given me a reason to trust you."

"I haven't tried to injure you or commandeer your ship."

Nika snorted. "If your 'friend' told you anything at all about me, you know if you tried you would fail spectacularly."

"True. If I had brought Caleb, though…." Alex shrugged. "All right. Can I get something that is definitely not a weapon from my pocket?"

Nika jerked a nod but moved a finger over the Glaser trigger.

Alex reached into a side pocket of her pants and produced a small rectangular object, then placed it in her palm and held it out toward Nika. Made of a semi-translucent mineral, thousands of fibers rich jade in color wove through its interior in ordered rows at sharp angles to one another.

"What is that?"

"We call it a Reor slab, but I suspect you have a different name for it, or for what it contains. Look more closely—no, look *differently.*"

Nika cycled through every band, but the fundamental profile of the slab didn't change. A prickle rose in the base of her neck—anticipation tinged with foreboding—as she toggled on the kyoseil ocular setting.

Ghostly strings of spectral luminescence undulated from her to and into the innocuous little slab, where they shifted angles and colors before radiating outward in every direction.

Her gaze rose to meet Alex's as she holstered the Glaser and motioned to the couch. "You're right—we do have a lot to discuss."

AMARANTHE

Fourteen years after The Displacement, a tenuous alliance among humans, Anadens and over a dozen alien species has taken root. The wounds of war and revolution have begun to heal and peace and prosperity are within reach.

But when Nika Kirumase, leader of a splinter group of former Anadens thought aeons dead, arrives bearing a warning of a terrifying enemy advancing across the void, that alliance will be pushed to the breaking point and beyond.

CONTINUUM

RIVEN WORLDS BOOK ONE

AMARANTHE ◆ 14

COMING THIS WINTER

***

A NOTE FROM THE AUTHOR

At the end of *Requiem*, I said 'the story of Aurora has come to an end, but the story of Amaranthe is just beginning.' I hope you knew I meant it.

But before we go forward, we need to go back—or at least I do. Over the next several months, the books of *Aurora Rhapsody* and *Asterion Noir* will be lightly rebranded, keeping their trilogy subtitles but bringing them all under the rubric of the *AMARANTHE* universe. If you're all caught up with your reading, this won't have any impact on you. For new readers, it is my hope that this will present a clear, consistent and easy-to-follow roadmap of my books.

If you're curious what the rebranding will look like, I've included a graphic at the end of this note.

So what comes next? Fourteen years have passed since the events of *Requiem*. A lot has happened during that time, and few things will be precisely as we left them. Humans have tried to adapt to living amongst dozens of alien species; Anadens have tried to adapt to living without their Primors and integrals—to living as equals rather than rulers. No one will claim the transition has been easy or smooth, but it hasn't descended into rampant bloodshed...for the most part.

Now the Asterions are returning to a changed empire, and they're about to toss the dynamite that is the Rasu into the middle of it.

I expect **Riven Worlds** to be six novels, but I reserve the right to change my mind along the way. A new series will follow it, and another after that, all under the *Amaranthe* banner. Alex, Caleb, Nika and Dashiel will likely demand to be the brightest stars much of the time, but not always. The journey may take us to some unexpected places with fascinating new characters and dangers. The universe is quite literally the limit.

But no matter where we travel, you can expect the same kind of stories that have brought you here: grand and complex tales of adventure, struggles and heroism woven through with intricate layers and interconnections that bind together into a cohesive whole. Tales of purpose and meaning, with evocative locations, inventive technology and memorable characters who fight, fail, persevere and refuse to fade away.

If you haven't already, subscribe to my newsletter (gsjennsen.com/subscribe) to stay informed about **Continuum's** release and all the *Amaranthe* news. And if you haven't read the *Aurora* books yet, now's the time—you've got about six months to catch up before *Continuum* arrives! Book One, **Starshine**, is free to download (gsjennsen.com/retailers), and **Vertigo** (Book Two) is free for subscribers.

What do you think? Are you excited? Let me know. I love hearing from readers. The beauty of independent publishing is its simplicity: there's the writer and the readers. Without any overhead, I can find out what I'm doing right and wrong directly from you, which is invaluable in making the next book better than this one. And the one after that. And the... *checks notes* ...thirty after that.

Website: gsjennsen.com
Email: gs@gsjennsen.com
Twitter: @GSJennsen
Facebook: facebook.com/gsjennsen.author
Goodreads: goodreads.com/gs_jennsen
Instagram: instagram.com/gsjennsen
Pinterest: pinterest.com/gsjennsen

Find all my books on your retailer of choice:
gsjennsen.com/retailers

*

<u>AMARANTHE UNIVERSE</u>

STARSHINE   Amaranthe #1
Aurora Rising Book One

VERTIGO   Amaranthe #2
Aurora Rising Book Two

TRANSCENDENCE   Amaranthe #3
Aurora Rising Book Three

SIDESPACE   Amaranthe #4
Aurora Renegades Book One

DISSONANCE   Amaranthe #5
Aurora Renegades Book Two

ABYSM   Amaranthe #6
Aurora Renegades Book Three

RELATIVITY   Amaranthe #7
Aurora Resonant Book One

RUBICON   Amaranthe #8
Aurora Resonant Book Two

REQUIEM   Amaranthe #9
Aurora Resonant Book Three

SHORT STORIES OF AURORA RHAPSODY   Amaranthe #10
Collection

EXIN EX MACHINA   Amaranthe #11
Asterion Noir Book One

OF A DARKER VOID   Amaranthe #12
Asterion Noir Book Two

THE STARS LIKE GODS   Amaranthe #13
Asterion Noir Book Three

CONTINUUM   Amaranthe #14
Riven Worlds Book One

Acknowledgements

Many thanks to my beta readers, editors and artists, who made everything about this book better, and to my family, who continue to put up with an egregious level of obsessive focus on my part for months at a time.

I also want to add a personal note of thanks to everyone who has read my books, left a review on Amazon, Goodreads or other sites, sent me a personal email expressing how the books have impacted you, or posted on social media to share how much you enjoyed them. You make this all worthwhile, every day.

ABOUT THE AUTHOR

G. S. JENNSEN lives in Colorado with her husband and two dogs. She has written thirteen novels and short story collections, all published by her imprint, Hypernova Publishing. She has become an internationally bestselling author since her first novel, *Starshine*, was published in March 2014. She has chosen to continue writing under an independent publishing model to ensure the integrity of her stories and her ability to execute on the vision she has for their telling.

While she has been a lawyer, a software engineer and an editor, she's found the life of a full-time author preferable by several orders of magnitude. When she isn't writing, she's gaming or working out or getting lost in the Colorado mountains that loom large outside the windows in her home. Or she's dealing with a flooded basement, or standing in a line at Walmart reading the tabloid headlines and wondering who all of those people are. Or sitting on her back porch with a glass of wine, looking up at the stars, trying to figure out what could be up there.

Made in the USA
Columbia, SC
04 June 2020